There are two main paths and intertwined side-trails running through this novel. Behind each cover is a possible starting point for the action. Where you begin reading is up to you, or to chance. You can follow the narrative on one side until you get to the middle of the book, then flip it over and continue reading from the beginning of the other side. To follow one of the side-trails, turn the book over after each chapter, and continue reading where you left off before. Of course, you're also free to find your own way.

Amnon Zichroni

We do not know what is true,
you say. We can only say
what counts.

1

For a long time I believed that I had something like a sixth sense. Not that I saw dead people or anything that might have been considered supernatural. It was more the opposite. I thought I had a feeling for what was truly vital in people, a sense of what drove them, or prevented them from doing things, a feeling for that core in them that, in a moment of candor, they might have described as their true self.

The essence of a person isn't written on their face. It can't be picked up from the sound of their voice. You can't smell it, and there's no taste, not even in the drop of sweat on someone's temple in a moment of fear. If you relied on touch, you would be completely lost, because the person doing the touching and the one being touched commingle when they make contact, and in such moments, it's impossible to know whether you're perceiving more of yourself or of the person you're trying to connect with. It's not a mixture of all those things, either.

No, what I'm talking about here can't be grasped with the senses that are normally available to us. It's the mélange of all the touches, smells, sounds, images, and tastes that our senses have encountered over time, the ones that haven't been forgotten. It is our memories that make us what we are. Our minds are where our selves truly reside.

But memory is volatile, always ready to change. Each time we remember, we reshape, filter, separate and connect, add in, take out, and replace the original bit by bit over time through the memory of a memory. Who, then, can say what really happened?

Forgetting is the scab of the psyche, some of my colleagues like to say. But just as new skin grows under a scab to complete the healing process, something new also comes into being beneath forgetting. I have observed this again and again among my clients. As for that sixth sense, upon which my success as a psychoanalyst was based, and upon which I could always rely: it was—a sense of memory.

I smelled, tasted, felt, heard, and saw other people's memories. I am not sure if I should call it a gift. If I did, I would have to ask who bestowed that gift. Where I come from, there's only one answer to such a question: *Hakadosh Boruch Hu*—the Holy One, blessed be he—or Satan, the eternal tempter, and it would have fallen to me alone to provide evidence of the actual origin of this gift. And every gift, people would have told me, contains both a streak of good and of evil, and in the end it's up to the recipient to make that gift into a blessing or a curse.

I was fifteen when a flood of images, sounds, smells, and feelings flowed into me like molten metal, burning every trace of childishness and every remaining bit of childhood out of me. I was sitting before my father, head bowed, expecting him to pronounce a punishment that I assumed would violently and irrevocably change my life.

I think I need to back up a bit so I can explain the nature of that moment, which may have determined the course of my life, and so that I can convey an impression of the kind of punishment I was prepared for on that day. When I say violent, I don't mean corporal punishment. It was more the violence of a heart that, out of an absolute feeling that it is doing the right thing, smothers every conflicting emotion in itself.

I was born in Mea Shearim, Yerushalayim. After three daughters I was the first son, and I was five-and-a-half years younger than my oldest sister. That wasn't unusual in our neighborhood. Only the age of my parents might have been considered noteworthy, since they were a good bit over thirty. In a place like that, there could only be three explanations for this. Either they had married late because something in their respective families wasn't completely kosher—the ominous workings of the evil eye, for example, a synonym for life-threatening melancholy, or perhaps untamable *tayves* that, God forbid, had led a member of the family away from the one true path of Torah. A second possibility that people took into consideration was that it might not be their first marriage. And the third possibility, that their Jewish roots didn't reach all the way back to the foot of Mount Sinai, would hardly have amounted to less of a stigma.

In a society with such strict norms, even a small deviation from what's expected is enough to make people suspicious. And perhaps that was the reason I often had the feeling that my parents were always doing a bit more than seemed necessary, they were always a little more eager than other people to follow the strictly predetermined line of what was expected—in order to be, if not respected, then at least accepted.

My parents' apartment was small. There were three rooms. The girls stayed in one room. The second belonged to my parents and was locked. In the third room, the largest, there was room for a cupboard, a bookshelf with the Rashi and Gemara editions, a foldout dining table, and chairs for every family member, plus one or two for guests. This was where family life took place, because the kitchens—there were two, *fleishig* and *milchig*, to the right and the left from the hall—were so tiny that there was just enough room in each for a sink, a stove, and a narrow counter.

My birth was a welcome occasion to look for a new apartment. I couldn't possibly share a room with my sisters, and my parents' room was off-limits. It was always locked. Even if they had wanted to put my bed in there, that would only have been a short-term solution, since children weren't allowed to sleep in their parents' rooms for longer than one, maybe two years.

The new apartment was only a few streets away from the old one. For the move, my parents rented a wooden cart. Two boys from next door helped them, even though the neighbors openly disapproved of the fact that we were leaving the quarter. The new building was only a little more than two hundred meters away, but it belonged to another world.

We moved to Rechov Malchei Yisrael, to Geula, which means redemption. We not only crossed a language border—the people there didn't speak Yiddish, they spoke Ivrit—we also traveled forward in time about one hundred years and unpacked our belongings on another continent of the Jewish world. In Geula you didn't see only black hats. And the fact that my father opened a store and now spent only one or two hours in the evening sitting over the holy books, instead of from morning until evening—in our new neighborhood, no one saw that as a reason to end a friendship.

I have known since that moment, which came before my punishment was proclaimed, that the move saved not only my life, but my parents' lives as well. They must have felt infinitely better being just a few hundred meters away from the center of holiness, under much less pressure to prove themselves and, as I now know, to disguise themselves.

For years, however, I didn't have the faintest idea about any of this. After all, it wasn't as if my father got rid of his caftan. And, of course, he still sent me to cheder in our old neighborhood, where I learned to read, and I studied the types and order of sacrificial offerings in the ancient temple. It was also understood that, since I studied hard and never caused any trouble, the yeshiva right next to the cheder was the only one that my father would consider for me. And surely everyone assumed that, when I was nineteen or twenty and married with a new baby, I would study at the same kollel as my father did every evening after he closed the store.

Everything was just the way it was supposed to be and as if nothing had changed, except for the fact that Hashem had not seen fit to find us an appropriate apartment in Mea Shearim and had therefore sent us into exile to Geula—perhaps as a test, who could know?

It was easier to answer the question of what was hidden behind the door to my parents' room. The answer was laid at my feet, literally, in the form of one of the two keys that my parents usually carried around with them at all times.

At first I didn't know whose key I had found; it was lying directly in front of the mysterious door. I really wanted to know, because I could hardly believe that, after so many years, it could have fallen into my hands out of carelessness. When, after hesitating for just a moment, I finally opened the door and entered the forbidden room, I found it even harder to believe. After a few seconds and hurried glances, and without having changed anything in the room or even touched anything, I discovered what the secret was.

It was December. The sky hovered cool and clear above the gates of the quarter, and the sunlight swam into the small room through the windows that looked out onto the street. It illuminated what was hidden, it led me directly to it. The light seeped over the walls, the wardrobe, the bed, and led my gaze to a narrow, floor-to-ceiling shelf filled with books—goyish books, forbidden books.

The shelf was a shelf of dreams, filled with the knowledge that I had been longing for, knowledge that blew up the cosmos of the narrow streets and lanes of our quarter and could take me beyond the strict boundaries in which I lived. In the rows of books before me there were volumes by authors my father had told me about just a few days before, as if he had an urge to set me on the right path, to incite me, to air the secret and open these books like a door to a previously forbidden and carefully locked room that had long been reserved for others.

The names had come up—Freud, Jung, Poe, and Wilde—in a conversation about the Talmud tractate that I was studying at the time: *Berachot*. I had almost finished it, and after many large folio pages full of tricky law derivations, I had come across one of the most popular and exciting aggadic passages: not laws, not calculations, but stories, stories about dreams, their interpretation and meaning, two things which, as I learned from the Gemara, are thoroughly different.

The sentence that introduced this particular passage had caused me trouble. An uninterpreted dream, it said, is like an unread letter. And it went on: All dreams follow the mouth. The wise men taught that no matter what we may see in a dream, it only obtains meaning through interpretation. Once it was spoken, however, the interpretation would endure and come true.

Why, then, I asked my father, should you open the letter at all? And if you should, why would you have another person open it, if the interpretation could lead our lives in a fatal direction that it wouldn't have followed if we hadn't had the dream, or at least not had it interpreted?

I also couldn't understand how a dream could have no value in and of itself and yet, following the mouth of the interpreter, have the power to change our lives, to bring good luck or misfortune over us, as if God had rolled the dice without being the slightest bit interested in how they would fall. And if that was really the way it was in the end, I asked, should we dream at all?

Of course, my father said. Dreams, he insisted, absolutely had the power to change our lives. There's plenty of evidence of that, and also good reason to entrust the interpretation of our dreams to others, he said. We ourselves can only see in them what we are prepared to see. And many souls are unfortunately conditioned to see catastrophe in every sign, like a cloud of ink in the clearest water. And then there are others who wouldn't notice the shadow of a gigantic cliff, even if it were looming above them and everything around them were being plunged into darkness.

What kind of evidence is that supposed to be? I asked. I wanted more concrete examples than the ones in the Talmud, which seemed to me to be too old-fashioned to be reliable. And my father told me about Poe's "The Pit and the Pendulum" and connected the story with the healing of the psychotics in the snake pit, with the wolf-man in Oscar Wilde's *The Picture of Dorian Gray*, a novel in which a knife stuck into the heart of a portrait kills the man shown in the picture.

I didn't have the slightest idea how my father knew about all of this. Poe and Wilde appeared neither in the Torah nor the Midrash, and poetry was mentioned in the yeshiva only if it had something to do with hymns to the cherubim and seraphim that hovered around the throne of Hashem.

I listened carefully to my father. How important it is to dream, he finally said with raised eyebrows, we know from Isaiah. For the prophet says that the word dream means nothing other than: May you strengthen me.

May you strengthen me . . . I said it to myself in a whisper. Since I was standing in front of a shelf full of dreams and only needed to stretch out my hand in order to be strengthened, I did not want to wait another second. My eyes rushed over the spines of the books. Holding my breath, I reached out and grabbed a narrow volume that I figured I could hide easily.

The picture on the cover showed a young dandy. He was sitting in a leather armchair in front of an easel, smoking. His cigarette was in a long silver holder. Between his fingers it looked like a jauntily-held paintbrush. But he wasn't painting. Instead, he was contemplating a delicate black cloth that shrouded the painting on the easel; it was left to the observer to speculate about what might be depicted on the canvas behind it.

This book, I thought, was meant for me. I had the absolute feeling that I had made the right choice. I decided to steal *The Picture of Dorian Gray*, and I hoped that my transgression would only be visible as a purple gleam on a carefully veiled canvas, instead of on my face, so that no one would see my crime.

I stuck the book under my shirt, made sure that I hadn't touched or changed anything else, and I left the room without looking back again. I closed the door as quietly as was possible, turned the key, pulled it out, and put it back down in the same place I had found it, just inches from the doorway.

I hid the book in my bed. For the rest of the day, I ran around with cold hands and a racing heart. Now and then I passed by the door of my parents' room, as if by chance, to make sure the key was still on the floor. At some point in the evening, when everyone was back at home and I went looking for it one more time, it had disappeared. No one mentioned it, neither that the key had gone missing, nor that it had been found again. If it hadn't been for the stolen book waiting under my mattress, I wouldn't have been able to say with certainty whether the key had ever been in front of the doorway, or whether I had really entered the room. It all could have been part of a dream I'd fallen into while reflecting on the words of my father, who considered dreams to be medicine.

I read the first pages of the book at night in the bathroom. Even at night, however, I was afraid someone would notice if I stayed in there too long. I didn't dare to read it in bed, either, because we weren't allowed to read holy books in bed. If someone came into my room and found me reading in bed, I would have to explain myself then and there. If they found me at my desk pondering the Talmud in the middle of the night, they would probably believe it—but they would worry about what I was losing sleep over. That could easily result in a minor interrogation, during which I might possibly betray myself.

No, I couldn't read the book at home. But I couldn't take the suspense. I had read just enough that I'd made a fleeting acquaintance with the painter Basil Hallward and Lord Henry Wotton and taken a brief look at the just-finished portrait of Dorian Gray—an innocent picture that at this point didn't provide even the slightest indication about what it was going to develop into. I wasn't able to follow the conversation between Harry and Basil when I was flying over the pages in the bathroom. I had to start again and read, read, as soon as possible.

The evil inclination can drive a person mad. I had heard the rabbi say it often enough. It lodges itself in us and whispers arguments in our ears, wraps us and our minds around its finger, finally clouding our spirits completely and taking possession of us. This is how we begin to do evil, firmly convinced the whole time that it is not wrong at all. So shrewd is the Troubler and Tempter. And precisely for this reason, one must be vigilant and resist him, no matter where he raises his whispering voice to lead us astray.

Today I couldn't say with certainty when and what he whispered in my ear. But I know that I did not resist. Out of curiosity, I listened to every word and willingly followed every line of argument that he trickled into my ear. I certainly remember the moment of his first real victory: that moment when I turned the key in the lock of the forbidden room. And I also remember the triumph of the Tempter when I took the book off the shelf and put it under my shirt. He must have been laughing. Just how quickly my judgment would go downhill, however, I could not imagine.

By the next morning, I could no longer endure it. I took the book out from under the mattress and brought it with me to the yeshiva. Once I'd gotten there, I hid it under my Talmud volume and waited longingly for the rabbi to walk out of the room after his morning droshe, leaving us to our memorization of the daily folio.

When he had finally left, I took *The Picture of Dorian Gray* out from under the folios. I placed my Gemara, which was opened to the correct page, onto my bookstand. I put the stolen book in front of it. And I believed in all seriousness that no one would notice that I was not studying the ways of God, but, instead, the ways of literature.

In the deep silence of the study hall and in my false sense of security, I progressed quickly. I flew through the book, line by line, page by page, drinking in the words. Now and then I closed my eyes so that I could vividly imagine a scene that Wilde described. And I succeeded.

For a moment I even thought I was no longer in Yerushalayim, but in Basil Hallward's studio or in Dorian Gray's salon. And I believed not only that I could see the portrait directly in front of me, but also that I could even touch it. I touched the first small scarlet stain that appeared on the picture; and I wasn't sure whether the transgression that had become visible and palpable was Dorian Gray's or my own.

I had closed my eyes. I was in a dream. It felt warm, real, and electrifying. I had crossed over into another world.

The rabbi, however, was not dreaming. When I suddenly felt his heavy hand on my shoulder, I opened my eyes. But I didn't look at him. I didn't move. There was still a slight chance that he hadn't noticed what was happening with me. After all, it's not unheard of for a student to nod off over his books. He took the book, opened it, and gave a cursory glance at the back cover, where the title would have been if it had been a Hebrew book. I believe he did so automatically, since that was presumably the side from which he had opened every book he had ever considered worth reading. But on that page he found only the book number and the name of the publisher—Penguin Books—nothing else. He paused for a moment, and I could literally feel the contempt welling up in him.

You, he said, very, very quietly as he bent down to me. You will pack your things now and go home. And then you are to send your father here. He can pick up the book from the Rosh Yeshiva.

You . . . and he whispered it exactly as he had whispered the first *you*, then he hesitated for a moment . . . you are obviously in the wrong place.

What happened? asked my father, as I dutifully reported that I'd been sent home and that he was to go see the Rosh Yeshiva.

I was daydreaming, I answered, which wasn't really a lie. My father took his glasses off and looked me in the eye.

Is that all? he asked.

Yes, that's all, I lied, adding another heaping portion to my transgression. I couldn't imagine the kind of punishment that was waiting for me. But I had to assume that it would be a punishment of biblical proportions. After all, I had not only brought disgrace upon myself; I had also damaged the reputation of my family. What would people think of a mother and father who couldn't keep their child away from the filth of English-language novels? What would they think of parents who weren't capable of preventing me from bringing that kind of book to the yeshiva, recklessly exposing my fellow students to the same destructive influence?

For a few hours, maybe even until the next day, I would be able to continue my previous life, albeit in a state of fear, because my crime hadn't yet been made public. A black cloth still shrouded the painting with the image of my soul, which was already polluted by dreams and the whisperings of the Tempter. Only for a little while longer would I be a normal fifteen-year-old from a Haredi family in Geula . . .

The reprieve only lasted two-and-a-half hours. My father hadn't wasted any time and had made his way to the Rosh Yeshiva's office immediately. What exactly they discussed there, I would never know.

I waited in my room. I sat on my bed with my legs tucked up, and I stared through the open door at the deserted table in the living room, the plastic table cloth, for weekdays, with the red hollyhock pattern, and the silver bowl that was in the middle of the table and was filled with apples. I tried to imagine how the Rosh Yeshiva would receive my father, how he would begin the conversation, and how my father's face would change as the Rosh Yeshiva slowly pushed the book across the large desk toward my father, who would recognize it—that dream in the form of printed pages, which I, his son, had pilfered from the secret treasure chamber.

When he finally came back, I could only hear him at first. He put his hat down on the cabinet next to the door, took off his caftan and hung it carefully on a hanger. His movements, from what I could tell just by listening, seemed slowed down somehow. Maybe, I thought, he also wanted to stop time, or at least stretch it out, smooth out its wrinkles, so that he wouldn't see me and have to speak to me immediately. In fact, he didn't come into my room. Through the open door I could see him sit down on his chair at the dining table. He put his elbows on the table and buried his head in his hands.

I don't think he was crying. But he was surely mulling over the possible outcomes of this story, which I had brought upon myself, him, and the whole family. And I am sure that he knew very well that I was sitting on my bed watching him.

Maybe, I thought, this was already part of the punishment: making me see his helplessness and endure his silence. There was nothing in the midst of that silence now except, like a small planet in limitless space, my father's hands holding up his head, in which there were surely thousands of thoughts racing around, and in which there was whispering, maybe also screaming, and in which punishments and tokens of love were being considered and rejected, and accusations and reassurances battled for dominance.

I couldn't stand it. I got up from my bed, walked through the door toward my father, very slowly, and sat down with him at the table. For two minutes, maybe three, I sat beside him without speaking, silence against silence, as if time had frozen between us and now stood still. One of us, I thought to myself, would have to budge, to decide on a move, a word, and break through the silence. And the sooner that happened, the better.

But my father didn't budge. He hardly seemed to breathe. Maybe he wasn't even there anymore but had gone on a trip, away from me, away from this room, the neighborhood, our quarter, possibly even away from the city entirely. I wanted him to come back and speak to me, no matter how terrible and irrevocable what he had to say might be.

I could utter the name of Hashem, I thought. It might possibly be a good omen and wake him up. It could bring him back from his absence, since he would have to answer. And so I reached out for the silver bowl in the middle of the table. I took an apple and whispered: Blessed are you, Lord our God, king of the world, creator of the fruit of the tree.

It worked. My father answered.

Amen. He said it quietly, as if it were only a timid attempt at an answer. And when I bit loudly into the apple, he raised his head, opened his eyes, and looked at me.

Later, I would ask myself again and again what might have triggered the storm of images, sounds, and feelings that followed. Was it the name of Hashem? Was it the penetrating sound of the apple splitting between my teeth, which broke through the silence that just a moment before had been insurmountable, like a wall between my father and me? Or was it that the unbearable suspense I'd been enduring for hours, and which had suddenly dissolved with the bite into the apple, had prepared me for this moment, when I would learn what was for me a previously unfamiliar, thoroughly new way of seeing, tasting, smelling, hearing, and feeling? I don't know.

I couldn't chew. The piece of apple burned on my tongue, and soon my mouth was overflowing with saliva. But I couldn't swallow, either, so the liquid flowed out of the corner of my mouth while my gaze, controlled by an insurmountable force, was fixed on my father's pupils. It was as if I was penetrating him with my gaze, plunging into his eyes and sinking in them. I floundered and sank, enveloped by the smell of countless hollyhock bushes, immersed in the acid of the green apple in my mouth. There was a silver gleam before my eyes, and when I closed them—the light was blinding me—I heard from a distance, or rather from an unreachable depth, the sounds of a violin.

I saw my father packing boxes. Behind him, unnaturally small and as if hovering over his left shoulder, I saw a boy. He was playing; but my father was listening to the sound of the pages he was organizing. He was busy taking papers out of binders and tearing them into tiny shreds, pile after pile, binder after binder. Afterwards he turned around and took books from a shelf. He packed them carefully in boxes, but only after he thumbed through them quickly, perhaps to make sure there were no more notes stuck between the pages. This much was obvious: the papers in the binders belonged to him. Or rather: they *had* belonged to him, and now he was in the process of giving up that property and destroying anything he might once have written down on all those pages.

He piled the books in crates. One after another, they were carried away by an invisible hand. And finally he stood amid a pile of paper shreds in an empty room. The snippets of paper disintegrated; and only when there were just a few left, perhaps two handfuls, he bent down and gathered them up. He held them as if he had drawn water from a well. And to make sure the precious remnants of his fit of destruction didn't slip through his fingers, he raised them to his lips and licked them with his tongue. He put the paper shreds in his mouth and chewed, very slowly and for a very long time, and swallowed . . .

The mixture struggled to move through his chest like tough mucus and took the form of a key in his stomach. He opened his shirt, raised his undershirt, and took a firm hold. His fingers bored through his skin. He grabbed the key, pulled it out, and held it tight in his bloody hand. The hole in his abdomen closed slowly. I heard rattling in his breathing that was gradually drowned out by the moan of a violin. And when the wound in my father's belly had closed again and there was nothing, no blood, not even a scar, to serve as a reminder that he had pulled something out of himself—at that moment a narrow female hand appeared in the picture and reached for the key. Since my father wouldn't let it go, the key stretched until it finally broke. Water from a jug was poured over hands. The violin fell silent.

My father turned away and put on a caftan, which was apparently new. He wrapped himself in the shiny black fabric as if in a curtain. He put the belt around his hips and pulled on it, perhaps a little too tightly to breathe freely, but just tightly enough that the words he would have liked to say remained bound up inside him. Then it became dark around him, not really black, only dark.

I could still taste the sour apple, but it was milder now, as if someone had dipped it in honey. It was quiet inside the black room, until a door opened, the door to my parents' room, first just a crack, then all the way. I saw my father standing at the doorway. December light flooded over him from behind. He stepped out of the room, closed the door, and reached into his pants pocket for his key. He hesitated, trembled. The key fell to the floor, just inches away from the door. But my father did not bend down to pick it up.

•

I opened my eyes and dropped the apple. It fell down onto the hollyhocks, rolled a little way across the table, and fell on the floor with a thud. My father stood up. He came over to me and took my head into his large hands. Now, I knew, he would render his judgment. But I was not afraid.

Amnon ben Yehuda, he said, and it was the first and only time that he addressed me with my name and patronymic, You can't stay at the yeshiva. You can't stay here at all. I am going to call Uncle Bollag in Zurich. The best thing for us to do, he concluded, is to send you to Switzerland.

2

My father's decision to send me away was—and I'm not exaggerating when I say this—the greatest act of love that I have experienced in my life. One might think it was a major departure for him, too, but I believe instead that, by deciding to send me to live with my Uncle Nathan in Zurich, my father actually stayed right where he'd always been.

No one in our quarter knew where I had gone. The official story was that I was studying at a strict yeshiva in Brooklyn, New York. If anyone asked why I always arrived via Zurich when I visited my parents—which wasn't all that often—we would tell them that my father had family in Switzerland, aunts, uncles, and cousins who also wanted to see me when I was in Europe.

The truth is that Nathan Bollag was not my father's brother. We weren't related at all. He was actually a close friend of my father's from the time before he married my mother and went with her to Mea Shearim to start a family there.

Uncle Nathan had no children. He lived alone, which occasionally raised some eyebrows. No one could explain why he hadn't found or even looked for a wife, since there didn't seem to be any discernable reason why he had remained alone.

Nathan Bollag was born the same year as my father. They knew each other as children, lived in the same building, and went to the same school. But at a certain point in their lives, they had made different decisions about the future. While my father chose Yerushalayim and sought out a wife who would go with him to Mea Shearim, Uncle Nathan decided to apprentice as a stone cutter with a relative in Antwerp. He learned everything there was to learn about diamonds and other precious and semi-precious stones. He learned to give them ornate facets and to set them in pieces of jewelry that were so valuable that no one we knew personally would ever have been able to afford even one of them.

When he had finished his apprenticeship, he traveled first to Namibia, and not long after that to Russia, as he had developed a passion for a very special kind of gem. His enthusiasm was for the demantoid garnet, a stone ranging in color from light yellow-green to a rich brown-green. On rare occasions it could be found in emerald green. Uncle Nathan discovered his love for these stones when they were still scarcely known. And from the beginning, he deliberately looked for rare samples that were over one carat, especially those from the Urals. They stood out because of their golden yellow chrysolite inclusions. These impurities, called horsetails, looked like tufts of gold thread, causing the stones to shimmer multifariously between gold and green.

The thing that delighted Uncle Nathan so much about demantoids was the fact that they obtained their special beauty from something that sharply reduced the value of a diamond: those embedded impurities. For Uncle Nathan, demantoids were the palpable proof of his theory that a life completely and exclusively for and with the Torah, a life like the one my father had chosen, was not the most that a person could aspire to. He was firmly convinced that one had to combine the feeling for holiness, and the awe of it, with a proper bit of the unholy world. In short: secular education and a profession, skill in several languages, and intimate knowledge of philosophy and art were, in his opinion, indispensable if one's life were to sanctify Hashem.

The success of his business seemed to prove him right. He made a name for himself in Zurich as a jeweler and sold primarily demantoid pieces he designed himself. That was his way of making his convictions public, for good pay.

He definitely wasn't alone in his views, which were part of a long tradition, especially in Germany, where his family originally came from. And yet, in the consistency with which Uncle Nathan lived out his conviction there was something extraordinary, something that from time to time even lent him a libertine streak. In Nathan Bollag's apartment, which looked more like a library with places to eat and sleep, there were books of every type imaginable, displayed openly on the shelves. Anyone who had a problem with that didn't get invited back. Of course he went to the theater and the opera and had a weakness for paintings.

But it was literature that was the most important thing for him, right after demantoids. He was the gatekeeper of a whole treasure chamber full of dreams, so to speak. The basis for his passion was that he considered all artists to be spirits that were subservient to Hashem, the moment they created something of unmistakable depth and beauty. It hardly mattered whether it was music, a picture, a specially cut stone, or a poem. In every true work of art he saw the face of Hashem shimmering; and so art was liturgy for him, and the artist was an assistant to Hashem in the unending work of perfecting the world.

I may have looked into my father's most painful memories on that December day in Geula. The fact that he sent me to Zurich instead of punishing me and subjecting me to strict supervision and inflexible rules, however, seems to me to be proof that he knew me better than I knew him, or even myself. Perhaps the green apple I had bitten into reminded him of Nathan Bollag's Russian demantoids, and he entrusted me to his care because he knew that my uncle would put the finishing touches on me and make my secular inclusions shimmer.

Nathan Bollag did not hesitate when my father asked him to take me in. He even refused to allow my parents to pay my board and tuition. I think he liked the idea that he was effectively adopting me—as minor compensation for the sad fact that he didn't have any children of his own. Having to take care not only of his gems, but now also of me, the black sheep of the family who'd been sent abroad—that was just fine with him, because looking after my education and upbringing gave him the opportunity to put his views to the test.

You could find Hasidic boys with peyes, caftans, and hard round hats in Zurich, too. Still, the clothes I had brought from Yerushalayim never made it out of the armoire. Uncle Nathan had bought me a black suit with a vest and a smart, stiff Borsalino hat. Cutting my peyes was out of the question, since they were in a certain sense my ticket home and provided cover for the story about my being sent to a Hasidic yeshiva in New York. But from now on, they were no longer carefully put in curlers every night, and during the day I kept them pinned up under my kippa. This way I looked like a devout Swiss Yehudi rather than an emissary from a shtetl a thousand miles to the East and a hundred years in the past.

I was immediately enrolled in the Jewish boys' school *Beis Sefer Le-Bonim* on Edenstraße, a day school which, in addition to in-depth instruction in the holy subjects and Hebrew, also offered German, English, French, and the secular curriculum to the end of secondary school. I had to start three grades below my age level just to be able to catch up with the Swiss curriculum. It wasn't exactly a walk in the park. Even so, I had less trouble with the language than I worried I would. Back in Mea Shearim, I had spoken Yiddish with my friends and during the day at the yeshiva. Now, in Zurich, I could understand almost everything. Still, I couldn't make myself understood very well in the beginning.

On Edenstraße, the day started just after seven with the morning prayer. Classes lasted into the evening. From eight to ten on weeknights, and on Sunday mornings, a tutor came to our house and helped me review the material that hadn't been emphasized at my previous school.

Uncle Nathan still went to the theater and the opera by himself. I didn't get around to reading novels, either. As soon as I went to bed around eleven o'clock at night, my eyes closed, and I immediately fell into a death-like sleep.

I studied without taking any breaks, and I worked every day until I couldn't fit another thing into my head. I caught up quickly and was able to switch to the graduating class at seventeen, one year earlier than expected.

Uncle Nathan was very proud, and so was I.

Of course the clothes weren't enough to make me Swiss. I may have gone to school in Zurich, but I didn't really live there. Our apartment was in the Enge, a predominantly Jewish quarter near the lake. I didn't experience much of the city beyond what I got to see while traveling the triangle between home, school on Edenstraße, and the synagogue on Freigutstraße.

The regimen was strict, in school and at home. The days were planned out with almost no gaps, and everyone expected punctuality and accuracy. There was no time for daydreaming.

You came here to study, my uncle liked to say, whenever I expressed the desire to see more of the city or the region, to go to the lake or to the mountains. To *study*, he would say, pointing to the pile of schoolbooks on my desk. That, he said, was the best thing I could do at my age.

I had almost no contact with strangers. Though Uncle Nathan proudly described himself as Modern Orthodox, that didn't mean he didn't make a point of staying with his own kind, that is, among Yehudim, to use his term. That way there was less danger that I would even come into contact with the temptations of a modern European city—with what Uncle Nathan called *goyim nakhes*, which was meant to be as derogatory as it sounded. The theater and his books, which would have been put in that same category in Geula, were exempt for him, of course.

In that sense, it hardly made a difference whether the room where I studied was in Zurich or Yerushalayim. It was nevertheless clear to me that, even with my rigorous schedule, workload, and isolation, I was living in a different world than before, a world that was so different that I never felt like a prisoner. For the time being, it was enough for me to get my knowledge exclusively from schoolbooks.

Shortly before my exit exams at *Beis Sefer Le-Bonim*, however, I did make one escape attempt. It was completely clear to my uncle that I would get my *Matura* certificate and then continue my studies. I assumed the same thing. But we had never talked about which school I should attend to complete my *Abitur*, so I could qualify for university. There was no Jewish preparatory *gymnasium* in Zurich. Many families sent their children to London or France to Jewish boarding schools they considered trustworthy. But I thought Uncle Nathan would want to keep me with him; and that would mean switching to a regular *gymnasium* in Zurich. I was looking forward to that, because at the *gymnasium* I could finally make a connection to the non-Jewish Zurich, satisfy my curiosity, and discover the surprises that life outside the Enge held in store.

It wasn't as if I was hoping for anything scandalous. But for starters, there was the fact that classes at a *gymnasium* wouldn't be segregated by sex. Also, the hours of the day that were the most productive for me, from morning until early afternoon, would be reserved for secular subjects. The holy books, on the other hand, would have to be content with whatever was left of my attention in the evening. Also, for the first time in my life, I would not be under religious supervision from morning to evening. Not that I was planning to stray from the right path. But I would have been more than happy to live without the feeling that I couldn't take a step without being observed.

And so I asked Uncle Nathan which *gymnasium* he'd found for me in our area.

He gave a quick laugh. You must be out of your mind, he said. There's no *gymnasium* for you here in Zurich. And after this statement, which put an abrupt end to my hopes for a little more freedom, he revealed how he imagined my immediate future.

My father may have given him a free hand as far as my education was concerned, he told me. But I shouldn't delude myself: it was absolutely out of the question for me to attend anything other than a religious school that would lead to the *Matura* certificate, according to the standards of *Beis Sefer Le-Bonim* at the very least. I would therefore have to prepare myself to go to a boarding school for the next three to four years.

It didn't take long before I found out just what Uncle Nathan had in mind for me. At the end of one Shabbos, right before school vacation, he came into my room. He was holding two airplane tickets—to America. Right after the last day of school, we would be on our way, to pay a visit to my new school. My uncle said he was certain that he'd found the right place, but the director insisted that we introduce ourselves in person. And besides, he thought it proper to go and get an impression of the institution for himself.

The institution he was talking about was a campus with a high school and secondary yeshiva in the modern style in Pikesville, Baltimore. The complex was founded in 1933. It still exists. Today there are around seven hundred young men studying there, and at that time there were at least five hundred.

The educational concept came from Yeshiva University in New York. Students there receive primarily Orthodox instruction and delve intensively into the written and oral tradition, without having to forego a university education. A lot of students do in fact spend their time in Pikesville preparing for YU in New York, so they can go on to become lawyers, doctors, rabbis, or religion teachers.

The director in Pikesville was quickly convinced that I would fit in at the school. Uncle Nathan had already told him where I came from and how hard I had worked to make up for all the material I had missed. That impressed him. And he didn't seem to consider it a problem that I was almost two years older than the rest of the students in my future class.

I still didn't know what I planned to study later on, my uncle told the director—without having discussed it with me beforehand. It might be too early for that, he said. My education in Pikesville should leave all possibilities for the future open to me, he told the director. After all, it was possible that I might choose an academic career.

Even though my uncle was running roughshod over me, it actually comforted me a little. I had the sense that he at least wanted to leave the decision about my future profession to me. I hardly believed I could soften his resolve to send me to Pikesville. I would try. That was my plan. But I didn't think there was much of a chance that I could change his mind. As a result, I toured the campus in Pikesville with the feeling that I was scouting out the corner of the world that I would be assigned to for the next few years.

The schedule the director outlined resembled the one from my school in Zurich. In Pikesville, the day also began around 7:30. And here, too, the morning was reserved for Jewish studies. English, meaning the secular subjects, was taught only after 2:30 in the afternoon, and only for four hours, including breaks. The sedorim for Talmud and Mussar began right after dinner at seven. And it was expected that students would continue studying until nine o'clock. Many students even sat over their books until eleven or midnight. And that, the director said, is the way we think it should be.

Television was forbidden, along with newspapers and magazines, with a few exceptions. Secular books had to be submitted, so the contents could be reviewed. Any trip into the city was subject to approval and was frowned upon—the director was quite clear about that.

Life at the school revolved around the campus. Even students who lived in Baltimore or had family there were only allowed to spend one Shabbos a month away from the yeshiva. There were hardly any vacations during which students could go home—only three weeks in the summer and ten days each for Pesach and Sukkot.

Young people, the director said in closing, came here to study, not to have fun.

Uncle Nathan smiled when he heard that, which didn't surprise me. The words could have come out of his mouth. Inwardly, I prepared myself for the fact that I would have to wait for at least three more years before I would be able to broaden my studies beyond religion.

The decision not to ban literature outright was a clever move. But if I hoped to be master of my own reading material in Pikesville, I would have to operate outside the law. And that might end the way it had in Geula, when I was fifteen and got caught reading *Dorian Gray*. But with one difference: I couldn't hope for a second stroke of luck. If I came to Pikesville, I couldn't stand out. I would have to fit in and wait patiently. The prospect of all that waiting didn't make me especially happy.

Back in Zurich, I did undertake one timid attempt to change my uncle's mind.

Why, I asked him, should I spend three-quarters of my time with the twelve volumes of the Talmud and other religious books when an unbelievable abundance of secular knowledge and a whole universe of great literature were waiting for me? I hardly had any idea about how to get around out there in the world or, above all, about what really made things happen in that world. Presumably it was not the Talmudic subtleties that I would be memorizing day after day.

I was almost nineteen and knew nothing. That's the way it seemed to me, anyway. I thought of Uncle Nathan's demantoids. And I said so, too.

Was there anything about me that shimmered? There was no trace of brilliant cut to be found. I had no color. I felt like a magnifying glass, nothing more than a simple convex piece of glass over the tightly printed lines of a Talmud page.

Uncle Nathan listened patiently to what I had to say. He didn't contradict me or raise his voice. It seemed that he took me and what I was saying quite seriously. He didn't seem annoyed; instead, he seemed pensive.

We'll talk about that, he said. He asked me to come to his shop the following day. He said I should get there just after closing time. He had something to show me.

I was agitated the following evening as I waited in front of the display window of the jewelry shop. The grates had been rolled down, and the decorations had been reduced to the few pieces that could stay in the dimly lit display overnight. Inside the store, it was dark. I paced back and forth in front of the window for a while, until something stirred inside.

I heard a set of keys rattling. With a dull clunk, the steel bolts released the door. And for a moment, it was as if Uncle Nathan wasn't just opening his store for me, but was allowing me to enter the fortress of his emotions and his often impenetrable thoughts, so I could see for myself the things that moved him, which had now led him to decide whatever it was that he had decided.

He didn't say a word when he finally stood before me in the open shop door, those two small steps that led up to the store, looming above me in such a way that he looked like a giant in the half-light of the doorframe. He waved me in, closed the door, and told me to follow him.

We walked through the store, past the empty showcases and into his office. One of the vaults where he kept valuable pieces was open. Uncle Nathan walked right up to it and took out a small case, a simple jewelry box made of black cardboard. He opened it, and inside, on a red velvet cushion, I spied a deep dark-green demantoid that was surely three to three-and-a-half carats.

What do you think of this stone? I heard my uncle ask.

That surprised me. I had seen a few pieces before, but never so closely or with the kind of attention to all the detail of color, inclusions, and cut necessary to make a well-founded judgment.

Uncle Nathan took the stone out of the box, asked me to come closer, and held the demantoid in the warm, bright light of the work lamp on his table.

The color of the stone was intense, clear, and completely even. I looked carefully at the inclusions, a bundle of the finest small gold hairs, all of which emanated from one point and fanned out into a bushel that was slightly twisted into itself. When he turned the stone over in the light, it seemed as if sparks from fireworks had been captured and had solidified inside it, without losing any of their fire or brilliance.

It's beautiful, I said, and I was a bit ashamed, because here I was, effectively the adopted son of the area's greatest demantoid specialist, and I couldn't think of anything more precise to say.

Yes, said my uncle, and it didn't seem to bother him one bit that I had remained so vague with my opinion about the stone.

Yes, he said again, and after a brief pause, he continued by holding the stone directly in front of my eyes again. How much space, he asked, does the chrysolite take up in this stone?

I hesitated.

Maybe five percent, I answered, possibly ten.

Not a quarter? my uncle asked. Couldn't it be a quarter or even more?

Absolutely not, I replied. The stone would look stuffed if it were that much.

I think so, too, said Uncle Nathan. The flying spark effect could never occur if the inclusion didn't have its own space in all the green.

He brought his hand down and laid the stone back on the velvet cushion. And while he closed the box and carried it back to the safe to lock it up there, he added: That's a fine lesson on the subject of proportionality.

So that was his final decision, I realized. I was going to Pikesville, Baltimore to study three-fourths kodesh and one-fourth English for at least the next three years.

For a moment, I felt as if I had been forced into a cage. On the scale of religious consistency, when I came to Zurich I had been somewhere between my father and my uncle, who had seemed like a savior to me. Since then—I couldn't interpret my feeling of trepidation any other way—I must have moved far away from Geula, further and further in the direction of my uncle. And now I was standing right in front of him, eye to eye, and I wanted to get past him.

But he would not budge.

3

I only went to visit my family in Geula for a week that summer. I can still remember the shimmering air that hung over the quarter like a glowing dome that August, slowing everything beneath it to a near torpor: the steps of the passers-by, the gestures, even the flow of conversations.

After a few hours of bustle in the early morning, the streets emptied out by noon. The cats lay around lethargically in shady doorways. There wasn't even the slightest breeze. The air was filled with the sour odor of sweat-soaked wool and dust. It smelled strongly of people, even though there was hardly anyone outside. It was only at night that a bit of life returned to the streets, but even then it still felt like the city was on the brink of heat stroke, unconsciousness, and paralysis.

It was as if we were looking through veils, and every sound that reached our ears was muffled by cotton balls. We drank cool mint tea and vast quantities of cardamom water. But every sip we took seemed to follow a direct route through the skin and out of our bodies, so our thirst was never really quenched.

In the heat of that August, no one wanted to talk much, and I suspect that was precisely the reason I would always remember this visit with my family as peaceful and easygoing.

My father was very happy about my graduation from *Beis Sefer Le-Bonim*, and no less so about the arrangements Uncle Nathan had made for the coming years. Just how much he agreed with Uncle Nathan's guidance, he showed me on the last day of my visit.

I spent the morning with him at his business, a shop on the main street of the quarter, where he sold talesim exclusively. They hung in plastic bags folded over small hangers in long rows of shelves. You couldn't take a walk around the store without being amazed by how many types of prayer shawls there were. Of course my father carried all sizes—from a tallis for the Bar Mitzvah boy to the oversized specimen that was stretched as a chuppah over the wedding couple by friends of the groom. Most of them were classic white with black stripes on the sides. But they differed from one another in the number, the width, and the array of the stripes. In this matter, everyone follows very particular traditions and attaches special meanings to the various patterns.

For the High Holy Days, there was another whole collection in pure white. Right next to those were the items preferred by the mystics, in different shades of white, with or without shiny silk stripes woven in.

For the less tradition-conscious clientele, my father also carried models with embroidery in silver and gold, as well as other colors, such as blue and white for the Zionists, wine-red stripes for the secret kings, or the rainbow look for incurable individualists.

Displayed in glass showcases were the especially expensive items, like the ones interwoven with thick threads of silver, or those that had atarot made of silver platelets in all kinds of shapes and patterns, which kept the tallis lying flat and firm on the shoulders. One would be justified in saying that you could find the right tallis for every taste and every budget at my father's store.

In addition, however, my father offered a special service. However nice, or even extravagant, individual items in his collection might have been, it couldn't be forgotten that there is really only one reason to wear a tallis, and that is to fulfill the holy commandment of the tzitzes, which, in keeping with the instructions of the Torah, are to be attached to the corners of any four-cornered garment. The only way to fulfill this obligation is to actually wear such a garment. But for anyone who came to my father's store to buy a tallis, choosing the appropriate type was only the beginning.

Every tallis was already fitted with tzitzes. But the vast majority of my father's customers would never have dreamed of actually using those tzitzes. There were different reasons for this. It definitely mattered where they came from, what kind of wool they were made of, how long and how thick the individual threads were. For many of the customers at my father's shop, even the question of whether all the people involved in the stages of production—from the sheep-shearing and the spinning to the completion of the tzitzes threads—had been aware of the fact that they were contributing to the fulfillment of a mitzvah was of fundamental importance. But the most important thing for them was how, and by whom, the tzitzes were tied.

Countless types of tzitzes sets hung on the wall behind the cash register. They came in various lengths, qualities, and shades of white. Once a customer had chosen a suitable set, my father would cut the machine-tied tzitzes from the newly-bought tallis and tie new ones on by hand.

The tzitzes that he cut off ended up in the shaimos, a big cardboard box that was under the tzitzes sets that hung on the wall. This was the place to deposit all the things that couldn't be left for the garbage collectors: holy books that were no longer legible, for example, and all printed matter that was no longer needed but which contained some variant of the name of Hashem. When the cardboard box was full, it was taken to the cemetery and its contents were buried.

Some customers may have hesitated, wondering if they should have their tzitzes tied by my father, or whether it wouldn't be better to do it themselves. But when they saw the shaimos with the cut off tzitzes, they knew they were being served by someone they could trust.

Depending on the background of the customer, the tzitzes for the tallis would have to be tied differently. Every thread, every knot, and every coil had a meaning assigned to it.

For certain Hasidim and the mystics, my father had to poke a second hole in the material at each corner of the tallis and sew stitches around the hole. Once that was taken care of, he opened the newly purchased tzitzes set and inspected each of the sixteen threads. He made sure that four of the threads were about a third longer than the rest, and he laid those over his shoulder. Only then did the procedure really begin.

The corners of the tallis were laid over one another and placed in a wooden clamp that was fastened to the edge of the table. Then he took three of the shorter threads, and one long one. He combined four ends of thread and pulled them flat. Then he threaded them into the hole at the corner of the tallis and pulled them about halfway through. He clamped those ends with a clothespin, which he wore on the lapel of his caftan at other times during the day, when he didn't need it for tying tzitzes.

He left a loop as long as a half a centimeter over the edge of the corner and took the threads, which now lay before him in two pairs of four, and tied them to a first double knot, so that he now had eight threads in front of him—seven of equal length and one a few centimeters longer, which he needed for the tying. This longer thread had to be wound counterclockwise around the remaining seven that were tied together, in a spiral, so every coil remained clearly visible.

After a certain number of coils, the threads were once again divided into two pairs of four threads each, followed by a second double knot, then another section with coils and a double knot, and so on, until there were four coiled segments and a total of five double knots. If everything was tied properly, in the end the excess length of the eight threads would be just enough for the coils, and the ends of all eight threads would be equally long.

When I was a boy, my father had told me about the deeper meaning of the tzitzes, of the type and number of coils and knots. They are all symbols for words, and they connect those words inextricably with their meanings.

There are different views on the exact number and sequence of the coils, which provide a coded answer about why people keep the laws. The Sephardim tie ten, five, six, five coils—in that sequence. The numbers correspond to the four letters in the name of Hashem.

The Ashkenazim, on the other hand, coil the thread only seven, then eight, eleven, and thirteen times. The first two segments stand for the first pair of letters in the holy name, the third segment for the second pair. The fourth segment, finally, has the same numerical value as *echod*—one—such that the combination of coils stands for *Hashem echod*—the Lord is one.

I am sure that there are even more variations of knots and coils, but clandestine ones, worn secretly by those who truly know. But people like that wouldn't have their tzitzes tied by someone else, not even by my father.

I always loved watching my father do his work. He was unbelievably skillful and experienced and probably could have tied tzitzes in his sleep. What I liked was the idea that, with a thought and a few movements of the hand, very simple things could be imbued with deeper meaning. I liked the reverence for a single letter, a knot, or a number, because they were the smallest components of a great work that *Hakadosh Boruch Hu* created through his will and his word.

My father wore his tzitzes in the Sephardic way. That wasn't our background, but I also wore them that way—in accordance with the stipulation that the father's custom is the children's law. He never explained to me why he did this, and I never saw anything more in it than a small freedom that he allowed himself, a completely harmless rebellion. Along with all the rest of the traditions and practices, he of course bequeathed this small rebellion to me, his only son, and I stuck with it, the way a son should.

But on that last day of my visit in Geula, everything changed, with a wordless gesture from my father. He had asked me to come with him to the shop because he wanted to give me a new tallis. I was to take it with me to the yeshiva in Pikesville and wear it there for the first time. It would be a good omen for my journey to Baltimore and my studies there, a sign that I was beginning a new chapter in my life.

I was expecting that my father would pick out a tallis for me. But that was just the thing he didn't want. He stood in his shop and waved his arm from one end of the collection to the other. I was free to choose.

In that case, I said to myself, I didn't want one of the usual types I'd always worn: ivory-colored with wide black stripes on the sides. If it was going to be a symbol of my wishes for the years ahead, then I would have to look on a different rack.

I went to the purely white talesim with the cream-colored silk stripes, the ones worn by those who delve into the wisdom passed on to us through stories. In other words, the men who discover whole worlds in numbers and words, and who make whole worlds visible by way of numbers and words. I was well aware that my choice could possibly be presumptuous. But how could anyone object to the fact that I was making plans, that I had wishes and interests and also hoped to be able to pursue them?

My father didn't comment on my choice. That is to say, perhaps what followed was in fact his comment on it, albeit a silent and symbolic one. After he had unfurled the tallis and held it up to the light to examine it, he turned around and went to the table next to the cash register, to the wood clamp, which he needed to secure the corners when he tied tzitzes.

As for the tzitzes, my father said, *I* would like to choose them.

I agreed. He took a set with long and relatively thick threads from the wall behind the register. They were of a somewhat more yellow white than the tallis. They would be heavy tzitzes, and they would be conspicuous at the corners, which would direct a potential observer's attention to the part of the garment that was the whole reason for wearing it.

He showed me the threads, and I nodded.

Silently, he began his work, cut the old tzitzes off and threw them in the shaimos. Then he opened the set with the wool threads and examined it. For a moment, I was distracted by noise from outside. I looked through the display window onto the street. By the time I turned back to my father, he had already tightened the first double knot and was coiling the shamash, the longer thread, around the cord of the other threads, with his usual seasoned panache. But he didn't stop after ten coils, as I expected, but after seven, and he secured the first segment with the second knot. He followed this with eight, eleven, and thirteen coils between the remaining knots.

These were Ashkenazi tzitzes, like the ones Uncle Nathan would have ordered from my father.

When he was finished with the first corner and had inspected his work and counted all the coils of the threads between the knots one more time, just to be sure, then I started to think he might have done it consciously. And when he silently repeated the procedure on the remaining three corners of my new tallis and at last presented my gift to me with a smile, I was sure that it had not been a mistake.

Not a word. Just a smile—and a gesture that an outside observer wouldn't even have noticed. But for me, it meant a great deal. I hugged him tightly before I took my gift and walked out into the street.

Back in Zurich, I proudly showed my gift to Uncle Nathan. He was definitely struck by the fact that, in the future, I wanted to wear white. He didn't notice the tzitzes, though. I had to call his attention to them. He pursed his lips in amazement.

That's just like your father, he said. When it comes to the really important things, he can't find the words. But don't go thinking he considers you a grownup and that you'll be left to make your own decisions from now on.

That remark hurt my feelings. He had no way of knowing how my father's gesture and embrace had felt.

But Uncle Nathan went on: As it should be with proper tzitzes, your father has sent you a coded message with them.

I was surprised by this. After all, I thought I had understood quite well what my father had meant. And the fact that he had said nothing and left it at a gesture seemed especially tender to me.

My uncle explained that my father had learned how to tie tzitzes relatively late, sometime in his mid-20s. He had registered at a yeshiva for baalei teshuva, that is to say, for men who were returning to their faith, or rather, to an observant life. While there, he was assigned a Moroccan Yehudi as a study partner. He, too, had only immigrated to Israel a few months before, but he knew what my father still needed to learn. And he helped him wherever he could, with great dedication and unfailing patience. My father, Uncle Nathan said, had often spoken of his chavrusa partner and was convinced that he had him to thank not only for his knowledge, but actually, for his whole new life.

Out of gratitude, my uncle continued, he wore his tzitzes like this Sephardi from Morocco—so he would always remember that he had made a conscious decision to follow this path.

By tying different tzitzes for you now, my uncle said, your father is sending you on your way with a well-intentioned piece of advice—and a wish. The advice is this: in your new yeshiva, choose your chavrusa partner judiciously. What you learn now counts for more than where you come from. And his wish: that this friend will stand by you, just as your father's Sephardic friend stood by him.

This disclosure did not trouble me. It seemed to me only that one more secret had been revealed.

But there was one thing I did find unsettling. It was now clear to me that everything I had seen and felt when I was sitting across the dining table from my father, none of it was the product of an overactive imagination. The books, the torn-up papers, the key, and the bloody hands . . . I had seen my father's memories.

4

My uncle's little lesson on the proper relationship between Torah study and secular education wouldn't be his last word on the subject of Zurich *gymnasium* versus yeshiva. I've often wondered why he didn't bring it up again directly, instead of taking a detour through literature. Perhaps he thought that anything he said would be more likely to stick in my mind if I had some associations to connect it with. And if I was correct in my assumption, he was right, because I still remember his explanations well.

Uncle Nathan advised me to take it easy during the last days before the new school year, go down to the lake, take in a movie, and perhaps also—read. He even personally chose a book for me from his library, a Russian novel.

He said he would love to talk about it with me when I was finished reading it.

I didn't waste any time. My uncle had finally opened the treasure chest of his library for me. And he had obviously handed me one of its jewels. Never before had I obeyed him so willingly. I took the book and headed for the lake to find out what my uncle would have me discover.

I left the Enge, went down to the Mythenquai, and sat down on a bench in the sun. Without being aware of it, I placed myself in the exact same situation that the book started with.

The setting was not Zurich, but Moscow in the last days of the 1920s—on an unusually hot May evening, on a bench near the Patriarch's Ponds. On the bench sat two men of letters, Mikhail Alexandrovich Berlioz, editor of an important literary journal, and the poet Ivan Nikolayevich Ponyrev, who wrote under the pseudonym Bezdomny, or "Homeless."

The promenade along the avenue, which was shaded by large linden trees, was almost deserted, which was quite unusual for that place and time. The two men did not notice this, however, for they were absorbed in a literary discussion.

Bezdomny, it turned out, had been commissioned by the editor to compose a long anti-religious poem. The artist had portrayed the protagonist, none other than Jesus of Nazareth, in very dark hues. But Berlioz was not at all pleased with the work, much to the author's amazement.

The text has to be completely rewritten, the editor declared. In the poem, he lectured, the figure of Jesus had turned out to be altogether alive, not at all sympathetic—oh no—but *alive*! And precisely therein lies the problem, Berlioz concluded.

Ponyrev alias Bezdomny didn't completely follow his critic. Given that he had made the subject true to life and therefore believable, how could anyone say he had failed?

The problem, Berlioz explained, starts with the fact that Jesus of Nazareth never existed. Bezdomny shouldn't have depicted him as a disagreeable person, a reactionary, or a debaucher, he said. Instead, he should only have reported the fact that this Jesus, whose name half of humanity calls upon in religious delirium, never lived. He is fiction, Berlioz continued, a pure figment of the imagination and the backward need of the masses to believe in something or someone—or both at the same time.

There is not a single Eastern religion, Berlioz said, where you will not find an immaculate virgin giving birth to a god. The Christians didn't come up with anything new, they just created their Jesus by following the same legend.

Your main thrust should go in that direction, Berlioz instructed the poet.

Bezdomny was about to have an epiphany. But at that very moment, something interrupted their conversation. A man was approaching them, obviously a foreigner, since he was wearing shoes and gloves to match his expensive suit, and he had a walking stick with a black knob that was shaped like a poodle's head. This foreigner, who had come out of nowhere, took note of the editor's remarks with gentle amusement.

The stranger asked whether they were atheists. And both of them, Berlioz and the poet alike, affirmed this fervently. Not without exhibiting a certain educated arrogance, the two stood firm when the foreigner got on the subject of the well-known five proofs of God's existence.

Those so-called proofs, Berlioz retorted, have been adequately refuted by science. In response to the peculiar foreigner's next question: Who then—if not God—controls the fate of the world in general and of humanity in particular? Berlioz answered, with deepest conviction: Man himself, who else?

This was an opinion that the foreigner could not accept without objection. In order to control something, he argued, be it one person or even masses of people—not to mention the universe—one would need a definite plan for a fairly decent period of time. But it is in fact the case, he said, that human beings are mortal and, on top of all their misery, sometimes die very suddenly.

For example, he continued, it can absolutely happen that a certain gentleman, while he is making plans and thinking he is in control of his own life and other people's lives, slips on the street—say in a puddle of sunflower oil that Annouchka accidentally spilled—and meets a sudden death, because a fast-approaching streetcar severs his head from his torso.

And in such a case, the stranger asked, do you seriously believe that this man was in control? Don't you think it would be more appropriate to assume that someone else determined his fate?

The two men of letters were silent. They had become uneasy.

As for the question of the existence of Jesus Christ, the foreigner contradicted the editor quite forcefully: This Jesus of Nazareth, there can be no doubt that he really existed. Anyone who suggests otherwise is a fool at best. The foreigner continued that he not only knew him; he had even met Jesus himself in his own time.

This made the men of letters feel better. For it was now obvious that the stranger was not only a foreigner, but completely crazy to boot. They nonetheless listened to the stranger's account of the meeting between the aforementioned Jesus and the great Procurator of Judea, Pontius Pilate, for the narrator depicted it no less realistically than Bezdomny portrayed Jesus in his tendentious poem. They could see the blood-red lining of the Procurator's white cloak before them. They could hear him walking with the shuffling gait of a cavalryman when, according to the foreigner's report, on the fourteenth day of the spring month of Nisan, he came out into the covered colonnade of the palace of Herod the Great.

Poetry, the editor-in-chief said to himself appreciatively: reactionary, completely anachronistic, to be sure, but poetry!

But whether it was poetry or not: after the foreigner was finished and they had all said their goodbyes, Berlioz took a few steps and, his convictions notwithstanding, slipped in a puddle of sunflower oil. He fell onto the streetcar tracks, and an oncoming car of the Number 4 line ran him over and severed his head from his torso. And while the stranger simply considered this to be a further, absolutely valid proof of the existence of God, the poet Bezdomny lost his mind on the spot.

Berlioz was, incidentally, not the only person in the book to meet a sudden death. And one could almost say that fate was good to him, since he was at least allowed to die without his life first being dismantled and ravaged, as happened with some of the other protagonists. Because in that early summer in Moscow, taking the form of the black magician Woland, none other than Satan himself was afoot—immortal, ruthless, and certainly not an atheist. He turned the scientific materialists' world upside down in a way that no Muscovite could ever have imagined.

I didn't leave my spot on the bench at the Mythenquai until the sun was going down and I had finished the book. I was delighted. My head was spinning. It was as if the world was teetering around me.

My uncle could hardly believe that I had devoured Bulgakov's *The Master and Margarita* in a single day. But the slightly feverish look in my eyes convinced him. He nodded appreciatively. He seemed pleased that I was so enthusiastic about literature. But he didn't want to talk about it with me that evening.

That, he said, can wait until your head has cooled down a bit. And he said it with a smile that I didn't know how to interpret.

The next morning at breakfast, however, he guided the conversation directly to the Master, to Berlioz, Bezdomny, and Woland, that foreigner who had overturned the orderly socialist state of affairs in Moscow so completely. He wanted to talk about Berlioz and Bezdomny and the conversation that the two of them had with the foreigner, while Annouchka was unsuspectingly spilling her sunflower oil.

Just as the black magician Woland invaded the world of the two Russian men of letters, my uncle told me, others would soon try to invade my world.

Once Uncle Nathan got going, he delivered a veritable presentation about the mania of the *Yevonim*, as he disparagingly called the Greeks, that is to say, those who brought us the *gymnasium* and the universities, certainly, but also what was in his opinion an extraordinarily dangerous and untenable view of the world.

You, he said, looking at me with a mixture of concern and vigorous fervor, you will meet a lot of *Yevonim* who will sneer at you and your views, for whom *Hakadosh Boruch Hu* is just a figment of the imagination and who consequently—just like Bezdomny and Berlioz in Bulgakov—are firmly convinced that man and man alone controls his own fate.

Short though their yardstick may be, they measure everything. They categorize, sort, assess, and squeeze things into charts and tables. And this seems to be reasonable, very sensible, and all for the purpose of gaining knowledge. Unfortunately, they consider their piecemeal measurements to be a mapping of the universe and insist on treating their theories as established facts, as long as a new theory doesn't come along and succeed in taking over as the next established truth.

It is much too seldom, my uncle said, that people like Woland turn up at universities. Much too seldom that the unfathomable breaks into the edifice of those supposedly secure theories and hypotheses. And it will happen again and again that you will be derided if, for example, you consider a flower to be the epitome of Hashem's creative power and not, as those scholars see it, the product of a process that's essentially dependent on inconceivably long evolutionary developments.

Everything that is vague, or doesn't fit into the current theory, or defies measurability and categorization, in short, the fantastic, or let's call it the magical, which has moved the mystics of all religions for millennia—there is no room for all that out there in the *yevonish* world of the supposedly precise sciences. And people will hold you up to ridicule if you persist in believing that there is something superior to you and other people, and that we humans can at best be partners of Hashem, but certainly not the ones steering or controlling, the ones with the overarching plan.

The treacherous thing about this isn't that they take a different view. What's treacherous is the fact that they continually try to put their minor insight on display as truth. But this truth does not exist. It belongs to no one. We all hold only fragments of it in our hands. And because we do not know what is true, we have to decide what counts for us. And whether something counts or not doesn't depend on measurements and certificates. It's weighed on a different kind of scale: meaning against emptiness, for example, or the idea of an eternal will outside of us, against sheer nothingness.

Since it was my uncle who was saying this, his choice of words couldn't have been a coincidence. When he said *Yevonim*, what resonated in that word was the whole fatal meaning of *Malchus Yavan ha'reshaah*, the wicked Greek kingdom, as it is called in the *Al HaNisim* prayer for Chanukah: *In the days of the Mattisyahu, the son of Yochanan the High Priest, the Hasmonean, and his sons—when the wicked Greek kingdom rose up against Your people Israel to make them forget Your Torah and compel them to stray from the statutes of Your will . . .*

The destruction of the people through assimilation was the name of the game in those days. Athletic competitions instead of

Torah study, philosophy in place of the divine laws. So when my uncle spoke of *yevonim* and the dangers of *yevonish* ways out there in the halls of academia, then that could only mean that he really considered those influences a potentially deadly threat to the Jewish soul of his foster child.

Wasn't this the language of the fearmongers, the sentences I had heard so often from the mouths of my teachers at the yeshiva in Mea Shearim? I could not believe that my uncle was making common cause with those who believed that any deviation from the prescribed path inevitably led to the fiery abyss of Gehinnom: a skirt that was too short, for example, an exposed female collarbone, not to mention a woman's singing or the sight of a married woman's hair.

No, if my uncle said such a thing, even with all his education, then that could only mean that it was of sacred importance to him, because the thing he was warning me about really was a threat to my life. And so I believed him, and I resolved to beware of *yevonish* thinking and its temptations. At the same time, however, I decided to sharpen all my senses for the immeasurable and unexplained things in people and in the world.

I would be lying if I said I decided at that very moment to dedicate myself to the human psyche and, in particular, to its disorders and their cures. Even the *Yevonim* were—at least back then—still prepared to perceive and accept a vestige of the fantastic and the unreal in the psyche. Still, when I thought of fantastic things, then I thought of pictures growing old in place of the people portrayed in them, or I thought of spilled sunflower oil—in short, I thought of fiction, of magic that possibly emanates from the human imagination, but maybe not.

•

Uncle Nathan's speech on the eve of my departure produced a noticeable effect: I was determined not to view the yeshiva in Pikesville only as a transfer station on my way to the university. He had succeeded in curbing my curiosity with a bit of fear, just enough to direct my energy back to Talmud study.

The first semester at the new yeshiva was hard for me nonetheless. The days were endless. That may have been mostly due to the fact that, during the first six months I spent in Pikesville, neither the coded wish of my father nor the fears of my uncle came true.

I hardly retained any of the tractate that we were discussing during that time. We were learning *Kiddushin*—betrothal—probably so that we would be prepared for the obligations that awaited us—preferably soon after our graduation.

We weren't allowed to choose our study partners. They were assigned to us. The rabbonim followed a carefully considered approach. They assigned the boys to one another according to country of origin, native language, and religious background. They preferred to match boys who did not share the same native language, and thus didn't generally come from the same country. After all, they were supposed to speak Hebrew with each other and not English, French, or Yiddish, like at home.

The rabbonim also preferred it when the two did not come from the same religious environment. There was a good reason for this, as well. In Pikesville, things were done the Litvish way, everything according to the views and educational methods of the old Gedolim from Lithuania. Our teachers were clearly inclined to this school of thought, even when there were differences to resolve among the various customs. When both study partners came from different religious circles—one with a Hasidic background, for example, and the other Yekkish, the way Uncle Nathan had raised me—then the students were less likely to form alliances with each other in opposition to the school doctrine. Since it often happened that neither boy's customs matched those favored at the school, it was a similarly difficult exercise for both to submit willingly to the education that we had all been sent to Pikesville to receive.

My chavrusa partner came from France. He was short and slender, shy and not at all talkative. He wasn't just childish physically. He wanted to be called Dani, even though his name was surely Dan or Daniel. I can't even say that for sure anymore.

Studying with Dani was not a pleasure, because he was something like a storage shed for words. He could memorize things quickly and thoroughly, both the texts and their approved interpretations. He wasn't much for discussions, for the simple reason that, in his eyes, there was nothing to discuss, since all the relevant questions and their answers could of course easily be looked up in the books and memorized.

The chavrusa sessions with Dani were tiring. I was always only half awake, even though I made a renewed effort each day to study vigorously and stay focused. It just didn't work out. Dani could never be tricked into going someplace new with an idea, not even once. Every time I tried it, he promptly interrupted me and said: But that's not what it says in the book.

It's hard to have to spend the better part of the day with someone you can't remotely imagine as a friend. Of all the things that were on my mind, there was nothing that I would have wanted to share with him. Requesting another chavrusa partner was completely out of the question, however. For one thing, Dani had a better command of the material than I did. So the rabbonim would surely have pointed out that I was the one they would expect to benefit from this study partnership. Furthermore, it would have hurt his feelings.

5

Like me, Eli Rothstein was older than the other students, because he had also lost time. That's what people might have thought, anyway. Of course, he didn't think the year he had spent in various clinics and at home in bed was lost time.

Shortly after his seventeenth birthday, he began to feel an unusual pressure in his eyes that continued for days. He didn't take the symptoms seriously. Even though they were uncomfortable, he thought they were nothing more than an allergic reaction. It was spring, and Eli's mother had begun feeling the effects of the first airborne pollen from the birch and boxwood trees. She'd had hay fever for years. Eli figured he had inherited her sensitivity and that, from now on, he would have to spend the spring months the way she did, blowing his nose and rubbing his eyes. It wasn't anything he would have gone to see a doctor about.

But a family friend who spent his free time reading the medical writings of Maimonides told Eli and his parents that the pressure could also have been caused by a dysfunction of the right kidney. His remarks got Eli's mother worried, so the only thing to do was to go to the doctor. He couldn't explain the strange eye pressure. He didn't think much of the kidney theory, but he agreed to do a blood test and send Eli's urine to the lab to be examined.

Just one day later, the doctor called and asked Eli to come to his office. Traces of blood had been found in his urine sample, and now there really was suspicion that something wasn't right with Eli's kidneys. From the ultrasound, it was clear just what was wrong. An ulcer was growing on Eli's right kidney.

A few days later, Eli packed a small suitcase for his first stay at the clinic. While he was on the operating table for open back surgery, the histologist confirmed after a quick incision that Eli's tumor was a carcinoma. The kidney and the surrounding lymphatic tissue were removed. And since the doctors couldn't say with certainty whether the cancer cells had already spread to the adjacent tissue or even into the bloodstream, it was only after the operation that the real torture began. Since he was young and in good physical condition, they put him through everything they could to kill off the cancer, wherever it might have spread. It started with chemotherapy. After that he had to submit to radiation therapy, and it continued with an autoimmune treatment stretching out over several months.

Eli took all of this stoically, though he sometimes felt that they were poisoning him with the radiation and the drugs, either on purpose or by mistake. All he had felt was some pressure in his eyes, which he would have been prepared to ignore. But now there were some days when he actually felt close to death. And when he looked in the mirror and saw that he was bald and had no eyebrows, there was no doubt that he was seriously ill.

There were days when the thought that he might die young, through no fault of his own, made Eli burn with an absolute rage at Hashem. Wasn't there something wrong with divine justice if Hashem was sentencing him to death without cause, before he even had a chance to really live and do anything to deserve such a punishment?

After a day of severe vomiting and headaches, he asked to speak with the rabbi, because he was hoping for an explanation for everything that was happening to him.

His rav didn't spend a lot of time beating around the bush. If there were any explanation at all, he said, Eli would perhaps find it himself, maybe only years later. The only thing he could do now was hang on and marshal all his physical and mental forces to beat the cancer.

The rav also said that Hashem takes care of anybody who is prepared to fight with him for his own life. Eli should read tehillim whenever possible, he said, and he should learn Mishna, since every mishna he studied would have healing properties—not just for him, but for everything around him. One cannot rule out the possibility, the rav continued, that the sickness was not intended for him, the seventeen-year-old Eli, but instead for something else near him that was in need of healing.

Perhaps this was the explanation that Eli was longing for: that Hashem had chosen him for this task, precisely because he thought him capable of mastering it. If he studied and repaired the possible damage in his surroundings, the rav said, the cancer might disappear as well.

Eli wasn't really convinced. Still, his rabbi's interpretation contained a potential explanation for the disease, and that was more, and at any rate better, than being helpless and exposed to the illness solely as a victim. If there was a chance that a tikkun through study could improve the world around him and also indirectly improve his own condition, then he wanted to do whatever was necessary.

He didn't want to rely only on pleading by saying tehillim. He decided he would learn as much mishna as his current condition would allow. And if the idea was a tikkun, he also wanted to learn something that was associated with mending and building. And so he chose *Masechet Mikva'ot*, a tractate which, like no other in the Talmud, connects very practical questions—in particular on the construction of immersion baths—with profoundly spiritual questions of ritual purity and impurity.

Eli had barely begun studying when he realized that he had actually had chosen the topic most appropriate to his condition. A mikvah has to contain water from a source that has not been touched by humans, whether it be a drop of rain, a pool filled directly from a natural well, a river that hasn't been straightened, or also the sea. The "living" water has the power to absorb all traces of destruction, particularly traces of death, like a filter that binds and neutralizes destructive energy, even transforms it into something constructive, as it changes from tumah to taharah, impurity to purity.

Several folios delve solely into the question of just what tumah and taharah really mean. The interpretation of tumah as a destructive condition that develops through contact with death seemed to Eli to be the most likely, at first glance. He had learned from his own experience that an encounter with death, the feeling of having been brushed by the wings of the angel of death, can change a person fundamentally. After an experience like that, you can be waylaid by timidity, fear, and great weakness, and you can easily wind up close to death yourself.

It stood to reason that water was only suitable for a mikvah if it hadn't traveled through man-made pipes or been handled by people in some other way. The real tumah, it seemed to Eli anyway, was in the *fear* of dying and in all those destructive psychic processes that emerge from contact with death. It was, then, a profoundly human phenomenon.

What also made sense to Eli intuitively was the fact that even though the smallest drop of "living water" absorbs tumah, its ability to transform it is a matter of quantity. "Living water" can only transform tumah if the volume is sufficient for an adult to be completely submerged. Just as contact with death permeates the entire soul, the water that purifies it of that contact must envelop us entirely.

Eli was sure the tikkun through study had much in common with immersion in a mikvah. But just learning a Mishna was not enough to heal the internal and external wounds of his body. And it was especially not sufficient to flush the fears out of him entirely, nor to wash out the chemotherapy poisons that were being pumped into his body week after week—and which had afflicted him so severely that his hair still wouldn't grow back months later.

So Eli studied, as much as he could, everything he could possibly learn about mikvaot, their construction, and the laws pertaining to them. He spent the long hours of his sick days reading countless books, and he studied every day until he fell asleep on top of them.

His studies had an immediate effect: he no longer had the feeling that he was losing time in the possibly short life span that was allowed him. For one thing, he was convinced that, by studying, he was fighting, and that each minute of study could add days, if not years, to his life. For another thing, he strongly believed that even if the studying itself could not save him, he would still be engaged in a great tikkun and would in this way at least deny death a victory over his soul.

Since Eli was immersed in the subject of the mikvah and the transformations that were possible through "living water," it was inevitable that he would realize that only a tevila could heal him in an effective way. He decided not to let anyone in on his plans for the time being. He wanted to look for a mikvah that was beyond reproach. He would only consider a mikvah appropriate if it had already existed in the days of the Holy Temple and had been used for the immersion of the Kohanim. After all, the priests who served in the temple and whose lives depended on their appearing before Hashem in a state of true purity would have been just as unwilling as he was to rely on dubious sites. Eli told only one person about his desire to find such a mikvah: that friend of the family who studied Maimonides's medical writings and had therefore sent him to the doctor with the completely accurate diagnosis of a kidney problem.

What Eli didn't know was that this friend had been blaming himself ever since. For he also adhered to the conviction that diseases that devoured people from the inside take possession of the body through the antennae and ways of the psyche. And so, deep down, he was unsure whether Eli had really been sick already when he made his diagnosis, or if instead, by uttering the conjecture, he had planted the disease in Eli's body.

There was still some residual doubt. And perhaps it was in fact the result of the encounter with Eli, his inexplicable eye pressure, and the tumor, an encounter with death, which has slipped into a young, barely adult man: the source of his very personal tumah, which now clung to him in the form of self-doubt.

He was immediately prepared to help Eli find a suitable mikvah, and he even promised to travel there with him.

Since they were both searching feverishly, they soon found a place that seemed suitable. It was a mikvah in a grove near Yerushalayim. It was made up of three natural stone pools, each about six feet deep, arranged to form terraces. The highest of these was supplied by a well that originated in the ground, and all three were connected by spillways. The pools had been in use as a mikvah more than two thousand years ago. For the priests back then, that meant a walk of several hours from the temple and back. If they went to such lengths to immerse themselves there, even though there were several mikvaot along Yerushalayim's outer city wall, then it must have been a place that even then was considered special and qualified beyond any doubt.

The decision to travel to Yerushalayim was made quickly. In many conversations with the doctors and Eli's parents, the family friend allayed all concerns that taking a trip in his condition would weaken Eli too much. On the contrary, he assured them: he was certain that he would bring Eli back so healthy that people would no longer be able to tell what he'd been through during the past year, or that he'd even been sick. The doctors and the parents finally consented, even though they didn't seriously believe for a second that he would get better by taking this trip.

The two of them didn't waste any time and went directly from the airport in Tel Aviv to Motza near Jerusalem. They didn't stay long. At dawn, the pools looked like deep black holes under a mirror. Eli undressed silently and jumped naked into the mikvah. He submerged twice and made sure to hover underwater for several seconds with his fingers and toes spread out and his eyes wide open, without touching anything. His face was glowing when he climbed out of the pool. He reached for the towel and dried himself off hurriedly, even though he wasn't cold. He was—this is what he believed he felt—no longer the same person he had been when he arrived.

Of course, nobody knew whether Eli Rothstein was really cured. And if that was in fact the case, who could say if he owed it to the various therapies of the doctors, or indeed to his tevila in the waters of Motza? But one thing was for sure: Eli himself was completely convinced that he had climbed out of the mikvah into a new life, a life without toxic medication, without sickness, and above all, without any fear of death. And that was the only thing that mattered.

For a year and a half, he hadn't been able to go to school, but he had come to know more in that time than he could have learned at any school in this world. It was no wonder then that he didn't even remotely consider these months to be lost time.

He came to Pikesville in the middle of the semester. When he appeared before the Rosh Yeshiva along with his parents and introduced himself, he exuded such a force of will that the Rosh Yeshiva had no doubt that Eli could make up the material he had missed.

After all the fears and battles he had endured, he made a decidedly more mature impression than the other students in our class. Because Eli Rothstein, perhaps due to a whim of Hashem, had suffered, since he had done battle with death and had therefore missed a year and a half of school, and because he was, like me, considerably older than all of our fellow students—for that reason, the Rosh Yeshiva decided that from now on, he should learn with me as my chavrusa partner.

Unlike Dani, Eli wasn't just prepared, but happy, to question every detail of the material we were studying. I am sure that the rabbonim didn't know what Eli thought of our curriculum. Otherwise they would have classified him as a dangerous influence and maybe even expelled him from the school.

The core of his thesis, which he readily presented to me after only a very short time, was that we hadn't really been sent to Pikesville to learn Torah. The real purpose of our education, he said, was to indoctrinate us, stuff us to the brim with ideology, but in a way that seemed natural to us, so that we would absorb everything they taught us with the feeling that we were drinking directly from divinely inspired sources, and that nothing but pure, unadulterated truth was being jammed into our heads.

Eli didn't denigrate all of it. It may well be good for something, he said. But he wasn't about to submit to brainwashing.

If you really care about Torah, he said, if you're really interested in truth, then you have to understand and keep in the back of your mind that that's not what we're learning here.

Why, for example, does Torah study for children begin with *Vayikra*, the third book of Moses, and not with the first? Children learn all the details about the offering of sacrifices in the Temple, a bloody business, and barely comprehensible for five- or six-year-olds. It would be more reasonable to start the lessons with the story of creation and the lives of our forefathers.

But then, Eli said, they would find out about Cain's murder, Noah's alcoholism and his inhuman curse of Ham's descendants, about Lot's incest with his daughters, Jacob's betrayal of Esau, the whorehouse visits of Yehuda, who was, after all, the ancestor of Jewish kings. And then it would be difficult for them to believe a certain interpretation of reality blindly, and they would ask questions from the very beginning.

I was prepared to agree with Eli. He could have sown doubt and seriously shaken all of my previous convictions. But he did not do that. He replaced the illusions that he took from me with something incomparably more valuable. Through his crisis and experience at Motza, Eli Rothstein had become a squire, if not a knight, of Hashem. But he was firmly convinced that true learning begins only where ideology ends, when it is no longer about power and advantage in the clash of interests, but only about the individual and Hashem and the piece of worldly reality in between.

I was excited by Eli's way of looking at things. And I believed him completely and without hesitation when he said that there was more truth in the mysteries of the living water than in the bloody works of the priests and in all of the complex laws derived by the wise men from the smallest letter in the Torah.

My suspicion of every ideology came from him. What I didn't understand then, and wouldn't comprehend even many years later, however, was the fact that it is precisely those ideologies that set the tone in the world, not the mystics, and that it is the ideologues who write history and who therefore ultimately decide what is designated as true and what is not.

Eli Rothstein came from New Jersey. But luckily for him, one of his mother's sisters lived in Baltimore. As a result, he had permission to visit his aunt's family on the one free weekend we were allowed to spend outside the yeshiva each month. Since Eli's aunt didn't mind putting me up for the weekend along with him, my friendship with Eli came with the perk of being able to leave campus at least once a month.

But it wasn't just because we got to leave school behind for two days that I so enjoyed going with Eli on those weekends. And it was only partially due to the fact that we could do whatever we wanted on Sundays: swim, read, play chess, go to the movies, or whatever else we could think of. Most of all it was because of Eli's cousin Rivka, with whom I fell deeply in love.

When I think of that time now, it seems to me that, from the age of fifteen at the latest, my life followed a plan that was mapped out precisely by Hashem, who pieced together all the details of my story in such a way that I advanced, step by step, encounter by encounter, toward my purpose in life. I was virtually pushed into my sense of memory. And I owe it to Eli that I finally began to believe in it and to accept it as a gift from Hashem.

Though Eli had told me all about the intimate details of his illness and his almost mystical experience in the mikvah at Motza without reservation, I had remained reticent and hadn't told him anything about my own experiences, which could also have been described as mystical. I had concealed from him what had happened that day in Geula, when I sat across from my father at our dining table. And I had also kept secret that everything I had seen during those moments later turned out to be true.

The fact that I did end up speaking to Eli about that experience had to do with the unconditional trust he had shown to me. And it was because of the circumstances under which I fell in love with his cousin Rivka. For that love also began with a vision.

That is: I cannot say with certainty whether I fell in love with Eli's cousin because of the vision or if the vision itself was caused by the feelings that came crashing down on me at the moment when we first met.

We never touched. That would have been unthinkable. And yet, the first time I found myself face-to-face with Rivka (at an appropriate distance), I knew within seconds how her hair smelled, how her hips felt through the fabric of her dress—and how her lips . . .

It was my first kiss. And I experienced it under the eyes of Rivka's entire family. I experienced it, even though I must have been standing two meters away from her and wasn't even looking at her. I had immediately averted my eyes from hers. When Eli introduced us, I looked *him* in the face, and it was *his* lips that I watched while he said my name. And it was with *his* arms that I embraced her. It was through *his* nose that I drank in the smell of her hair and her neck, and with *his* tongue that I tasted the kiss that she had shared with him, Eli, perhaps a year before, or maybe only recently.

Perhaps the arousal I felt was so overwhelming precisely because I experienced it through his memory, in which he felt it again and again, and in which it may have become more intense every time he remembered it, before it intermingled with my own arousal.

He's shy, said Rivka. She flashed her eyes at me and laughed, presumably because I was standing in front of her, red-faced and sweating, and probably looked as if I might fall over any minute.

When I came out of it, two things were clear to me: first, that I had fallen deeply in love with this girl on the spot, and second, that I had once again become immersed in someone else's memory, which meant that my ability was something special and was somehow similar to Eli's experiences in the waters of Motza.

I couldn't possibly speak to my only friend about these two insights. It would have been difficult enough for me to let him in on the fact that I was in love. But it seemed much harder, completely impossible even, to tell him that I not only knew about the kiss, but that I had kissed Rivka along with him, with his lips and every facet of his experience.

That weekend I did at least tell Eli about my first vision and about the fact that Uncle Nathan later confirmed every detail of what I had seen, heard, and felt.

I asked Eli if he thought this could be something like a special gift.

Of course, he answered, without seeming to spend even a second wondering whether he should believe me, or consider me a show-off.

After he had answered, he paused for a moment and scrutinized me. I smiled, as if to show him that he was in no danger. Whether or not I knew what had happened between him and his cousin, nobody was going to hear about it from me.

As if he understood it all, Eli smiled, too, and said: Rivka is really adorable.

I know, I answered.

6

There are some matters, Eli always said, that you can only approach if you're prepared to question everything—and even smash some things and leave them behind. His sudden cure in the mikvah was the clearest proof for him. If he had put his faith solely in the scientific consensus and had only allowed doctors to operate on him and stuff him full of drugs, he wouldn't have survived. He was convinced of that.

What had happened with him at Motza had taken place beyond all scientific knowledge. It couldn't be explained or repeated in measurements or clinical experiments. It had come from inside him and had been set in motion by his trust in Hashem and his strong will. In the healing of his body that came from his own soul, the waters of the mikvah had merely acted as a catalyst. The mental act had conquered and transformed the matter. No one could have convinced him otherwise.

And yet, it remained unclear to Eli whether it was only a coincidence that he had succeeded in focusing his mental powers to such an extent, or if there was a principle behind it that he still needed to discover and understand, so he could help others the way he had helped himself.

Anyone eavesdropping on our conversations at that time would surely have considered Eli precocious, and me too uncritical of what he had to say. I saw things differently, of course. I had a million questions that our rabbonim left unanswered—just as my father and my Uncle Nathan probably would have avoided giving an answer—because such questions led to the outer limits of what was sanctioned religiously.

In my eyes, Eli was courageous, more than anything else. He wasn't afraid to look for answers and to give them, regardless of whether his views would have been considered suspect if he had aired them in public. His handling of the sources, his relentless search and the conclusions that he drew from his findings, appeared to me even then to be an expression of wisdom—the kind that you cannot earn, but which you may at best receive as a gift after many years of living, or else in the form of especially impressive experiences. From the wealth of historic rabbinical personalities, he had chosen two role models: Eliezer ben Azarya and Elisha ben Avuya.

Eliezer ben Azarya had been appointed Nasi and chief of the Sanhedrin in Yavne when he was just seventeen. After he was chosen, Hashem turned his hair and beard white overnight, in order to silence the incorrigible and scornful people who considered Eliezer too young and inexperienced and therefore opposed his selection.

Elisha ben Avuya was known in the Talmud only as Acher, the Other One, for his name was no longer to be mentioned and would thus be blotted out. He had succeeded in doing something only three other rabbonim before or after him had accomplished: to ascend to the seven heavenly palaces, solely on the strength of his mind, to approach the throne of divine splendor in the Pardes and behold Hashem amidst the band of angels.

This ascent, or actually, descent into the depths of mystical experience was not the cause of his ostracism, however. He was called Acher because he had strayed from the path of Torah after his return from the other side. It wasn't that he had lost his respect for the law; on the contrary. As one of the greatest teachers of his time, he continued to instruct individual students. The Talmud tells of an event that caused Eli weeks of reflection: One Shabbos, Elisha ben Avuya was riding through the city, publicly desecrating the holy day of rest. One of his students was walking beside him, and Elisha was teaching him the law that he himself was breaking at that very moment. When they came to the Shabbos boundary, which the student was not allowed to cross, Elisha stopped his horse and pointed out that the student would not be allowed to follow him any further. The student turned around. Elisha himself rode on.

The Gemara does not provide an authoritative explanation for Elisha's lapse from the law-abiding life. Even so, there is one story that tries to discern the cause in a paradoxical incident that Elisha ben Avuya is said to have witnessed.

There is hardly any mitzvah where the Torah mentions a potential reward. In two cases, however, it explicitly promises a long life: for the commandment to honor one's father and mother, and for the mitzvah of *Shiluach Ha-Ken*.

Just as it is forbidden to slaughter a young animal on the same day as its mother, the Torah prohibits taking fledglings out of a nest if the mother can see it. She must be chased away, so she will not have to watch as her offspring are taken.

In the story about Acher, a boy goes for a walk with his father. The father sees a nest in a tree and asks his son to catch the fledglings for him, so he can make a tasty meal out of them. The boy does not hesitate to fulfill his father's wish. He climbs the tree and courageously tries to scare away the mother, who is prepared to defend her young. When she finally gives up and flies away, the boy tries to take the little birds out of the nest. But he falls from the tree and dies.

Elisha ben Avuya, as the story has it, observed this scene from a distance. The fact that the boy died at the exact moment that he fulfilled both mitzvot, for which the Torah expressly promises a long life, is assumed to have robbed Elisha ben Avuya of his faith and caused him to become that Other One.

Eli didn't think much of this explanation. He wondered: Could someone who had gotten as close as possible to Hashem lose his faith in light of a simple paradox?

Eli didn't just learn Gemara, as was expected of us. With great effort at times, he also consulted the writings of Reb Isaac Luria, the *Book of Creation* and the *Zohar*, mystical books that were actually still forbidden to us, since we were young, unmarried, and childless.

There was scarcely anything that made him more furious than the term "loving God." If Hashem was supposed to be all-encompassing, and humankind was created in his image as well, then he would have to contain all the conceivable attributes of humanity within himself. People who spoke of a "loving God," Eli postulated, were turning a blind eye to the true recognition of Hashem, who could be just as cruel, jealous, angry, and unjust as caring and was therefore, on the whole, unpredictable.

Someone like Elisha ben Avuya would not have seen it any differently. Surely he would not have lost faith in Hashem and his teachings because of such an experience. If it had been that way, Eli maintained, he would not have propagated the tradition by continuing to take on and instruct students. It seemed much more likely to Eli that Elisha would have comforted the father.

Perhaps he would have told the father that his son, having simultaneously performed the two mitzvot whose fulfillment was expected to bring longevity, had immediately received the greatest possible reward: his eternal share in the world to come, which he could no longer forfeit through any transgression or omission in this world, since Hashem had allowed him to die at the very moment his life had been fulfilled.

Eli therefore considered it a red herring that the Talmud presented this story as a possible explanation for Elisha ben Avuya's straying from his faith. Since Eli was prepared to ascribe any characteristic to God, he considered Hashem capable of anything, no matter how improbable, or even absurd, it might seem.

Eli was by no means planning to leave behind the law we had been raised to follow. But he had decided never to settle for the obvious answer. He had decided to assert his right to doubt and to question. And he would always be more likely to prefer an interpretation that went beyond the obvious, thereby revealing the poetry in divine action—a poetry that could likewise be a poetry of horror.

While Eli pursued his studies with an almost holy seriousness, for me the weighing and juggling of possibilities was more of a game. Eli was convinced; I only flirted with his views. The emphatic way he pushed every boundary, and sought to be consistent by aligning his actions with the insights he had gained, sometimes seemed downright radical to me. That was not my style at all, because I have never been a fighter. I was also never sure enough of myself and my possibilities that I could be assertive and present myself in such a distinct manner as Eli did.

My insecurity was most obvious when it came to my "sixth sense." First of all, I still didn't want to believe that it was really a gift. Not even Rivka's kiss, which I had felt so genuinely on my own lips, as if I had actually taken Eli's place, not even the thrilling experience of that kiss could convince me. I didn't want to remind myself or Eli about it, not even with the slightest remark, question, or allusion. I was prepared to discount both visions, which had taken place years apart, as sheer coincidences. I would much rather have been completely average, instead of having to accept that Hashem had given me a gift that I didn't know how to deal with.

When I actually did imagine even for a moment that there could be more to it than I was prepared to admit to myself, I was immediately filled with inner turmoil, fear really. Hadn't I penetrated into my father's memories and thus intruded upon his soul? By not only observing the affection of Eli and Rivka but also experiencing it along with them, hadn't I disturbed their intimacy? It seemed to me that I had taken secrets, secrets I should never even have known about, from both my father and Eli.

Intimate memories and personal secrets may be shared with a very close friend. But it is always a gift. People decide, speak, and reveal only as much as they themselves want to. But I hadn't even asked for permission. None of them had meant to share their secrets with me. They had been stolen and left at my disposal. I couldn't say whether I stole them, or if perhaps Hashem was the thief. But in any case, I was the one who received the stolen goods: sensations I had never felt, experiences I had never had, suddenly belonged to me.

I couldn't imagine that such a talent, if it was one, could have come from Hashem. I would more likely have identified it as a disorder or a sickness to be overcome, or a temptation to be resisted.

Of course I was not able to forget those incidents. And Eli also didn't forget what I had told him in that careless moment. I don't know how many months or even years had passed when he asked me about it directly. He wanted to know whether I had had more visions, and if I had thought about how I wanted to use my gift.

At first I tried to evade the question. But Eli wouldn't let it go. And so I confided in him about what I had seen when he introduced Rivka to me.

At first he said nothing and seemed taken aback, but he quickly regained his composure. The fact that I was only coming out with it now was proof enough for him that he could count on my discretion. For his part, he was now entirely convinced. I, on the other hand, was still wavering. What if it was just the fear of punishment on that day in Geula, and then later, after the first meeting with Rivka, only my erotic imagination, combined with a dash of jealousy, that had triggered the intense fantasies?

I just don't believe that it was more than a coincidence, I said.

Eli shook his head emphatically. If in my visions I had—and he assumed this—really felt with all my senses what he felt when he kissed Rivka, then I couldn't possibly have any doubt! No one, he said, could imagine a kiss like that in such a lifelike way, the way it actually felt. And if it had been possible for me to live at the heart of his memories, as if I were in his skin, Eli said, then that couldn't possibly have been a coincidence. Hashem had opened his hand and presented me a gift that I only needed to accept.

Even if that's true, I objected, how should I know whether the gift wasn't in fact a curse, perhaps, or a test? How could I be sure that it wasn't—and I faltered here—a sin to use this talent instead of suppressing it?

This objection made Eli almost furious. He told me I was faint-hearted and maintained that Hashem would not endow someone with such a talent if he didn't want it to be developed, refined, and used. As for sin—as long as I was using the word—it would only be a sin to reject it, to refuse to believe in it and to let it wither, Eli said. That would be no different from refusing to eat or breathe— an outright rebellion against His will.

If I followed Eli's line of reasoning, my gift was a mission. But what was that mission supposed to involve? I couldn't imagine what purpose my ability could serve.

Eli, at least, had an idea.

There are so many people who are trapped in their memories as if they were in a dungeon, he said. The psychiatric clinics are full of patients who suffer because they can't make themselves and their memories known, he continued. Patients no one believes, or who don't even believe themselves, because their memories are too horrendous to be credible.

They wouldn't have to tell you anything, Eli said. You would only need to look at them and establish contact with their memories to really understand. And understanding is the first step toward healing.

The idea of being hurled into the darkest chasms of the human experience again and again while sitting across from such patients—not only observing them, but also taking their place and becoming immersed in their memories—made me panic. I was supposed to voluntarily relive strangers' agonies, through every part of my senses, in order to help them? Eli had argued himself into a state of great agitation.

What immense possibilities! he raved, not noticing at all how much the idea horrified me.

Eli turned out to be right. No matter how great my fear was, there was no point rebelling against Hashem and the plan that he seemed to have for me. It took a long time for me to understand this, and even longer to accept it. And it was Eli who helped me, by providing proof that coincidence had nothing to do with it. This proof nearly cost us our friendship. A few weeks after our conversation, in which Eli had argued his point so heatedly and, instead of encouraging me, had scared the hell out of me, he knocked on my dorm room door late one evening.

Don't open the door, he said, when I was just about to turn the knob to let him in, Wait!

What's the matter with you, I asked, pressing my ear to the door.

I need advice, he said, his voice barely audible from outside, Something's happened.

It didn't sound like he was kidding. That wasn't his style, anyway. But I really didn't understand why I shouldn't let him in so I could talk about the problem with him.

Why don't you want to come in? I asked.

It was quiet out in the hallway for a few seconds. Then it sounded like Eli was propping himself up against the door with his hands, and with his mouth close up against the wood, he whispered in my ear as if through a muffling membrane.

Can you see me, Amnon? he asked.

Of course not! I responded.

And you can't feel anything, either? he continued.

No, I answered . . . except for the fact that you're weird.

If you open the door and look at me, I heard Eli whisper, you'll probably find out what kind of shape you're in, I mean, as far as your visions are concerned.

If this was supposed to be a test or a game, I didn't like it. But I wanted to know what had happened and why Eli was behaving so strangely. So I didn't wait any longer; I opened the door with a jolt. Then everything happened very quickly, and I'm not sure if I remember every detail, or only a few images and the all-pervasive and charged atmosphere of the moment when Eli entered, approached me, and grasped my upper arms with both hands.

It hurt, but it wasn't Eli's firm grip that caused the pain. It was what happened next.

As soon as he touched me, I found myself in a dark, strange room. I couldn't see anything, but I felt someone else's skin against my thighs, my belly and my lips. I was sweating. A wave of tremendous desire welled up in me and surged a moment later, like a shivering fit through my stomach and my head. Someone was holding me in a tight embrace, and my hands were also grasping a slender, tense body. We were panting quietly, moving and thrusting, as if each of us wanted to disappear into the other.

Until then I hadn't had any idea that, and how much, I was still in love with Rivka. The desire was overpowering, and her tenderness only stimulated it more. Slowly, yet inexorably, something crept through my chest, like a viper that's been heated up in the blazing sun and, withdrawing into the shade, leaves behind a winding line in the sand. It crept deep inside me and remained cowering there.

At least as strong as my longing was the jealousy I felt when I realized that Rivka wasn't giving all her affection to me, but to him: Eli.

I can't say what happened next. When I opened my eyes, I was lying on my bed with bare feet and my shirt unbuttoned. It was dark, the door was closed. I was alone.

I did not believe for a second that I could have been dreaming. When I closed my eyes, I could still feel Rivka's body against mine, her lips on my skin and her long, tender fingers running through my hair. The jealousy was still there, too, but it was now changing into a wild rage.

How could he have done this to me? a voice inside me clamored. As ridiculous as it must seem, at that moment I actually thought only of myself, the humiliation I felt, and my disappointment. Eli couldn't even have known that I was in love with his cousin. I had never told him, and had even tried to hide it from myself.

Apart from that, Eli and Rivka now had the much bigger problem. They loved each other. I had felt it so intensely that there could be no doubt about it. It was obvious that my feelings for Rivka could not be compared with what was between them. I could not imagine that I had ever been loved, or would ever be loved, the way Rivka loved Eli. For her it was about him, and for Eli, about her. I could only think of myself, there was no denying it, and the fact that I was in danger of getting lost in jealousy and envy made it plain to me that I was perhaps not even capable of being a true friend. I had never felt worthless before. Now I did.

I claimed to be sick and stayed in bed for two days. Eli came by several times and knocked on the door. But I didn't answer. I didn't want to talk to him, and I certainly didn't want to see him. The mere thought that my last experience with him could recur made that acrid mixture of envy and jealousy well up in me again. I had to get rid of it before I could look my friend in the eye.

On the third day, Eli slid a letter through the gap under the door. At first I wasn't sure if I should read it, but I couldn't resist.

I had no idea what the two of them were planning. I wasn't even sure whether Eli had expected he wouldn't have to tell me anything. I assumed so. After all, he had implied something along those lines when he stood outside my room that night and asked me not to open the door yet. But one thing I really did know now was how things stood with me—not only in terms of my visions, but also when it came to my qualities as a person. I wanted to know if Eli had guessed how close I had come to him and Rivka. I couldn't find any indication of that in his letter. I even believe that he didn't have the faintest notion of what it really meant not only to watch another person, but to become one with the person in that kind of vision.

The letter was short and unemotional. He and Rivka were going to get married very soon, he wrote. He absolutely needed to speak to me, not only because he wanted to be sure that I didn't despise him and wasn't rebuffing him because of his transgression, but also because he wanted me to be his witness when he signed Rivka's ketubah.

Our friendship, I decided, would never have been a true friendship if we allowed this to pull us apart. Eli was not at all at fault. He could not have known what I felt for Rivka; and even if he had known, their love didn't have to accommodate my infatuation. I wrote a reply, explaining myself and asking him to give me a few more days, and asked my next door neighbor to bring Eli the letter.

Nobody, except for the bride and groom themselves, was excited about the news that Eli and Rivka wanted to get married. The Torah doesn't explicitly prohibit marriage between cousins. Still, it was a union that any rabbi would have advised against. The two mothers grumbled, Rivka's father was quite firmly opposed, and the rest of the family shook their heads disapprovingly.

Eli would not have been Eli if he had let anyone deter him from marrying Rivka. He had slept with her and whispered the words of betrothal in her ear. The only thing they still needed was to wrest consent from their parents and rabbonim. The two of them had made no secret of the fact that they had been together; they had admitted it openly. As a result, Rivka would only be able to marry another man if she officially received a letter of divorce before a rabbinical court. Eli would have to sign the get and present it to her. But no Beis Din could force two lovers to declare a divorce and accept it if they were not forbidden to each other as marriage partners.

Eli described the legal situation to Rivka's father in a private conversation. He was anything but amused, of course. Aside from the problem that the couple could not be forced, he was frightened by the idea of having to hash out an embarrassing debate like this virtually before the eyes of the whole community. He could only choose between his own disapproval and the outright indignation from members of the congregation and the families. So he chose the lesser evil and resigned himself to the inevitable.

The fact that they loved each other had become impossible to overlook, since they were no longer making any effort to hide it from others. And so, at least his daughter would get a loving husband whom everyone had known—and indeed cherished—since he was a child. And, to top it all off, he had become a Talmid Chochem who felt at home in the most remote corners of the law, just as comfortable as they themselves felt in their own living room. He had proven it during that private conversation.

I had shut myself away for a week. Now I believed that I could leave my room and see Eli. I looked for him and found him in the library. We embraced, and no further explanation was necessary. We had a free weekend ahead of us. Eli invited me to spend Shabbos with him at his aunt's house.

Rivka will also be there, he said, and he asked if that would bother me . . .

No, I was relieved to be able to tell him. I might still have a crush on his cousin and future wife, but she belonged with him.

Good, Eli said, sounding just as relieved as I was. We'll have Shabbos afternoon all to ourselves, though, he told me. We have a few things to talk about.

We certainly do, I agreed. During the week of my retreat, I had become aware of many things that I really wanted to discuss with a friend.

And so, on Erev Shabbos, we went to Eli's aunt's house. When we got there, Rivka was sitting in the living room reading. Eli waved to her to come outside. Rivka closed the book, stood up, and blew him a kiss, but she didn't come closer. The whole evening, they exchanged long glances and spoke quietly, but they didn't touch each other once. After everything I had experienced along with them, it was incomprehensible to me how they managed to follow the laws and avoid all touching.

Of course, in Rivka's presence, or even in the presence of anybody other than Eli, I could not talk about what had happened. It was only on the next day, after we had eaten and slept for a bit, and we left for a long walk around Baltimore.

Was it possible for now, Eli asked, to ignore the content of my latest vision and get enough distance to contemplate only its course and inner nature?

I had spent the greater part of the past few weeks trying to do just that. It had become clear to me that I had a long way to go before my ability could be useful to anyone. To begin with, I didn't know whether, when, and under what circumstances I was going to see things. Once again, as with the two previous times, I had been overrun by the images. I was at the mercy of events, without even the slightest chance of controlling their course.

But what seemed most problematic to me was the fact that, although I had inhabited another identity, I had not completely ceased to be myself. I had felt Rivka's skin and Eli's desire and love for her, as only he could have felt them. And yet, that viper had crept through *my* chest. This overlapping of other people's emotions with my own made it plain to me that I couldn't help anyone with my gift, at least not at the moment. This time I had known which feelings were mine and which were not. But I was not sure that I would always be able to tell the difference. If I didn't know whose thoughts I was actually thinking and whose emotions I was feeling during such a vision, the image unfolding before me would always be a vague collage of myself and others.

That, Eli replied, is exactly what he meant when he said that Hashem expects us to work on our talents. The first step, he said, is to accept them and to understand their true nature. And once you've succeeded in doing that, he continued, you can make progress, grow, and refine your own abilities.

At the moment, you're still standing in your own way, he told me. You haven't succeeded in withdrawing far enough that you and your feelings can dissolve completely in the vision. But withdrawal, Eli said, is an exercise that the law demands of us anyhow.

He called it *Bitul Atzmo*, which essentially means self-restraint, or more precisely: the diminution of one's ego. If I wanted, he promised me that he would put aside his mystical writings for a while and learn Mussar with me. We could begin with the *Mesillat Yesharim* of the Ramchal, an ethical text that describes the *Path of the Just* as a gradual process of self-awareness.

Bitul Atzmo does not mean disappearing as a person, but reaching a level of humility that still allows one to strive for a goal, but free of all self-involvement.

I was surprised to hear him use a term like humility. I would more likely have assumed that I needed a dose of "Greek knowledge," as my uncle Nathan would have phrased it, a scientific education, in medicine for example, in order to gain at least a rudimentary understanding of what was happening in my body and what made me different from Eli, who had never in his life had to deal with other people's memories being transferred onto him. But humility? That term surprised me, coming from him of all people.

Eli admitted that he, too, had a long road ahead of him. He knew that, he said, and it couldn't hurt either of us to think about humility, and to try out a few of the exercises recommended by the Ramchal.

Are you sure? I asked, still skeptical.

Of course, Eli said, looking surprised that it was not immediately apparent to me. How much more proof do you need? he asked. Hashem works in the world like an artist, in whose hand even a simple grain of sand can turn into a gem.

I thought back to the evening in Zurich when my uncle told me to come to his shop, so he could show me his most beautiful demantoid. Uncle Nathan had tried to get across to me that secular insights would do me no good if I did not wrap them in a cloak of Torah knowledge. And now Eli was explaining that if I wanted to help anyone with my gift, I had to follow the Mussar teachers on the path of *Bitul Atzmo*.

The wedding of Eli and Rivka was celebrated a few weeks later with immediate family. I accompanied Eli during his Aufruf, signed Rivka's ketubah as a witness on the day of the wedding, just as he had requested, and stood with the couple under the ruby-red chuppah when he put the ring on her finger and the ketubah was read aloud.

Not all marriages are made in heaven, as the saying goes. But watching the way the two of them looked at each other, spoke to each other, and touched with discreet tenderness as they passed each other, there was no doubt that their connection had been determined and sealed by a higher authority.

Even though Eli and I were both over twenty, we were still in school. Not for much longer, though. Eli's wedding was not the only decisive change in our lives. Six months later, we would be graduating from Pikesville, so there was an urgent need for us to think about what we wanted to do after school.

Eli decided to attend the rabbinical seminary at Yeshiva University in New York. He had relatives there who had a big apartment on Amsterdam Avenue in Manhattan, not far from YU's Wilf-Campus, and they had agreed to take Eli and Rivka in.

I wanted to continue studying with Eli, but I did not believe that Hashem had a life as a congregational rabbi, mashgiach, or Mussar teacher in mind for me when he endowed me with my unusual talent. Luckily, along with rabbinical studies and liberal arts, Yeshiva University also offered a pre-med track. That, I thought, could be just the right combination for me: I could prepare for medical school and continue learning Torah with Eli.

Uncle Nathan had explicitly promised me years before that, after my graduation in Pikesville, I could decide for myself what and where I wanted to study. My decision went beyond his expectations. Becoming a doctor, he said, could not be wrong in any case. But the fact that I also wanted to begin my studies at a religious university left him convinced that he had given me appropriate advice before he sent me to America.

He readily agreed to pay for my studies and my housing in a Yeshiva University dormitory. After my graduation from the yeshiva in Pikesville, I went to visit him in Zurich and he presented me with a gift: it was the black cardboard box in which—I remembered it well—there was a large, emerald green gem on top of a velvet cushion.

I asked my uncle to keep the demantoid for me until I completed my studies and could stand on my own two feet. He agreed. I

7

We spent that year's High Holy Days in New York. Eli and Rivka had moved to Amsterdam Avenue. I lived in a dormitory near the university. I had been assigned a room in one of the buildings on West 187th Street between Amsterdam and Audubon Avenues. Ten students shared a spacious apartment with four rooms, a common living space, bathroom, and kitchen. Compared with the dorm on the campus in Pikesville or even with our small apartment in Geula, it was paradise.

Uncle Nathan had arranged everything, from getting me registered and finding me a place to live to paying my tuition and housing fees. I didn't even know how much my studies cost. When I asked him about it, he dismissed the question with a wave of his hand.

As long as you study hard, he answered, every single dollar will be well invested.

The daily routine at YU was nearly as strict as it had been in Pikesville. Attendance and participation during lectures and seminars were mandatory. But as rigorous as the programs for prospective doctors and lawyers were, religious studies certainly weren't treated like a minor. Everyone who'd come here had, in a sense, willingly chosen a double major. There were no compromises; inattentiveness resulted in an immediate warning and, if necessary, harsh consequences.

It wasn't easy to satisfy my desire for cultural education on top of the pre-med track and my studies in Torah, Talmud, Midrash, and Halacha. Luckily, I had no difficulty learning the skeletal parts, the names of the blood vessels, and the structures of the brain. Learning things by heart, and repeating them almost playfully so I wouldn't forget them, was something I'd been trained in every day since childhood. I could have completed my basic medical studies in less time. But instead, I used the free hours to continue educating myself in cultural matters.

My uncle wasn't only generous when it came to tuition and housing in New York. The way he saw it, by graduating from Pikesville, I had earned my share of secular education, as well. Whether it was visits to the Museum of Modern Art, classical music concerts at Carnegie Hall and Lincoln Center, or the acquisition of particular books—Uncle Nathan gladly covered the cost, as long as I could document what I was spending the money on.

One hour a day was strictly reserved for joint studies with Eli. We never skipped a day. On Shabbos we even studied a little longer. We systematically worked our way through the books of the great Mussar teachers, debated a lot, gave each other tests, and watched as we slowly made progress on the path of *Bitul Atzmo*, that exercise in humility we had chosen so that we could prepare for the moment when we might have to prove ourselves. Perhaps we wouldn't know enough or be capable of enough at that moment, if it ever came, but at least we wouldn't be blocked by our own overpowering egos.

If it hadn't been for those sessions with Eli, New York might have been my undoing, because from the very beginning, my study of medicine, my forays into secular art, and my experiences in that metropolis brought me moments of profound insecurity.

It started with the Big Apple itself. Never in my life had I been so close to the modern, non-Jewish world. I only had to leave campus and go a few blocks. Though I had never been conscious of living in a ghetto, I now felt like I came from one. Whether it was in the isolation of Geula, on the campus of the yeshiva in Baltimore, or even in the Enge in Zurich, I had always lived in a relatively protected habitat, where the Torah dictated the rules, and even the animals and plants seemed to submit to the will of Hashem.

Manhattan was different. I was not prepared for the sensations that other people are able to absorb and process over several years. Along with the half-naked girls sauntering past me with their exotic scents, I came across men holding hands and outsiders of every type imaginable, and from a variety of backgrounds. The advertisements that practically screamed from the newspapers, the radio, and the huge neon signs promoted a lifestyle that was the exact opposite of what Eli and I were studying during our evenings. It was a world where humility not only had no place, but was even frowned upon as a personal obstacle on the road to individual fulfillment. What unsettled me most, because—naïve as I still was—it surprised me, was the seemingly complete absence of Hashem and His Torah among the lines of cars, the hot dog vendors, the people handing out fliers, the glamour, and the sex. Wearing a black hat and having your tzitzes blowing around on these streets was like being an emissary from another world, carrying a message that hardly anyone wanted to hear.

All the same, there were islands, individual quarters in this alien world—like Williamsburg or Washington Heights. But I couldn't help wondering every day just how much longer the moloch would tolerate these islands. I was convinced that the only reason they were tolerated at all was precisely because they were islands, which could of course be circumnavigated, and which were also occasionally known to disappear into the sea of the mainstream.

•

Just as irritating as the unfiltered sensations of the goyish Big Apple was the strictly deterministic view about the mechanics of the human body that I was being taught. To my great surprise, according to the science, there seemed to be no connection between consciousness and being. The human body was regarded as a highly complex machine, though the experts believed they understood most of its details well.

Whatever took place in this biomechanical system could supposedly be explained using physical or chemical formulae. How is the arm raised? How does the heart rate accelerate or decelerate? What makes a bone age?

Diseases were systemic malfunctions, brought on by intruders like viruses, bacteria, or chemical substances. Occasionally some screws came loose in the machine, or there wasn't enough oil. The remedies created still more formulae, and countless pharmaceutical products that were developed on the basis of those formulas.

Everything we were learning ruled out phenomena like Eli's cure in the mikvah at Motza. The science was miles away from the ideas of Rambam, which held that a person could completely renew every cell of his body within seven years—a process that could only be controlled through consciousness.

Medicine, with its mechanistic reasoning and its trust in devices and substances, seemed to me to be a fascinating but ultimately erroneous thought experiment that didn't add up—the variable of the divine spark was missing from the equation.

Sometimes it seemed to me that even our lecturers weren't truly convinced of what they were teaching. There was no other way for me to explain some of the deviations from classroom theory that people allowed themselves in their lives outside the university.

Our anatomy professor puzzled me most. He only taught half days, from early in the morning until around eleven o'clock, Monday through Thursday. On Sundays and weekday afternoons, he took care of his patients, who came in droves to his ear, nose and throat practice at the corner of Park Avenue and 86th Street.

The secret of his success with his Upper East Side clientele was revealed to me once when I had a sinus infection, and I had to ask him during a lecture break if he would let me leave early. Professor Freedman gave me his card and told me to come to his practice that afternoon for an examination.

At the doctor's office, there were hardly any medical instruments. Of course, he shone a light into my nose, throat, and ears. He even took an ultrasound image of my nasal cavity and my sinuses, which made him sigh, since they were swollen, apparently infected, and completely phlegmy. But he conducted most of the examination by touch, with his bare hands.

With my shoes, socks, and shirt off, I lay on my back on the examining table, and Freedman felt around in search of the true cause of my condition. He was definitely interested in my lymph nodes, but mostly in certain lines on the inside of my right forearm and in the area of my left heel.

After he had spent several minutes gently touching different places, massaging them in circles and briefly applying pressure, constantly and attentively observing me as he did so, he took a warmed metal rod, and for about a minute he pressed the end of it against the back of my left hand, into the hollow between the thumb and forefinger. The constant throbbing in my temples and the strain under my eyes abruptly became less intense.

Professor Friedman seemed satisfied, and he told me I could put my clothes back on. He prescribed an herbal tea.

That will help your body get rid of the mucus, he said. But you have to go to a dentist immediately. One of your upper right molars seems to be dying; probably a hidden cavity. It may be that it's already dead, and that's why you don't have a toothache. It looks like an infection in your jawbone is to blame for your discomfort.

I nodded in amazement, but the appointment wasn't over.

The professor said he could help me with the headaches if I stayed for another half hour, and then came back to the practice on each of the coming days for forty-five minutes of acupuncture.

Some things I would have expected, but definitely not that my anatomy professor from Yeshiva University would figure out that a molar was silently rotting away by feeling his way around the meridians of my body, and then, to top it all off, that he would offer me acupuncture to get my chi back on the right path and free me from my headaches.

I didn't know whether I should feel redeemed or conned.

The professor led me into a different room and asked me to have a seat in a big leather armchair and put my feet up. While he was placing the needles at my temple, the wing of my nose, and the nape of my neck, he told me about his first encounter with Chinese medicine.

Fifteen years before, during a time of great personal difficulty, he had experienced a sudden hearing loss, and as if that wasn't bad enough, he could hardly move his head, either. Back then he was a research physician at Mount Sinai Hospital in New York, and he was always bleary-eyed and stressed out. Of course he had himself checked out thoroughly. But none of his colleagues at different clinics around the city could figure out what was limiting the mobility of his cervical spine. The cause of his hearing loss also remained unclear. They prescribed infusions and a few days of rest.

After those days off he could still barely hear anything with his right ear, and he continued to move as if he was wearing a neck brace. When there still hadn't been any improvement fourteen days later, his doctor handed him a business card after an examination.

You may think it's hocus-pocus, he whispered to the professor, but my wife swears by this man. Go see him, it couldn't hurt. I'm afraid I can't do anything else to help you.

The man the doctor's wife swore by was a Manchu in Chinatown who was at least ninety years old. His office was a storeroom behind a fruit and vegetable market on Elizabeth Street, halfway between Canal and Hester.

The business card was simple. Printed on it were three characters that might have meant a name, then the name of the store and the street, and the instruction to "show card at counter."

Freedman was exceedingly skeptical, but even the slight chance of relief for his symptoms made it worthwhile for him to take a trip to Chinatown.

He showed the card at the front desk, and he was directed to the back and asked to wait by himself for a moment in the storeroom. In fact, it took almost twenty minutes, and he was tempted to leave several times, before the Manchu turned up to ask what ailed him. The old man's face displayed no emotion at all as he listened to Freedman's vague theories. He asked him to undress his upper body and lie down on the table on his stomach. First he felt around Freedman's spine. Then he asked him to sit up, turned on a bright light, and approached him. He pressed his index fingers against Freedman's eyebrows and pulled his lower eyelids down with his thumbs. After a few seconds, he lowered his hands and stepped back.

The Manchu said quietly, but decisively: You must change the direction you are looking in. Your head will follow—slowly, but it will follow.

Freedman thought that sounded like something out of a fortune cookie. Even though he thought he must have looked quite flabbergasted, he got no further explanation, only the terse instruction: *Fifty*.

Mechanically, Freedman took the five bills out of his briefcase and put them in the hand the Manchu was holding out. The old man took the money and told his patient to lie down on his stomach again. With a few movements of his hands, he loosened the blockage in his cervical vertebrae, said goodbye, and left the tiny examination room before the professor could put his clothes back on.

Professor Freedman could move his head again by the time he left the store on Elizabeth Street. That evening he could feel his hearing slowly returning in his right ear, and two days later it was fully restored.

This recovery made a deep impression on him, and that, more than anything, was why he was prepared to heed the old man's advice: he decided to change the direction he was looking in and monitor whether and how his head, that is to say his views, would follow that movement.

He put in for a sabbatical, and he went to Taiwan for several months, so he could become initiated in the basic principles of traditional Chinese medicine. When he came back, he quit Mount Sinai and applied for a half-time position as a professor of anatomy at Yeshiva University, so he could use the rest of the time to deepen his studies in alternative medicine.

Two years later, he opened the practice on the Upper East Side, and from then on he treated patients who would not, under any circumstances, have put themselves in the hands of a ninety-year-old Chinese man in the back room of a store in Chinatown, but who completely trusted him, the distinguished Jewish professor, and came to him for treatment, even with the needles, teas, and homeopathic remedies that he used to supplement the therapy.

It had simply become clear to me, the professor said, how insane it is, for example, to prescribe powerful medications to lower a patient's blood pressure. If the body is creating pressure, there's a reason for it. The body is compensating for something that has become imbalanced. We must promote the restoration of this balance, he said, and help the body help itself, instead of preventing it from doing so.

After he had said this, he patted me on the shoulder and told me to relax while the needles took effect. After about twenty minutes, he said, he would come back to remove them.

When he left the room, I immediately fell asleep, and I didn't wake up again until he spoke to me quietly.

I am going to remove the needles now, he said. After that, feel free to stay seated here for another fifteen minutes, then come back tomorrow.

I nodded. But there was still one thing I wanted to know.

Why, I asked him, weren't we learning anything at all about this knowledge in our program? Why was he practicing something completely different from what he taught at the university?

I'm not, he objected. Look, my young friend: I have my patients and a peaceful life. Even my colleagues from the university come to me first when they don't feel well, so they can be treated. But back in the late Sixties, if I had—or even today, if I were to express my appreciation for Chinese medicine in an article or a seminar, it wouldn't be long before I lost my teaching position, and maybe even my license to practice medicine. Even the Chinese have tried several times since the revolution to ban the practice of acupuncture and other balancing therapies. These ancient methods, which are hardly verifiable scientifically, collide with the western understanding of medicine much more than they do with the communist understanding of it.

No, he concluded, that would have meant nothing but trouble. I teach anatomy, he said. As you know, that's basically the undisputed foundation of every type of medicine. I don't have to make any claims I can't stand by, and with my impolitic knowledge, I help many patients here. I think that's a very balanced compromise.

I went to the dentist the very next day, as the professor had recommended. I was not in any pain, so I asked for a thorough checkup to start with.

The dentist could find no evidence of cavities, and he was ready to congratulate me and send me on my way. But since I was sure that there must be something to the professor's diagnosis, I pretended to feel a slight pain in the area of my upper right molars.

Isn't there any more precise way to examine that? I asked.

Of course, the dentist said. If you'd like, I can take an x-ray. Then we can see if something isn't right.

I asked him to take the x-ray. When it was ready and he put the image up to the light, he let out a quiet whistle, as if in admiration. Sure enough, under an old filling in the first molar on the top right side, a cavity had eaten its way deep into the tooth. The inflammation in the jaw bone around the root of the tooth was also visible as a light shadow, and above that, as a dense cloud, my completely clogged maxillary sinus.

That, he said, really doesn't look good.

Using a coolant spray, he checked the vitality of the tooth. I couldn't feel anything. The bacteria had already narcotized and destroyed the nerves. The tooth was dead.

I would be spared the pain of a root canal, then. But the doctor said he was uncertain about whether he could save the tooth, given the infection in the bone. It could take months to heal completely, he said, if it even went away without the tooth being pulled.

We decided he should try to save the tooth anyway.

The acupuncture sessions of the following days took away my headaches. The tough, glassy mucus soon drained away. The dental treatment, on the other hand, took nearly six months. The dentist's bill was considerable. The treatment from my professor hadn't been pro bono, either. Nevertheless, the money that Uncle Nathan wired to me was, when I really thought about it, an investment in my education, just like costs of the concerts I attended and the yearly MoMA membership.

The treatment from Freedman, and the story he had told me, changed my attitude about medical school completely. I still wanted to complete my training. But I told myself that I wouldn't let anyone turn me into a conventional doctor.

After I completed my undergraduate degree and moved on to Yeshiva University's Albert Einstein College of Medicine, I took as many courses as I could in neurology, psychology, and psychiatry. In a discipline where even my professors admitted that science was not sufficient to penetrate the complex structure and workings of the subject matter, I felt more comfortable than I did in pure biomechanics.

Specialization did nothing to lessen my uncertainty, however. In light of the admission that what we were learning was sound but at best superficial knowledge, I was surprised by the curriculum and the actual state of therapy research. In some courses on the practice of psychiatric treatment, I felt more like I was in a chemistry seminar than one on the healing of the human soul—and I had never been able to conceive of the psyche any other way.

If Freedman had considered the use of blood pressure medications questionable, clinical psychiatrists were viewed almost as poisoners. The syndromes weren't very sophisticated. Besides schizophrenics and manic-depressives, there hardly seemed to be anything else. The medications either kept people quiet or brightened their moods. They made the patients manageable. But I couldn't imagine that they promoted the healing of a wounded soul. Some of the current treatment methods the patients were subjected to— from immobilization and ice baths to electroshock and lobotomy— seemed to me more like medieval torture methods than therapies.

I had wanted to avoid the biomechanists, but I ended up choosing a subject where their views found especially drastic expression. The human machine had to work. If it was out of order, crude instruments were tried, so that these patients at least would not do any harm or, better yet, could be reintegrated into societal processes as a sort of auxiliary engine with limited performance. People who in other cultures would have been revered as saints with second sight were locked up in clinics and chemically sedated, so no one would notice them.

This idea of humanity was foreign to me. How could someone who, like me, also considered human beings to be created in the image of God, contemplate surgically removing whole areas of a patient's brain and making him into a creature with almost no will? In reports from the Third Reich, such methods wouldn't have been astounding. But in medical studies by American and European doctors who were entrusted with clinics, they surprised and horrified me. And yet, this subject was being taught at a religious university. In my eyes, that was as great a paradox as the one Elisha ben Avuya is said to have once faced.

At that time, if I wanted to become a psychoanalyst, there was no getting around psychiatric training. I had no choice but to study the entire topography of this hell if I wanted to make my escape at some point and get into psychoanalysis.

I often wondered if I myself wasn't in danger of one day ending up as a patient in this medical Gehinnom. If I ever confided in a psychiatrist, my visions would promptly be classified as a symptom of schizophrenia. The medication would be determined in the blink of an eye, and right along with it the prognosis of probable incurability.

At such moments I felt transported back to that green bench on the summery Mythenquai in Zurich, where years before I had read Bulgakov's *The Master and Margarita* in just one day—and the imponderable, which defied precise natural science and which I had encountered in my visions, and my image of the mechanical man who believes he can control his and the world's fate with substances and ideology, were sitting next to me: Woland and Berlioz and Bezdomny. I knew that Annouchka had already spilled the sunflower oil. And it really almost drove me out of my mind that I didn't have the slightest idea how to save Berlioz from losing his head when he so persistently refused to at least accept that something else was directing people's lives—namely, the sometimes grim, poetic hand of Hashem.

By the time I arrived in Portland to begin the General Psychiatry Residency at the Maine Medical Center, Eli already had his smicha and was allowed to call himself a rabbi. He had two children and planned to move with his family to Israel, where he had the opportunity to work as a part-time Mussar tutor at a well-known yeshiva.

Shortly before they left New York for Israel, Eli and Rivka came to Portland with their children to visit me and say goodbye. Rivka seemed exhausted, but she was still beautiful. Eli was bursting with energy, as always.

I didn't show them the clinic. It probably would have been upsetting, and not only for the children. But I spoke to both of them and shared my anguish about my endless passage through the Gehinnom of psychiatry. I had the feeling that I was going to have to waste several years in institutions whose methods I detested and condemned.

At the same time, the center in Portland was something like an oasis of paradise in the middle of Hell. Therapies that were ultimately geared toward breaking the will and personality of the patients were frowned upon. Still, even there it was understood that chemistry ruled the bodies and souls of the patients.

It seemed to me that, with my gift, I possessed a valuable treasure that no one wanted. I even had to hide it, so that I wouldn't unexpectedly end up as one of the patients. What was the point of my gift, what was the purpose of my studies with Eli and our efforts to prepare ourselves for the day when we would be challenged, if none of it counted for anything out here, and I had to accept that I could never really help any of the patients, who were mostly classified as hopeless cases?

Eli tried to calm me down. Patience, he said, is also one of the exercises on the path of the pious. Impatience always comes about when your ego cares more about itself than it does about the task that's intended for you. And because it was his profession, Eli told me a parable from the Midrash to help me to find my patience once again, and my place in Hashem's plan.

In Galilee, Eli told me, there once lived a merchant. Business was good. He made enough money to build a house. He became wealthy and built a bigger house. And when he had become even richer, he built himself a palace worthy of a king. His success led many people to envy him and wish him ill. The merchant had no choice but to build a wall as tall as a man all around the palace. He lived this way for a number of years, and he was happy. One day, when the summer sun was especially scorching, a beggar came by the palace. He had nothing but a small piece of bread in his pack, but he didn't complain. Still, he was hot, terribly hot. He sat down on the ground in the shade of the wall, and he ate, and when he'd had his fill, he thanked Hashem—for the bread and the shady spot He'd allowed him to find. Then he rested for a while in the cool shade of the wall, and finally he continued on. The beggar had hardly left the place when the earth began to tremble. The palace collapsed along with the wall, and the merchant died beneath the ruins, which also buried his wealth. He had lived, his business had been good, his affluence had become wealth and then even greater wealth, and the neighbors had become envious—all so that he could build the wall, and Hashem could allow that beggar who thanked Him for the piece of bread and the cool shade to rest for an hour; and no one ever heard about it.

When Eli had finished telling his tale, we were quiet for a long time.

I knew that he had learned his lesson. I still hadn't learned mine.

8

Hashem, it seemed, had compassion for me, or understanding. He didn't make me wait long for an opportunity to prove myself. Maybe he did it out of sympathy for his impatient student. Or maybe he just wanted to protect me, since it must have been obvious to him what kind of danger I was in, walking the halls of the clinic in Portland and counting the days until the end of my residency, which was still a long way off. I felt helpless and angry, because I thought I was completely out of place there.

At the time I was accompanying doctors on their rounds. They talked to me about symptoms and therapies that had already been tried and had failed, while I marveled at the frighteningly high percentage of patients who were considered incurable and classified as hopeless cases. They didn't even have a chance of ever getting out of this clinical antechamber of Gehinnom and returning to the world.

I took blood pressure and pulse readings, gave injections, helped the nurses feed immobile patients, and took care of the harmless cuts and stab wounds that other patients had given themselves on their arms, wrists, and legs. In the mornings I helped put together the medications that patients received each day and had to swallow under supervision.

The clinic had many more nurses than therapists, and most of them had acquired their credentials by taking a one-semester supplemental course during their psychiatric training. The group sessions and half-hearted attempts at behavioral and occupational therapy seemed to me to be a fig leaf that was supposed to hide the fact that we were really just detaining most of the people who were stuck there, to protect them from themselves, or to protect society from them.

In that atmosphere of routine immobilization, who would ever have approached the patients and tried to get to the bottom of the fear that, in one way or another, had control over all of them? And who was supposed to try to truly understand their apathy or aggression, their compulsions and delusions—as strategies that their psyches had chosen, so they could at least maintain a fragile emotional balance?

When I looked into the eyes of those patients or even touched them, chasms of fear and loneliness opened up, a chaos of emotions they couldn't express, because they had never learned how, and had probably never been allowed to learn. But there was almost always a small, abandoned child crouching and shivering behind the demonic curtain of fear, longing to be accepted, held, and comforted, frantically wrestling with its own emotions, which could hardly find shape or direction. It was that child, I felt instinctively, that I had to reach. I had to join forces with that child, so it could grow and become strong, so it could find its way out of this fearful hell.

At least I learned to deal with my gift more effectively, so that I was no longer helplessly exposed to my visions and the sounds, smells, images, and feelings from other people's pasts that came flooding into me.

Thanks to the exercises in self-examination and self-withdrawal that I had begun during my Mussar study with Eli and was still practicing, I quickly made notable progress. I had discovered that I was more or less receptive to the transmission of other people's memories depending on my condition on any given day. I also learned how to consciously open myself up, and how to close myself off.

I had figured out that I only truly melded with someone's remembered self if I touched that person, and there was direct contact with the skin. If I limited myself to eye contact, it was possible for me to immerse myself in the world of my counterpart's memories purely as an observer. So even when I was standing in the middle of a landscape of terror and could hear the demons salivating and snorting, I remained myself and knew that it wasn't me that they were after.

Still, even those experiences were hard to take. Afterwards I was often plagued by nightmares where the demons attacked and tried to kill me, because they sensed that I was there and was planning to come to the defense of their victims. The scenes I found myself in were like war zones. People were being murdered and tortured. Some of the children I saw were sitting in their own blood and excrement, faceless or disfigured by wounds. They screamed, or they were silent. And always, the children were alone with their fear.

If I had had to experience the torture and fear first hand during every immersion into a patient's memory, it would have been unbearable.

During that time I began to wear gloves made of thin white cotton, so that I could at least shake hands with the patients or stroke their foreheads if I upset them, so they could calm down. Of course my gloves elicited astonishment and disapproval from the staff. I claimed that I was allergic to one of the disinfectants they used and that I would suffer from a permanent skin irritation without the gloves. They believed me. The patients understood almost instinctively that I was protecting myself. Some even envied my second skin, stroking it searchingly while giving me an approving wink.

When I try now to remember the names of all the people I have treated over the years, it isn't easy for me. I've forgotten many of them, and I actually wanted to forget the things that happened to some people, and the scenes I had to witness, because in the long run, no one can live with such a crushing abundance of memories.

I destroyed my notes. During my Pesach cleaning eight years ago, I took everything that might have reminded me of my old job and, along with the rest of the chometz I needed to get rid of, I burned it on the street—all except for one comprehensive case study that I once wanted to publish as a book, something that never happened.

In that study I had described my first case, a therapy that I actually never should have performed, because I started it in Portland, when I was still nothing more than a prospective psychiatrist in a residency. I didn't burn that study. But it should have been the very first thing I threw into the fire.

The fact that I even considered describing the case in a book should have made me wary. But at the time I was still so excited about the success that I had achieved with my very first patient that I argued, to myself and her, that there were dozens of reasons why the public had a right to hear about her case.

She finally consented.

The fact that I never did publish the study was perhaps a result of the setbacks that I had to accept after that initial triumph. The therapies didn't always turn out well. I do believe that every individual I worked with benefited in one way or another, even if that benefit wasn't always as great as I would have hoped. Some of those scared children in adult bodies even preferred to go to their deaths in the end, rather than be tortured by their memories any longer.

I myself always considered their deaths to be a personal failure, a failure before Hashem, which then made me feel unworthy of my gift. There are three cases—if you can call them cases—that I will never forget as long as I live, as much as I sometimes secretly wish I could. I am even sure that if I ever ended up confronting myself in one of my visions, it would be the faces of Lauren, Minsky, and Wechsler that I would see first—even before those of my father or Uncle Nathan.

Lauren's return to life made me euphoric. The collapse of Minsky, for whom I hadn't even been a therapist, but simply a friend, cost me my reputation, my practice, and my research position in Freiburg. With Wechsler I might possibly even have become a criminal in the end. I say possibly, because I don't even know for sure whether that is indeed the case.

I met Lauren at the beginning of my second year in Portland. I had been transferred to another ward, and I saw her the very first day, in one of the bright, long corridors, which were subdivided into manageable sections, with automatic double doors at regular intervals. If there was ever a problem because a patient was aggressive or injured, these doors could be closed in a few seconds. This kept everyone from converging on the scene so they could see what was going on or even helping their fellow patient, who was being restrained by the nurses and had to be secured before being brought to the isolation room.

The doors were made of unbreakable glass in a steel frame and were about six feet wide. They opened and closed in opposite directions. This reduced the danger of an accident if the alarm went off and there was still someone trying to slip through the half-closed passageway.

When I first saw her, Lauren was standing up against the wall, right in front of one of those doorways, teetering slowly from one leg to the other, frantically shaking her head over and over again.

Her nightmarish indecision was not, however, the first frightening thing I noticed when I saw her. I couldn't tell how old she might be. Her hair was close-cropped, and some patches on her head were completely bald. Her eyes lay deep in dark sockets. Her head, arms, and legs, which were naked and peeking out from under a blue gown, were like those of a mummy, utterly without flesh, the one difference being that the wrinkly skin over her knees was not dried up. Lauren was emaciated to such a degree that I could hardly understand how she managed to stay on her feet.

I began to walk more slowly on the opposite side of the hallway. I looked at her for a long time and tried to concentrate on her completely, so that I might catch a fleeting glimpse of what was inside her. I wanted to know what was preventing her from moving on.

I didn't manage to connect with her immediately, since she was completely lost inside herself. Actually I don't even think she had noticed me. It wasn't until I approached her at her level, stopped and tried for a few seconds to look through the deep, dark circles into her eyes, that I heard an almost imperceptible whispering.

I'm going to get stuck, something was saying to her insistently: I'm just too fat. It's totally impossible for me to get through this door. I'm going to get stuck.

She stopped teetering, paused for a moment and turned around, as if in slow motion. After a moment she began taking short, shuffling steps the few feet back to the next door. Once she'd made it there, the scene repeated itself. She stopped, hesitated, and, after a while, began teetering from one foot to the other again.

I could no longer see her eyes, and I couldn't hear anything, either. But I was sure that the voice inside her was again speaking to her insistently: I'm going to get stuck, I'm just too fat!

Lauren had been admitted to the ward at her own request a few weeks before, but she hadn't spoken to anyone since her arrival, and she was steadily losing more and more weight. Since her insurance wouldn't pay for more, her care was limited to a medical escort for her slow demise. There were already days when she couldn't get out of bed. If she was feeling well, she took a few steps, but they were endlessly exhausting for her.

As I later found out from the ward physician, they only gave her a few weeks. She had been starving herself for years, even if she had never reached the type of dramatic stage she was at now. Her spine was already irreparably damaged, and it was only after taking painkillers that she could sit or stand up. Sooner or later, her organs would stop functioning. And then, the ward physician said, it'll be over. No one believed that she might still have a chance to decide to live and start to eat normally again.

It's not against the law to starve yourself to death in the United States. If relatives—the parents or spouse—don't have the patient declared incapacitated and request a feeding tube, the doctors won't do anything to provide essential nourishment for the body against the patient's will.

Lauren, however, was on the ward at her own request. Her young son—I also found this out later, but from her—lived in foster care, with her ex-husband's parents. She had broken off contact with her own family years ago and had moved from Arkansas to Maine, so she could get far enough away from her father and the people and places from her childhood in a strict Pentecostal church. She had come to the clinic to die, and since no relative seemed to have an interest in her continuing to live, there was also no one to stop her from putting her decision into action.

I continued to watch Lauren for some time that first day. After several minutes of desperate indecision, she turned around again and shuffled back toward the doorway that I was standing in. She still took no notice of me, behaving as if I wasn't there at all and she was all alone in the corridor, and maybe even in the world.

By the time she had made it halfway back, however, her strength was depleted. She stopped and faltered. She had probably become dizzy. I ran right over to her so I could prop her up and help her get back into her room. I picked her up and held on under her armpits. Beneath my hands I could feel her ribs clearly. Her body was light as a feather. Only then did she notice that she was not alone. She raised her head and looked at me through dull green eyes, frightened and alarmed at first, but finally with great gratitude.

I saw Lauren in the middle of a large crowd, outdoors, in front of some kind of enclosed platform that had a microphone and two big loudspeakers set up on top of it. The preacher of the congregation was in position at the microphone, and his words, when amplified by the speakers, towered over the assembled crowd like a tidal wave, finally plummeting down and hitting each person with full force.

With a powerful voice that nonetheless cracked repeatedly, the preacher sketched out for his spellbound congregation a picture of the terrible agonies that all those who had violated the eternal and one true law of the Lord could expect after the return of Jesus and the Day of Judgment.

Lauren was maybe seven. She was shivering, because—I sensed it clearly—she was convinced that on Judgment Day, which was possibly close at hand, she would inevitably be cast into the fiery abyss of damnation. She had been born a sinner, and every day since then her parents and her siblings had given her the tally of her transgressions, which were piling up higher and higher, causing even the prospect of redemption to recede into an unreachable distance. If she should ever meet the Lord, he would be her executioner. He would grab her with red-hot forceps and deliver her to the eternal torments of fire and brimstone.

That's why Lauren was shivering. That's why she spent every day living in fear of the return of the Redeemer of the Righteous, whose appearance would mean only the sealing of judgment for her. Nothing she did could remove the mountain of transgressions. Not enduring beatings or shunnings, during which no member of the family was allowed to speak to her, because she had eaten too noisily, spilled milk, or not paid attention during grace and hadn't said *amen* at the right moment. It also wasn't enough that she diligently learned her psalms and Bible verses, no longer contradicted her parents, and only floated through the house like a cringing, subservient spirit, so as not to disturb anyone. There was nothing—they had made it clear to her—that could make up for her worthlessness and the extent of her sin.

When I picked up Lauren in her exhaustion in the ward hallway, I did not know yet how close the connection was between the preacher's sermon and her starvation. I only sensed her despair and guilt. Everything in Lauren was guilt and felt guilty, a feeling so overpowering that it utterly displaced every other emotion.

I spoke to her reassuringly. I explained to her that I would give her support and walk with her. She nodded. I brought her close to me, put her arm over my shoulder and held her hand.

After a few steps, I heard the sound of squealing tires, followed by the thud of a collision. Instead of the weakened Lauren, I was suddenly holding a screaming baby in my arms. Before I even realized that I was losing contact with myself, I had already become the twenty-year-old Lauren. Carrying my son, who was frightened and screaming, I was running in a state of panic through my parents' house.

My heart was racing. I rushed down the stairs to the ground floor and across the stone path past the hedges and oleander bushes to the garden gate. I sensed what had happened.

I had just been sitting with mother in the room I'd lived in as a girl. She was watching me nurse my child, and she hadn't been able to take her eyes off me and the little one. I had never seen my mother this way. I couldn't remember her ever having looked at me with such affection. When I asked her if she wanted to hold the baby, she trembled. But finally, when the little one was snuggling in her arms, she became quiet, smiled, and, after taking a walk around the room with him, gave him back to me.

I think he's tired now, she said. And so was she. She wanted to go downstairs and lie down.

Not even five minutes had passed since then. When I carefully opened the garden gate and stepped into the street, I held the baby tightly to my breast. In the middle of the street was a red pickup. The driver had gotten out and was kneeling on the pavement next to a strangely twisted body that was wearing my mother's dress.

I didn't scream, didn't panic. I didn't cry, either. The only thing I felt was guilt. I had killed my mother. She lay lifeless in a glossy pool of dark blood, and it seemed like my body was stretching out and becoming wider and heavier than it already felt to me.

We were standing in Lauren's room by her bed. I must have let go of her hand, because her arm went slack, slipped off my shoulder, and fell down.

While I was busy with pills, bottles, and cups for the afternoon medication, I had taken off my gloves. They were still in the pocket of my white coat. I lifted Lauren up, anxiously trying not to hurt her, and certainly not to touch her skin again. Once again she looked deep into my eyes, but I looked away immediately. I was exhausted. Lauren smiled and fell asleep.

That same day, I spoke to the ward physician to find out more about Lauren and her clinical history. I asked if I might work with her more closely. He took my interest to be naïve ambition. But he didn't have any objection to me staying an extra hour after my shift to talk to Lauren and perhaps make an attempt at therapy.

The things I had learned about Lauren during those first minutes of our acquaintance made me aware once again of the limits of my gift. I could become a witness to events from long ago. I could even experience those events authentically in other people's bodies and with their senses, the way they were preserved in their memories. But I had no way of recognizing connections if the person didn't make them at that moment.

I had learned that Lauren blamed herself for her mother's death. Why she felt responsible for the accident, however, I didn't know. Lauren would be spared having to describe the scene outside her parents' house on the day of the accident. Still, I had to bring it up, in order to find out from Lauren herself why she thought she was at fault for the death of her mother.

At least I had the advantage of knowing what had happened. As a result, I was able to steer the conversations that we finally had, and the association exercises she agreed to, toward the themes that made up the core of Lauren's suffering.

At first, we spent days talking about nothing but Hashem. That is to say, we talked about Lauren's Lord and my God, as if they were completely different things. I told Lauren about my childhood in Geula and my expulsion from the yeshiva, and she couldn't believe that I hadn't been punished by my father.

As far as our understanding of Hashem was concerned, we came from opposite ends of the universe. Not for a single day of my life had I seen God as an executioner. He might occasionally be brutal, but whenever I had the feeling that he had abandoned me, that would be followed by another experience that completely convinced me that I was accepted and guided by him, caringly, if not even lovingly. With every mitzvah I performed, I was able to establish closeness, and the smallest step that I took toward Hashem each time balanced out the transgressions and omissions that no human being can get through life without.

Lauren had never had such experiences. She knew only the threatening, fear-inspiring, and ever-admonishing figure of the superior and implacable God. There were transgressions, and the punishments that followed were inevitable. It was not possible to atone, unless she made herself so small and weak that she disappeared and ceased to exist as a person. That was the reason she was starving herself. But even disappearing, she said, was something she couldn't seem to manage.

Mornings and evenings, Lauren ate a cup of oatmeal, with some water and a teaspoon of milk mixed in. She stretched these meals out over an hour, chewing for ages and swallowing slowly, so that she could begin to feel full. But she considered even this small amount of food to be wrong, and every spoonful of oatmeal that she ate only served to enlarge the mountain of guilt that nothing could take away.

In her own eyes, Lauren was immensely fat. It was her guilt that had made her body so bloated beyond measure that she could not bear it. The sluggishness that had afflicted her because of her extreme hunger, she attributed to the hundreds of pounds that, in her opinion, she was carrying around with her in the form of gargantuan folds of fat. Taking up so much space only increased her guilt before God. She didn't deserve more than the teaspoon of milk that she mixed into her oatmeal every morning and evening. Actually, she didn't even deserve the air that she breathed, as long as the mass of fat on her body had not disappeared. And because she couldn't manage to avoid eating altogether, she didn't stand a chance. With every breath, and even more so with each spoonful of oatmeal, her guilt grew, and her body got bigger, heavier, and more immense.

When I told her that she would die if she didn't eat something, she believed me, even though she also couldn't comprehend how a person could starve while carrying around so many folds of fat. Still, she confided in me that death would actually be salvation, because even though in the afterlife she would be cast into damnation, at least in the torments of hell she could atone for her sins. And she thought she could see a blessing in that, since redemption was something she just couldn't find in life, no matter how she tried.

I took notes during our conversations at that time. I logged every important train of thought, every theme worth pursuing, every bit of progress, no matter how small, and also the countless setbacks. Since Lauren was struggling primarily with God, I thought I could help her by letting her share in my interactions with Hashem, which seemed almost informal. Perhaps God would value her efforts, her doubts, and her sincere distress more highly than she had ever thought possible. Perhaps, unlike what people had always told her, he was in fact much more willing to overlook a transgression and forgive a debt.

Of course those conversations were only a kind of key to open the door to a possible cure for Lauren's sorrows. It took months before she believed me that God would not hold it against her if she mashed up half a banana and put it in her oatmeal at breakfast from now on. Even so: the door was open.

After several weeks of a half a banana per day, Lauren told me why she felt responsible for her mother's death. Actually, she claimed, her mother took on the punishment for a transgression that Lauren had committed.

Lauren was the oldest of three siblings. Her brother and her sister were blond and light-skinned and had dove-gray eyes like their father. Lauren's hair was black, and her eyes were green. Her skin turned brown like coffee with cream if a single ray of sun hit it. They'd always suspected something wasn't right with her.

Don't look at me like that with your sinful eyes! her mother had often said to her. What she meant by that, Lauren did not quite understand. But she learned to keep her head down and never look anyone in the eye, even if she was speaking to someone.

Once before, she told me, she had stood at the garden gate, staring at the street, distraught like on the day of the accident. She was maybe six and couldn't understand what the kids meant when they cried out in unison from the other side of the street: Lauren is a bastard! Lauren is a bastard! She understood only that it was meant to hurt her feelings, and she suspected that it would hurt her feelings when her parents told her what the word meant.

You are a child of sin! her father shouted when she came crying to him one night and told him about it. And he smacked the table with the palm of his hand. That's how Lauren found out that her parents weren't her parents and that they had taken her from the orphanage when she was two years old.

I adopted you, her father informed her. *I* did. And: the children were right that she was a bastard. There was no reason to blubber about it. She should be happy to have a family, he said. But Lauren was not happy. She didn't feel thankful, either, as hard as she tried, and she added the ingratitude to the mountain of her transgressions.

Long after she'd left Arkansas, Lauren told me, she once read a story about a bird-catcher who was in love. Whenever he had spent a day waiting in vain for his beloved, he painted one of the captured birds with bright colors and set it free. The bird would then fly up into a tree and attract other members of the same species with its song. But when they got there, and he wanted to join the swarm, the other birds would not recognize him as one of their own, and they would peck him until he fell to the ground dead. In the painted bird, Lauren said, she saw herself. She said she couldn't have described her own childhood more accurately.

The green of her eyes, which irritated her mother so much, couldn't be cried away. Once she went down to the river and scrubbed her skin until it was bloody, but the dark color of sin remained.

When she was seventeen, Lauren met a married man in a near-by town who gave her compliments and was the first person who ever really paid her any attention. He liked her eyes. He liked it when she looked at him. She agreed to a date and let him have his way.

When she missed her period, she was panic-stricken. Her father would never allow her to bring such shame on the family, and abortion was considered murder. They would send her away, so that she could bear her child without the knowledge of the congregation. But then they would take the baby away from her and put it in a home, just as she herself had been put in a orphanage by her mother—another painted bird. She couldn't think of a worse punishment.

Lauren decided to take action. She went to a young man from the neighborhood, a man she found reasonably pleasant and whom she trusted for some reason, and convinced him to marry her. She kept it a secret that she was expecting a child. Why he didn't become suspicious, and why he immediately agreed, remained a mystery to Lauren. But the question of why didn't trouble her. She would be able to have her baby and keep it. That was the only thing that counted for her.

On that day when her mother ran in front of the red pickup, Lauren was visiting her parents for the first time since giving birth. She let her mother hold the baby, feeling like she had prevailed, because she had escaped punishment. She had outwitted the merciless Lord and saved her child.

Your mother has died for your sins, and you're not just going to get off scot-free, either! Those were the last words her father said to her when she finally left the community. Since then, Lauren believed that her mother had run out in front of the truck intentionally. She must have realized that her daughter had committed the same sin as she had once brought upon herself, but that Lauren had been prepared to commit another sin, and if necessary many more sins, to protect her child.

I had refused, Lauren told me, to atone for my sin in life. And I pulled through because of it. That's why my mother died. She took on my punishment.

The extensive study that I later assembled from my notes is still in a box in my basement. I didn't burn it with the other records from my previous patients. Why I haven't been able to get rid of the study to this day is something I can only explain in a way that doesn't make me look very good. I am still proud of Lauren's cure. I still consider it to be a personal achievement. It's flattering to me that I was able to help her. It was for that completely selfish reason that I took such thorough notes and wanted so badly to turn them into a book, so that the experts would hear about my success. At some point I realized this, and I decided not to publish the study. But the fact that I could never destroy it proves to me that, in this matter, I have never managed to see myself purely as an instrument of Hashem, who merely had mercy on Lauren and on me and brought us together for that reason.

I didn't help Lauren because I saw it as my duty. I did it for myself—if not exclusively, then at least partially.

That is the reason why I don't want to go down to the basement now to open the box, take out the study, and recall every detail of my protracted efforts, through which I finally succeeded in getting Lauren's perception of her own body back in order, so that she gradually began to eat more, regained her strength, and was able to leave the clinic. It's enough for me to remember my visit with her some years later in a small town in Maine, where she was living with her son, who was taking care of her.

When I said goodbye to both of them back then, I remembered the merchant from Eli's parable, his palace, and the wall that was as tall as a man. Now, I thought, my heart could stop beating, my plane back to New York could crash, or some other unexpected event could end my life. I truly believed that I had already done everything that I was destined to do.

But I'm still alive, which goes to show how presumptuous my feeling of triumph was back then, beneath the orange-red foliage of the maple tree in front of Lauren's house in Maine.

9

For years I hardly had any contact with my family. Occasionally I wrote a few words to my father, who answered with even fewer words, to let me know how proud he was that I was studying hard, and how relieved he was that I had not left the ways of Torah.

During my studies, it went without saying that I spent the holidays with my uncle in Zurich. He still lived alone, and he was happy when I came to see him for a few days. In Geula hardly anyone noticed when I wasn't there. I was only in Yerushalayim once during that time, when my oldest sister got married. Among the hundreds of guests, I felt like a stranger who had been invited by mistake. It wasn't just the neighbors from the quarter who eyed me suspiciously. My siblings, and even my parents, also seemed unsure if I was still one of them.

How was I supposed to feel comfortable with them? The connection was broken. There was now too much between us that was unknown and imponderable. If I hadn't wrapped myself every morning in the white tallis that my father had given me years before, I might never even have written those rare letters to my father. The people I really considered to be my family were Eli, Rivka, and the children, even though they also lived in Israel, and of course my uncle Nathan. The things I knew and the experiences that I remembered fondly were associated with them. It was with them, and not in Geula, that I felt at home.

Whenever I went to see my uncle during semester break, he would rent us rooms for a week or two at the Hotel Dan in Lugano, or the Edelweiss in St. Moritz, where there was kosher food, accommodations that were suitable for Shabbos, and a daily minyan right in the building. We went for walks and talked for hours. In the morning we learned Mishna, in the evening the daily page of Gemara, and my uncle always amazed me with his sharp logic and inexhaustible knowledge.

The late evenings were reserved for literature. Music and books made up half of our baggage on those short trips. My uncle knew them all. He read to me, or had me read to him, and he often repeated particular sentences or verses from memory, just to listen to the sound of them, or to let a thought hover in the room for a few moments, before we came to the next one.

Uncle Nathan had bought a Sony CD Walkman, which was brand new at the time, and he had started buying CDs of the best recordings of his favorite classical pieces, which at home he only played on vinyl. He mostly listened to the CDs in his workshop, while he was working on his jewelry. The dust from the stone-cutting couldn't harm the CDs, and thanks to their sturdiness and to the portable player, you could even travel with them.

There was hardly any style within classical music that my uncle rejected. During one of those literature-and-music nights at the Hotel Dan, he even introduced me to twelve-tone music; and he went so far as to describe Schönberg's "Moses and Aaron" as one of the most profound Perushim about Aaron's inglorious role in the sin of the golden calf. In Geula he would have run the risk of being ostracized by making such a statement.

It was only with Wagner that my uncle had problems. Not because of the music, but because of the themes: in Wagner's operas, he said, he couldn't identify even the spark of a thought about Hashem. On the contrary, he saw an estrangement from him. That didn't fit with Uncle Nathan's conception of art as a never-ending continuation of creation, a conception that was unthinkable without a connection to Hashem.

My story, on the other hand, would have delighted my uncle as a theatrical production. The sequence in which everything had occurred and continued to occur would have pleased him, because it suggested that Hashem was directing from a well-thought-out script. Even the horrible twists and turns would have met with his approval, not only because they seemed necessary, but because they revealed a deep poetry about the divine hand in our fate. Yes, he would have liked that, despite the fact that he would not live to see the continuation and the (at least temporary) end of my story.

Nathan Bollag died after I had come back to Zurich as a newly licensed doctor. Once again I was reminded of Eli's parable about the merchant and the beggar. My uncle went, as we say in our circles, with a kiss from Hashem: quickly, painlessly, and peacefully.

I found him in the living room. He was sitting in a rocking chair, wrapped in a blanket, with his feet up on a stool. From the speakers I heard Fritz Kreisler's "La Gitana," played by Kreisler himself, a live recording that my uncle put on often. A book of Poe's poems was open on his lap. He had been reading "The Raven": *And his eyes have all the seeming of a demon's that is dreaming* . . . My uncle's eyes were closed as if he had just dozed off while reading. But even though he was still warm, I sensed when I touched him, immediately, that he was not simply sleeping.

I took off my gloves and reached for his hands, which had become heavy, as if they were made of stone. I couldn't feel a pulse;

and even when I closed my eyes, I could see only an impenetrable nothingness, a room that contained nothing but the echo of Kreisler's "Gypsy Dance." Perhaps he was still there, in that room, in that apartment, watching me, but he had left his body.

I put the book aside and turned the music off. Then I opened the glass door of the grandfather clock and stopped the pendulum. Now it was completely silent.

I had to call the emergency services, even though I knew it was too late. But how was I supposed to talk? I felt like screaming, but I wasn't able to do that, either. I knelt next to the rocking chair and held Uncle Nathan's hand for one moment more.

The darkness and the silence, from which not even the smallest signal made it through to me, made me furious. I stood up, and with a single pull I tore the lapel of my jacket and the collar of my shirt. Then I took my shoes off and went to the telephone.

While I was making the call, with my eyes fixed on my uncle's body, I heard myself speaking as if I was listening to someone else. My voice sounded calm. I gave the address and informed the emergency services—speaking as one doctor to another—that it was no longer urgent. Then I hung up, went to the bedroom, and got white sheets out of the large chest under the window, so I could cover the mirrors in the house.

When the emergency physician arrived and asked me if I was a relative, I nodded and said: I am his son. While he examined Nathan Bollag and filled out the papers, I sat motionless on the floor in front of the open grandfather clock, holding tight to the book of Poe's poems. The doctor and his assistants seemed to me to be ravens in red coats that had broken into this place to take my uncle. But they didn't get him. It felt as if he was sitting next to me and we were watching them do their work, quietly and without a trace of anger.

When the police came after being called by the emergency physician, I remained seated. The officers conferred briefly with the doctor. They only asked me if I had changed anything. I held up the book that had been on Uncle Nathan's lap.

And when did you find him?

I pointed up at the face of the clock that I had stopped.

The officer who had asked me nodded. Then they left.

Did I need any help? one of the red birds asked.

I shook my head. The paramedic team's driver was Jewish. You have to call the rabbinate, he said. They would inform the chevra kadisha, he said, which will take care of everything. He bent down to me and said: May you be comforted among the mourners of Zion and Yerushalayim.

I nodded and wanted to stand up so I could bring the talking raven to the door. But he flapped his wings and they all disappeared. The door clicked shut, and I sat motionless beside my uncle for what must have been an hour before I called the community officials.

The taciturn men from the chevra kadisha took my uncle with them. I spent a sleepless night on the couch in the living room, in the depths of silence. At dawn I finally got up, set the clock, wound it up, and set the pendulum in motion again.

Around two hundred acquaintances, friends, and customers from Zurich and Basel gathered at the cemetery two days later, to say goodbye to Nathan Bollag. All of them, even Uncle Nathan's brother Josef, who had come in from Basel, treated me like the surviving son.

It goes without saying that for the next week men from the neighborhood came to Nathan's apartment at around eight every morning to daven shachris with me. It didn't bother anyone that

I was sitting shiva and saying kaddish for my uncle the way a son would for his father, even though in reality I hadn't even been related to him.

I had become a Bollag. That was the feeling I was getting from everyone. But it was only several days later that I found out just how much that feeling matched up with the facts. I got up from shiva and began to worry about what was to become of me. I was living in my uncle's apartment. The only asset I had was a three-and-a-half-carat demantoid that I had no intention of selling now of all times, after Uncle Nathan's death. Other than that, I had only my American certification as a psychiatrist, which I still needed the Swiss officials to recognize. I didn't have the slightest idea what I was going to live off of, or what I was supposed to do next.

Josef Bollag had handled the official matters: death certificate, notice of departure, account cancellations, probate court—all kinds of requirements that only a Swiss citizen could take care of. Nonetheless, Uncle Nathan's lawyer contacted me first and asked me to come with Josef to his office in the Pelikanstraße for the reading of my uncle's will.

As it turned out, from the time I had come to live with him, Nathan Bollag had not only treated me like a son. During my first year at *Beis Sefer Le-Bonim*, he had drawn up and lodged a will that granted me all the rights of a biological son in the event of his death. He had never told me about this. Perhaps he would have considered it a bad omen to talk about matters of inheritance while he was in the best of health. It is more likely, however, that he wanted to fulfill his promise to my father to take care of my education even in the event that something happened to him while I was still in school. He had also stressed to me time and again that you can only be proud of something that you've earned through your own hard work. He would never have run the risk that the prospect

of a sizable inheritance might weaken my resolve to build a successful future for myself. So the lawyer's disclosure surprised me, and
since there was no letter to me enclosed in the will, I also never
found out just what led my uncle to appoint me as principal heir.

This utterly changed situation left me feeling just as over-
whelmed as the uncertainty had made me feel before. The business,
with its stock of jewelry and raw materials, had to be appraised and
sold. I had to sort out my resident status and my study or work
permits, and there were various contracts to terminate or transfer. I
had a deep knowledge of Talmudic contract law, but I didn't have
the slightest idea about civil business matters. The only option I
had was to entrust my uncle's lawyer with the liquidation. For my
part, I advanced myself a thousand francs and shut myself away for
weeks in the apartment I had shared with my uncle for so long.

Every morning and evening I went to the synagogue to say
Kaddish. But in my prayers I fought with Hashem. I had been
rescued from Geula and delivered into a modern life, I had gotten
an education, and now I was well taken care of. But if Hashem
was really following a plan by endowing me with a sixth sense and
arranging everything for me, then my uncle's death was a cynical
twist—just like the earthquake in the Midrash about the beggar
and the merchant, which knocked down the wall around the palace
once it had served its purpose. Cynical and cruel—as if my uncle
had been nothing more than a character in a puppet show.

And how heavily that idea weighed on me! If Nathan had really
lived his life only for my sake, how could I ever be worthy of that?
How many desperate people would I have to cure, and in how much
time? Or whatever the task was that Hashem intended for me. I
still had no idea what he expected of me. But my uncle was dead,
and now the lawyer was presenting me with the statement for a
fortune that I had not earned, an amount that made my head spin.

·

If you pick a fight with Hashem, your chances of success are slim. I recalled my studies with Eli and our exercises, and I decided to give in. If I wanted to find out what was expected of me, I had to take a look at the situation Hashem had put me in.

During my time as a student I had already begun to concern myself with different variations of psychoanalysis. With most of the patients I had dealt with at the clinic in Portland, the causes of their disorders—I preferred to call them difficulties—could be found in the past, in their memories, which they had sometimes unknowingly shared with me. It was plausible, then, that a form of therapy could be based entirely on plunging into memory and leading patients to the places and events of their pasts.

I was convinced about the methods. I didn't get so much out of Freud's interpretations, though. His focus on the sexual seemed obsessive to me. Jung's views were much closer to mine. But I was especially fascinated by the technique of free association based on dreams, which I felt was meditative and creative at the same time.

Often the patients were not aware of the events that I witnessed in my visions. It was only in their dreams that splinters of those memories emerged—usually in guises that left them barely recognizable. It often seemed to me that the dreams were an attempt by the psyche to reshape the memories that had been banished to the unconscious, and to imbue them with new meanings. The path the psyche took was often a detour, if not the wrong way.

What I liked especially about psychoanalysis was the fact that, as a therapist, you could step back completely and help the patients help themselves—so they could remember and, in the process of remembering, give the past a new meaning. After all, many patients suffered from the fear of being helpless and at the mercy of the past and their situations. In analysis, you could put the reins back in their hands—or rather, the pallet and the paintbrush, so they could set a new tone on the canvas of their memories. You could even become a canvas yourself, a projection screen where the patients could sketch possible alternative drafts and try out new ways of entering into relationships with other people again. In the process, they roamed around thousands of possible worlds, just as people do when they become immersed in books or music.

In psychoanalysis, therefore, I saw nothing less than the natural link between art and healing. The idea was not to extinguish or get rid of something, but to collect and restore what was broken. It was a tikkun that gathered up the scattered sparks from the dreams of an unhinged self and then provided a new vessel to contain them. And when you did that, you restored a bit of creation that had been damaged, perhaps even nearly destroyed.

I had long considered it impossible to continue my education to become an analyst. The cost was so high that I didn't even dare talk to my uncle about the mere possibility. The most expensive thing was the training analysis that you had to undergo: up to 1,500 hours that you had to pay for yourself. Where was I supposed to get that kind of money?

But now I had the means for that training. And I was in Switzerland, which isn't the worst place to learn about Jung's analytic psychology.

Of course, all that training analysis took time. You had to budget four to five years. I had already spent six years in internships and lecture halls. I wasn't thrilled about the idea of spending that same amount of time studying and waiting again.

In general, the large amount of time you had to invest in analysis to achieve any progress seemed like a problem to me. Over the years, it wasn't my only criticism of the process, but it was the most important one. So when I decided to begin training analysis, I also resolved to find an institute that would allow me to conduct research. I wanted to look for ways to make it easier for the patients to reach the doors of the unconscious and walk through them. My notion of expanding and supplementing the classic method, which was only vague at first, soon took on concrete forms. The way I imagined it, I wouldn't have to reveal my gift to my patients, but I would allow them to share in my experience of immersing myself in their memories. In this way, I could accompany them through the situations they remembered, thereby taking away their greatest fear: that they would have to relive everything on their own.

I found what I was looking for at the very first place I went, the Institute for Parapsychological Studies and Frontier Areas of Psychology, across the German border in Freiburg im Breisgau. There the focus was on developing and conducting tests for people who claimed to have paranormal abilities. I was especially interested in their research on clinical hypnosis. They investigated this area primarily with regard to pain therapies, since pain brought on by stress could often be relieved through an induced trance and the deep relaxation that came with it.

Given that it was a psychological institute, the people who dealt with hypnosis were, of course, not interested solely in the possibilities of pain therapies. They also investigated different variations in the application of trance states within the framework of psychotherapy. The research topic that I submitted as a project proposal for my doctorate was a perfect fit: I wanted to measure and observe the brain activity of patient and therapist in the course of a hypnosis session and examine whether the therapist was able to put himself into a trance along with the patient, even if not as deeply, so that he could accompany the patient to the gates of the unconscious and, if necessary, lead him there.

I never would have gone so far as to mention my visions before the scientific advisory board. But an institute where the staff members regarded such a phenomenon with a certain skepticism, but not with utter rejection, seemed to me to be the most suitable place to deepen the investigation of my gift and the possibility of sharing it with others.

The project was approved.

Even today I think that I learned and gained more for myself and my patients from my research in Freiburg than I did from the training analysis that I completed at the same time. I have often wondered if it was because of a shortcoming on part of my supervisor, or a flaw in the method, that during a total of 1,200 hours of analytical efforts, there were two things I never talked about: my sense of memory, and my fear of not being ready—or failing—when it really mattered.

I had put an end to my dispute with Hashem. But the idea that my uncle had died of a stupid blood clot just so that every imaginable possibility for higher education would be open to me, that was an idea I couldn't let go of. And it is because of that very thought that I am so unforgiving today when I look back at my own failure. For eight years I practiced as an analyst in Zurich, and I was successful in my work, even with the patients my colleagues had given up on long ago. Eight whole years, after eleven years of study and research, and even more years of preparation and doubt. Eight years. And I can't shake the impression that the cause of my failure was nothing other than carelessness.

After that day of reading during the last summer vacation before I left for Pikesville, my uncle had warned me about the *yevonish* world. Because that warning was so important to him, he had entrusted me with Bulgakov's novel and had made sure I had read it attentively. But I underestimated the import of his warning during all the years that followed. I had forgotten, and I remembered it again only when the medical council advised me to give up my practice and threatened to revoke my license outright if I didn't give in voluntarily. And I remembered it when the scientific advisory board at the institute in Freiburg froze all funding for my research projects and expelled me from one day to the next, because if an institute is already being watched suspiciously by the scientific community, a scandal is the last thing it needs. The charge that was filed against me was unprofessional and unethical conduct in the course of a therapeutic treatment, during which I was said to have led a patient—Minsky—to personal disaster. It was only at that moment that I remembered my uncle's warning.

10

For more than five years after Uncle Nathan's death, I lived in his apartment without changing a single thing. I continued to sleep in the room where I had lived as a teenager. The furniture stayed where it was, and my uncle's room remained untouched. The cleaning lady vacuumed and dusted. I didn't even look in his closets.

I never sat in Uncle Nathan's rocking chair. But on the days of his Yahrzeit, I put on "La Gitana," sat down on the floor in front of the grandfather clock, as I had done on the evening of his death, and read poems by Poe. I liked the idea that, in a way, he was still present.

The apartment also included a compartment in the attic where my uncle had stored several boxes of things, a few pieces of furniture, and some lamps—things there was no room for in the apartment, but that my uncle didn't want to part with. That was another area where I never looked. I only went up there twice a year: before Pesach, so I could stow away some opened bottles of single malt, and after Pesach, so I could bring them back down. Those bottles had also belonged to my uncle, who had never been ashamed of his weakness for single malts.

Because the bottles had been so expensive, Uncle Nathan brought them up to the attic every year for Pesach. During the festival, you weren't allowed to own them, and they were sold temporarily, so he wouldn't have to pour them out or give them away. On the morning of Erev Pesach, the rabbi received a contract empowering him to sell the entire attic and its contents to a non-Jew. We stored the key somewhere out of sight.

Of course the rabbi didn't just sell Uncle Nathan's single malts (and the wooden bread boards and bowls that we stored in the attic) because we couldn't kasher them for Pesach. Whole shops, warehouses, and even wheat futures changed hands every year before the holiday, for a fixed amount. On the day after Pesach, when owning chometz was allowed again, the rabbi bought everything back, and everyone automatically retook possession of all the things they had needed to get rid of before.

In the years after Uncle Nathan's death, when I carried the boxes up to the attic, the thought always entered my mind that this would be the year when something would go wrong with the buying back of the chometz. The attic, and everything my uncle had stored there that I had never looked at, would not return to my possession, and I would therefore be spared having to go through everything and sort it, in order to sell it, give it away, or dispose of it. That, I thought, would perhaps give me the strength to finally say goodbye.

Of course that never happened. After Uncle Nathan's death, the rabbi still proclaimed on every 22nd of Nisan after the evening prayer: All the chometz that has been sold will be bought back at midnight tonight. And the following morning, he confirmed that it had happened. The first year, the second, and the fifth, as well.

It was an acquaintance from the synagogue, who visited me and was appalled that I hadn't changed anything in the apartment, who finally convinced me. He owned an antique shop and offered to send two men over to help me clear everything out and sort it, if

I named him a good price for the things I didn't need that could be sold.

I sold the rocking chair that my uncle had died in. I offered his suits and shirts to a man with about the same build as Nathan Bollag, and he was happy to take them. I gave his shoes and linens to charity. As for the personal items—a few notebooks, a pad with ink and pencil drawings, and two packs of letters wrapped in ribbons—I put those in a package and sent it to Josef Bollag in Basel. In a second package I placed my uncle's design books, which documented his works as a jeweler: materials, preliminary sketches, detailed scaled drawings, and photographs of his pieces of jewelry, which he had mostly produced as unique specimens. I wrote Josef to say that I was sorry that I was only sending these books now, and that, while I hoped they would remain in the family's hands, it would also be all right with me if the Bollags sold them.

The men from the antique store took most of the furniture from the attic. The things that seemed unlikely to sell they hauled to the municipal waste incineration plant. The only thing I kept for myself was a black violin case that we found while we were clearing out the attic. At first I assumed that it was empty. But when I opened it, I actually found an instrument inside. It was in pitiful condition. The bridge and the strings were missing. The varnish was chipped in several places, and a piece of the carved scroll had a broken off.

The movers would have taken the violin along with the case. But I wanted to keep it. When I held it in my hands for the first time, I immediately heard Kreisler's "Gypsy Dance" again. I was saying goodbye to my uncle, but that didn't mean I couldn't hold on to a keepsake that reminded me of the day of his death and the moment when I found him.

I decided to have the violin appraised and repaired. Since my uncle had kept it in the attic for years, I did not suppose that it was a valuable instrument. But apparently he had held on to it so that one day he could have it repaired. I liked the idea of completing something that he must have planned years before, even if he had never gotten started on it.

And so the violin stayed with me, at first assuming a place on top of the serving cabinet in the living room. I wanted to take the time to look for a suitable violin maker who could repair the instrument.

But first, I needed to move some furniture. My old bedroom became a guest room, which was used maybe three times over the years. I moved into my uncle's former bedroom, replacing only the bed and the curtains. I had the writing desk moved into the library, which from then on I called my office.

The hardest thing for me was changing the furnishings in the living room, which we had always called "the salon." Even so, I exchanged the ceiling light for one of the lamps from the attic, and I had the grandfather clock moved to a different wall. Since the rocking chair was sold, the image I had visualized so often since my uncle's death, and which I had even repeatedly reconstructed on the day of his Yahrzeit, finally began to vanish.

The clock wouldn't work in its new location. Again and again, the pendulum stopped moving after a few minutes. I would have had to call in a professional to get it straightened out. But I accepted the clock's refusal, set the hands to twelve minutes past ten, and let the pendulum rest for the first time after so many years. The silence that came over the room was the biggest change. Without the constant ticking and the chimes on the half hour and the hour, it was no longer the same room, and my uncle was gone once and for all.

But the violin case was there to remind me of him. Of Nathan Bollag and of my plan to do him one last favor by achieving a tikkun that he might have intended to perform while he was still alive.

Minsky was recommended to me by a young patient who played the violin and had been taking lessons from him for years. Minsky, he reported, was not only an accomplished violinist; he also routinely appraised and repaired vintage instruments, and more recent ones, in his workshop. Minsky could be reached in the evening from Monday through Wednesday in his small apartment on Neptunstraße, he told me. During the day he taught at the music school, the patient added, but every Thursday afternoon he headed out to the Vallée de Joux, where he owned a house and devoted himself to his instruments.

I decided it was destiny, and I called him that same day. Minsky's voice sounded delicate and quiet, but full of energy.

Of course, he said, I could come see him and show him the instrument. He would be happy to examine it. He wanted me to be aware, however, that he kept all of his tools and books in his workshop in L'Abbaye. As a result, he told me, he wouldn't be able to make a diagnosis or do any repairs in Zurich.

Still, he concluded, go ahead and come by with the piece, and we'll take it from there. If you want to have it repaired, I'll just have to take it with me. The instruments mend much better in the Jura region than they do here, anyway.

He gave a quick and inviting laugh. I agreed, and we made an appointment for the following evening.

When I got back home, I opened the case I'd found in the attic, took out the instrument, and gently ran my fingers over the chipped varnish and the damaged scroll. I caught myself talking to the violin.

Soon you'll make music again, I said, listening to the deep silence of the room, trying to hear whether any sound was discernable. But it remained silent.

The first thing I noticed when I rang Minsky's bell on Neptunstraße the next evening was the big, splendid mezuzah on the doorpost of his apartment on the third floor. My patient hadn't mentioned that Minsky was Jewish. When Minsky opened the door, I was confused, because on his right hand, which he cheerfully held out to me, he was wearing a signet ring with a Star of David, but he had no kippa on his head.

I have always made an effort to approach non-observant Jews without resentment. But with my upbringing, it isn't easy for me, even now. It triggers a reflex of indignation in me when people use symbols to display their affiliation with a tradition that they no longer follow or have never followed. Then I usually try a positive interpretation, telling myself that at least the connection to the tradition isn't broken yet. There's still a link, and therefore the hope of a return. Besides, in the end, everyone has to decide for himself how to live. Still, as much as I try to be contemplative, I am not unbiased on this matter.

Minsky's apartment was small and piled high with books. They didn't just fill the ceiling-high shelves along the walls; they were also stacked up on the table and the floor. Minsky took my coat, asked me to have a seat, and cleared off the table. Then he held out his hands to accept the case.

Why don't you let me have a look, he said.

His eyes gleamed, and he smiled when he opened the case and took a look at the violin. Just as I had before, he ran his finger gently over the chipped varnish, examined the damaged scroll, tapped several times on the top of the violin and checked to see that the neck was securely glued. Then he sat down and held the violin almost tenderly on his lap.

He could certainly repair it, Minsky told me, but I should expect to pay about four thousand francs. The bridge and the strings are the least of your worries, he said. But the restoration of the scroll should be true to the original. Fixing the cracks in the top would be the most difficult thing, he told me. We'll have to remove the top and glue and reinforce the cracks. Then we need to put the violin back together and touch up the varnish. Finally, I will need to fit a new bridge and sound post.

I must have looked horrified. I hadn't expected it to cost so much.

But it's worth it, Minsky hastened to reassure me. It's a beautiful instrument and certainly worth the investment, he said.

That surprised me. I would have thought it was just an ordinary violin, off the shelf, as it were, but certainly not valuable, since my uncle had kept it in the attic for years.

Terms like valuable are always relative, Minsky said. It's certainly not a priceless instrument, but it's more than a hundred years old.

He was sure that the piece in front of him was manufactured in Germany, a violin from the late Klotz dynasty around 1850-1870, from Mittenwald in Upper Bavaria. You can easily tell from the shapes, he said, which are inspired by the aesthetic of Stainer, an Italian violin maker, who was once as revered as the now-almost-proverbial Stradivari. Of course you can't make a direct comparison between this instrument and the ones the old Italian made, Minsky said. But these later instruments from the Klotz family, which were made entirely by hand, also have centuries of experience in them, and a loving attention to every detail. The value, he continued, is certainly somewhere between twenty and thirty thousand Francs. He told me he could only assess the actual damage to the top and the varnish, and the exact cost of the restoration, in his workshop. But a repair would certainly pay off, he said.

How about this, Minsky asked, you give me the violin, and then visit me in L'Abbaye in two or three weeks? In the workshop, I can show you the state of the varnish and the damage precisely, under a special light.

I hesitated, although there was no reason to. Of course I could have gotten a second opinion. But I had no cause to distrust Minsky. It was obvious that he knew what he was talking about, and he was excited about the instrument, as if it was a child who required his undivided attention in order to recover from a long, serious illness. In a way, Minsky had already adopted it, simply because it needed help. I liked that, because it reminded me of my uncle. And so I entrusted him with the violin.

The only thing that worried me was the idea of visiting Minsky at his house in the Jura Valley. It was pretty far off the beaten track. I wouldn't be able to get there and back in one day. Where would I be able to stay and cook for myself?

At my house, of course! Minsky cried out enthusiastically. You have my invitation. This put me in an even more embarrassing position.

Please don't take this the wrong way, I said, but I wouldn't be able to eat at your house.

I'm Jewish, Minsky replied with surprise.

Now I was completely unnerved.

That certainly may be, I answered—and I could have kicked myself for my choice of words—but you see, and this is in no way intended as a criticism, I have to assume that you're not observant.

Minsky scowled.

You're right, he relented. For a moment, he said nothing and bowed his head as if he was listening to what was inside him. When he raised his head, it seemed to me that there were tears in his eyes.

That's a difficult story, he said, and he stood up from his armchair, slowly and with great effort, as if suddenly afflicted with pain. Perhaps I'll tell you about it another time, he said.

I raised my hands apologetically.

But I am prepared for Orthodox visitors, he said. I have glasses and disposable tableware. If you can help me out by bringing your own sandwiches, I would be truly happy to have you stay with me. It isn't just because of the violin. The story, also . . . I would like to tell you the story.

To this day I don't know why I agreed to visit him. It could be that I just wanted to end the conversation. But it's equally possible that I was interested in the story he mentioned, which he seemed to blame for his undecided religious lifestyle. But maybe I was just following a momentary impulse.

Apologizing again for having caused him embarrassment, I agreed to call in a few days and set a date for my visit to L'Abbaye.

Wonderful, Minsky said, giving me his hand. It's settled then. Thank you.

I distinctly remember that this statement also confused me. What was he thanking me for? Why was it so important to him that I come visit him in the Jura? There was something hanging in the air that left me feeling more interested than suspicious or worried. And that was evidently enough to make me get more involved with this new acquaintance.

•

Two weeks later, I visited Minsky at his house in the Jura. He offered to drive me there from Zurich, but I declined. I took the train to Geneva and enjoyed the taxi ride through the rugged landscape to the small town on the lake, where Minsky stayed on weekends.

He welcomed me effusively and brought me to the kitchen first. He had indeed gotten shrink-wrapped disposable tableware and had even purchased a new coffee machine, which he asked me to take out of the box. That made me uncomfortable, and I assured him that it really wasn't necessary. But he put me off with a decisive wave of his hand.

Of course it is, he said. You're absolutely right. It's no trouble at all. Please don't worry about it. And once again he smiled as endearingly as he had two weeks before in his apartment in Zurich, when he had been so insistent about inviting me.

We drank our coffee in the workshop. He had set it up in a one-story annex that had three rooms. In the first, which was his office, the walls were covered with technical drawings of various parts of violins. Hanging on the front wall, directly above the desk, was an enlarged drawing of an Amati from 1660, and next to that a technical drawing of a violin model that Minsky had designed.

Minsky told me, with great enthusiasm, that he didn't only repair violins and violas. He also manufactured his own. He said he was almost obsessed with the pieces by the old Italians. He was an historian, he told me—also a long story—and by coincidence, while he was looking for documents, he had stumbled upon a report that a group of violin makers in Berlin had compiled in the twenties. They were of the opinion that the body form of the Amati violins followed the laws of the golden mean. Using modern centimeter rulers and compasses, this form could be precisely analyzed geometrically, he said, making it possible to construct plans for so-called "half-instruments"—violins, violas, and cellos—based on the Amati prototype. The technical drawing over the desk showed such a construction, assembled from triangles and compass arcs.

He was still experimenting, Minsky conceded, but he said he was determined to apply for a patent soon. With that, he directed me to the second room in the workshop, where wood was stacked on shelves, along with half-finished and finished components, like tops, backs and carved scrolls. On another shelf were violins in various stages of completion.

He had nearly completed one of his "new Amatis," Minsky whispered. It just had to be "dressed," he said, winking at me cheerfully.

Come see, he beckoned. It's in my "alchemist's kitchen." With that, he opened the door to the third room, from which a bluish-purple glow emanated. I followed him in.

The room was filled with intense smells: wood, resins, and solvents. This was where Minsky experimented with varnishes. For centuries, he explained, violin builders used spirit varnishes in which resins and dyes dissolved easily and dried quickly. But the violin makers from Cremona, like Amati and Stradivari, used only oil varnish, he said. This was his hobby, in a sense, Minsky informed me. He wanted not only to recreate the forms, but also to work with the varnishes and glues that at least came close to ones used by the old masters.

The tone, he said with an almost holy seriousness, requires all the components to make up a harmonious whole. It needs the appropriate, properly aged wood, the perfect form for the body, the right glue, and the appropriate varnish, Minsky continued. An unvarnished—or, in a sense, naked—violin never produced a good sound, he said. It needed to be moderated by the varnish, and he was convinced that using the historically accurate glues and finishing materials was the best way to get close to the sound of the real Amatis.

He did a number of things to accomplish this, starting with the glues, which he made with lime and casein from dissolved milk curds. When its consistency was thick, he used the mixture as glue. When it was diluted, he used it as a primer for the body, because the wood needed to be sized with it before he could apply the varnish.

The production of the varnish really was reminiscent of alchemy. He had spent a long time looking for the right oils to start out with, which had to be boiled for what seemed like an eternity, then strained several times. The resins he used—mastic, sandarac, and copal—were ground until they were as fine as sand before he mixed them into the oil. He added madder root and saffron for the slightly reddish amber color, but just a little bit, because he applied the colored varnish in up to fifteen ultra-thin coats.

This is the thing that pains me, he said. In Italy, the coatings dried in the sunlight and fresh air. I only have an ultraviolet light. It really is alchemy, Minsky continued, I've read up on it and had it confirmed by various chemists: when exposed to UV light, the oil is oxidized—just think about it—and it hardens in the process. I always imagine that back in the old days, in the light of Cremona, the atmosphere of the region was absorbed into the varnish. Of course, you can't replicate that . . .

But look at this, he said, holding the nearly-finished Minsky-Amati up to the light before my eyes, almost the same way my Uncle Nathan had with the demantoid years before in his workshop, What a color! What warmth!

But he refused to play the violin.

Oh no, he said, it's too soon for that. It isn't ready yet. It still needs several more coats, he told me, and then I have to warm it up. But one day, who knows, I'll play something on it for you. Just have a little patience.

All of a sudden, he was in a hurry to get out of the "kitchen." He led me out, closed the door, and waved me back into his office.

Come with me, he said. I have your Mittenwalder here. I am sure it's an instrument from Bavaria. I've examined it. You should definitely have it repaired!

I followed him. In the office, Minsky went to a cabinet and took out the violin case with my instrument. Under a UV lamp, he showed me the damage to the varnish and explained all the things that needed to be fixed. Would he also coat this violin with his magic varnish? I asked.

Absolutely not, he fired back. Instead, he would make a spirit varnish similar to the kind the violin makers from the late Klotz dynasty in Mittenwald would have used. He was very precise about such things, he said. It was important to be authentic, especially in the details.

I knew he was right. He had infected me with his enthusiasm, and I completely trusted him to restore the violin from Uncle Nathan's attic to near original condition, so it could be played again.

Back in the house, Minsky passed me a contract and an estimate. He told me I could pick up my violin in three weeks. I signed immediately, but I asked if he couldn't bring the instrument back to Zurich and give it to me there.

Oh, you know, Minsky said, there is still the story that I would like to tell you. It's really weighing heavily on my mind, but I don't have the strength to tell it today. And certainly not in Zurich. That city is associated with too many terrible memories.

Suddenly, Minsky slumped. It was a sharp contrast to the man I had experienced up until that moment, who was vigorous in spite of his short stature. A slight wince came over his face, and once again his eyes looked the way they had in his Zurich apartment, blurred by an onslaught of tears.

Please come, he said, come back here one more time and listen to me then. Please.

These last words were only whispered, and I was overcome with an ominous foreboding that I didn't know how to classify.

I spent the next three weeks wondering about this story that Minsky absolutely had to tell me. I assumed that it was something very personal. I could only speculate. In any event, he had aroused my interest.

Three weeks later, when I returned to his house in L'Abbaye, it was a broken man who opened the gate. I was appalled. Minsky looked haggard and bleary-eyed, as if he had neither eaten nor slept since my last visit. Without speaking, he invited me in and led the way to the house slowly, propped up by an old-fashioned cane, dragging his left leg as if he had injured it.

What's wrong with your leg? I asked with concern. Did you fall?

No, no, he replied, almost inaudibly. It just hurts. It's an old pain that's returned. But come in. You have no idea how relieved I am that you're here.

Once in the house, he invited me into the living room, collapsed into his armchair, and lit a cigarette. During the whole day I spent with him, he smoked incessantly, and he told me, with many long pauses, about Auschwitz and Majdanek, about the picture of his father, who he said was murdered in front of him and his mother by White Russian soldiers near Minsk, where he was born. He talked about the barracks at the camp, about the ever-present death and the rats, about his rescue and the years he spent in a children's home in Poland and, finally, in Switzerland, where he had been taken, as he put it, as part of a kidnapping meant to rob him of his past.

I was incapable of any kind of response.

I was not even allowed to remember during all those years, Minsky whispered. I know I am Jewish and come from a village near Minsk. I know that I went through hell. When I play a note on one of my violins, I hear my father's voice. He's speaking Yiddish with me. But you know, no one believed me. My passport has a false name in it. My papers tell a falsified story. Everyone is dead, and I am alone.

I need to rest, he said. Would you mind if I lie down on the sofa?

I nodded silently.

Minsky trudged from the chair over to the sofa, lay down, and fell asleep immediately. For about a half hour, I sat next to him without moving, and I let the images of what I had just heard wash over me, watching his breathing and guarding his sleep, in which he had, it seemed to me, found peace for the first time in days. Most of the time he lay quietly. There were only two times when he stirred for a moment, and he kicked wildly, as if he were fighting off the rats he had told me about.

When I think back on that half hour now, I am still overcome by the horror of the images he depicted. The annihilation had not left a void in our family. My grandparents and parents came from Switzerland. Even though no one would believe this later, I had never been to Yad Vashem before, and I had always avoided documentaries about the Holocaust. The most vivid impression that had ever been conveyed to me about the camps came from Minsky's story. I didn't doubt him for a second.

It was also not doubt, but a desire to really understand Minsky and his sorrow, that led me, after that half hour of sitting silently, to remove my gloves and touch him. It wasn't that I needed to make sure he had told me the truth. I was certain of that. I only wanted to descend into the abyss of his memory myself for a moment, so I could realize that everything that I had not wanted to think about had indeed occurred in all its unimaginable savagery.

It was the first and only time that I touched Minsky. When I placed my hand on his forehead, I was seized by panic. I was crouching, curled up in a ball, on a coarsely timbered plank floor under a low table. It was dim, and a woman was stomping through the room, shouting. I could only see her legs, in rough rubber boots, the kind farmers wear. She kept shouting that she would tear me to pieces if she found me. All the while she was banging on the table and against the walls with a stick or a rod. The fear of being discovered was so overwhelming that I stopped breathing and pressed my hands over my eyes, hoping to disappear.

When I came to, I was sitting in the armchair, and Minsky, propped up by his cane, was standing before me and holding out my gloves. He seemed like a ghost from the cave in which I had just been sitting as a frightened toddler.

Leather boots, Minsky said, as if I had asked him. The Blockowa wore shiny polished leather boots, the stick was a riding crop, and every blow was like a branding iron against my skin.

That's what I remember about that day in L'Abbaye. Nothing else. Not what else we talked about, how I received my violin, or how I got back to Zurich. Nothing.

What Minsky needed was attention and a friend. A few weeks after my visit to L'Abbaye, I met him again, this time at his apartment in Zurich. I had my Mittenwalder with me. I wanted him to play it for me.

Why? he asked.

I can't play it, I replied. But I would like to hear how it sounds.

Why don't you learn how to play? he asked. I could teach you. It's not too late, if you want to.

I was puzzled, but I imagined myself playing "La Gitana" some day. And so I began taking lessons from Minsky. And every time the hour was over, we talked about the investigations that he was pursuing to track down the people and places that were part of the nightmares that had tortured him continually since childhood.

Yes, I accompanied Minsky to Poland, to the archives, which he looked through almost maniacally in search of clues about his origins, to Majdanek and Auschwitz, where he wandered about as if sleepwalking in search of the barracks where he had lived and trembled before the Blockowa. I also helped him with his search for the orphanage in Krakow where he had spent eleven months after the liberation, before he came to Switzerland, holding the hand of the woman whose picture and name were indelibly, and thus irrefutably, etched in his memory.

I did all that as a friend who was watching a friend recover, bit by bit, an identity that had been robbed from him. Many things were unclear and remained vague. He never disputed that. His life, as he described it to me on our way back from Poland, appeared to him like a canvas, like an oversized, forged painting. He was stripping away the colors in order to reveal the primer coat, the first five years of his life, that had been crudely painted over. He tried to the find and sharpen the contours. He relied on archival materials, records and reports. He visited the places where things may have happened and tried to square them with his slivers of memory, in an effort to fit them into the picture that, according to him, really looked more and more like him, instead of that other person he was supposed to be, if you believed the authorities and the reports of his deceased adoptive parents.

Minsky's search and his work on the image of his identity were as earnest as the work of an artist hoping to find the one true expression for a buried, but still present, horror in the depths of the self. It was the same earnestness he had displayed in his alchemist's kitchen when he was boiling varnish for his violins, the same earnestness with which he had spent countless hours referring to old studies and using his ruler, compass, and triangle to reconstruct their exact geometry.

The more progress he made, the more he was able to sharpen and verify the image, the better he was able to sleep at night and keep his fears at bay while he was awake. He healed the old wounds by painting them. He exorcised the horror by assigning it a space on the canvas of his self, a space where it seemed to belong. Who would have been better able to treat his sorrow than Minsky himself?

For more than ten years, I have asked myself almost every day where my guilt lies in this whole matter. I don't see myself as free of it. After all, I was the one who encouraged Minsky to write down his memories, so that he might keep track of them more effectively. But it's not as if I had a book in mind. As a matter of fact, I was alarmed when he faxed me the first few pages just one day later and asked for my opinion. It was clear to me that he wasn't only writing for himself, that he had started a book. Still, I didn't advise him against it.

I also didn't caution him when the book came out to rave reviews, and people started inviting him to readings and lectures, events he could barely cope with emotionally. I didn't caution him when inquiries about translations came in from more than ten countries, and he was showered with praise and awards.

I pushed aside the memory of my uncle's warning that truth is always a matter of your point of view, and that, as soon as you enter the public sphere, you become subject to their point of view. And just as it was by the Patriarch's Ponds in Bulgakov's book, what counts out there today are the views of the editors and the essayists.

First they called Minsky a liar and a crook, and in the end, they said the same things about me. The charges varied only when it came to the question of which one of us had distorted the truth, and who had merely believed the distortion.

I, they charged, had encouraged Minsky to go public with his story. That was not quite true, but it could still be interpreted that way. I had accompanied him on the road to fame. That was certainly accurate. According to the completely unfounded but eagerly circulated view of some reporter, I had supposedly also performed therapy on Minsky—using hypnosis, in violation of all the rules of classical analysis and my duty of care as a therapist. That seemed more like deliberate backstabbing from one of my colleagues. It was said that I had encouraged Minsky to remember the images that he recalls in his book. That's ridiculous, completely ridiculous. But people considered it plausible.

When the first malicious article by Wechsler came out, and Minsky collapsed under the ensuing media onslaught, I felt as if I was awakening from a trance. Wechsler invoked the truth. But what was he talking about?

Of course he didn't mean the poetic truth—that a knife used to destroy the picture of a person will kill the person in the picture. He meant the truth of the scientists, who finally concluded, through a court-ordered DNA analysis, that Minsky's father was a

Swiss citizen from the Jura Valley. Just as a carbon analysis would have proven that of all of Minsky's violins, which were built over several weeks according to the attentively reconstructed proportions of Amati and sealed with fifteen ultra-thin coats of the finest oil varnish, not one of them was a real Amati—even if they looked and sounded just like one.

What—this is another question I am still turning over in my mind after more than ten years—is the value of a truth that kills, compared to a truth that allows a person to live? None of the journalists who pounced on us like a pack of rats has ever provided an answer.

11

I am reading from the *Mesillat Yesharim*, the first Mussar book I studied with Eli in New York. With each chapter I read, it becomes more and more clear to me how much I have failed. The reason is obvious. I only need to turn to the foreword and read the opening sentences.

"I have written this work," Rav Moshe Chaim Luzzato begins, "not to teach men what they do not know, but to remind them of what they already know and is very evident to them, for you will find in most of my words only things which most people know, and concerning which they entertain no doubts. But to the extent that they are well known and their truths revealed to all, so is forgetfulness in relation to them extremely prevalent. It follows, then, that the benefit to be obtained from this work is not derived from a single reading; for it is possible that the reader will find that he has learned little after having read it that he did not know before. Its benefit is to be derived, rather, through review and persistent study, by which one is reminded of those things which, by nature, he is prone to forget and through which he is caused to take to heart the duty that he tends to overlook."

This is a book that I should have studied not just once, but again and again over the years. I neglected to do so. When I go through it now, with nearly every sentence, Luzzatto shows me the true magnitude of my failure, and it's difficult for me to make an argument in my defense.

It started with the arrogance I displayed in the case of Lauren. It continued with carelessness, for it was nothing but carelessness during my friendship with Minsky that caused me to drift on the wave of my admiration and ignore all the signs of the approaching catastrophe. And it finally ended in anger.

I thought I had long since overcome the anger, and the bitterness with which it was always intermingled. But I was wrong. For it is just as Luzzatto says: The exercise must be repeated constantly. Anger will grow again if the causes remain. And they have, both the external causes and the ones within me.

I have never been quick-tempered, like the furious man who, as it is written, would destroy the entire world if it were within his power to do so, for he is, in the truest sense, as devoid of reason as any predatory beast. I, on the other hand, have always considered myself to be one of those who are "difficult to arouse and easy to appease," as it is said in the Verses of the Fathers. But in fact, as I have recently learned, that's not the way I am at all.

I have to accept the fact that I am one of those people whose anger is not easily aroused and who do not abandon their intelligence, but who continue to nurse their wrath. And that is the danger. The anger settles in as a permanent guest. You get used to it, and after a while, you hardly notice it anymore. But amid your carelessness, the fury continues to smolder, and one day it can suddenly ignite again and cause a firestorm that devours your whole being.

I'm not exaggerating. I have crossed a line that I should never have even approached. Things only got this far because I was not mindful of the smoldering fire of an old, bitter anger. And so I have every reason to pore over Luzzatto, even if I don't believe that Mussar studies can save me now.

The hounding of Minsky started with an article by Jan Wechsler that appeared in the spring of '98 in a German newspaper. It was short and hard to outdo in its venom and malice. What followed was an outcry across the media landscape. Wechsler had set the tone. The chorus of so-called journalists eagerly joined in.

It wasn't long before everybody started dropping Minsky, one after the other—first the press, then his agent and the publishing houses, his acquaintances, and finally, his few friends. Minsky was sued for damages, even though no one could prove that any damage had been done. On the contrary. The publishers profited considerably from the turmoil of the first few weeks after Wechsler's revelations, selling every last hardcover edition before they started acting like they were the aggrieved party and announced that they had pulled the book from the shelves.

As time went on, the wave of public denunciation bore increasingly strange fruit. Various literary prizes that Minsky had been awarded were revoked. There were even demands that Minsky pay the prize money back, as if the book did not exist at all, as if he had never really written a word of it. I started to get the impression that he had never been honored for his book as an author, but only as a victim to be paraded around so everyone could show their concern and feel sorry for him—something the public apparently had a great need for.

I didn't comprehend just how much the tide of malice had taken on a life of its own, and how irrational it had become, until I found myself in the media's crosshairs. When they began to claim that I had treated Minsky and invented the memories in his book for him and with him, I grasped once and for all that this whole matter was not, as everyone vociferously claimed, about documenting the truth. Every rumor, whether it was verifiable or not, was eagerly taken up and passed along. As long as there was demand for it, the reporters fed stories and legends to their shocked and indignant readers. Books came out. Everyone made money off of Minsky's downfall. Which of the allegations were true, and which were only presumed to be true, or even completely made-up, did not matter in the slightest.

In all of this there was a hero, who was more than happy to bask in his success, and in the general recognition that he deserved the credit for bringing Minsky to justice. That was Jan Wechsler, who had gotten the witch-hunt rolling.

The first time I saw Wechsler was in the spring of '96, at the Leipzig book fair. Minsky's book had come out the previous autumn. He had already received his first awards. Everyone was talking about the book, and Minsky had several events to do at the fair. It was obvious that all the excitement was going to push him to the limits of his emotional capacity. I didn't try to talk him out of going to Leipzig, but I did go with him, as was so often the case before that, and afterwards.

The main event for us was a double reading by Minsky and Wechsler, which was held on one of the last evenings of the book fair, in a big hall. There must have been two hundred people in the audience. Wechsler went first, reading from his novel, which had also come out the previous autumn. In it, he evoked the panorama of a Jewish family that for the most part had survived in communist exile in the Soviet Union, a scintillating, magical story that was put together imaginatively. The applause was cordial, but brief.

Minsky's book stood in stark contrast to Wechsler's. As always, Minsky did not read himself. His voice would have failed him. He needed someone who could go to the podium and read from the book on his behalf. Usually, before a talk began, Minsky played one or two short pieces on the violin. During the reading itself, he would sit off to the side and listen with his eyes closed, as if he was far away, traveling through the places in his memory once again.

The standing ovations the authors received at the end were really meant for Minsky. The television cameras were also aimed at Minsky. Wechsler was nearly lost in the shuffle. Every time I recall that scene, I can't resist the idea that the only reason Wechsler embarked on his research, unearthed the facts from Swiss government files, and then publicized them with such powerful eloquence and personal disapproval was because he had been completely overlooked in all the excitement about Minsky.

The campaign against Minsky, a fight that Wechsler provoked and would soon reignite with his supposed documentary book *Masquerades*, must have given him great satisfaction. The amount of attention it brought him went beyond anything that ever came his way before, or later, when the public began to forget about the case.

Minsky was destroyed in that campaign. When I called him a day after Wechsler's article appeared, no one answered, neither in Zurich nor in L'Abbaye. I assumed that he had sought refuge in the Jura, so I went there immediately. There were already a few reporters hanging around, but at that point, they still had enough decency to keep their distance from the house. The housekeeper let me in. Minsky was in bed and refused to leave his room. He would stay there for weeks, frightened, panic-stricken, and completely disoriented. He didn't have the slightest grasp of what was happening, and it would take months before he would be able to leave his room without having a severe panic attack.

•

A year and a half later I called it quits. I gave up my practice in Zurich. Half of my patients had stopped coming after the allegations, which were also directed at me. I also had to disappoint the patients who still believed in me and refer them to other doctors. The medical association left me no other choice. I was no longer able to practice. And after the scandal and my expulsion from the institute in Freiburg, further research was also out of the question; there was no more work for me in Switzerland.

I would have had to go through one lawsuit after another to clear my name. My attorneys said that although it might take some time, I had a chance of success. But I couldn't imagine that anymore, after everything we had been through over the past several months.

And so, I decided to go back to Israel and try to make a new start. I sold most of my possessions. It pained me to think of spending the rest of my days more or less idly, living off my uncle's slowly dwindling inheritance. Even so, it was a possibility.

I saw Minsky for the last time in the fall of '99. I visited him again in L'Abbaye, where he now lived permanently, so he could stay as far as possible from all the turmoil. He had nobody. Everyone had abandoned him. He lived by himself from a small pension and what remained of the inheritance from his adoptive parents.

He spent his days and most of his nights in the workshop, where he continued working on his project to make a faithful reproduction of an Amati. I'm no expert, but I loved those instruments. When I saw them for the first time, I hardly dared to touch them, they seemed so delicate, fragile in a way—just as fragile as the man who had built them. The sound was unparalleled. He never sold a single one.

We talked on the phone for a few minutes once a month, usually right before Shabbos. There were some weeks when that was the only conversation he had at all. He still felt persecuted, and he wouldn't even speak with the cleaning lady, because he had come to view her as a hired spy. He watched over her while she cleaned. He never let her out of his sight, but he didn't say a single word to her. She was not allowed to enter the workshop.

My visit with him was short. I only stayed for a few hours. When I said goodbye, we embraced for a long time. I think it was clear to both of us that we were never going to see each other again.

We have spoken on the phone occasionally over the last few years. But he has never wanted to visit me, and I have never felt the need to return to Switzerland, even just for a visit.

In Israel I bought a small house and a plot of land. It's in Ofra, a yeshuv northeast of Yerushalayim, in the middle of the West Bank, surrounded by walls, high fences, and Arab villages. Land and housing were still affordable when I got there.

The landscape is rugged, and the climate is comfortable for someone like me who has spent most of his life in Switzerland and the northeastern United States. There's always a mild to strong wind. The summers aren't too hot. In the winter, it snows. I read a lot and work in my garden, where I'm trying to domesticate various exotic fruit trees. They need care, attention, and a lot of time. That's something I've got plenty of.

Occasionally Eli and Rivka come visit for Shabbos. I enjoy those days. Having friends like them is a great comfort.

Twice a week I go to Yerushalayim for the day. I share a practice there with a colleague. Something I once picked up as an additional tool of the trade has now become the basis for my modest occupation: I help people quit smoking—through hypnosis.

I don't want to have anything more to do with other people's memories. I no longer perform therapy, though I could, since the Israelis recognized all my degrees and certifications without objection. But I can't bring myself to do it. I, too, am still afraid that maybe things have only calmed down temporarily, that I'm still being watched—by colleagues, by the press. I just don't have the peace of mind to be able to help other people.

Ofra is closely guarded. It's not advisable to go outside the yeshuv on foot or venture into the surrounding Arab areas. Even so, it's a quiet life. At least it was until two weeks ago.

When I came back to Israel, I changed my last name. The authorities granted me that privilege after I made the case that it was the only way I could protect myself against stalkers from foreign countries. But now, that name change has become my undoing. Without it, I probably would never have come across Wechsler again. He would have steered clear of me, instead of visiting me in Ofra.

I myself didn't have the slightest idea what was in store for me. I had unsuspectingly agreed to have him stay with me over Shabbos, and I had even gone so far as to suggest that I could take him to Motza on Sunday. There were three degrees of separation—a friend of a friend of a friend had asked me.

A visitor was in from Germany, they told me. He couldn't understand a word of Ivrit, but he was frum, they said, it was his first time in Israel, and he was on a tour, visiting historic mikvaot, a hobby of his. They also told me he really wanted to visit a yeshuv in the West Bank and spend Shabbos in a place where everyone keeps Shabbos. They said they thought of Ofra, and of me, of course, since I spoke German and had occasionally talked about that ancient mikvah in the grove near Motza.

Apart from that, they also told me that the young man was very friendly and uncomplicated. His name, they said, was Jan.

I agreed. Never in a million years would it have occurred to me that it could be Jan Wechsler I had just invited.

I stood at the gate to the yeshuv waiting for the bus from Yerushalayim that my visitor was supposed to arrive on. He was the last person to get off. The young man was over forty, and I recognized him immediately. I should have turned around and walked away, maybe. But I didn't.

Aside from me, there was no one waiting at the gate. Wechsler walked up to me, greeted me exuberantly, and thanked me profusely for having him. He said the bus ride had been exciting in and of itself: bulletproof windows and Arab villages on both sides of the road. He said he could barely contain his excitement about spending Shabbos in Ofra.

He clearly had no idea who he was talking to. I had seen him once, during the reading in Leipzig. I was sitting in the audience. When Minsky went to have a vodka with him afterwards, I had already gone back to the hotel. We were never introduced. There was no way he could have recognized me.

Wechsler appeared to be in disguise. He was wearing a black suit with a vest, a white shirt and tie, and a yeshivish hat on his head. He looked frum. That didn't fit the image I had of him. In Leipzig, he had stepped up to the podium in jeans, a T-shirt, and rumpled sport coat, unshaven, his hair dyed blond and wild, as if it had been teased out—to me he looked like a madman. Still, his clothes notwithstanding, it was him. I was absolutely sure of it.

Wechsler never stopped talking. He talked on the way from the yeshuv gate to the house. He talked while I set the table and put the food for the next day on the plata. He talked on the way to the synagogue and on the way back home from the synagogue, before Kiddush and after Kiddush, and during the meal, incessantly.

But it wasn't his own family history that he unfurled for me. He claimed he was telling me about his grandparents, but I recognized them as characters from his novel. He repeated the stories from his book to me as if they were his own memories. Every word that he said was a lie.

Of course, he didn't talk about his other book, *Masquerades*. He didn't mention Minsky, either. It was unbearable.

After the meal, I interrupted him and suggested we go back to the synagogue. Three paytanim from Bnei Brak had come to sing the *Shirei ha-Vakashot* at midnight. Luckily, he did not object and came along.

The paytanim could have been grandfather, father, and son. Whether they were actually related, I don't know. They alternated, singing from the bottom of their hearts, every single intercession was a love song extolling the King of Kings. We stayed for two hours. And at least during that time, Wechsler was silent. He didn't talk on the way home, either.

There was no way I could sleep that night. Wechsler slept. I lay awake, got up, paced, lay back down again, and then got back up and sat awake at the table until dawn.

It was Shabbos. We were both stuck in Ofra. Neither he nor I could leave. And there was no other place for him to stay. There was no way I could tell him who I was. I had to endure his presence, his lies, and his lightheartedness, at least until the sun went down.

We were in the synagogue until noon. Then we sat down to eat. Fortunately, he drank some wine, got drowsy, and fell asleep in an armchair for a while after the meal. When he woke up, I showed him my garden. I told him about every tree, bush, and weed, just so I wouldn't have to listen to him any longer.

It was the longest Shabbos I have ever experienced. When it was finally over, I suggested that we set off for Yerushalayim immediately. We could take my car, I told him. I would go with him to Motza, I said, and then take him back to his hotel.

In the middle of the night? Wechsler asked, astonished.

I assured him that at night the atmosphere in the grove near Motza was incomparably more powerful than it was during the day. The illumination from the headlights of just one car made the mikvah look like a passage to another world, I told him. He had to see it, I said, since mikvaot were the reason he had come to Israel in the first place.

Wechsler agreed. We packed a few towels and headed out. I calmed down a bit during the ride. Wechsler fell asleep and didn't wake up until I had passed Yerushalayim on the Tel Aviv highway and taken the rugged exit, which was easy to miss, and turned onto the road through the woods that leads to the mikvah.

I parked the car in a place where the headlights illuminated the entrance to the highest of the three pools. We got out. It was bitterly cold. There was an icy breeze. Glimmering through the treetops from the deep black sky were tiny white sparks and the fine crescent of the moon, which looked like a heavy eyelid closing over a tired eye.

I'll pass, I told him, saying it was too cold.

Wechsler didn't wait a second. Standing by the open passenger door, he undressed and tossed his things into the car. He took off his glasses, his rings and his watch. Then, standing naked and shivering in the headlights, he started to babble.

If you're supposed to feel reborn after the tevila, then it could also feel like death, he said. He was already standing at the edge of the pool. I watched as he tentatively gauged the water temperature with his toes. He hesitated, and I asked him if he was really sure.

Of course, he replied, and he climbed down the well-worn stone steps into the water.

I kept my eye on him as I approached. And there it was again, all of a sudden, the old, bitter anger that had gone unnoticed. It wasn't a spark. It wasn't the kind of flame that flickers on a candlewick, either. It was a fire that came over me, burning a hole somewhere between my stomach and my head.

Did this man think he could start a new life in the waters of the mikvah, a different life than the one he'd been trying to lie his way out of? Did he think he could wash himself clean of the act of destruction that he had caused and could never make up for? How was that supposed to be possible? He hadn't even grasped that he had committed a crime, neither in his head nor in his heart.

The water in the mikvah must have been freezing cold. Wechsler panted when he climbed down and crouched in the water for the first time, just for a few seconds. Then he stood back up, crossed his arms in front of his chest, and closed his eyes.

While he was preparing for his tevila, I took off my gloves. Wechsler took a deep breath and submerged. I knelt down at the cold, wet edge of the pool and stretched out my arms. When he resurfaced, huffing and shivering, I looked right into his eyes and grabbed his head. I held it like a ball between my hands and pushed it slowly, but as hard as I could, back into the water.

Yerushalayim/Ofra
Sh'vat—Av 5768

Glossary

Aggadic: from *Aggadah*, Aramaic for tales or lore. Rabbinic texts on biblical characters and ethical ideas recorded in the Talmud and **Midrash**.

Arizal: Yitzhak Ben Sh'lomo Luria Ashkenazi (1534-1572), a rabbi and mystic in the community of Sfad in the Galilee, considered the father of the mystical discipline known as **Kabbalah**.

Ashkenazim: Jews descended from the medieval communities along the Rhine in Germany and Northern France. Used broadly to describe the Jews of Central and Eastern Europe, and their descendants.

Atara (*plural* Atarot): crown. A neckband on a **tallis** (prayer shawl).

Aufruf: Yiddish name for a ceremony held just before a wedding, where a groom is "called up" to recite a blessing over the Torah.

Bracha (*plural* Brachot): Hebrew, a blessing

Chavrusa: Yiddish/Ashkenazic pronunciation of Hebrew *Chavruta*, from the Aramaic for "friendship" or "companionship." A method of Talmud study where two students discuss a text.

Cheder: an elementary school where children learn Hebrew and the basics of Judaism.

Chometz: Yiddish/Ashkenazic pronunciation of *Chametz*, leavened foods prohibited during Passover. Describes any product made from one of five kinds of grain, which has been combined with water and left to stand raw for longer than eighteen minutes. Must be removed from the home before the holiday and sold temporarily to a non-Jew, because Jews are not allowed to own *chometz* during the eight-day festival.

Droshe: Yiddish/Ashkenazic pronunciation of *d'rash*, a sermon or brief exposition of the Torah portion or rabbinic literature.

Gedolim: Plural of the Hebrew *Gadol*, or "great," a term used mostly by Haredi Jews to refer to revered and learned rabbis of their generation.

Gehinnom: the name given to Hell in rabbinic literature.

Gemara: From the Aramaic "to study," the component of the Talmud that comprises rabbinical analysis of and commentary on the **Mishna**.

Get: a document presented by a husband to his wife to effect a divorce.

Gilgul ha-Neshamot: Kabbalistic concept of the reincarnation of souls.

Halacha: the collective body of Jewish law.

Haredim: Jews associated with the most conservative forms of orthodoxy.

Hasidim: literally "the pious." Jews associated with orthodox movements of Eastern European origin that promote mysticism along with strict adherence to Jewish law.

Hechscher: a kosher certification.

Ivrit: the Hebrew language.

Kabbalah: literally "receiving." An overarching term for a range of mystical activity in Judaism.

Kasher: to make kosher.

Kashrut: Jewish dietary laws.

Kohanim: Priests, direct male descendants of the Biblical Aaron, the brother of Moses and first high priest.

Kollel: an institute where married men study Talmud and rabbinic literature.

Mashgiach: person who inspects and supervises the production of kosher food.

Mezuzah: literally "doorpost." A piece of parchment inscribed by hand with two portions of Torah, contained in a small case which is affixed to doorframes in Jewish homes. The portions are the *Shema*, Deuteronomy 6:4-9 and 11:13-21, both of which include the verse: "And you shall inscribe these words upon the doorposts of your house and upon your gates."

Midrash: from the verb "to investigate" or "to study." A form of storytelling, a tool of interpretation that explores ethics and values in biblical texts.

Mikvah (*plural* mikvaot): ritual bath.

Minyan: Congregational quorum of ten adult (traditionally male) Jews required for a public prayer service and certain other religious obligations.

Mishna: literally "repetition." Judaism's first major canonical document after the Bible. The written compilation of the oral laws known as the "Oral Torah."

Mishteret Yisrael: The Israel Police. Its duties include crime fighting, traffic control, and maintaining public safety.

Mossad: Israeli secret service.

Muezzin: Arabic for the person who leads the call to prayer at a mosque.

Mussar: literally moral conduct, instruction, or discipline. An ethical movement that developed in 19th century Eastern Europe. The term is used for didactic Jewish ethical literature.

Peyes: Yiddish for sidelocks or sidecurls worn by some Orthodox Jewish men.

Perushim: commentaries to the Bible and the Talmud.

Pesach: Passover.

Peytanim: a cappella singers who perform liturgical poems.

Piyyutim (*singular* Piyyut): Jewish liturgical poems, usually sung or chanted.

Rav (*plural* rabbonim): rabbi.

Ramchal: an abbreviation for Rav Moshe Chaim Luzzatto (1707-1746), a prominent Italian rabbi, philosopher, and Kabbalist whose magnum opus is the ethical treatise *Mesillat Yesharim* (1740).

Rega!: Hebrew, "Just a moment!"

Rosh Yeshiva: The dean of a Talmudic academy.

Sanhedrin: from the Greek *Synhedrion* (assembly or council). The high court in ancient Israel, made up of seventeen judges.

Shabak: an acronym for *Sherut haBitachon haKlali*, Israel's internal security agency, also known as Shin Bet.

Shachris: Yiddish/Ashkenazic pronunciation of *Shacharit*, the morning prayer.

Sheitel: Yiddish name for the wig worn by some married Orthodox Jewish women.

Shuk: Hebrew rendering of *souq*, the Arabic word for market.

Seder (*plural* Sedorim): order or sequence. In this case, a study session at a Yeshiva.

Sfardim: Descendents of Jews who lived on the Iberian Peninsula before the expulsion in 1492, many of whom later settled in North Africa, Turkey, Greece, and other parts the Ottoman Empire.

Slicha Adoni: Hebrew for "excuse me, sir."

Smicha: Hebrew for "leaning (of the hands)." Formal ordination of a rabbi. Grants authority to give advice or judgment in *Halacha*, Jewish law.

Sukkot: "Festival of booths" or "Feast of Tabernacles," a Jewish holiday celebrated for seven days. Commemorates the forty-year period when the Israelites wandered the desert and lived in temporary shelters.

Tallis: Ashkenazic/Yiddish pronunciation of the Hebrew *Tallit*, a prayer shawl. In Yiddish, the plural is *Talesim*.

Tateh: Yiddish for "papa."

Tayves: Yiddish, morally questionable urges.

Tehillim: psalms.

Tesbih: Islamic prayer beads.

Tevila: immersion in a ritual bath.

Tikkun: Hebrew for "fixing" or "rectification." Often used in the phrase *Tikkun Olam*, or "mending the world," a concept central to **Kabbalah**.

Treif: Yiddish for not kosher.

Tzaddik: Hebrew for "righteous one."

Tzahal: Hebrew acronym for the Israel Defense Forces.

Tzitzes: Ashkenazic/Yiddish pronunciation of the Hebrew *Tzitzit,* knotted ritual fringes on the four corners of the prayer shawl (**Tallis**) or on a *tallit katan,* a garment worn under or over a man's shirt.

Yeshiva: a Jewish school where students focus on traditional religious texts. A *Yeshiva Bocher* is a young man studying at a Yeshiva.

B enjamin Stein was born in East Berlin in 1970. He has worked as an editor and correspondent for various computer magazines, and has been a corporate IT advisor since 1998. He owns the author-run publishing house Edition Neue Moderne and writes the literary weblog "Turmsegler." Benjamin Stein is married with two children and lives in Munich.

B rian Zumhagen has been a weekend anchor at WNYC since 2003. In the the 1990s he worked as a reporter, producer, and fill-in anchor at KQED in San Francisco. Most recently, he won a grant from the Arthur F. Burns Fellowship to produce radio features for the 20th anniversary of the fall of the Berlin Wall. Brian lives in Queens with his wife and children.

Benjamin Stein was born in East Berlin in 1970. He has worked as an editor and correspondent for various computer magazines, and has been a corporate IT advisor since 1998. He owns the author-run publishing house Edition Neue Moderne and writes the literary weblog "Turmsegler." Benjamin Stein is married with two children and lives in Munich.

Brian Zumhagen has been a weekend anchor at WNYC since 2003. In the the 1990s he worked as a reporter, producer, and fill-in anchor at KQED in San Francisco. Most recently, he won a grant from the Arthur F. Burns Fellowship to produce radio features for the 20th anniversary of the fall of the Berlin Wall. Brian lives in Queens with his wife and children.

BENJAMIN STEIN THE CANVAS

TRANSLATED FROM
THE GERMAN
BY **BRIAN**
ZUMHAGEN

OPEN LETTER
LITERARY TRANSLATIONS FROM THE UNIVERSITY OF ROCHESTER

Library of Congress Cataloging-in-Publication Data:

Stein, Benjamin, 1970-
  [Leinwand. English]
  The canvas / by Benjamin Stein ; translated from the German
by Brian Zumhagen. — 1st ed.
    p. cm.
  ISBN-13: 978-1-934824-65-8 (pbk. : acid-free paper)
  ISBN-10: 1-934824-65-8 (pbk. : acid-free paper)
  I. Zumhagen, Brian. II. Title.
  PT2681.T36428L4513 2012
  833'.914—dc23
                                        2012006422

Partially funded by a grant from the
National Endowment for the Arts, a federal agency.

NATIONAL
ENDOWMENT
FOR THE ARTS

The translation of this work was supported by a grant from the
Goethe-Institut which is funded by the German Ministry of Foreign Affairs.

GOETHE
INSTITUT

Printed on acid-free paper in the United States of America.

Text set in Caslon, a family of serif typefaces based on the designs of
William Caslon (1692–1766).

Design by N. J. Furl

Open Letter is the University of Rochester's nonprofit, literary translation press:
Lattimore Hall 411, Box 270082, Rochester, NY 14627

www.openletterbooks.org

There are two main paths and intertwined side-trails running through this
novel. Behind each cover is a possible
starting point for the action. Where
you begin reading is up to you, or to
chance. You can follow the narrative
on one side until you get to the middle
of the book, then flip it over and continue reading from the beginning of
the other side. To follow one of the
side-trails, turn the book over after
each chapter, and continue reading
where you left off before. Of course,
you're also free to find your own way.

Jan Wechsler

Do you want to take the ravine
or the river? (no one pays
the ferryman with love)

1

Normally we don't open the door on Shabbos if someone buzzes our apartment. Family and friends wouldn't ring the doorbell. We'd be expecting them, and around the appointed time, they would wait on the other side of the street, so we could see them from the window and go down to let them into the building.

Hashem arranged it ingeniously: during every meal and on Shabbos, we're reminded that we live among strangers, in exile. Our Catholic neighbors don't hang out the wash on their holy Sunday, but that would hardly stop them from writing a letter or driving the car out to the country after mass. The students who share an apartment one flight down have only a very vague idea of God, I'm afraid. In German cities, he's not really fashionable. Nowadays, people around here don't want to hear too much about someone who makes such elaborate and restrictive demands, like keeping Shabbos.

Of course there are exceptions, like José Molina, a slightly overweight, tremendously friendly musician who lives with his boyfriend in the apartment next door. We've never asked him where he comes from. I've always liked imagining that he's a Chilean exile. Of course that has something to do with his name, the *Kiss of the Spiderwoman*, and his accent, which is difficult to place geographically. Though I'm not sure where Molina comes from, I do know that he has traveled widely and spent a few years in New York. He lived in Brooklyn, in a predominantly Jewish neighborhood. We found that out one Friday, when we had to ask him to accept the delivery of our new washing machine. They were supposed to bring it early in the afternoon, but Shabbos was about to begin and they still hadn't come.

Molina knew just what to do. He gave the delivery men all the necessary paperwork, signed the receipt, and even gave them both a tip. We didn't have to explain anything to him. He just laughed and said: I never dreamed that I would come in handy as a Shabbos goy again in Germany!

Neighbors like José Molina are rare. If you want to keep Shabbos in this country, you have to build yourself a fortress. As soon as you step outside your door, you walk into a religious minefield, and it's just as dangerous when someone enters from the outside—by ringing the bell, on Shabbos, at our door.

Thanks to my wife, I no longer feel cornered when this kind of thing happens. Just don't answer, she said one time, when I was trying to get rid of yet another mailman, because I wouldn't have been able to accept the package or sign for it.

How do you explain yourself at a moment like that? It throws me off completely. I feel like an idiot. It's embarrassing. And on top of that, I'm ashamed that I'm embarrassed. Embarrassed to explain to a complete stranger what Shabbos is, that it's Shabbos *now*, and that that's why I can't accept the package, but I can't ask him to take it back, either.

When I feel embarrassed, I become unfriendly. And my rudeness then makes my wife uncomfortable. And so, when the bell rings on Shabbos, the door stays closed.

And it would have stayed closed yesterday, if I hadn't been playing with my kids in the hallway, horsing around and giggling so loudly that we could be heard in the stairwell. The door would have stayed closed if the man who was trying to come up to see us had been standing outside at the building entrance and not right in front of our apartment, knocking and calling out for us to open up. Ignoring him when he knew someone was home just seemed too impolite. And so I opened the door.

The guy waiting in the stairwell was—what else?—a courier. He seemed annoyed. I didn't see a package or a letter. But he had a suitcase and the inevitable clipboard with the receipt that was waiting for my signature, which I was going to have to withhold once again. Still, I decided not to say anything for the time being.

The courier explained that he'd come from the airport. The airline regrets the delay, he told me. But your luggage has finally been found. Here it is, he said. I just needed to sign for it, then he could be on his way. He told me he still had a lot of stops to make.

I exhaled. This time the problem was easy to solve. When you consider the extensive security measures at Ben Gurion Airport in Tel Aviv, where every piece of checked baggage, and every carry-on bag, is tagged with a barcode sticker, it seems impossible that they could lose a piece of luggage, or that it could get lost and end up unclaimed somewhere, waiting to be recovered.

I'm not missing a suitcase, I told him.

That can't be right, the courier replied. Wait a minute, here it is: January 7th, TUIfly Tel Aviv—Munich. You reported the loss.

I couldn't recall doing that. There must be some way to verify that I only checked one suitcase, I said.

That's not my department, the courier told me. He said he only delivered the bags when they'd been found. And he said they tend to turn up even when they've been lost for weeks. Some bags end up going halfway around the world, he told me, because someone mistakenly loaded them onto the wrong plane.

Be that as it may, I assured him, the suitcase is not mine.

You've got to be kidding me! the courier shouted. I could understand why he was getting angry, because he showed me the address tag, which certainly looked like I had filled it out.

I gave the bag a closer look. It was a pilot suitcase, black, presumably faux leather with riveted bronze-colored code snap locks.

But the locks are broken, I said.

Yes, the courier conceded, the airline apologizes for that, too. But there are no exceptions, he said. Customs and Border Protection have to inspect every piece of luggage that is reported lost and then reappears. All of that's explained in the cover letter, he told me. I'd have to read that later, he said, because right now he really didn't have time to go over everything with me.

I'm just the courier, you know, he continued, now sounding perhaps just a little bit desperate. If you want to file a complaint, call this number, he said. And he pointed to a number starting with 0180 at the top of the cover letter, which I was just as reluctant to accept as I was to take the suitcase itself.

To top it all off, now my kids were getting curious. They were sneaking a peek at the suitcase through the open apartment door.

Are there presents in there, Papa?

What presents?

You know, all the presents you bought for us in Israel!

I already gave you those!

But look, Papa, there have to be more presents in the suitcase. Yay!

Yes, kids, the courier said, the suitcase is definitely full of presents for you, and your papa just didn't want to tell you, because the suitcase was lost. But we found it, and I've brought it back, with all the presents inside. There's nothing missing.

If someone had told me before about the kinds of underhanded tricks couriers are prepared to play to get rid of suitcases, I would never have believed it.

My son could no longer restrain himself. He jumped around the suitcase excitedly, lost his balance, and fell over it, thudding against the door of our neighbor Molina, who was practicing on his violin. I absolutely had to restore the balance of power, so I resorted to a ruse of my own.

Why don't you go in, I said to the kids, and ask Mama if she has another dessert for you?

That worked. The children dashed into the apartment, shouting. But it didn't do me any good. As soon as they were gone, José Molina opened his door, violin in hand.

He probably thought I had knocked. I noticed the friendly gleam in his eyes that I remembered from the Friday with the washing machine. With one look, he grasped the situation.

Oh, he said, they brought your suitcase! And then he turned to the courier and asked if he couldn't sign for me, since he was practically part of the family.

Of course, said the courier, relieved, and he quickly held out the clipboard. Molina added his signature to the list, took the suitcase, and, without being asked, carried it through our doorway and put it down in the hall.

So that's it, right? Molina called toward the hallway. But the courier was already on his way out. You could hear him half a flight down, mumbling: *It takes all kinds* . . . And before I had a chance to explain myself, my neighbor patted me on the shoulder sympathetically. A few seconds later, he had disappeared into his apartment with the violin and the feeling that he'd done a good deed.

There was no dessert after dessert. My wife is unrelenting about such things. The children didn't get any presents, either, which really disappointed them. Today, a few days after it was delivered, the suitcase is still sitting there, unopened, in my office. After all, it is simply a fact—and I would swear it in court—that I have never seen it before.

The days have turned to weeks, and then to months. The suitcase is still in my office. I haven't opened it. It's right next to my desk, and my eyes are invariably drawn to it if I look up from my work for a moment, if I stop staring at the screen and the keyboard and allow my eyes to wander. I have begun to hope that maybe it will merge with its surroundings, become one with the desk, disappear among the piles of books and become invisible, like so many of the things that surround us day after day, things we get used to and then at some point no longer notice.

But in this case, it seems that my hopes are in vain. This suitcase is something like a spike in my flesh, the splinter you get when you're absentmindedly walking along an old dock. It's just a little prick, but it startles you and disrupts your thoughts, which in my case means being jolted out of my routine daydreaming.

I am a publisher and an author. For many hours of the day—some would even say: without any interruption whatsoever—I am occupied with stories, biographies, and incidents, both outrageous and mundane, but in any event with material, nothing but scraps of reality that deserve, one and all, to be lovingly fictionalized. Or that already *have been* fictionalized. No one knows better than I that the boundary between reality and fiction in every story runs meanderingly through the middle of language, concealed and incomprehensible—and movable. Even the word "actuality" leads to uncertainty. Who can say whether it's a synonym for reality or instead stands for everything that acts—a very subjective picture that depends more on the eye of the beholder than it does on the object being observed.

The fact that this suitcase is here means that a boundary has been crossed. It really shouldn't be here, reminding me each time I see it that something isn't the way it should be. The splinter is in my foot. I can bear it; it wouldn't be worth mentioning if I didn't need to pull it out to keep the tiny wound from getting infected. And if it weren't for my undeniable fear of that small, insignificant operation—the moments that stretch out intolerably as you sit there with tweezers and a sanitized needle, trying to get the tiny little piece of wood out of your flesh.

The fact that the suitcase is here, with its tie-on address label filled out in my handwriting, the fact that it's here, even though I am still convinced that it doesn't belong to me and has never belonged to me—none of this is a big deal. But the fact that I am afraid to open it and find out what's inside, that's anything but insignificant.

What is true is that I have had very similar suitcases twice in my life. I got one shortly after I accepted my first permanent position as an editor at a magazine. That was a good fifteen years ago; but I still distinctly remember buying it.

It was my first acquisition in Munich, where I had just moved from Berlin to take the position—temporarily, of course. At least that's what I told myself at the time. As a Berliner, you don't move to Munich permanently. You're just there temporarily, for a visit. And when you say you're going home, even after several years in this transient state, you still mean Berlin, even though you've given up your apartment there for financial reasons, and you have to spend the weekend at a hotel or a friend's place.

Back then I didn't have a car or a license, and since I've never liked long train rides, I had to fly. Given my editor's salary, I could only afford the trip over a long weekend once a month, but that solution had the undeniable advantage of being quite comfortable.

What I really needed was a suitcase with the maximum allowable dimensions for carry-on luggage, a bag that could hold a lot but wouldn't have to be checked, so I could be spared all the waiting around at the baggage claim when I reached my destination.

The monthly trips home weren't the only reason I bought my first pilot suitcase. As part of the job, I had to go out of town at least once a month for a day or two, and sometimes even a whole week. The conferences and press events, where I reported on companies and the products they were introducing, were held regularly in all kinds of cities in Europe and the United States—I went to those places by plane, too.

At that time I was fascinated by electronic gadgets, and since I worked for a computer magazine, I always had to be equipped with the very latest laptop, electronic organizer, and mobile phone. (Not that anyone equipped *me*. I equipped *myself*, which, despite certain press rebates, meant that there often wasn't enough money left at the end of the month for the flight home. And so, instead of flying to Berlin, I would end up spending the long weekend in my "transitional" apartment in Munich, studying product manuals and transferring data to my latest acquisition.)

Given my almost emotional attachment to these technical devices and the considerable amount of money they consumed, it was hard for me to leave my mobile office in the hands of those rough baggage handlers. I couldn't run the risk of anything getting damaged or ending up lost on the other side of the globe because someone forgot to load my bag onto my connecting flight. As a result, having a suitcase that would allow me to travel around the world for several days with only one carry-on was more important to me than having food in the house. So, on one of my first lunch breaks as an editor, I bought that first pilot suitcase, which bore an uncanny resemblance to the one here today.

It looks like it, but it's not the same one. I know this because my old suitcase met a similar fate—it also went missing, because, in a careless and lazy moment, I had decided to check my bag on a flight from Los Angeles to Munich via Atlanta.

I got it back. A courier from the airline brought it to my door, but only after two endlessly long weeks of uncertainty. Customs had opened it, the combination locks were intact, but the face panel, which was made of firm cardboard covered with leather, was torn up. Nothing was missing, and the contents of the suitcase weren't damaged. None of my luggage had gotten lost. But the suitcase itself was finished.

It wasn't a real loss, because I quit my job at the magazine a few days later. At the moment I can't remember why I quit. Why didn't I want to work as an editor anymore, and why, of all times, after that trip to America? I don't know. I even have to admit that, at present, I can only *assume* that I quit. I'm not certain of it.

I can still see myself coming down the stairs with the damaged suitcase, intending to throw it into the garbage bin in the court-yard. I was sure that I no longer needed it. I wouldn't be flying again anytime soon. That was exactly what was going through my head as I opened the lid on the trash can. It was empty and smelled musty, slightly sour, like spoiled milk. It was drizzling. I remember it clearly. Every detail is present. It's all the more incomprehensible that it's just not coming back to me why, on that evening, I believed that the suitcase, damaged or not, was expendable.

Maybe I am wrong and I had already quit. Or there was an incident that left me convinced that it was going to happen inevitably. That's just as possible. Strange. I can usually rely on my memory.

The second pilot suitcase I can verify that I owned was a present my mother gave to me—to celebrate the founding of my publishing company. I had told her the news while I was visiting her in Berlin.

Now you're going to have to fly a lot again, she said, when she gave me the gift the next day. She seemed more worried than excited.

I don't know where my mother gets her information about the day-to-day life of publishers. Whatever jet-setter she had in mind couldn't possibly have been the owner of a small literary press. Still, it's widely known that maternal care has an infinite half-life; what's more, rebelling against it is as futile as fighting the forces of nature. Objective reasoning will only lead to complications. After all, a moment like that involves a mother's noble feelings, and it's best not to hurt those with petty objections.

Wow! That's really nice, I said. I used to have one just like it. Do you remember?

Of course I do. But you can't take care of anything. The old one must be completely run down by now. You really have to pay more attention to your appearance. You can't possibly travel with a worn-out old suitcase. What are people going to think about you? Such sloppiness! That's going to reflect negatively on your books and their authors. Then you'll be finished in no time, and the poor authors will be finished right along with you. You're responsible for them. You can't just think of yourself anymore!

I am over forty, married, the father of two children, but in my mother's eyes I'm apparently egocentric to the point of being asocial, and completely irresponsible. And a *schlomp*. And so on and so forth.

Customs ruined the suitcase, Mama, I objected timidly.

Excuses, excuses! You can wipe those right off your face! With books, everything's in black and white, and it's eternal. It has to be truthful. Just think of the press!

I lost her train of thought there. Veracity and the press, books and eternity—I didn't quite get the association. But anything I said would have put me even more on the defensive. You can't resolve a situation like that by arguing. It must have been during a similar conversation with my mother that I started to accept that my years of transitional residence in Munich had become a permanent condition.

As for my mother's gift, she was indeed proved right. The suitcase didn't last long. For a few months it just sat in the attic, until I finally put it in the overhead bin of an airplane one single time, during a trip to Spain.

When I went on that vacation to the Costa Blanca, I took a pile of unsolicited manuscripts with me—which is a more apt description of my daily life. In my rush to get ready for the trip, I must have made a mistake while I was setting the combination for the suitcase lock. When I got to the vacation apartment, the locks wouldn't open. After about a half an hour of futile attempts, I thought it over for a moment; then I sacrificed the suitcase.

I read some of the manuscripts by the pool, and I flipped through the others under an umbrella at the beach. I wrote a handful of rejection letters and left the suitcase with its broken locks and its carefully shredded contents in Spain. On the flight home— I'll admit it—I felt relieved.

I have never told a soul about this. Not that I think anyone would have held it against me. My mother? The authors? I can hardly imagine that. The suitcase had to bite the dust because I'd made a blunder. It certainly wasn't a crime for me to dispose of the rejected manuscripts. And suitcases, unlike women, don't take revenge for the abuse they've suffered.

If someone's really trying to get me in trouble and planted this suitcase on me, it would be better to open it and get some assurance. Besides, I can't give it back. The airline says it can prove that I checked it myself in Tel Aviv. The address label doesn't exactly back up my story—that I couldn't have packed the suitcase myself because I've never seen it before. In any event, it's much too late now to make any kind of claim, months after the courier delivered the suitcase to me, and my neighbor Molina signed the receipt.

And still, I hesitate to open it. Just now I was unable to recall why I quit my first job as an editor, or even whether I quit or was fired. It simply escapes me. And that's not all. It is as if all the events and perceptions that must have led, or at least contributed to, the conclusion of my career as a journalist have been erased from my memory. That's not normal. The thought that this might not be the only gap in my memory frightens me.

It's one thing not to remember events from years ago. And I concede that it must seem unusual that I have forgotten essential facts about an obviously significant turning point in my life. But the idea that, just a few days after coming back from Israel, I would be unable to recall buying a suitcase, one I bought specifically so I could fill it with various things, things that I also can't remember . . . that sounds eerie.

I'm not sure I can trust myself anymore. Where was I when? What had I done when, and why? Maybe the *Shabak* was already looking for me because I had left behind a dead body in the Holy Land; and maybe it was only my guilty conscience, leading to a kind of traumatically induced amnesia, that was preventing me from becoming aware of my crime.

Making the suitcase disappear by throwing it in the garbage is no more an option than giving it back to the airline. The way things are, I'll never have any certainty or find out the truth, and from now on, I'll have to live day in, day out with the fear that maybe I'm a murderer, and my guilt just hasn't been uncovered yet.

No matter how much you deny yourself, how long and how strongly you've fought the impulse to do a certain thing—in the moment immediately after an unavoidable act, you're always amazed at how easy it was, how quickly it happened and how little there ultimately was to crossing the boundary. It was difficult, a gigantic obstacle, and overcoming it was unimaginable—before it was done. Seconds later, it's just mundane.

I opened the suitcase and unpacked it. I can recite the things that were inside one by one, nothing more than a list of personal effects: a pair of white gloves made of sheer cotton; four books (a large format hardcover and three paperbacks); a bundle of newspaper clippings in a white envelope (DIN A4 format); the manuscript of a medical case study, about two hundred pages long; a worn jewelry box, apparently decades-old, made of black cardboard. Inside the box, on a ruby-colored velvet cushion, there was an emerald green precious or semi-precious stone with gold-colored inclusions in the form of sheer threads, round, faceted, about a centimeter in diameter. The books and the jewelry box were wrapped in three pieces of clothing: Jellabas (without hoods) made of a cheap blended fabric, in a deep shade of dark green under gold-colored appliquéd patterns, which match the gem.

I don't feel relieved at all. I can't claim that these items have nothing to do with me. I don't know what to say about the gem;

I've never seen it and can't even say what kind of stone it is. I am sure that I have never collected newspaper clippings. But then, what good are my assertions when it's possible that I just don't remember anymore, as if a part of my memory has been abruptly erased?

I have to proceed in a calm and collected manner. I have to rule out the possibility that someone or something has torn holes in my memory, as if he (or it) had taken an eraser and wreaked havoc on a pencil drawing, leaving behind large, white spaces, and the best I can do is try to reconstruct the previous content on the edges of those spaces—vaguely, if at all.

Let's take the large-format book, a Hebrew art print edition, which is about ten years old and has apparently been read many times, or at least thumbed through. The title *Mikvaot atikim b'eretz Yisrael* (Ancient Mikvaot in Israel) is displayed over a black-and-white photo of the Arizal mikvah in Sfad.

Yes, I am interested in historical mikvaot. And during my last stay in Israel, I did visit a few of these baths, some of which are thousands of years old. But I'm not familiar with this book. It doesn't belong to me, and I have never seen it.

The first of the paperbacks, which I examine more closely, could actually belong to me: *The Picture of Dorian Gray* by Oscar Wilde. It's an old edition from Penguin Books, and it's familiar to me. It must be in my library, at least in a similar layout and comparable condition.

That will be easy to check, I think to myself, but then I stop when I look at the cover of the second paperback. The title—*Masquerades*—doesn't ring a bell, but the name is familiar to me: Jan Wechsler. That's the name that's written on the address label attached to the suitcase.

Jan Wechsler is me.

2

I'm not going to tell my wife anything about my discovery for the time being. Even though there doesn't seem to be any reason for me to be particularly hopeful at the moment, I do think that soon I will be able to find plausible explanations about the suitcase and the items inside it. Until then, it's enough that I'm worried myself. I don't have to infect anyone else with it.

At least I was able to find my Penguin Modern Classics edition of *Dorian Gray*, which I had immediately thought of when I was inspecting the suitcase and came across the Wilde novel. It wasn't with my books, though; it was on one of my wife's shelves. She has this funny habit of keeping the proof of purchase inside her books, whether it's a receipt, an online shipping invoice, or a delivery slip from an antiquarian bookseller. She thinks it's a nice thing to do in case she ever ends up selling a book. She says the receipt would give the new owner a kind of document showing a bit of the path that the book had taken.

I didn't understand this until one time when she was at a flea market and found a handwritten dedication in one of the books they were selling there: *My sweet Karin, because I love you so much, I want you to have this book of poems, as a token to express in words that very beautiful thing that's kept us alive. Yours, Martina.*

Some books tell stories that the author never imagined. This book seemed to have outlasted the love it was intended to prove. Or the life of the recipient; who could know? A dedication like that, and the circumstances under which my wife found the book, left plenty of room for associations and possible stories.

I guess sometimes love really is a second-hand emotion, she said, as she put the book on the shelf, not alphabetically, the way she usually does, but with the special treasures, those books that she would never lend out under any circumstances.

Just like a dedication, my wife explained, a receipt or a delivery slip is a personal note that gives a book's potential future owner more room to imagine. This had already been her opinion before. The loving dedication from Martina to Karin merely confirmed the feeling.

Aside from that, thanks to her receipts, she was also able to determine when and where she had acquired a particular book, even years after the fact. And ever since we moved in together, it's been a kind of insurance against the constant danger of my looting her collection. Time and again, I could have sworn that a certain book on her shelf actually belonged to me. But she would just give me a weary smile. Even though I could remember where and when I had bought it, she could prove it, and she proved to me, over and over, that my memories were anything but trustworthy.

It's not at all surprising, then, that these slight memory lapses might occur when I am faced with objects of unknown origin from a suitcase that was delivered to me by mistake. What is new for me is being completely and utterly incapable of remembering something. Usually, I can remember thoroughly and very accurately; but sometimes, what I describe from memory, often in great detail, never happened, or at least not the way I claim it did. And I owe this insight to the receipts that my wife has carefully kept with each of her books, and of course I owe it to her stubbornness. When I'm wrong, she likes to prove it to me.

But does it make me a liar that I'm wrong sometimes, and my stories don't square with verifiable facts? If anyone were to make that claim, I would dispute it. A lie has to have intent. And a purpose. If there's no intent, it could be considered a pathological defect, but not a lie.

In particular, there's a reasonable explanation for my tendency to appropriate my wife's books by remembering my own story about how they were acquired. It's an explanation that would absolve me of the charge that I am consciously seeking to enrich myself by lying. This explanation has its origins in my biography: I was born in East Germany in the 1960s.

The East ended for me at the Oder-Neisse "Border of Peace" with Poland. My homeland was red. I grew up under socialism, and socialism—I've never viewed it any other way—is a synonym for shortage.

Zbigniew Herbert, a Polish poet whose works I would read much later in West German editions—passed around only among the "faithful hands" in my close circle of friends—described it as only a poet could: *The inquisitors are in our midst. They live in the basements of huge tenement houses, and only the shop-sign WRINGER HERE betrays their presence.* In German, the word for "wringer" also means "shortage."

That's where I come from.

No, we didn't starve, even though some western propaganda films liked to make that claim. There was bread, butter, milk, even chocolate. And, contrary to the widespread perception in western Germany, there were also bananas occasionally, at least around Christmas time, oranges (full of seeds, bitter, Cuban), and mandarins, which tasted less bitter and whose origin was unknown to me. Nonetheless, there was always a shortage. But it was a shortage of another kind.

In the Small Country, everything was small: the horizon, the opportunities, and above all, the people. The dominant feeling of my youth was one of being closed in and limited. But the reason for that wasn't the mined border and the barbed wire that blocked the way to the West. It was more the way the peculiar society succeeded in seeing that small, restricted habitat as the entire world.

No, when I say "hunger," I don't mean material scarcity. It wasn't like the Korea of Kim Il Sung. People had enough to eat, places to live, they even drove cars—I mean: Trabants. But emotionally and intellectually, it was impossible for me to feel full. Perhaps that was the reason why my hunger was always tremendous. That may be.

In the seventies, our street had a laundry with a steam wringer. When I was a child, I liked to go there and look in the windows, watching as the women worked with what seemed to me to be gigantic machines. Of course, no one would have dared put a sign in the window that said HIER MANGEL. Because everyone would have understood the macabre double-entendre, and humor of that kind was not appreciated.

The bed sheets, which they carry out of the wringer-shop, are like the empty bodies of witches and heretics. That's how Zbigniew Herbert ends his poem. But from time to time, a witch or a heretic makes it through—almost unscathed—and isn't wrung out entirely. They still have enough liquid to rejuvenate themselves. And those hungry witches and heretics are the keepers of tomorrow's shortage—or they will abolish it.

It wasn't a cozy homeland, that Small Country, but it was still a homeland, something I no longer believe that I have.

Books offered a way out of the confinement. I grew up with them, I loved them. To this day I can remember which room of my parents' apartment I was sitting in, and under which lamp, when I read my first "big book." It was *Dr. Aybolit*, which was the Russian knockoff of *Dr. Doolittle*, something I found out only years later, to my great disappointment. I had taken it out of the children's library and didn't want to return it, because I kept going back to the first page every time I finished reading it. Of course I had to return it eventually and pay the painfully high late fee of ten pfennigs out of my allowance. After all, the book didn't belong to me.

In Berlin-Friedrichshagen, where I grew up, there were two libraries, one for children, and one for adults. The children's library was in a prominent location, right on Bölschestraße, which had once been Emperor Fritz's silk promenade down to the Müggelsee. I registered there as soon as I could read and the ABC books no longer sufficed. Things weren't so lavish for us, financially speaking; to satisfy my hunger for reading, library books would have to do. And they did, for a while. But at a certain point, just like a worm, I had worked my way through the whole collection. I also had literary interests that were inappropriate for my age. In short: I wanted to go to the other library, the one for adults, eighteen and up, which was down a side street off our boulevard. There was just one catch. I was only twelve. My mother realized that this could not be allowed to stop me. It took some effort on her part, but somehow she found a way to get me the library card I was longing for.

The first and closest source of reading material, however, was the library at home, my parents' bookcases and bookshelves. They'd inherited this library from my grandfather on my mother's side. (My other grandfather was still alive, was just as crazy about books, and perched on his treasures like a mother hen. I wasn't allowed to read his books until I was over twenty and inherited his estate—an involuntary loan, as it were.) My parents' library wasn't exactly a curated collection. It was more like a random assortment. Kneipp's books on neuropathic medicine were next to an illustrated edition of the Protestant Bible from 1832 and guidebooks by East Germany's star lawyer, Professor Friedrich Karl Kaul (widely known by the abbreviation F.K.K.—West German shorthand for nudism).

No book on my parents' shelves was taboo. I was allowed to read all of them. No one withheld any of the books from me, as long as I treated them with respect and care and re-shelved them in the correct order when I was finished reading them. As is the case with my wife's books today, these were arranged alphabetically on the one hand, while certain books were also sorted specially, according to the personal value that was apportioned to them.

There were some real treasures among the many dubious titles on the shelves. I have an almost tactile memory of one book. When I close my eyes and become engrossed in my memory, it's as if I can still feel myself thumbing through the yellowed pages. This book was an epistolary novel.

Letters have always held a great fascination for me. I have written countless letters myself. My first amours were long-distance loves. We'd only see each other every three weeks, and the time between each meeting was bridged by daily letters. Which means I have also received many letters. Always eagerly anticipated, they were often no less stirring when I read them.

But I was also, and especially, fascinated by letters that were neither addressed to me nor written by me—for example, the few letters that my great grandfather wrote to my great grandmother in March of '33 from the Gestapo prison in Leipzig, where he was murdered soon afterwards. Or the letter my father wrote just before his 25th wedding anniversary, in which he ended his marriage, a letter my mother later gave to me to read. But then there were also those "literary" letters that occasionally appear in novels—sometimes even an entire work is constructed around them.

There were some books that my parents kept inside a bookcase, instead of putting them out on the shelves. These were the collectors' items; it was important to keep them free from dust and out of the hands of children—which is to say the hands of my younger sister. Among these protected books, I found something very special one day. It was an edition of the *Letters of Ninon de Lenclos*, with light red printed etchings by Karl Walser. I had to work hard to read it, because the book was printed in old German Gothic type. What I found especially exciting were the fringed ends of the pages. They created the impression that the book was hand-made. And sure enough, I later learned that this copy was one of those books where you still had to cut open the pages.

At that time, I was just the right age (fourteen or fifteen, I believe) to use these letters from the seventeenth century to educate myself about the meaning, purpose, and nature of love. I read the book several times, and it was clear to me that one day I would take it from my parents' house, so that I could add it to my own library. And that's just how it happened. I managed to make a convincing case that I urgently needed to have the book, and eventually my mother gave it to me.

Unfortunately, a few years later, I made a fatal error: I lent the book to someone. And when, after some time, I tried to get it back again—inquiring tentatively—I got nothing but an aggravating denial: Never in a million years would I have borrowed that book from you, and so on. And with that, it was lost.

It wasn't long before I was living only with, in, and around books. I even walked out of the house in the morning with my nose in a book, which considerably prolonged the amount of time

I needed to get to the streetcar that I took to school—reading throughout the whole ride, naturally.

Of course I took part in our graduating class' elective literature course. All of the students who turned up for that class looked a bit alike: with our noses in our books, we were trying to expand our horizons. We read Salinger, even Kerouac, and we felt very subversive. When one of my friends discovered Rilke's "Panther" and read the poem to us, we all saw ourselves in it. Didn't that strength lie within each of us? And weren't we all afraid that one day it would peter out in that cage, behind the thousand bars that bounded our Small Country, beyond which we assumed the real world could be found?

We were not sure of our own selves. But when it came to books—and this was another thing we all had in common—we were willing to risk a great deal. We were fearless about this and would defy any ban. Reading—that was our modest revolt.

A classmate told me that her father had every book by George Orwell. Of course, I promised her everything under the sun if she would get me some of them. She was in love with me and couldn't say no. A few days later, she brought me a paperback edition of *1984*. Of course the book was banned in East Germany. I covered the book in newspaper and read it in the schoolyard during my lunch break. For my girlfriend—I don't know anymore whether I fell in love with her before or after *1984*—my boldness was anything but amusing.

Under the spreading chestnut tree / I sold you and you sold me—. In the book, the line isn't translated. In the German dub of the unsettling black-and-white film version by Michael Anderson, the line can be heard in German in a voiceover: *Im Café Kastanie sicherlich / verriet ich dich und du auch mich*—.

How is it, I still wonder to this day, that of all the depressing things that Orwell depicted, it was the betrayal of the lovers that touched me the most? It illustrates a tragic fact: we can't say for sure how we would react under certain extreme circumstances. Since then I have been very touchy when dealing with moralists. Whenever I encounter a betrayal, I can't help thinking of Julia and Winston, and I find myself wanting to defend the betrayer, inside of whom—I always assume—there is perhaps nothing but a desperate lover who can't find any other way out.

It was also a book that made the Stasi suspicious of me when I was barely eighteen years old.

Among the minor oddities of East Germany were the libraries which were open to the public, but which didn't allow you to borrow most of the books in the card catalog. And then there were other libraries where you could have taken out every book on the shelves, but you weren't allowed in. The Berlin City Library was in the first category: books published in non-socialist countries couldn't be borrowed without special permission. In the second category was the library at the American embassy in East Berlin. They were willing to loan all of their books. Entering the embassy, however, was unwise.

There was one particular book that made me decide to disregard the bans and taboos.

I first heard the name Cummings in a movie. Woody Allen's *Hannah and Her Sisters* was on television. Two of the protagonists, I think it was Elliot and Lee, meet in a bookstore. Elliot takes a huge tome off the shelf, an edition of the *Complete Poems, 1904-1962* and quotes from "somewhere i have never travelled": *nobody, not even the rain, has such small hands.*

I absolutely had to get *my* hands on this treasure chest of American poetry. And for some reason my mind was made up that it had to be that particular edition.

When the second-hand bookshops and libraries couldn't help me get that edition—the city library wouldn't let me borrow a book of American poems—I became desperate. I don't remember who the clown was who told me to go ahead and try the American embassy library. It probably wasn't meant seriously. But I didn't hesitate.

The oil in the gears of a dictatorship is the fear that its citizens feel. I certainly wasn't especially brave—naïve is more like it—but I had an objective. I wanted that book. So I sauntered into the American embassy like it was nothing. For the first time in my life, I went through a metal detector. The security agent at the entrance was friendly and pointed me in the direction of the library. But when I walked in, the librarian made it clear to me that I shouldn't have been allowed to get this far, and it would be better if I didn't stay too long. As for the book, yes, she said, she had it, and she pulled it down from the shelf for me.

There I stood, with a thousand pages of Cummings in my hands, and only a few minutes to look through it. The librarian didn't think I'd be allowed to come back to return the book. And so, for the time being, I would have to leave behind all those poems that were waiting to be discovered.

I may have walked into the embassy without any trouble, but I didn't come out that way. On the next corner, a policeman demanded to see my identification and asked what I was doing at the embassy.

I wanted to borrow a book, I said.

Aha, sure you did. What else?

Among the major oddities of East Germany was the fact that, as I learned years later from my Stasi files, even the slightest contact with a U.S. citizen could get you suspected of being an agent of the class enemy "in line with the Americans." Of course it doesn't look good when you visit the American embassy "to borrow a book," and then you can't even produce that book.

Nothing came of the whole thing. I finally ordered the book in 1993 through a shop in Berlin that specialized in American literature. I had to wait several weeks before the volume arrived from the United States. To this day, it's one of the books that I won't lend to anyone.

Shortage, borrowing—those are the definitive words. Almost none of the books that I devoured letter by letter, that I imbibed and ingested completely, almost none of those books belonged to me. They were borrowed. I read them, they became a part of me, but I never possessed them.

During the first years of my marriage, I lived with my wife and our two children in a tiny apartment. We have to live within walking distance of the synagogue. On Shabbos, driving a car and taking public transportation are prohibited. Anything you can't get to on foot is out of range on Shabbos. The stupid thing about this, at least as far as the apartment issue is concerned, is that nowadays all of the synagogues in Munich are located in desirable residential areas in the middle of the city. The rents are horrendous, and without the help of brokers, who mercilessly charge several months' rent for their modest services, you can hardly find a suitable place to stay.

In that tiny apartment, there simply wasn't enough room for me to accommodate all the books I'd bought over the years. Many of them spent several sad years packed in boxes in my mother-in-law's (fortunately dry) cellar. How many times did I curse when I remembered a book, wanted to open it up and read it, but was then unable to find it in the meager selection that wasn't in storage!

The books certainly weren't the only reason. But just as certainly, the unbearable fact that I couldn't have them with me played a substantial role in my motivation to make money. At some point we could afford to pay a broker, and so we got a place in the Glockenbach district, an apartment that we could live in, not just inhabit.

After our move a few years ago, I came to a bitter realization: most of the books that I had imagined I owned had in reality never been my property. I had borrowed them, from friends and from libraries. They hadn't been with me for some time, only in my head, where memory rewrites everything and sometimes distorts it beyond recognition.

But when I think of all the episodes about reading that I've depicted, when I think of the stories, people, and places that are connected with all those books, and which I distinctly remember, when I consider all of that—who could blame me if my memories go haywire when I look at my wife's bookshelves, and I discover this book, and that book, the edition of the Lenclos Letters, the collected poems of Cummings, or a clothbound edition (with a ribbon bookmark!) of Orwell's *1984*? If I told people that of course I never lent out the Lenclos volume that I bummed from my mother, and so I never lost it . . . If I were to say that the well-camouflaged Orwell book that I read in the schoolyard was not a paperback, but a first-class cloth edition, and that my childhood sweetheart gave it to me because owning it made me so happy . . . If I were to tell people that the librarian at the American embassy, profoundly impressed that my love for Cummings' poetry defied all danger, did not keep the *Complete Poems* from me, but instead, after some hesitation, lent the book to me after all, even though she probably knew that I wouldn't be able to bring it back . . . who, I ask, would not believe that it happened that way and only that way, and that the book in question belonged to me, just as surely as if I had been born holding it in my hand?

No one, I say.

Except, of course, for my wife. She knows me. And—she has proof. When I counter with my most truthful memories, which would back up my claim of ownership unequivocally for anyone else, she just smiles, opens the book, unfolds the receipt, and shows it to me. In the face of such evidence, not much remains of my memories other than a literary fallacy.

What I feel at those moments must be close to the emotion that filled Antonio when Shylock applied the knife. If it weren't my wife, and if it weren't for her love, which fills up the hole that the old shortage left behind in me—I wouldn't be able to bear it.

3

I wasn't aware that there's another German-speaking author with my name who has also worked as a journalist for several years, just like me. That may sound unbelievable, since this other Jan Wechsler is hardly an unknown author, as I find out from the blurb on his book *Masquerades*. He's about as old as I am, but he was born in Israel and grew up in Switzerland.

I do some research online. *Masquerades* is Wechsler's second book, published in 1998, three years after his debut, which was a novel. Both books were released by a Swiss publishing house that's well-known and highly regarded for its ambitious literary offerings, which still include *Masquerades*. The original edition of his debut novel, on the other hand, is out of print, as I quickly discover on the Internet. It's still available in paperback, though, and what surprises me is that there are three editions, all from different publishers.

Wechsler's debut must have gotten quite a response. The first paperback edition came out relatively late, almost at the same time as *Masquerades*. Apparently the hardcover had been so successful that the publisher was able to take more time than usual with the sale of the paperback license.

I don't understand why after a success like that, his second book was issued only in paperback. I'm holding the first edition in my hands, and the publisher in question usually releases those in a lovely, elaborate layout.

Shouldn't I have heard of my namesake before? Of course, I haven't been in the publishing business that long; in the last year alone, eighty thousand new titles came out on the German book market, probably by just as many authors. It would be impossible to know all of them. On the other hand, back then, nearly fifteen years ago, the glut of new releases every spring and fall wasn't as dramatic as it is now. I was intensely interested in everything literary, I kept up with the arts and literature sections, and I was always on the lookout for undiscovered talent. An author who not only has the same name as me, but who has also written a highly-regarded debut novel, seems like something I couldn't possibly have missed . . .

I was probably so preoccupied with my own manuscript at the time that I picked up much less of what was happening on the literary scene than I have always thought. My work on that little poetic novel cost me years. At seventeen I produced a few sketches, and at nineteen I completed a first draft of three hundred pages. Not long after that I disassembled the novel, shortened it, transposed it, and recast it. I was never satisfied. I repeatedly filed and polished particular passages, sentences, and sometimes even a single punctuation mark, a technique that I privately called "black polish."

I had read about it in a book on trade techniques of *haute horlogerie*. I collect books about the art of watchmaking, coffee table books with photos of historic factories, catalogs from various manufacturers, and of course also—and this is what makes my passion expensive—the watches themselves. There is hardly anything that can compete aesthetically with a successful poem. But the pleasure I feel when I examine a refined, complex watch movement under a bright light comes very close.

My profound attachment to mechanical watches started years ago, when I found out for the first time that I was going to be a father. It must have abruptly changed and refined my sense of time. Whereas before I had believed that I would not, and did not want to, live a long life, and yet at the same time miraculously thought I had an endless amount of time at my disposal—that feeling changed radically when I got the news. For the first time, I was interested in my potential life expectancy; I gave up smoking and got myself an expensive wristwatch. It came with three features that fit precisely with my altered sense of time. First of all, it had a second hand that swept around the face in 240 tiny, snappy clicks. It was propelled by a mechanical movement that took hours upon hours of dedicated handiwork to manufacture, and I saw it as a veneration of time that had, in a sense, become art. And finally: a mechanical watch ticks. It's not silent, and it isn't one of those quartz watches where the only sound you can hear is the tired flapping of a stepper motor; no, it ticks. Every fraction of a second leaves behind an echo as it disappears. That's a hundred ticking reminders per minute of the fact that, for me at least, time is not endless, and I hold the watch to my ear again and again so I can listen for a while to the elapsing of time that has become so audible.

During "black polish," various types of paste, wood, and other substances are used to finish the components of a mechanical movement. In the process, the surface of the steel becomes so even and smooth that it looks black when the light hits it at a certain angle. If you look at a component that has been polished in this way under varying light, after it's been fitted into the movement, at first it looks like a mirror. But the next moment, if you tilt it even slightly, it seems to absorb the light completely, and the eye of the beholder descends into that black mirror as if it were a deep crack that has suddenly opened up into infinity.

That was the kind of effect that I hoped to achieve with my writing, and I was not about to give up before my words at least began to get close to the ideal that I'd set my sights on. Art is not about modesty and humility. And the project that I was burning myself out with was about as modest as I was myself. Sometimes it even struck me as megalomaniacal, and the obsessive way I dealt with the words seemed pathological.

When I finally decided one day that I could stop, the characters and stories had already changed so often in my hands, my head, and my heart that I would no longer have been able to trace their genesis. I prowled around in my own text as if I were in someone else's house, a house where the walls were made of black polished steel. One moment I was standing before a mirror, looking right into my own eyes. The next second, however, there was nothing in front of me but deep black, an immense void that I was falling into.

I couldn't find an agent who would represent the book, or a publisher willing to print it. Perhaps I failed as an author, that may very well be. I would rather not be the judge of that, even if I could be. Becoming a publisher was certainly the right decision for me. I still work with words, even if they're not my own. I've grown fond of that work, and I pursue it with just as much attention to detail as a watchmaker disassembling an *ébauche* under the loupe, examining, polishing, oiling, and reassembling hundreds of parts, until they are finally joined together to form a perfect whole.

The fact, then, that in all these years I have never heard anything about the existence of this other Jan Wechsler is amazing, but not inexplicable. I can't find a picture of him in a book or on the Internet. The number of online sources about Wechsler himself is, overall, rather paltry. I find a great many reviews of his novel, and even more articles that refer to his *Masquerades*, which is apparently an exposé, a work of journalism, a research report . . .

•

That night I lay awake in bed next to my wife. I alternated between listening to what was going on outside and what was happening inside. From the street I could hear two drunk guys debating whether Katarina was faithful, or a slut. At some point they moved on. It got very quiet. Now and then I could hear a car or a streetcar zip past. I felt an urgent need to say something, to tell my wife that I had opened the suitcase, and talk about what I had found inside. I made several attempts, breathing in deeply, as if I was about to lift a heavy load, but I didn't even whisper her name, and then at some point I heard her breathing deeply and regularly next to me.

I asked myself again and again: What kind of masquerades had Jan Wechsler exposed in his book? I also wondered whose face he had pulled the mask from. What kind of monstrosity could he have revealed? And what did all of this have to do with me?

At around three o'clock, I was still wide awake. Since I wasn't going back to sleep anyway, I decided I might as well get up, get dressed, and go to my office. I only needed to open the suitcase, take out Wechsler's book, and skim through his revelations. Then everything would be cleared up, maybe in an hour. I could calm down and maybe still get a few minutes of sleep before the alarm went off or the kids woke us up.

And so I got up, got dressed, sat down in my office, took the book out, and began to read. I didn't need a lot of patience. Wechsler got right to the point.

The book dealt with a political issue. He began his report by recapping what was a hot topic at the time. The issue was Swiss "Jewish gold," those bars that had been melted down in German death camps in the forties from stolen jewelry and gold tooth fillings, and then recast so hastily and carelessly that, if you believe the reports, the shapes of teeth were still visible on some of them.

Those bars ended up in neutral Switzerland, and their purchase helped finance not only Hitler's war, but also the industrialized extermination of people at camps like Auschwitz, Bergen-Belsen, and Majdanek.

It soon became clear, however, that Wechsler was less concerned about the monstrosity of these facts than he was about the negotiations that various Jewish organizations were conducting with Swiss banks at the time to determine the type and amount of compensation for victims and their descendants. The gold was only the most recent example. He continued by describing various scandals that involved business dealings with the Holocaust. At first he limited himself to those well-known cases where it wasn't just Swiss banks that had profited, but other public and private entities, as well.

But then, the thrust of his argument suddenly changed: The business with the Holocaust never stopped, Wechsler wrote. On the contrary, it's still booming—only the other way around. Now, according to Wechsler, people make money off the cult of memory and presumed guilt. Negotiators haggle over billions of dollars in compensation, he wrote. Millions more are spent to hold design contests for Holocaust memorials, and then to build them. And on top of all that, Wechsler continued, newspapers, TV stations, movie producers and authors keep finding more buried treasure underneath the corpses of Auschwitz.

I couldn't shake the feeling that I was dealing with a demagogue. What, precisely, was this man's point? Was there no appropriate response to the phenomenon of Auschwitz and the millions killed there, other than to remain silent and let the survivors die without compensation? Shouldn't the facts be documented? And, if so, then only on a pro bono basis?

I decided it was because of the lateness of the hour that I wasn't able to follow his reasoning to its conclusion. His rants about the

Holocaust Industry, as he called it, were only the prelude to the actual exposé, the real subject of his book.

Wechsler was concerned about another author and his book. His name was Minsky, and his book was called *Days of Ashes*, a slim volume that had come out in 1995, at the same time as Wechsler's debut novel. In his book, Minsky, who was four years old at the end of the war, recounts his earliest childhood memories. Those memories created quite a stir in the public, primarily because they included scenes from the Riga Ghetto and various death camps.

Minsky had survived the selections at Auschwitz—as a child. By way of orphanages in Poland and Switzerland, and several foster families, he came to live in Bern with the family of an industrialist, who eventually adopted him. He had, as he himself wrote, escaped—unlike most others. He should have been dead; and yet he was alive. But Minsky also wrote that his ordeal did not end with his liberation from the camp. He was not allowed to remember what he had experienced or mention it to other people, such as his adoptive parents. It was just a bad dream, they told him. They had eliminated the traces, forged papers, and given him another name, to cut the connection to his past, to conceal his true origins and replace his identity with that of a boy who came from difficult circumstances at first, but ended up in a well-ordered Swiss home. And so he had not only endured the hell of Auschwitz; he also hadn't been allowed to remember it without putting himself at risk of further punishment.

Minsky's book became a sensation. Before long it was translated into several languages, published in large runs in Europe and the United States, and given enthusiastic reviews and awards all over the world. Minsky traveled extensively, accepted honors and gave talks, not only about his own case, but also about the techniques that had helped him take his undimmed memories and put them into words when he was an adult. What he had been through was not an isolated case, he declared. And there were many children who, even though they had not lost their lives, had lost everything else—parents, siblings, and above all, their identities—who were still waiting to be liberated: that is to say, waiting for permission to remember.

A bookseller had slipped Wechsler a copy of *Days of Ashes* during a book tour, when Minsky's fame was at its peak. He read it at his hotel one sleepless night—just the way I was now reading his *Masquerades*. And after reading a few pages, he was certain: Minsky was lying. His memories could not possibly be authentic.

The depictions of the atrocities in the camps struck Wechsler as bad writing, mere clippings of documentary sources taken from different sources and mixed with horror kitsch, legitimized solely by the fact that survivors weren't supposed to be contradicted—especially in this case, since it was precisely the constant doubts that people raised about Minsky's memories that accounted for the second great trauma of his life.

And this epic of suffering was making money for Minsky, and earning him accolades. That stirred Wechsler's sense of justice and brought out the journalist in him.

It couldn't be all that difficult to research the biographical information, Wechsler thought to himself. Forging an identity in bureaucratic Switzerland, without leaving any traces, the way Minsky claimed, seemed impossible to him. He made inquiries with agencies and departments, had conversations with friends and relatives of Minsky's, and before long he was sure he could prove that Minsky's Swiss background, his actual name, and his origins in the Swiss Jura region were not inventions, but established facts—and that Minsky's memories of Auschwitz must therefore be a masquerade, a contrived melodrama that he was using to cash in like an ordinary con man.

It was clear to Wechsler: Minsky was no Holocaust survivor. He had only seen the camps in Poland as a tourist, decades later, as a grown man. He had never been there as a child. He had never even left Switzerland, the country where he was born, and which had been spared the war and mass murder.

Minsky had to be stopped. Someone had to expose him and, along with him, the whole mob of people who were making money off the Holocaust, with their demands for compensation, the books, the movies, and all the other gruesome things.

Wechsler's exposé, which at first was nothing more than an article in a German newspaper, hit the literary scene like a bolt of lightning out of the blue. Minsky's publisher affirmed that it had checked Minsky's facts and stood by the author and his work. Still, once the last copies of the book were sold out, and more and more information started to emerge that backed up Wechsler's allegations, Minsky was dropped by his agent and his publisher.

The showers of praise for Minsky's book and the author's outstanding skills were followed by a wave of derision and hostile reviews. Suddenly Minsky had as many critics among the arts and culture editors as he had once had supporters. Some of them claimed that they'd always at least had an inkling, and now they ripped into the author, the book, and everyone involved with it. And then there were others who intoned helplessly: *How could we have been so wrong?* Lying the way Minsky had, and about something like Auschwitz, certainly no one should be allowed to do that, they all agreed.

It wasn't just in German-speaking countries that the book disappeared from the shelves. The foreign publishers also withdrew their translation licenses. It was only in the United States that the publisher hesitated: when he was asked about it on television, he said the controversy was making the book hotter than ever. It's literature of the highest caliber! he said. But he was soon isolated in this view; and so, in the United States, where Minsky had been just as celebrated as he had been in Europe, the author and his book fell into obscurity.

I stopped reading. Wechsler still had more to say in his *Masquerades*. But it didn't interest me. I had already found out everything I needed to know. I couldn't possibly be Wechsler. I didn't know Minsky, and I hadn't published a novel in 1995, gone on a book tour through Germany, read Minsky's book, decided it was a forgery, and launched an investigation. And I had certainly never publicly accused another author of telling elaborate lies, with such verve and malice.

It no longer surprised me in the least that there could be people who wished Wechsler ill and who might, for example, pack a suitcase full of objects that were meaningful to him and then send it to his house.

Who's to say, then, whether that courier really came from an airline? It could just as easily have been a Minsky fan who wanted to take revenge on Wechsler. Maybe the suitcase was just the beginning. They're mixing us up because I have Wechsler's name. They're coming after me because of a book I didn't write.

I absolutely had to do something, immediately, to clear up this mistake and get out of the stalkers' line of fire. No one else would be better able to get me out of this mess than the man who got me into it: Jan Wechsler, my namesake. Surely an investigative journalist like him wouldn't be scared of an anonymously delivered suitcase. He would go public about it and stick out his neck for me: Credit where credit is due, he would say. And it was due not to me, but to him, since he had gotten the ball rolling with the whole Minsky issue in the first place.

And so I wrote a letter to Wechsler, in which I explained my predicament, appealed to his sense of decency, and asked him to clear up the matter in public immediately. My name is my name. I can't just discard it because someone else who happens to have the same name has publicly styled himself as the unflinching defender of true memory.

I wrote the letter quickly. I found the publisher's address on the Internet. It was just after eight when I sealed the envelope. I set off immediately and waited anxiously on the sidewalk for the few minutes that remained before the post office opened. I was the first customer that morning, and I sent the letter as registered priority mail.

The reply came faster than I had expected. Less than a week later, I got a letter from Wechsler's publisher, and I tore it open impatiently while I was walking back upstairs from the mailbox.

What amazed me was that the letter was handwritten and several pages long. The greeting confused me: *My Dear Jan.* What gave Wechsler the idea that he could call me by my first name when he didn't even know me?

I skimmed over the pages, and at the end of the letter, I finally found the sender's name. *Yours, Franz*, it said; and it was only when I had begun to read that I realized that it must be Franz von Dennen, Jan Wechsler's publisher and the owner of that same respected literary house that had published Wechsler's first editions.

It was completely inexplicable to me what might have compelled von Dennen to answer my letter to Wechsler and address me so informally, and it made me worry that the misunderstanding about the suitcase, the shared name, and the presumptive stalker was not going to get cleared up, and it was likely to get even more complicated.

•

I gave in to the spontaneous impulse to open a bottle of wine, even though it was only noon, and it's usually only on Shabbos that I drink a glass or two of red wine. I poured myself a glass, took the bottle into the office with me, and closed the door. After I had taken a first strong gulp, I sat down at my desk, smoothed out von Dennen's handwritten pages and began to read.

Zurich, August 25th, 2008

My Dear Jan,

I don't know what to make of your letter. You know that our relationship was never just about business. Over all those years, I felt responsible for your work, and not only as a publisher. I was also always close to you personally and never made a secret of the fact that I sometimes felt more like a father figure than a publisher. I removed obstacles from your path wherever I could. And the important thing for me—and I'm sure you wouldn't disagree—was always to make sure that you were not only able to write, but also that you were doing well and that you were personally satisfied and happy, and without ever thinking about any benefit for myself. And now this?

So you've written yourself a letter care of the publishing house. There are quicker and less complicated ways to communicate something to yourself. You could stand in front of the mirror and just start talking—as far as I'm concerned you can close the door first so no one will hear you. But that's not what you decided to do. Instead, you wrote a letter, but you didn't put it in your own mailbox, so you could take it back out a few days later and read it;

no, you sent it here. So it could get to you through me. How else am I supposed to understand this?

When I think about it—and it does seem that you want me to try to get to the bottom of this—four possibilities come to mind about what you might be trying to accomplish with this letter. I have to start by saying that all four make me worry. But fine, I'll play along and let you know which guesses I made when I received your letter.

First: Maybe you're trying to test our internal processes to make sure that letters addressed to you care of the publisher actually make it to you. I can assure you that we've had that under control for years. We don't pass hate mail along to our authors, I'm happy to admit, because neither the senders nor the authors would be well-served by that. But inquiries, fan mail, and things of that nature, as well as serious, cultivated, and well-formulated criticism, are always forwarded to our authors. Why would we ever withhold those things from you?

Second: You sent your letter care of the publisher because you assumed that, given its contents, my secretary would show it to me, and I would read it. That would mean your letter to yourself is actually a message to me, and I just need to figure out how to decipher this coded message, and why you would even send me such a message. Even if you do want to tell me something, there are simpler ways—like picking up the phone and calling me. A direct, unencrypted letter would also have done the trick.

Third: You're tinkering with the plot for a new novel, and your letter, its contents, and my uncertain reaction are going to be part of the story. I really should be happy about this, because I still believe in your talent and believe that you will produce many more books—even though you haven't written a word in years, or else you've been keeping all of your new work from me.

W. 42

(As insulted as I am, that would make me happy, for the sake of literature.) But if that's the situation, I also have to give you a warning. I never wanted to become the subject of your writing. On the contrary. Some years ago, when I was looking over the most recent manuscript of yours that I am aware of, and I found details from my childhood, details that I probably shared with you after a few glasses of wine—but in confidence—I made it clear that I would not tolerate being misused as source material for your characters. I am happy living in the real world, and I do not have the slightest desire to be turned inside out in a literary work, put under the microscope and described in detail. I would not be able to speak freely with any of my authors, and I would never get a good night's sleep again, if I had to worry that I was going to show up as a character in a novel, in circumstances that I do not appreciate and cannot control. You had better believe that I mean this seriously, you of all people. It was a very difficult decision for me not to publish your last novel, even though it represented an important turning point in your work. (I know that very well.) But you refused to take the childhood memories you had stolen from me out of the manuscript. Perhaps you would call my reaction too harsh, and you have not forgiven me. I call it steadfast. I named my price and would not negotiate. I will not behave any differently if something similar is happening again now, that must be clear to you, if you are even the least bit in your right mind.

And that brings me to the fourth possible interpretation that went through my head when I read your letter: that you are completely confused and don't know what you're doing.

For the moment, I will leave unspoken which of the four possibilities seems most likely to me. Let us discuss your letter, the accusations, and the demands you make.

We had an agreement back then. Even though I did not completely approve of the project, I financed and produced Masquerades. *And why not? Everyone was waiting for you to speak out in detail. It was good for business. The sales gave you the financial leeway to spend years writing in peace. And thanks to the unexpected income, I was able to support and promote literary experiments that no one wanted to put on the market, and which I would not have been able to put out without a strong backlist title.*

But let me remind you that I was the one who reined in the pomposity of your writing just enough so we could print the book at all. It was clear to me, and I said and wrote this to you several times, that you needed to step away from this Minsky story immediately, and that you couldn't write any more articles or give any interviews, but that you should instead pull back, budget your funds, and focus on what you were meant to do: write books—and by that I mean novels, narratives, short stories, whatever comes into your head, so long as you get off the investigative journalism trip.

You didn't follow a single piece of advice that I gave you. You invested a considerable portion of your royalties in precious watches. Can you eat those? Do they help you send your kids to decent schools? Or take your wife on a well-deserved vacation? I have no idea what you were thinking. And then you put an additional portion of your money into useless research projects that didn't lead to anything, certainly not to anything literary.

And no, I haven't forgotten your last manuscript, one hundred pages that you struggled over for ten years. That's not even one page per day, if it's even one word per day. Maybe that was the reason why you didn't want to edit out my childhood memories, the ones you so generously helped yourself to. How many months' worth of work you would have had to destroy and invest in again, since there really wasn't anything more you could have cut from that little booklet.

Excuse me for being so blunt, but I have no other option if I want to preserve the one last hope for us to save you as an author.

It's one thing to reinvent oneself repeatedly as an artist. A skill like that is a priceless asset, and I take my hat off to anyone who manages to do it. But it's another thing entirely for a person to deny who he once was, to discard and disavow all knowledge of his past. That is not healthy, and no good will come of it.

I can only advise you to open your eyes and to get back to your life and your writing. Get help if you need help. Don't hesitate to let me know if there is any way I can support you. You are still my author.

But please, Jan, and I really mean this seriously: Spare me charades like these in the future. This is the last time I will take half a day to give you such a detailed and serious response to something so foolish.

Yours, Franz

I had to take several breaks while reading von Dennen's letter. I don't know how much time had passed. When I had finished reading, the bottle was almost empty, and I was drunk. I scanned a few sections of the letter again, and at some point I must have closed my eyes and fallen asleep in my chair.

My wife woke me up around five o'clock in the afternoon. She had picked up the kids from kindergarten. They were both standing in the doorway. My son, tired from playing, was whining; my daughter was waving at me.

What's the matter with you? my wife asked, pointing to the nearly-empty bottle of red.

You won't believe it! I blurted out. You remember the suit-case, right? It's all so crazy and confusing! I didn't feel capable of explaining. Instead, I picked up von Dennen's letter, which had fallen on the floor, and passed it to her. Read this, I said: I have no idea what this man is talking about.

Standing next to me, she began to read. Her face looked as if it had turned to stone, only her eyes were moving, hurriedly, and they darted over von Dennen's words as if something or someone was chasing her. She probably only wanted to get an explanation for my condition as quickly as possible.

Was she afraid when she got to the end? I wondered. And when she finally lowered the letter and said nothing, I really did get the feeling that something had given her a fright. And I also sensed what was scaring her. It was me.

4

Maybe it was a mistake to show my wife von Dennen's letter. Ever since she read it, she's been withdrawn and strangely cool to me. We met at the end of 1999, a year and a half after *Masquerades* came out. She probably thinks that I am the author of that book and just never told her about it. Now she'll be speculating about the reasons why. I don't know. She won't talk to me and is avoiding my gaze, and even more so my touch.

She had always wondered how I managed to live off my writing. I didn't even have a book I could show her. I only occasionally wrote articles for magazines here and there, and every year I compiled two or three manuscript surveys for a publishing house in Frankfurt. That hardly brought in anything.

The idea that I was able to make a living from those meager earnings was based on a misunderstanding that I just didn't want to clear up right away; at the time, I was living off money that I hadn't earned in the true sense of the word. I had gotten it as a gift. Or rather: I had won it.

It was a small fortune, even if it wasn't millions. I cherished the freedom that a lucky Lotto ticket had brought me. But I didn't go around telling everyone about the details of my win. I couldn't be proud of it, the way people are when they've earned their wealth. I had just been lucky.

The lottery is a tax on people who can't do math, as an acquaintance of mine used to say. And because that phrase had become firmly embedded in my consciousness, I was a bit embarrassed when I decided one day that I wanted to play the Lotto after all.

But, as they also say: Wealth and honor come from God; and I think that applies in my case.

It all started with a joke a friend told me at synagogue: Moishele goes to shul day after day and prays fervently. He shockels back and forth, raises his arms, and wrings his hands. Hashem! he cries, I have a wife and children, and the money is tight. So I ask you, Hashem, have mercy on me and let me win the Lotto! And so it goes, day after day, week after week. He doesn't let up with the pleading. Everybody knows what he's been begging for, and people are starting to roll their eyes and laugh at him behind his back. But then one day, just when he's about to give up, suddenly the angry voice of Hashem rises up, thundering loud and clear: Moishele! (Pause) I would really like to help you. But please, buy a Lotto ticket!

So, my friend told me, take a chance for once and get a ticket. You can't win if you don't play.

I didn't even pay for my first Lotto ticket. I found it in a parking lot. Someone must have lost it. Since I tend to go through life with my eyes closed, daydreaming most of the time, present only physically, but otherwise lost in my thoughts, the fact that I, of all people, even saw that ticket and picked it up borders on the miraculous. It was a Monday, and the Wednesday Lotto drawing was two days later. And the ticket was valid.

It was clear to me that I was going to win. I told myself that the only reason I had even found the ticket was *because* it was a winner, and it was meant for me.

That wasn't quite the way it turned out. The ticket I found was not a winner. I came away empty-handed that time, but I had acquired a taste for it. So I got a subscription, and from then on, I played the same numbers every week.

I decided on a subscription because it was personalized. The fees were deducted from my account every month. They had my address and cell phone number on file. Whenever I actually won something—and there were small wins even before my big ticket—I felt vindicated. I generally got a text message: *You're a winner! Your prize of x-and-such number of euros will be credited to your account.* The prizes weren't worth mentioning and didn't even come close to covering my costs. But one Thursday morning, everything changed. Instead of a text message, I got a call.

The Lotto company is familiar with the dangers that come with an unexpected windfall. When you win a considerable amount in the Lotto, you don't just get a text message and a bank transfer. Instead, you're gently prepared for it by psychologically trained employees of the Lottery company.

I'm not exaggerating when I say that I took the news very calmly. The hand I was using to hold the cell phone to my ear did shake a bit. But I didn't burst into delirious howls of joy, the way people sometimes do when they answer a trivia question on the radio and win tickets for a concert or a football game. What I felt was more like a glimmer of true awe. If Hashem had his hand in this—and how could it have been otherwise?—then I had undoubtedly just witnessed firm proof of his existence: Honor and wealth come from God. That's something you'd like to believe, especially when it happens so suddenly. Suddenly, yes, but not unexpectedly, since the basis—or, in a sense, the inspiration—for my decision to get what turned out to be my golden lottery subscription had been my friend's story about Moishele's pleas to Hashem. As a result, in my imagination the Lotto became firmly connected with God's workings in the lives of individuals. And it was precisely that fact, at least for me, that made the conversation with the employee of the lottery company into something like a mystical experience.

Lotto winnings are not tax-exempt. Any money that is not spent or invested in something tax-deductible within a period of two years is subject to various government charges.

I kept just enough to live worry-free for two years, and I put the rest in supposedly low-risk ship investment funds, and in shares of an Internet start-up. The dot-com rally was really starting to pick up speed at that point, and those investments promised terrific returns.

But I wasn't so lucky with all of my investments. By the end of the holdback period, during which the founders of the company and their initial investors aren't allowed to sell their shares, the Internet company was broke, and my investment was burned. The ship funds, on the other hand, yielded good dividends for more than two years, easy money that I spent hand over fist.

I developed a fancy for tailored suits and English welted shoes made of box calf or horse leather. Wearing those shoes was like walking on clouds, so I decided I needed at least one pair for each weekday and for special occasions.

During this time I had my hair and eyebrow color changed several times by one of the hottest stylists in Munich, whose salon was housed discretely on the second floor of an old bourgeois house in the center of town. Whenever I went to see him, I parked my car for free in one of the reserved spots in the opera's underground garage.

I tried to justify my weakness for this type of luxury with the excuse that I came from the Small Country and had the same birthday as Thomas Mann and Alexander Pushkin. Astrologically speaking, I should have been upper-class myself. Instead, I had grown up in more modest circumstances on the outskirts of East Berlin.

All through my childhood and my teenage years, I had worn ugly clothes, or hand-me-downs from third cousins in West Germany, which arrived in packages from time to time: shabby corduroy pants, washed-out T-shirts, and threadbare shirts, all of them out of fashion, though my mother at least tried to give them a touch of style by cutting the collars halfway off and sewing them into Nehru collars.

If you wanted to find clothing in the East that was distinct, if not exactly nice, you had to spend a long time looking. I bought my shoes—they were indestructible even with my powerful stride, which would have been worthy of a Mayakovsky—in a store that sold work clothes. They cost almost nothing, but you could drop a heavy load on top of them without damaging the shoes, or your foot getting injured. I purchased my coats in a specialty store for funeral clothing. Even though you might think people who buy coats like that don't wear them very often, they were just as durable as my shoes and lasted several years, even if you wore them every day like I did.

Taking all that into account, I felt almost no guilt about not being sensible. I thought I had a right to make up for some of what I'd missed.

It was during this time that I met my wife. At first she thought I was gay—a misunderstanding that was soon cleared up. If it hadn't been for that misunderstanding, though, she probably never would have gone out with me. When we first met, she didn't see me as a potential husband, or even a possible fling. And while I very quickly got the feeling that I was going to marry her someday, she fell in love with me in spite of all her original assumptions, and against the odds.

At least I could explain myself. My feeling that I had a lot of catching up to do in terms of material things was plausible, in light of my stories about the East. And maybe those stories and my unrestrained admission of neediness made her feel enough sympathy that she forgot about my lack of common sense and my unusual lifestyle. But since we were still getting to know each other, I didn't want to push it. It would have been awkward for me to admit right away that the wealth that allowed me to indulge in my extravagances was not money I had earned through honest and hard work, but was instead something I had only come by thanks to a lucky Lotto ticket.

Unfortunately, I also missed the opportunity to tell her in the years that followed. I was too busy with my literary ambitions, my wardrobe, and with being in love; or I was too naïve and careless about money matters. In any event, I had overlooked the fact that I was supposed to pay taxes on the dividends from my ship fund shares.

A mistake like that seldom goes unnoticed in the long run as it is, but when it's someone who's won the Lotto, after a short period of time the tax collectors become especially interested in what has become of the prize money and any investments made with it. If you don't have any evidence to give them, they'll promptly send you a bill, and you'll have to pay not only what you actually owe, but an amount that's estimated very generously in favor of the government—plus interest, penalties, and fees.

The tax assessment and the penalty notice were delivered to me when our daughter had just turned one, and my wife was pregnant with our second child. The large amount that I owed gave me something like the second mystical experience of my life, for in that moment I had the distinct feeling that Hashem was showing me, without warning and in no uncertain terms, the instruments that he had at his disposal to take away everything I possessed, in the blink of an eye. Wealth and honor come from God? Yes, indeed, but he also collects a fee for his services.

It was lucky for me that my wife isn't attached to material comforts. No more car? No problem. Having to move to a tiny apartment? It'll be all right. Pinching pennies and improvising? Whatever. What wife would say such things in a situation like that? Mine did. And I loved her for it, and it made me feel ashamed.

I had a hard time parting with prosperity. I had to sell most of my watch collection, which I had acquired in the initial phase of my enthusiasm for mechanical timekeeping, at a horrendous loss. Even leaving the good life behind wasn't free. Moving, renovating the old apartment, and the early termination of my leasing agreement on the coupe—somebody had to pay for all that. As for the ship fund shares, after the brokerage fees and the penalties for breaking my contract early, I only got back a fraction of my original investment. And that went right to the taxman.

Not that I was complaining. Just as I had previously felt that I had a right to have some of the things I'd missed out on, I now believed that I honestly deserved everything I was going through. It had been bound to happen. I had to accept it and tough it out.

But I certainly couldn't come out to my wife as a man who had burned through a fortune. I was too embarrassed. So I didn't talk much or explain myself. In general, it was a time of few words.

Of course I had to do something immediately. No bank would have loaned me money, since I no longer owned anything valuable and wouldn't have been able to provide any collateral. And the revenue office wouldn't have granted me a respite. The tax collector came every few weeks. The only items of value that I could have forfeited were two of my mechanical watches, which I had held on to and safely stored elsewhere as a last resort.

At least I had a plan. My suits and shoes, the shirts and ties, which I really couldn't sell, performed an invaluable service for me when I decided to become a consultant. A friend—I still had some—opened doors for me, putting his reputation on the line. And I got lucky again. Maybe they trusted my impeccable clothing more than my resumé, which didn't exactly make me look qualified to coach upper management. But that's precisely what I was offering.

While barely a word came out of my mouth when I was home in the evening, during the day I helped seasoned warhorses of management to recognize conflict situations, name them, and solve them. Often it was a matter of helping them deal consciously with their fear—fear of their own courage, fear of failing. I helped these men to trust their visions, and above all, to articulate them and make other people excited about them.

The per diem rates I got were substantial. Nevertheless, it took me years to pay off my debts with the tax authorities. It was only last summer that we were able to go on vacation again for the first time.

Things have gotten back to normal. At the beginning of the year, I scaled back my consulting business. I now reject most inquiries. For far too long I had too little time, and now I work, at least in that area, only as much as I absolutely have to. Instead, I started my publishing house and surrounded myself once again with literature, with stories. I was finally able to catch my breath and just live. And now this!

Of course, now that my wife has read von Dennen's letter, she thinks it's possible that I wrote *Masquerades*, and that it was that journalistic coup that provided me with the income I went on to spend so recklessly. If von Dennen's letter is really meant for me and not for some other author with my name, then it follows that she would doubt everything I have ever told her about myself and my previous life, my background, my parents, and my grandparents.

And she must be wondering who this person she's married to actually is. It's no wonder then that she's pulling away. I shouldn't have let her read the letter. But should I clear everything up now and tell her about the Lotto prize and the dividends I didn't pay taxes on? How believable will my story about a lucky ticket be against the reasonable assertions in a handwritten letter, and in a book that has my name printed in big letters on the cover? I would look like a fool or, even worse, a brazen liar who, even in light of overwhelming evidence, refuses to budge one iota from his story, even though it's been exposed as untrue.

My wife is able to endure many things in stoic silence, but not being deceived. If I don't find conclusive evidence that makes it abundantly clear that this is a mix-up, and von Dennen has sent me a letter that's actually meant for another Jan Wechsler, then that may well be the end of our affection and intimacy.

This all feels like a conspiracy to me, as if the events are following a cleverly thought-out plot, designed to erase me, or at least my past, my identity, and my memory. But for what reason? I'm getting all tangled up. If I had to describe my observations and conjectures to a psychologist, the diagnosis would surely frighten me. It's obvious that I am balancing close to the edge.

Last week my daughter reached into a box of Kellogg's Corn Flakes and pulled out a CD with a computer game on it. Of course we tried it out right after breakfast. You had to use the mouse to put a boy and a girl on a dance floor. Besides the music, you could also choose the type of lighting you wanted. We decided on the disco ball, along with a strobe light that flashed randomly from different directions. Then we made the figures start dancing: to techno, in a storm of strobe lights. My daughter was completely enthralled. Now she shows up in my office several times a day and asks: Papa, can I play again now?

She usually comes in at the worst possible moment, as if she were doing it on purpose. At least once a day I indulge her and leave my spot in front of the screen so she can play.

I now know that my daughter's desire to play computer games is already so strong that she also sneaks into my office when I'm not there. She still hasn't figured out how to enter the password and play the Kellogg's game by herself—not yet; after all, she's not even six. But once she's in the office, which is actually off limits, she finds ways to pass the time without the computer. She rummages through boxes and cabinets, tries out my fountain pen, rearranges stacks of manuscripts and staples them together at all four corners, or she takes invoices that are waiting to be sent to my bookkeeper and decorates them with elaborately drawn ornaments, flowers or Pippi Longstocking, fairies and cartoon characters, and whatever else is in her sticker album.

Today she went through the pilot suitcase, opened the notebook with the newspaper clippings, and scattered them all over the floor of the office. When I came into the room, I couldn't hear her excited babbling. I was too angry. My office is not a playground, as much as I respect her urge to explore. But I never had a chance to start shouting, because she was waving a big newspaper clipping in front of my belly, so urgently that there was no way I could have made her calm down.

Papa, Papa, she cried, Look! You're in the paper!

Children and fools tell the truth, as they say. I immediately forgot that I had wanted to yell at her. But the radiance abruptly drained away from her face. I must have been looking at her as if she had just pronounced my death sentence. I had only briefly gone through the notebook with the newspaper clippings, and I thought it contained nothing more than reviews of Minsky's *Days of Ashes*, reports about his trips and about the readings and talks he gave all over the world. If there was a picture of me in one of those articles, I was done for. I would never ever have been able to explain a coincidence like that. I tore the scrap of paper away from the girl, who now looked frightened and close to tears. I didn't see myself anywhere in the picture, which showed Minsky after a reading that was part of the Leipzig book fair in 1995. And yet, the caption read: *It was a full house at the joint reading by Minsky and Wechsler in Hall 4 of the exhibition center. The audience gave the authors standing ovations.*

I recognized Minsky immediately. He was looking directly at the camera as he walked out, waving to the applauding spectators. Jan Wecshler, on the other hand, was looking at the floor. I could make out a mop of blond curls. But half of his face was covered by Minsky's waving hand. I could only see part of his forehead, and a bearded chin. Wechsler was wearing tennis shoes, jeans, and a T-shirt with a dark sport coat over it.

Where do you see me? I asked my daughter, who was trying to get past me and slip out the door. I crouched down next to her and showed her the picture.

Right here, she said, looking at me in amazement and pointing at the mop of blond curls: But your hair looks funny, Papa, and it's yellow!

I got down on my knees and hugged her. Suddenly I understood that she had, without knowing it, just presented me with

5

During the past few days I have become very aware of just how much my emotional well-being hinges on attention from my wife, the intimate words, the small gestures, and the moments of tenderness. After we examined the picture of Wechsler that my daughter had discovered, and agreed that it must be someone else, we hugged each other. And later, when we had gone to bed, she snuggled up to me for the first time in a long while. After all the confusion of the previous few weeks, the doubt and suspicion, a bit of peace returned to my troubled mind. I assume it was no different for her.

I have never been what Kishon would call the "best husband of all," because it isn't easy to get close to me. When I say that in the early period of our relationship, I was busy being in love with my wife, that's a really good explanation of why living with me can be difficult sometimes. The thing I was busy with back then was the feeling of being in love, but I doubt that my wife had the sense that I was busy with *her*. The major part of the romance between us happened in my mind, and it took a rare moment of candor, where I was able to come out of myself momentarily, before she even realized how important she was to me.

I was so lost in myself that it didn't dawn on me for a long time that I was shutting her out. My emotions told me that I was showering her with love and attention. Every other thought I had was about her. She made me happier than anyone ever had before. And I just couldn't imagine that she wasn't aware of it, and that, on the contrary, she thought I was interested in every other thing imaginable, just not in her.

The world *within* me was, for me, the entire world. It was rare that anyone came to visit. It was even more rare that I gave out any information about myself and the reality I was living in. Given the closeness that I felt between us from the very beginning, it never even occurred to me that there might not be a link to that reality for her—unless I established that link, and not only in my dreams, but with words and deeds.

Occasionally it would happen that I surprised her with a remark that I considered completely insignificant, because it wasn't new at all. Naturally, I assumed each time that she must know what I was thinking and feeling, mostly because I was sure I had said it dozens of times. And then I found out that what I was saying was completely new to her, and I had only imagined that I had told her everything.

I was completely appalled one time, years after our wedding, when we were talking about the day I had asked her if she wanted to marry me.

I had always been certain that she was the one. But her comment that, if not for the aforementioned misunderstanding, she wouldn't even have gone out with me, continued to bother me. I felt her love, but I was always uncertain about whether she really wanted me.

On that day we had been driving for several hours. We had been keeping each other entertained by telling jokes and making plans, and I felt for the first time since we'd met that this could be the moment when she would say yes. So I asked, and she said yes. Six weeks later, we got married. We could hardly wait. It would have gone even faster if the jeweler hadn't needed six weeks to make the rings we had designed together.

That's how I remember that day and the few weeks leading up to our wedding. It sounded completely different when my wife told me how she experienced my proposal.

It was indeed true: I had chosen the right moment; but she hadn't said yes because everything felt right and there were no doubts. It was more because my question had totally surprised her. When I proposed, she told me, it was the first time since we'd met that she was sure that I really meant *her* and was actually interested in *her*. There couldn't have been more forceful proof that I was living in a different world than she was.

Even after that she didn't fare much better with me. At the time when the tax collectors were after us, I took every job I could get. I did everything I could not only to end the debt drama as quickly as possible, but I also tried to shield her and the children from the fact that our economic situation wasn't what it could be. I put the letters from the revenue service away before my wife was able to see them, I hid the bank statements, and I gave my wife the household money in cash. If there was a major purchase we needed to make, I figured something out. I never wanted her to feel like she had to go without anything—not counting the tiny apartment where we somehow managed to make ourselves at home, once we'd put most of our books in storage.

I remembered my childhood all too well, my parents constantly worrying about money, my father using his car as a gypsy cab, picking up fares at night after working all day, and the loans from friends, which my parents paid back in part by doing renovation work on weekends. Besides, one of my mother's favorite quotes kept haunting my mind: *Your honors, once my mother / put on me a terrible curse / She told me I'd end up in the morgue / or someplace even worse.* That was Brecht and had rolled off my mother's tongue repeatedly and very naturally, as if it were her own creation, ever since I had told her that I wanted to earn my living through literature.

And so I worked. But to my wife and children, I was more like a visitor who was seldom seen.

Now, as I've said, my wife isn't attached to material things. But she is romantic. What good is a man to her if she barely knows him because he's absent, either in fact, because he's out helping customers, or in spirit, when he's at home but won't talk about what's bothering him, because he's afraid to burden her with it?

Things didn't get any better once we had made it though the worst. I quickly resumed the work that I hadn't had time for over the past few years. I wrote, and I also kept an eye out for good authors and stories. Whatever I planned for any given day actually would have taken two or three days and nights to complete. Sometimes it seemed as if I was spinning a cocoon around myself with all my plans and activities.

Even though I am aware of all this now, it must still be a behavior that I have learned so well that I repeatedly fall back into the same pattern the moment I am confronted with anything I don't know how to deal with. It's still that way for me now. The reassurance I had felt after that evening when my daughter found the picture of Wechsler didn't last long.

A few days ago, I ordered Wechsler's debut novel. The book arrived today, and I started reading immediately. After only a few pages, a hidden fear came over me, and after reading for about an hour, I knew that this matter was far from over. Even in his novel, I encountered myself.

Wechsler's novel is a panorama of wild stories. It tells the saga of two families, the Regensburgers and the Markovás.

The Markovás were something like a dynasty of women. The only reason men appeared in the lives of these women from Prague, who had been blessed with impossible beauty and angelic voices, was to father children—girls, of course—and then disappear. All the men were cursed by the women they had abandoned; and the curse caught up with every one of them sooner or later: they were all burned alive.

There were also violent deaths in the other family. Hans Regensburger, for example, the son of an undertaker in Leipzig who was a secretary for the Communist party, died in Gestapo custody. He was said to have hanged himself in his cell with a handkerchief. When his widow was permitted to see the dead man again, he was covered with bruises and lacerations, but there were no visible strangulation marks.

Hans Regensburger's wife Anna, née Hiller, came from a carnival family. She was the only daughter of a carousel owner. After Hans' death, she and her son Max escaped into exile in the Soviet Union via Prague. She and her child were separated, because Stalin considered all Germans to be traitors, whether they were Communists or not, and he deported the children to the Crimea for re-education.

It would be twelve years before Anna saw her son again, and she didn't recognize him. He had become a man—on the surface, anyway. But just as the mother had missed her son, he had missed his mother. For the rest of their lives, both of them tried to make up for the time they had missed. Max was never really able to grow up. His mother took care of everything: weddings, divorces, moves. And although she didn't know it, as long as she lived, she also kept the curse away from her son. That was the connection between the two families: Max had gotten a Marková pregnant and, as Hashem or fate planned it for all the women of the dynasty, he had left her before he had a chance to find out about the pregnancy.

After his mother's death, the curse caught up with Max Regensburger, as well. One night he was three sheets to the wind, staggering around his weekend house looking for some cognac. He tripped over a wire, knocked over the electric bowl fire lamp as he fell, and hit his head against a table. While the red-hot electric coil was burning a black pattern into the carpet, which eventually caught fire, Max lay unconscious on the floor, surrounded by cognac bottles. The dacha burned to the ground, and everyone could only hope that he hadn't regained consciousness as the flames devoured him.

Where did Wechsler get these stories? They are, in every detail, just like the stories I was told by my mother, who claimed to have heard them from her grandmother. The supposed suicide, the dramatic escape across the Czech border, the separation of mother and son, and my grandfather Max's death in a fire—all of that is my family history. It belongs to me, not Wechsler. It's impossible that he could have come up with all of this in a novel, without even knowing me.

I was completely horrified when Wechsler recounted an incident at the library of the American embassy in East Berlin, where he claimed to have taken out a poetry anthology by Cummings. But if the few pieces of biographical information I have been able to find are accurate, he never lived in East Germany. He was born in Israel and emigrated to Switzerland with his mother when he was a boy. His grandparents died in Auschwitz. The things he talks about in his novel can only be fiction and are by no means autobiographical.

Of course I should have talked to my wife. Maybe she would have comforted me and offered me some explanations. And maybe they would have been plausible. Instead, I withdrew. I tossed Wechsler's novel in the trash, and I didn't say a single word about it to my wife.

Whereas before I had only suspected that the supposed coincidences and oddities that had burst into my life recently were part of a plot to replace me with another person, now I was nearly convinced of it. Wechsler must have been stalking and investigating me for years. He knew the experiences of my grandparents and great grandparents down to the last detail, and he hadn't shied away from marketing them as supposedly fictitious stories, in the form of a novel.

He had narrated *me*, without asking for my permission or even speaking to me. I had no doubt that he was going to push things even further. Someone who stole other people's identities wouldn't stop short of murder. Maybe his goal was to take everything away from me, to cast me out of my own life, so that he could put himself in my place and take possession of everything going back to my birth—and even further—everything that has been experienced and suffered and which belongs to *me*.

If that's the way it was, then sooner or later he was going to have to get rid of me physically, as well. When I read his book, I could feel the point of a knife against my back. Wechsler just hadn't stuck it in yet.

I don't know if I was more afraid of the possibility that Wechsler had stolen my memories, and along with them my very self, or of another possibility that seemed even worse: that I was the thief, and that sometime in the past ten years I might have adopted the Regensburgers, Hillers, and Markovás and turned their family sagas into the history of *my* family. If that was the case, then I didn't exist at all. Then I was made up only of the perception that I had of myself, and that others had of me. Then I was nothing more than a literary figure; and an author like Wechsler could do whatever he liked with me and my life.

6

needed a distraction. For years I'd been meaning to take a trip
to the Vallée de Joux, a rugged valley in the Swiss Jura Mountains,
not far from Geneva. Three of the most famous watch manufacturers are based there: Breguet, Jaeger-LeCoultre, and Audemars
Piguet. Along with the other adventures I'd dreamed about, like
driving a Jeep through the Sahara, or learning to scuba dive in the
Red Sea, this was another one I hadn't fulfilled yet. It seemed to
be as good a time as any.

One of the watches that I managed to hide from the tax collector and didn't sell is a *Royal Oak Chronograph* from Audemars
Piguet, a less flashy watch for everyday wear, but one where you
can still see how much experience, skill, and patience went into its
manufacture.

The movements of wristwatches are small, but their performance
is amazing. The balance wheel travels the equivalent of 5,200 kilometers per year. After six years in my possession, my *Royal Oak* was
due for an adjustment.

The dealer had recommended that I send the watch directly
to Audemars Piguet. That kind of an overhaul required a watchmaker with a good deal of skill and experience. So I left the watch
with the dealer, who sent it in to be examined. I got an answer
within a week. The balance wheel and escapement needed to be

replaced. The movement had to be disassembled, cleaned, oiled, and adjusted. The case and the band would also get a slight brush-up. I'd have to wait eight to ten weeks, but then the watch would come back just like new.

That was two months ago.

Now, there's one thing you should certainly never do: rush a watchmaker. Still, the chance to take a break, and fulfill a long-standing wish at the same time, by going to Le Brassus in person to pick up my watch at the Audemars Piguet workshop, was just too tempting. So I called their public information department and asked if it was even possible to visit as a private customer.

Of course! the press lady informed me. And as long as I was going to be there anyway, she said, they would be happy to take me through the workshops and the adjacent museum, if I was interested. I could even look over the watchmaker's shoulder during the final inspection of my watch.

It's a deal! I said immediately, full of anticipation, distracted from my current troubles.

When would be good for you? I asked.

Your watch is ready, the lady told me, after she had inquired with customer service, During the week you can come any time. But be sure to leave yourself enough time. The watches aren't the only things worth seeing here, she said. When you come, you absolutely have to see the countryside and take a walk along the lake, which has a view of the ridges of the Risoux and the Col du Mont d'Orzeires.

We decided on the day after next. I wanted to get away, get some distance, to be alone and get back to myself as soon as I possibly could. I wouldn't need more than a day to get ready for the trip, look up train schedules, buy the tickets, and book a hotel.

My wife didn't have the slightest objection. She also thought it would do me good to kick back a little. She only felt sorry that she couldn't go with me. She doesn't share my enthusiasm for watch-making, but the thought of a quiet day in the Jura Valley, and the picturesque lake between the ranges, was tempting to her, too.

I hadn't been able to find a kosher hotel in the area, unsurprisingly, so I had to bring my own food. My wife packed a regal lunchbox with boiled eggs, sandwiches, sliced fruit, and peeled carrots. For the second day, I took some pita bread, hummus, and tahini in two small cups, and a can of tuna. I wasn't going to starve, anyway. My bag was bulging from my provisions alone. I also packed my toothbrush and a book—the second paperback from the black pilot suitcase.

If the Vallée de Joux isn't located at the very edge of the world, it has to be close. The trip to Le Brassus was an odyssey. I left just after eight thirty in the morning and caught the train at Munich's main station. Just to get to Geneva, I had to change trains twice, first around noon in Mannheim, and then one more time at three in the afternoon in Basel. I didn't arrive until six o'clock in the evening.

For the last leg of the trip, I could have taken a taxi, but I wanted to get the view, so I decided to take the little regional train to Sentier-Orient, a station at the southern tip of the Lac de Joux between Le Sentier and L'Orient. The train rambled through the countryside, mostly along the water, on the northwestern side of the lake.

The bus stop in Sentier-Orient was right in front of the train station. I dozed on a bench for a half hour while I waited for the bus to Le Bressus via Chez-le-Maître. From there it was just a short walk to the Hotel des Horlogers, a tasteful vacation and well-ness hotel nestled against a rich green hillside, where most of the rooms have a scenic view of the lake.

I had chosen the hotel just because of its name. It was wonder-fully suited to the purpose of my trip. I hadn't had any idea about the sauna and jacuzzi, the elegant lounges, and the foyer, with its heavy, tobacco-colored leather armchairs.

When I got to my room, it was already well past eight. My trip had taken almost twelve hours. I took off my vest, my tie, and my shoes; threw myself onto the bed with my lunchbox and the book I had brought; and I started reading, while I nibbled on the apples, which had turned a bit brown, and carrots, which had gone a bit soft.

The title, *The Minsky File*, made it clear from the outset what the book was about. It was written by a Swiss historian by the name of Hans Macht. In the years following the Minsky scandal, he had collected, sifted through, and sorted out all the documents he could get his hands on. Macht followed up on every lead that Wechsler had chased down in his effort to expose Minsky's lies. But unlike Wechsler, who had pursued a particular goal, namely to unearth incontrovertible proof to support his thesis, Macht took a broader approach in his research. He seemed to have been interested in Minsky the *person*. Using photos, official records, school yearbooks, and eye-witness accounts, he constructed a much more detailed pic-ture of Minsky's real identity than Wechsler did in his *Masquerades*.

The facts and documents that Macht presented suggested that Minsky's Swiss background was beyond dispute. But in no way did they support Wechsler's version of Minsky—a carefree child of the Swiss upper class who coldly manipulated the sympathies of the public for attention and cash.

According to Macht, Minsky was the illegitimate child of a girl who had just turned nineteen at the time of the birth and came from a rural area outside Geneva. The father wasn't any older than Minsky's mother. He came from a middle-class family of watchmakers. A marriage between the two of them would have been unthinkable. And so the young woman remained alone with the child. The father's family even refused to pay child support and had to be ordered by a court to provide the girl and her baby with a small monthly sum.

When Minsky was six months old, his mother had a bad fall and suffered several complex fractures that had to be treated during long hospital stays, at great expense. It was then that Minsky was placed in a children's home for the first time.

In spite of the intensive medical treatment, Minsky's mother remained in frail health. She could only perform simple tasks for a few hours at a time. Given the circumstances, there was no way she could support herself and a small child on her own. An official guardian was appointed, and the boy was sent back to the children's home and later to various foster families, who apparently only took him in because the government compensated them for it.

The conditions were terrible for the most part, according to Macht, and evidently so problematic that the guardian finally urged Minsky's mother to give the boy up for adoption. If she wanted him to have a well-ordered, or perhaps even happy, life, then that was the only way, he told her.

When not long after that, a well-to-do childless couple expressed an interest in the boy, the mother agreed to place Minsky in their care permanently and said that she would not object to an adoption, if that was what they wanted. At that point, however, Minsky was already six years old, frightened, withdrawn, and difficult, as Macht had learned from the adoption agency records.

That didn't sound like a happy Swiss childhood. In his attempt to construct a psychological profile of Minsky, Macht drew primarily on his early years, where he saw the primal trauma that might explain Minsky's later role-play as a Holocaust survivor. Hans Macht presented the results of his research clearly and soberly. The second part of the book, by contrast, seemed muddled and dubious. Macht is an historian, not a psychologist, and with his speculations, he was encroaching on a field of study that he wasn't very familiar with.

The book concluded with an appendix of about ten pages that had been added during the reprint, and in which Macht reported, in a telegraphic style, how Minsky had fared since the revelations about his life story.

Contrary to what several journalists claimed, Minsky had never undergone therapy. He had never seen any reason for it, since he had been sure of his memories, in which he had found the explanation for all his troubling conditions, like panic attacks, nightmares, and his overall poor health. It was only after the media frenzy that followed Wechsler's exposé that he needed psychological care, because he was afflicted by severe, psychotic anxiety and was afraid to leave his room for months.

The mudslinging in the media was followed by legal altercations. Various prizes and awards that Minsky had received were revoked. Minsky was able to fend off the criminal trial and several civil suits that had been brought against him, however. Prosecutors were not able to convince the judges that Minsky was a cold-blooded liar and con artist that the public needed to be protected from.

The trials all had political overtones. After all, in the afterword to *Days of Ashes*, Minsky had accused the Swiss authorities of actively participating in the cover-up of his true origins by forging birth certificates and destroying files that could have proven his identity. Consequently, the government had a vital interest in proving his guilt beyond a doubt.

They ultimately forced the author to undergo a DNA test, under threat of imprisonment for contempt of court. They had tracked down the man presumed to be Minsky's biological father, whose family had at least temporarily been ordered to pay child support for the boy. The DNA test was supposed to prove to the public beyond a doubt that Misnky's parents were both Swiss citizens, not Jews from the Minsk region. The test was conducted and came back positive. Minsky was born in the Swiss canton of Waadt. There was no longer any doubt about who his biological parents were. And the Swiss authorities had proof that there had not been any irregularities related to Minsky's papers. They were authentic. The bureaucracy had functioned smoothly.

The last paragraph of the afterword startled me: *Minsky*, it said, *has not appeared in public since the court-ordered DNA test. He refuses all interview requests. Nothing is known about the current state of his health. According to his former wife, he now lives alone and in seclusion at his house in L'Abbaye in the Valée de Joux.*

I felt electrified as I started at those words. L'Abbaye—I had seen it on the map when I was planning my itinerary—was less than ten kilometers away from Le Brassus, on the southern edge of the Lac de Joux.

It was already well past midnight. Nevertheless, I went downstairs to the lobby. I asked the concierge to pour me a whisky at the bar, in spite of the late hour. He wasn't thrilled, but I managed to talk him into it.

Knowing that Minsky lived nearby threw me back into doubt. I remembered the horror I had felt reading Wechsler's novel. And once again I could see my daughter's face, the way she had beamed with excitement when she held up the clipping she'd found in the notebook, crying: Papa, Papa, look! You're in the paper!

I repeated the proverb: Fools and children speak the truth. My daughter, I thought to myself, couldn't have had anything to gain from finding me in *that* picture, of all places. She was innocent. She didn't even have any idea of what her discovery might mean. My wife and I, on the other hand, looked at the photo with anything but innocent eyes. We both *hoped* that it would show someone else. We didn't *want* to recognize me in that specter. And perhaps that, in the end, was the only reason we had agreed so quickly that it couldn't possibly be me.

Unfortunately, I didn't have the photo with me. I probably would have asked the concierge for a magnifying glass, so I could scan every millimeter of the picture.

But if I was really hoping for proof, it was now nearby. There weren't even ten kilometers between us. If there was anyone who could confirm for me straightforwardly and unequivocally that I was not Jan Wechsler, author of *Masquerades*, it was Minsky. It was to this place, near the edge of the world, that he had fled. And now, by coincidence, I was here, too.

Coincidence—that's a word that I hardly dare to contemplate anymore.

While the concierge filled my glass, I got a pack of *Parisienne Rot* from the cigarette machine. For nearly six years, since our daughter was born, I hadn't smoked. Now I tore open the pack and lit a cigarette. I didn't inhale. The smoke tasted disgusting. And it did nothing to calm me down. Still, I kept smoking. I washed down the stale taste with whisky. Then I went back to my room.

I spent half the night tossing and turning anxiously, even though I was wound up and overtired from the trip. My urge to visit Minsky, just so I could be certain, was selfish; I realized that. With someone who had a history like his, I couldn't possibly go to his house, ring the doorbell, introduce myself, and say flat out: Please tell me I'm not the one who destroyed your life!

If I wanted to visit him, I had to come up with a ruse, a harmless little white lie. The fact that I would be ringing the bell at *his* door, of all places, had to look like a coincidence. And strictly speaking, it was.

Coincidence—there it was again, that eerie and incredible word!

At some point I had thrown myself into the armchair and fallen asleep for a half an hour, or maybe an hour. I woke up with a horrible pain in my lower back and the taste of cold ashes in my mouth.

I didn't touch the pita bread, hummus, and tahini I had brought with me for breakfast. I couldn't eat a thing. I drank several glasses of water and went back to pacing between the bed and the window, as I had during the night.

And once again a memory flashed in my mind: *His vision, from the constantly passing bars / has grown so weary that it cannot hold anything else. / It seems to him there are a thousand bars / and behind the bars, no world.* I could see my classmates from the twelfth-grade literature course, the way we sat in a circle listening to the person making the presentation, giving one another meaningful looks. But maybe—I had to think it might be possible—this was just another one of Wechsler's stories and never happened that way in my own life. But today, I told myself, I could leave behind the Jardin des Plantes, all the bars, and the uncertain world. All I needed to do was go to L'Abbaye and face Minsky.

I got dressed, got my things together, and went down to the lobby. A young, taciturn woman was sitting at the front desk. She took my key without saying a word. I asked her to give my regards to the night concierge. Then I paid my bill and left the hotel.

I took a walk around Le Brassus for a while, and just before nine I arrived at 16 Route de France, where I was supposed to receive my watch. The manufacturer's head of communications was already waiting, and he seemed delighted to see me, as if private customers rarely came to Le Brassus personally to pick up a watch and tour the museum and workshops.

He spoke German and was exceptionally friendly and very well-informed. I forgot his name. In general I retained very little of what he told me about the history of the building, the special pieces in the collection, and the production process. I'm pretty sure he noticed how inattentive I was, how quickly I walked past the display cases in the museum, and how little time I spent watching the finishers, who were busy adorning bridges with Geneva stripes.

On any other day, I would have been full of enthusiasm and eager to hear about every detail. But not that day. In my mind, I was already in L'Abbaye.

It wasn't even eleven when we arrived back in the lobby. I asked if they could call a taxi for me, and while we were waiting, I apologized for being in such a hurry. I told them I absolutely had to visit a friend in a nearby town and get back to the train station in Geneva by two o'clock. I told them I would come back again and set aside more time. The taxi came. I said goodbye and jumped in.

L'Abbaye, s'il vous plait, I said. And without turning around, the taxi driver asked: *Oui, vous voulez aller chez qui?*

Who was I going to see? I thought it was odd that he didn't ask for an address, but only a name. I didn't realize that the place only consisted of a few houses, and my driver actually knew every resident personally, since he lived there himself.

Minsky, I said, after a moment of hesitation that was perhaps a bit too long. I had the feeling he had become suspicious and assumed I was one of those incorrigible journalists who were still stalking Minsky, trying to get an interview in the most adventurous way possible.

Do you have an appointment? he asked. Minsky doesn't receive visitors without an appointment.

I played dumb. Why not? I asked.

Oh, the driver said, shrugging his shoulders. He has his reasons.

The thing is, I conceded, I don't know Minsky personally. But I've heard that he restores and appraises violins. I inherited a very old instrument that I'd like to have appraised. It might need to be refurbished.

He still hadn't started driving. He turned around and looked at me. But you don't have a violin, he said.

It was the first time I had ever been interrogated by a taxi driver. I shouldn't have responded, but I had the distinct feeling that he wasn't going to take me to Minsky's house unless I convinced him that I was harmless and wasn't scheming against his neighbor.

Well, I replied, that's the first problem. I don't know the first thing about violins. I don't even know how to transport such an instrument properly. I hope Mr. Minsky will be able to give me some advice.

If you think so, the driver said. You can always try.

I'm not going to stay long. It would be nice if you could wait, and then take me to Geneva.

He finally started the engine. The prospect of a lucrative trip had obviously motivated him.

It was a short ride. Once we'd arrived in L'Abbaye, we headed right for Minsky's house, which was surrounded by a high wall. I gave the driver a hundred francs and asked him not to park in front of the house, but to go a little further down the road. I told him to wait where he could see me, and that I wouldn't be long.

He shrugged his shoulders again. He was probably still suspicious. But he agreed and didn't ask any more questions. I got out and let him go. I waited until he had driven about a hundred meters away, parked at the roadside, gotten out, and lit a cigarette, and then I went up to the wooden door, so I could ring the bell.

Minsky's name wasn't on the doorbell or the mailbox. On the gate, someone had written the word "Workshop" in big letters with a yellow crayon. A big arrow pointed to the doorbell.

I had to ring several times before I heard something stirring behind the gate. Someone was shuffling slowly toward me.

Yes? the voice finally said, tentatively, almost inaudibly, from the other side of the gate.

Please excuse me. I'm visiting L'Orient, and I went for a walk and got lost, I lied. Would you be so kind as to call a taxi for me? I've been walking for hours.

At first there was no answer. The man behind the gate seemed to be thinking. But he finally moved. A heavy bolt was pushed aside, and with a loud clicking sound, a key was turned twice, and then once more, in the lock. Then he opened the door, but only as far as the iron security chain would allow.

The man I spied in the narrow gap was short and very slender, around seventy, with thin hair, bald in the front. He didn't say anything when he saw me, but he became visibly ashen. For a moment it seemed as if he was going to crumple into himself. But then the tension returned to his seemingly brittle body. Never in my life had I looked into such a desperate and simultaneously hateful face.

No longer inaudibly now, but clearly and distinctly, he said, Clothes make the man, Mr. Wechsler, but they can't make you human. How could you even dare to come here?

He slammed the door as forcefully as a man of his size possibly could.

I think I stopped breathing. For a moment, it was completely silent. Then I heard the clicking of the lock again. The bolt slid back in, and Minsky shuffled back into the house.

I don't know how I managed to get back to Munich, how I found my way to the right trains in Geneva and at the stations where I had to transfer. I am sure I didn't speak to anyone. I can't remember anything. It was as if I had plunged into a deep well inside myself. I somehow continued to function, and I found my way, but I didn't take anything in. It was only hours later, when I was back at home and opening the door to my apartment, that I awoke, as if from a trance.

When I walked in, I stumbled over my wife's suitcase, which actually belonged in the attic. It was quiet, and the hall was dark. The only light was from the living room at the other end of the hall. I put my bag down, hung up my jacket and my vest, put my shoes on the shelf, and tiptoed down the hall to the kids' room.

The children's beds were empty.

Dazed, I continued into the living room. My wife had cleaned up. The coffee table, which was ordinarily strewn with pads of painting paper, dozens of colored pencils, and my wife's Moleskines, was empty. The only thing there was a small book, white and thin. On the cover was Minsky's name, and in gray, scrawny letters, the title: *Days of Ashes*.

My wife was sitting on the sofa and had fallen asleep. I went up to her and tapped her delicately. She gave a start, jumped up, and immediately cowered, as if there was something frightening about me.

What's wrong? I asked. Where are the kids? What happened?

My wife took a deep breath. I could see she was fighting back tears.

The kids are at my mother's, she answered quietly. And I'm going to leave now, too. I only waited so I could tell you myself.

I held my breath for a long moment once again, as I had once before that day. There was no way she could possibly know what had happened in L'Abbaye, I thought to myself.

I don't understand, I said.

And I don't understand *this*, Jan, she said. She went to the table, picked up Minsky's book, opened it, and held it out to me.

On the flyleaf, I found a handwritten inscription: *To Jan Wechsler, in friendship*. Underneath it was Minsky's autograph and a date: *L'Abbaye, May 27, 1996*.

Where did you get this? I asked. I wasn't familiar with the book. More accurately: I couldn't remember ever owning it or, as the inscription suggested, getting it as a gift from Minsky.

My wife pursed her lips, and her face became flushed. From your shelf! she sobbed. Jan, it was on your shelf. It's been there for twelve whole years!

A feeling of panic began to well up in me. Yes, it was strange that I had forgotten the book and the inscription. Maybe I really had been friends with Minsky and had simply forgotten. But was that any reason to end a marriage?

I really don't remember this book, I said. Baby, I've been forgetting a lot of things lately.

Don't call me baby! she snapped back. I'm a grown woman. You can't do that to me, Jan, not that!

What do you mean? I asked. Are you going to leave me because of an inscription in a book?

No, Jan, she replied. It's not because of the inscription. That's not all.

Well then tell me! I shouted. What is it?

Now the tears were flowing. She was determined to leave.

Your mother called, she said.

My mother called?! I repeated. So? Why is that so serious that you would take the kids away and pack your bags?

How could you ask me that? You've always told me you're from Berlin. But your mother speaks *Berndeutsch*. She's lived in Switzerland for more than thirty years. She's never been to Berlin.

I think that was the moment when she finally gave up. She reached for her bag and wiped her tears with her sleeve.

I'm leaving now, Jan, she said, before she passed me on her way to the door. I don't know who you are anymore.

7

Don't call until you're back to normal again, my wife says. We're standing in the hallway. She turns around and lugs her suitcase to the stairway. I offer to carry it down. But she shakes her head. Then she's gone, and I remain standing in the doorway until I can't hear her anymore. When I get back into the apartment and close the door, it's dark and eerily silent.

It all feels unreal, as if the hallway were a corridor in the house in my book. I'm standing in front of a black polished wall, staring into nothingness. *Berndeutsch*, she said, and I repeat it. The sound of the word is like a change in the light, and where there was blackness just a moment ago, a picture is suddenly taking shape.

I'm standing with my mother in her painstakingly neat living room. She's talking to me insistently. I say nothing and look past her out the window. Every time her emotions boil over and she starts yelling at me, I play dead the way a rabbit does when it sees a snake. I can't argue, maybe because I've never been able to get a word in edgewise. But this time I find my voice.

I'm going to Germany, I say, whether you like it or not. When I'm back here, I'll visit you. But it might be a while. I'm not going to give you my address or telephone number. If you find out what they are, I won't speak to you. No letters, no phone calls, and above all, no visits. Those are the rules, and there's nothing to consider or discuss.

Now she doesn't say anything. Her lower lip is quivering, and she looks at me as if I were a stranger. I don't care. Now I have to get my coat, leave the apartment, and get out of there. It's high time. I close the door to the apartment quietly. When I get to the front door of the building, I slam it with a crash. The cars parked in front of the building have license plates from Bern. It's snowing, and a biting wind is blowing.

Berndeutsch. I say it one more time, and once again the light changes at the sound of the word. The images slip into blackness. I am alone, standing in the hallway of my apartment in Munich. The children are gone. My wife has left. Don't call, she said, before she went down the stairs with her suitcase. That didn't sound much different from what I said to my mother in Bern years ago. If my wife is as serious as I was then, she won't be back.

I wish I could say that I didn't see myself. The memory came like a flash: words from a loudspeaker, staged images projected onto a screen—like a film showing my mother and me in another life. But as strange as it all feels, it surely wasn't a dream, but the flash of a memory that must have been in the murky waters of the unconscious, waiting to surface again one day. *Berndeutsch* was the fishing rod that pulled it out.

I rifle through my bag looking for the pack of *Parisienne* that I got out of the machine at the Hôtel des Horlogers last night; I light a cigarette and look around the kitchen for anything I can use as an ashtray. In the refrigerator, there's a bottle of vodka. One glass for the ashes, one glass for the vodka. I sit at the table and smoke and drink until I don't have to think anymore.

Sometimes it's good to live in a close-knit community. I haven't been to shul for three days. That's unusual, and the rabbi calls to make sure I'm all right. I have no idea what time it is, and I don't sound very convincing when I assure him that everything is just fine.

Really? he asks, sounding worried.

Yes, of course, I say. My wife is out of town with the kids, and I was traveling myself for two days, in the Swiss Jura, a gorgeous, almost unreal place.

Our rabbi spent many years in Switzerland. As soon as I mention the Valée de Joux, he starts raving about the place.

You must have had a wonderful time, he says, seeming relieved. Next thing I know, he's invited me to a Shabbos meal with him and his family.

It wouldn't be right to leave a weekend widower by himself! he says. Come on over to our house. We'd be glad to have you.

It feels good to know that I'm surrounded by caring people. He has no idea that this Shabbos will be only the first of many that I'll have to spend alone. Before he says goodbye, he asks me to come back to shul soon. It's too strange to see your seat empty in the morning, he tells me.

Of course, I assure him. I'll be back tomorrow. Don't worry.

Kol tov!

Kol tov!

Then I hang up, and I'm appalled at the silence that surrounds me. I've gotten so used to my kids giggling, chattering, and horsing around—now that they're gone, I feel like I'm in a cemetery. I trudge into the kitchen, drink two glasses of water, and go to bed. In my condition, I figure, I'm incapable of doing anything anyway. I might as well sleep and postpone the moment where I have to begin to do something.

I don't know how long it's been since I allowed myself to sleep for such a long time, and during the day at that. I don't sleep soundly.

It's more dozing and catnapping, and I keep falling into prolonged dreams.

In one of those dreams, I see myself, well-toned and sweating, in a skiff. One look to the side, and I know that I am on the Große Krampe, a narrow lake between Schmöckwitz and Müggelheim in southern Berlin. I am out by myself. There are no motorboats or excursion boats in sight. I listen to my breathing, the slide of the seat, the sculls that creak in the oarlocks with each stroke, and I can hear the water lapping against the boat. I am rowing quickly, with quiet, powerful strokes. The wake cuts a sharp wedge into the water. To the right and left of the trail, little puddles swirl slowly. My rowing is like meditation. I am absorbed in the repetition of the movements, the tensing and relaxing of the muscles and my deep, steady breathing. Suddenly there's a dull crack, and a jolt goes through the starboard scull. Then a duck floats by me with no head, lifeless. In a panic, I look at the oar blade to my left, and I see a bloody feather. Another stroke, and the blood is washed off. For a moment I wonder whether I should stop to have a look at the duck. But I keep rowing like an automaton: catch, drive, release, recovery, roll, roll and so on. From one of the puddles that my oars leave behind, a thin hand is stretching out, with its fingers spread, as if it were grabbing at me. But I row away, and it disappears.

I remember the scene. It was almost like that. But it wasn't on the Große Krampe. It was in the Dahme-Spree Canal somewhere near New Venice. And of course there wasn't a hand grabbing at me trying to pull me under water.

I was eleven when I joined a small rowing association in Friedrichshagen. Not long after that, I switched to a sports club in Grünau. It was one of those meat grinders of the East German sporting world, where you trained six days a week so that, someday, you could win an Olympic gold medal for the socialist fatherland. I left the house every morning at six and didn't get home until nine o'clock at night. After dinner I would fall right into bed and sleep like a dead man.

The streetcar connection between Friedrichshagen, where we lived, and Grünau, was bad. I had to change in Köpenick, but I usually missed my connection by about a minute and had to wait fifteen more minutes for the next streetcar. I made up for it by reading. At no other time in my life have I read as many books as I did on those streetcars and on that platform, as I made my way between home, school, and the boathouse.

I also wrote back then—poems and short stories—mostly in class at school, or during the breaks between training sessions. I didn't need more than those few minutes. The poems and stories developed in my head during the many hours I spent rowing on the lakes of Berlin. When I was back on land, all I needed to do was write them down.

That's still the way I write now: on the go, without a notebook or a pen. Characters and stories, rhythms and words, live in my head. They float around, come together in a magical way, and I just have to transfer them to paper at some point. It's no wonder that I usually walk around like a dreamer, more or less absent, traveling through the magical parallel worlds in my head.

I chose rowing because that sport seemed to be the quickest way to fame. I'm sure I wouldn't have admitted that at the time. But now it I can hardly deny it. Even early on, I wanted to be the center of attention.

I remember playing a secret game when I was a child. Back then we had a small cottage in the woods. My great grandmother had rented it for us. We didn't have a car. If we wanted to get to the cottage, we had to take the S-Bahn to Erkner, and then take a bus for about a half an hour. The bus was never full. Oftentimes I was able to sit down by myself in the back row, look out the window, and daydream.

The drone of the diesel engine became the subtle purr of a twelve-cylinder government limousine. I was sitting in the back seat, being chauffeured around a major city—not someplace like the Karl-Marx-Allee in East Berlin, though—more like the Champs-Elysées. A convoy of heavy motorcycles was driving ahead of us, in arrow formation. The limousine followed, and I waved to the crowds by the side of the road. That was pretty much the way I had seen it on television. And even though I would never have admitted it, I was determined that someday I would be important enough that I would get a police motorcycle escort, like during a state visit.

When I think back to my first book of poems by Gabriela Mistral, a few verses of her "Death Sonnets" come to mind. But most of all, I picture a scene that's described in the afterword of my first Mistral anthology. After several years abroad, the writer returns by ship to Chile, a country that reveres its poets like heroes. Having received the Nobel Prize, she has long been a celebrity in her native country. At the port, masses of people have gathered to receive her: schoolchildren, workers, intellectuals. Half of the city has come out to welcome her. As the ship enters the harbor, Gabriela is standing at the railing with a friend, marveling at all the people.

There must be someone very special on our ship, Mistral is said to have remarked to her friend. And the story has it that she couldn't believe it when her friend replied: Gabriela, these people are all here for you.

If I had been in Gabriela's shoes, I would have known who they were waiting for. When I read that story, I was fourteen and so convinced that I was going to be famous one day that I couldn't think in any other way. The idea of a writer like Gabriela knowing nothing of her own grandeur seemed like a fable to me.

I was impatient. To this day I don't know of any poet who has achieved worldwide fame while still a teenager. Gabriela, Bachmann, Celan—my heroes seemed overpowering to me. It would take decades before my writing could even come close to theirs. And no matter what I tried to do, there was always the possibility that I lacked the thing that they had all undeniably had: talent.

The idea of becoming a famous athlete was appealing to me primarily because I assumed that I needed nothing more than ambition, effort and an absolute will to win. Of course I rowed solo from the very beginning, since I wasn't about to share my fame with anyone.

I remembered a poster that hung on the door of the boathouse that showed three-time Olympic gold medalist Pertti Karppinen in a race. When you looked at that Finn's face, there was no doubt that he could win any race. He pulled the sculls through the water with such powerful force that they bent like willow branches. I thought that the photo showed him at the beginning of a race, during the first strokes. The caption disabused me of that notion.

Pertti Karppinen in the home stretch, it said.

Approaching the finish line with the determination and strength that others brought to the starting line . . . that poster became the standard for me. I don't think any of my fellow athletes could muster anything approaching my ambition. It paid off. I soon experienced success, even if it tasted different than I had imagined.

There must still be a picture of me from that time. I was only fifteen, but I was built like a tree. The photo shows me during the victory ceremony at the East German Spartakiad games. I remember the race well. I had overexerted myself to the point where I could barely make it to the victor's platform, and I had to be lifted out of the boat. When I tried to stand up, I doubled over and fell to my knees. The stands echoed with laughter. I think it was only my fury about the laughing that helped me to get back up when the fanfare sounded and my name came over the loudspeakers. I kept the medal. It must be in one of my desk drawers. It's been a long time since I held it in my hand.

A year after that victory, I quit the sports club. At the time, we were subjected to all kinds of elaborate endurance tests and measured extensively by sports physicians every few months. Based on the length of our phalanxes, the thickness of our skin folds, and the test protocols, they calculated whether, and how much, we each could be expected to grow. A rower's potential is measured in centimeters of height. In my case, the doctors' judgment was devastating.

I had stopped growing, I was informed when I was sixteen, and that meant I was at least fifteen centimeters too short. My competitors would soon surpass me, even those with more moderate ambition. I was no longer eligible and was eliminated.

I think it was around this time that I began to consider the existence of God to be a possibility. Up to that point, he hadn't figured into my life. My rethinking of the idea of a creator began with the sudden insight that, no matter if you have the greatest ambition and you summon up all your strength, you can't achieve everything, in rowing or other endeavors, if you're missing the ingredient that can only come from the outside: a gift—even if it only consists of long arms and legs.

I took up literature, though it was clear to me that the decision would demand a lot of patience on my part.

Ever since then, I have lived in constant doubt. I have put myself completely in the hands of the one who distributes the gifts that enable each one of us to do something special. If the prospect of fame was his bait, I swallowed it whole. The less of it I get, the more religious I become. A bad deal, you might say. But I know it isn't like that.

Honor and glory come from God . . . they come from him, but he doesn't just give them away for the asking. Only a naïve person would be comforted by the joke about Moishele begging to win the Lotto.

I'm going to lose my wife and the children if I can't sort out who I once was, and who I am now. And I need evidence. My wife is no longer going to be satisfied with mere assurances.

I pick myself up and go to my desk to look for my Spartakiad medal. Gold is worth something. That would certainly be suitable as evidence, I tell myself. But I can't find the medal.

Once I'm at my desk, however, another idea comes to me. If I were Swiss, my wife would have to have noticed a long time ago. It's only been in the last few years that officials have relaxed the residency requirements for Swiss nationals in the EU. At the time when we met, as a Swiss citizen I would have had to report to immigration officials every few months to have my residence permit extended. Furthermore, it wouldn't have been easy to get the papers together for the wedding. And above all, as a Swiss citizen I would also have a Swiss passport. How could that have escaped her attention during our vacations?

And so I open the drawer where we keep the passports, and I find all four of them—mine, my wife's, and the children's. They're red EU passports with the gold embossed eagle of the Federal Republic. I am a German citizen with a regular German passport. Isn't that proof enough?

In another drawer is the strongbox with our documents. It contains our family register with a handful of documents that prove not only my identity, but the whole family's: the children's birth certificates, our marriage license, my wife's ketubah . . .

Last but not least, since 1990 I have also kept my voided East German passport in the strongbox. I never wanted to throw it away. I got it in November of 1989, right after the borders were opened. There were dozens of people waiting outside the passport office, and I had to wait hours before it was my turn. I didn't just get the passport. I also received a permanent visa for travel to West Berlin and West Germany, the only visa that was ever stamped into that passport. Just ten months later, the Small Country ceased to exist. As a new citizen of the Federal Republic, I was supposed to surrender my blue East German passport. I refused. The officer smirked, took out a puncher and made a few holes in it, then stamped every page with the word VOID in red ink. Then he handed it back to me.

In November of '89, I went from the passport office right to the train station, got on the S-Bahn, and went to Friedrichstraße. As long as I'd been alive, that had been the end of the line.

Gray gray gray tangle / from which no trains depart where a giant raven / perches black between the tracks / train station that's the coldest of all places at night / no one sleeps. I had read those lines by Hilbig, one of my favorite poets, whose books you could only get as bootleg copies in the Small Country. And I couldn't help thinking of that poem as I pushed my way through the catacombs of the Friedrichstraße station, on my way to the other side of the world, which was actually just the other side of the same platform.

I rode the train two stations in the direction of Wannsee, got off, and went to the closest bank to get my "welcome money," one hundred West German marks. The bank was full. You didn't get your money from a register. The tellers were standing in the middle of the bank with thick bundles, handing out blue bills.

I remember hitting all the bookstores I could find that day in the hopes of getting a Hilbig book. Every bookseller offered to order one for me. But I wanted it right then, immediately, without having to wait any longer. And it was inconceivable to me that, in a country where people were allowed to read Hilbig, his books weren't on display in every bookstore. I might even have said so. The clerk at the shop on Savignyplatz certainly looked at me like I was crazy.

At another bookstore, I did at least buy a novel: Salman Rushdie's *The Satanic Verses*. It had just come out, and the fatwa had been issued, forcing him to go underground. A book that was about life and death in the truest sense was something I simply had to own.

I stayed on the other side until late that night. I had taken the U-Bahn to Kreuzberg, and my plan was to cross the Oberbaum Bridge back into the East. The Oberbaumstraße, which runs from Skalitzer Tor to the bridge, was nicknamed the "column of ants" back then. It was closed to cars during those days. Thousands of people walked down that street at all hours of the day and night, loaded down with plastic bags full of the fruit, chocolate, coffee, and cigarettes they were hauling back to their homes in the East. On that night, you could hardly get through. Eventually I made it to the banks of the Spree. But I couldn't get any farther.

Back then, the bridge was still a high-security area. Massive steel grates blocked the roadway on both the eastern and western side. The gate that the crowds had to push through was no bigger than a door. But that door was also closed.

We stood there for more than an hour, and nothing happened. More and more people kept coming. The crowd started pushing and jeering. I was standing on the banks of the Spree, with *The Satanic Verses* under my arm, staring over at the back of the Wall, and I was convinced that the border had been closed again, and we were locked out. The panther wanted to get back into the cage, and they wouldn't let him in.

So there I was with nothing more than the clothes on my back, plus a novel I hadn't read yet, and 40.75 West German marks. I don't know how my great grandmother felt in 1933, when she walked through the forest in the dead of night to cross the Czech border, with a suitcase in one hand, and her young son holding onto her other hand. But what I went through that night on the Spree felt like exile, a taste of a future without a home or family, on my own in a loud, colorful city that had the same name as the place where I had grown up but had absolutely nothing to do with my home.

It took an eternity for the situation to get resolved. Several welders were called in to remove the bars from the huge grates. The door had only been closed so that larger gate could be opened. I will never forget that night. That's the kind of thing that you either experience, or you don't; but why would you make it up?

The passport will prove my origins, I tell myself. I hurriedly take out the strongbox and open it up. The family register is on top. I take the strongbox into the living room, empty it out, and spread everything across the table, so I can get a good look. All of the sudden a feeling of euphoria comes over me. I tell myself that all of this will be cleared up soon.

I find my old passport; only it isn't blue like I thought; it's bright red, with a white cross on the front. I look inside, and I barely recognize myself in the picture, which is almost twenty years old. I look like a fop with my blond hair teased out. But it's me, no question about it. The date of birth is also correct. Only the place of birth is not.

Of course I want to make sure immediately. I check my German passport and my marriage license. I find the same entry everywhere.

If the documents are to be believed, I was Swiss, at least at one time. And I wasn't born in Berlin, but in Ramat Gan, Israel.

My German passport was issued in 1999. I hadn't been living in Munich for very long at that time. How could a Swiss citizen get a German passport in such a short time?

It's two p.m. If I hurry, I can make it to the registry office before the close of business. I want to know what information they have on file about me. When I finally find myself sitting across from a clerk on Poccistraße, I explain myself this way: I'm doing research for a novel, and I need some information about my records.

In literature, you can't just make assertions that you can't back up, I tell her. After all, it has to be realistic. Otherwise, no one will believe it. So if I'm going to describe a scene like this, it has to hold water, you know what I mean?

That's fascinating, she replies, giving me a smile. She pushes a few buttons on her terminal and pulls up the data.

Could I see your identification? she asks.

Of course, I tell her, and I hand over my EU passport.

She appears satisfied, and I write along while she reads out what she's found in the system about me: Born in Ramat Gan, Israel on June 6th, 1965. In Switzerland beginning in 1968. Last registered Swiss address in Bern-Elfenau, at the home of Wechsler, Edda, on Willadingweg. Relocated to Munich in 1998. Resided in Vaterstetten, Alpspitzstraße, later at three different addresses on Klenzestraße and Fraunhoferstraße. Married in June of 2001. First child born in September of 2002. Second child born in October of 2003. Both children have their own passports, and their names are listed in the passports of both parents. No record of any prior convictions. Naturalized in February of 1999 following accelerated proceedings, in accordance with the statutory rule on descendants of German nationals stripped of their citizenship during the Third Reich . . .

The clerk looks up.

You know, she says: I would have kept my Swiss citizenship if I were you. It's such a beautiful country. And after everything that happened . . . She shakes her head, as if she can't fathom why a descendant of Jewish refugees who had been stripped of their citizenship by the Nazis would want to apply for a German passport.

You know, my wife and children . . . I say, trying to come up with a plausible explanation. The clerk nods.

Yes, that's always complicated, she says.

Tell me about it, I sigh. I thank her for her help, say goodbye, and go to the checkout to pay the inevitable fee.

I make my way home like a sleepwalker. My records are unambiguous. The things I have told people cannot be true. It stands to reason that my wife would pack her suitcase and get herself and the children away from me. I'm a liar, or I'm completely insane. What else am I supposed to think?

8

In the middle grades, we always started our day with a song. When the teacher came into the classroom, we would stand up in our places. What we sang on any given day was something the girls worked out beforehand in the schoolyard. The class speaker—it was always a girl—would inform the teacher which song they'd chosen. Then the teacher started us off singing.

There was one song that I loved and hated at the same time. It wasn't a march like most of the songs we learned in music class, or even a song with verses and a chorus. It was a flowing tune set to words written by a young poet.

Our homeland, it is not just the cities and villages / Our homeland is also all the trees in the forest / Our homeland is the grass in the meadow, the grain in the field, and the birds in the air, and the animals of the earth, and the fish in the river are our homeland . . .

I loved the song mostly because of the music. But the words, when I sang them with my eyes closed, also sent me on a journey through the landscapes of the Small Country. I roamed through the forests, wandered through the fields, pulling down ears of corn and twisting cobs off the stalks. Or I rowed my boat across Berlin's lakes in the silence of the morning. When I saw all those things, I felt the meaning of *homeland* clearly. It had nothing to do with parades, Young Pioneer neckerchiefs, and collecting scrap paper for the Solidarity Fund. My homeland was the place where I had to belong, because otherwise, I probably wouldn't have loved it so much. The fact that it was sealed off from the rest of the world by walls and barbed wire was not the most important thing. The emotion was stronger.

I hated the song because of its closing lines: *And we love our homeland, the beautiful, and we protect it, because it belongs to the people, because it belongs to our people.*

Those final words were the only reason they taught the song at school. The feeling of having a homeland served a purpose. It was drilled into us, and we were reminded of it again and again, so that one day we would eagerly reach for our Kalashnikovs and serve with honor in the army. The defense of the nation was directed inward, however. Everyone knew that. At the border, shots were fired *into* the country—not at aggressors, but at people who wanted to leave.

I cursed the man who wrote those words, because I considered him a traitor to poetry. He had expressed something true, and then rendered it void. I cursed the composer, as well. The song's melody progressed so logically toward its wonderful two-part ending that I always found myself singing along with the final lines. It created a vibration in me and made it ring in such a way that I had no choice but to keep singing.

When it was your birthday, you got to stand in front of the class in the morning. Everyone would wish you a happy birthday, and you were allowed to pick the song of the day. Students often chose the Homeland Song, because most of us liked it.

There was one girl in my class who stood up front two days in a row. On the second day, she didn't get to request a song. And no one wished her a happy birthday. Instead, the teacher reprimanded her for lying. The day before, she had only pretended that it was her birthday, and she had smiled when we sang for her and the teacher gave her a warm handshake. Now she was crying, and she had to apologize in front of everyone for lying.

To this day a feeling of outrage wells up in me every time I recall that scene. What kind of person lies so she can be the center of attention for two minutes while people wish her a happy birthday? I have often felt needy myself. What she went through when the teacher humiliated her for that neediness, I went through right along with her.

We don't learn for school, we learn for life. That slogan was written on a faded banner over the entrance to the auditorium. The lesson was clear: lying has consequences if you're not experienced at it, and you tell a lie in a moment of weakness. Whereas if you lie deliberately and with a persuasive aesthetic style, students will learn the lie by heart and begin each day by singing it eagerly.

A liar is unpleasant enough. But a liar with a bad memory is a disaster, because he can neither admit the truth nor continue to lie.

I drank again yesterday. I needed to be a little numb before I could sleep, after all the discoveries of the day. I lied. She caught me and is making me feel her disapproval.

Actually, I should say: I *must have lied*. Because I'm still not sure what's true and what's a lie. I am what I remember. I don't have anything else. If the documents now appear to prove that a large part of my memory is unreliable, then I myself am unreliable. I could be called on to apologize publicly, to admit to the lie and wipe the slate clean. I suppose my wife is waiting for me to do something along those lines before she'll be willing to speak to me again. But if I did that, it would just be another lie, pure lip service, of no value whatsoever. I would have to admit that I don't exist.

I don't love all of my memories. Some of them are terrible. But they belong to me. It is in them that I exist. If I were to deny them by admitting that they're nothing but staged illusions, that would be a betrayal like Winston's betrayal of Julia in Orwell's novel. A betrayal like that is something that no one can demand of me.

I have to assume that the reason I raked Minsky over the coals in those articles and in that malicious book was because he refused to betray himself. I also have to assume that I have wiped out the traces of my background and slipped into someone else's life. Whether that's really the case, I can't say with certainty. I'm also in the dark about the potential reasons. If I no longer know what I have concealed and why, I can't keep up the lie.

If I were a criminologist, I would have to start looking into the five W's: *Who? What? Where? When? Why?* The question of *Who* is one that I'll have to put aside. Who I am is the most uncertain thing at the moment. As for the question of *What*, at least I have a guess. I even have a handful of guesses. I don't like any of them. Everything points to the case of Minsky, and I can't imagine any version of the story where I'm innocent, the way my memory would have me believe I am.

If I want to find out what happened, I have to try to accept, without emotion, that the life I remember is not *my* life. I am reluctant, but I have no choice but to follow the clues, which all suggest that I am someone else. To sort out the question of *What*, I'll have to ask someone who has known me longer than my wife has. Two people come to mind: my mother and von Dennen.

As a source of information, my mother is out. I know not very long ago I claimed that she gave me that pilot suitcase when I visited her a year and a half ago, the one I left behind in Spain with the locks broken open. I still believe that. But it's also equally true that I don't know where I visited her at that time.

I can't find an Edda Wechsler in my address book, neither in Bern nor in Berlin. I didn't notice any Swiss numbers on the list of calls on the telephone. So I can't contact her. Besides, a mother's naturally subjective view of her only son's personal history might just create more confusion. I need solid information, nothing personally biased.

Von Dennen is the only one left, then. Judging by his letter, he used to know me well, before I forgot him. I take out his letter and read it one more time, and then again. I know I could be in for a rude awakening if I talk to him. But after two days in an empty apartment, the prospect of spending the future without my wife and children is worse than anything that von Dennen might reveal about me.

Nevertheless, his letter also makes it clear to me that I can't possibly give him my version of the truth. If I ask him to tell me as much as he can about my life because I can no longer remember, I hardly think he'd give me any information. For him, that disclosure would be definitive proof that I belong in treatment and am not worth his time.

If I want to learn the truth, I'll have to keep lying. That's quite an insight all by itself. Of the four possibilities that von Dennen entertained in his letter, I will choose and embellish the one most likely to arouse his interest as a publisher: a new book. Of course I'll have to assure him that details from his life won't figure into the book in any way. I'll trot out a story that won't make him suspicious but that will pique his curiosity. I don't have to think about it for long. I have another vodka—my last, I solemnly swear to myself—and I dial the number of the publishing house from the letterhead.

The secretary seems dismissive. I announce that I'm one of the publisher's authors, but that doesn't impress her much. You can't expect to be put through to the publisher just like that, she says.

Even so, when I repeat my name, she seems to sit up and take notice, and she agrees to pass along a message.

I thank her, then I dictate my message and give her the bait: "It's about a book. Please call back."

All right, the secretary says, but I can't give you any guarantees.

Neither can I, I say, trying to make a joke. To my surprise, von Dennen calls me back just five minutes later.

Wechsler, I answer, clearing my throat.

Hello, Jan, is the reply from the other end. It's the voice of a resolute old man. Though I'm talking to a stranger, von Dennen seems to know exactly who he's talking to.

I'm glad you called, he says. I didn't believe you were actually doing research for a book. Good Lord, it's been almost ten years since the last time we spoke.

I don't feel comfortable calling von Dennen by his first name, but I figure I have to, so he won't get suspicious. Without a long run-up, I tell him that I'd like to meet him, precisely because we haven't seen each other in so long, and a lot has happened since then: I got married, had a couple of kids . . .

And the book? von Dennen asks. What kind of book is it?

I throw out a name: Do you know Raymond Queneau?

Of course, he replies condescendingly.

Queneau's story is simple. I have read it so many times that I can quote it from memory, which, when it comes to literature, evidently hasn't failed me: *On the S bus, at rush hour. A chap of about twenty-six, felt hat with a cord instead of a ribbon, neck too long, as if someone's been having a tug-of-war with it. People getting off. The chap in question gets annoyed with one of the men standing next to him. He accuses him of jostling him every time anyone goes past. A sniveling tone which is meant to be aggressive. When he sees a vacant seat he throws himself on to it. Two hours later, I meet him in the Cour de Rome, in front of the Gare Saint-Lazare. He's with a friend who's saying: "You ought to get an extra button put on your overcoat." He shows him where (at the lapels) and why.*

In his *Exercises in Style*, Queneau tells the story in more than a hundred variations. And he doesn't just switch the styles, tenses, and chronology, but also the perspectives. The events are described by various participants and observers, and often it seems that they're telling completely different stories, given how much the characters and the meaning of certain details change, depending on who the narrator is.

So? von Dennen asks.

Which of the stories is true? I ask in reply. He is silent for a minute.

Who knows? he finally says.

They're all true! I say, as contradictory as they may appear. In one version, the fact that a man has a cord on his hat makes him a Bavarian, but another time that makes him a dandy. For yet another narrator, it's an unmistakable sign that the gentleman hasn't kept up with the changes in fashion. And all these versions are true. The story happens not just once, but as many times as it's observed. And it is only in the observers' perception that the story takes place at all.

That's a bit lofty, von Dennen interjects.

But I'm not ready to give up yet. I have a great plot, I say, continuing with my lie: I'm going to tell the story from the point of view of the different characters, through the filter of their perceptions, as it were—a breathtaking experiment. It will be like nothing you've read before, by me or anybody else.

Good, good, von Dennen says. That's interesting. How far along are you? What can you send me?

I'm still experimenting, I admit. That's why I called. I need to do a few exercises of my own. At the moment I'm narrating *myself.* That is to say, I'm narrating the way other people narrate me. That's why I'd like to meet with you. Just tell me what you know about me, and then I'll re-tell it. It's an exercise. Once I feel secure in the form, I'll be ready to tackle the plot.

Once again von Dennen is silent for a few seconds.

Isn't that a bit inconvenient? he asks. I mean, do we really need to get together to do that? I can just as easily tell you what I know about you over the phone. It isn't an awful lot.

He's taken the bait, I think to myself. Now it's time to up the ante.

I have to watch you while you do it, I tell him. Facts alone don't make a story. For that you need a situation.

Like I said, it's a bit lofty, von Dennen sighs. But fine, let's meet. I'm game. But I don't have a lot of time. Tomorrow I have to be in the Lake Constance area. We could meet in Lindau around noon, for two hours at the most.

Great! I say. Tomorrow is absolutely perfect.

Tomorrow it is, then, von Dennen says. Let's meet at noon in front of the restaurant at the train station. Does that work for you?

Of course, I say, thanking him in advance for his help.

Then we say goodbye, and I hang up the phone with a feeling of triumph.

I have done something. I am taking back the reins. That's how it feels, anyway. And that's why I don't have any trouble pouring the rest of the vodka down the drain and falling asleep without being numb. Still, I sleep fitfully and have a lot of dreams. The headless duck keeps showing up in different variations.

In one of the dreams, I'm wading frantically, with all my effort, to get through a ford, and the water is up to my chest. A crocodile is swimming slowly behind me, snapping in the air. It only veers off when we reach the bridge at the beginning of a regatta course, and the starter says into his megaphone: *Ready, steady, . . .* The word *go* is drowned out by the starting gun. The crocodile yawns and submerges. Then the blade of an oar smacks me right across my forehead, and I float unconscious between the buoys of lane 4.

While I'm floating, the image cross-fades into the entryway of an old synagogue, which I recognize immediately. It's the Rykestraße synagogue in Berlin's Prenzlauer Berg district. I can hear my voice in a chorus of echoes. *Through your abundant kindness I will enter Your House; I will prostrate myself toward Your Holy Sanctuary in awe* . . . That was certainly a lie. When I prayed in that synagogue, I must have been sixteen, and I had no concept of awe.

Being different is a problem in every dictatorship. In the Small Country, being Jewish was the ultimate kind of difference. When I found God at the end of my sporting career, I didn't talk about it with anyone. My grandparents were dyed-in-the-wool Communists. After they returned from exile, they held important positions in the state apparatus. They never entered a synagogue. For one thing, religion was the opiate of the masses, according to Marx. And for another thing, Jews in the Small Country only came in three varieties: gassed, locked up after show trials, or forced to flee the country. Those weren't categories anyone wanted to end up in.

All the remaining people, who gathered together in tiny congregations, must have failed to grasp something vital. The small community I sought to connect with didn't make it easy for me when I tried to find out where and when services were held. But eventually I experienced my first Friday evening service at Rykestraße. I sat in my coat on the edge of a chair in the back row of the tiny weekday synagogue. It was also used on Shabbos and festivals. There were maybe forty seats, and usually not even a third of them were full. The larger synagogue was in serious need of renovation and was only used during the High Holy Days.

The fact that I felt at home at Rykestraße goes to show just how confused my sense of home must have been. I went back a week later. This time I took off my coat. But on that evening, and what must have been fifty Fridays after that, no one said a single word to me. I didn't realize why until years later. The congregation had about three hundred members. Many of them, especially the majority of the board members, were "unofficial employees" of the Stasi. Of all the religious groups in the country, the Jewish community was probably the one that was spied on the most, and everyone suspected everyone else of being an informant. If somebody new came around and nobody knew him, it was almost a given that he'd been sent in. So I shouldn't have expected a warm welcome.

I learned to read Hebrew with great effort over a period of several months, just by listening and comparing the sounds with the unfamiliar letters. I expanded my vocabulary at a snail's pace with the aid of the synagogue's bilingual prayer book, which of course I didn't dare to take with me, so my lessons were limited to the one hour each week that I spent at Friday evening services. It was more than a year before I started meeting people, and it took even longer to make friends. Hardly any of us knew what we were. The only connection we had to what we might have been was the old prayers and the remains of a tradition that most of us barely knew anything about. What we did have was the feeling of not being at home with ourselves—a feeling we already had anyway in the Small Country, which only needed its tiny Jewish community to demonstrate its tolerance.

Religion mattered only to a few of the people there. Most were searching, sincerely and with great difficulty, for identity. But under the constant suspicious observation that made every conversation hazardous, there was hardly any way to find anything that felt even remotely like identity.

Years later, an author friend of mine confided to me that in West Germany his Jewish identity only had two anchors: Israel and Auschwitz. Neither was an option in the Small Country. In the concentration camps and the prisons, it was the Communists who had suffered. That's what we learned in school. We read about it in novels and saw it in movies. Jews had also died, of course. But the Communists had fought back. In our self-proclaimed nation of resistance fighters, it was hardly possible to invoke Auschwitz thirty or forty years after the end of the war in an effort to bring focus to your self-image. And Israel was completely out of the question. The "Zionists" were imperialist barbarians who were taking everything that rightfully belonged to our proletarian brothers in Palestine at gunpoint. The only thing we were able to feel for them was loathing, and we were expected to express it with the deepest conviction.

My image of Israel was made up of the television scenes of heavily armed occupation soldiers and scant bits of information about the kibbutzim, where everything supposedly belonged to everyone equally—right down to every pillow and each individual sock. I had read about it in a book by a renegade Mossad agent, published by the East German Military Press under a pseudonym. It described the training methods of the Mossad and the way the military pervaded the whole country. I read it during breaks at school, and a teacher asked me: Isn't it awful, what's happening there? They're acting just like the Nazis, don't you think so?

I didn't think so. But in my mind, Israel was a heavily-armed country full of communes. The guys were coarse and violent. The girls had hairy arms and patrolled the beach in uniform, their Uzis at the ready. For me, Israel was just another Small Country full of absurdity and brutality that I certainly didn't need.

Not long after that, the same teacher very politely pointed out to me that "in this country," it was customary for people to take off their head coverings in enclosed spaces. At the time I had begun wearing a hat, and I ran into him at the entrance to the school building.

At the end of my dream, I was standing with that teacher in a colossal doorway. I was holding my hat in my hand, staring at the green-and-white emergency exit sign.

Von Dennen was not able to tell me as much as I had hoped. My train arrived in Lindau a half an hour before we were supposed to meet, so I took a seat at the train station café. At five minutes before twelve, an older but quite vigorous gentleman came in, wearing an open coat and a silk scarf, with a briefcase and publisher's catalogues under his arm. I could only assume that it was von Dennen. He, on the other hand, recognized me from a distance and headed right over. It was only when he was standing right in front of me that he paused briefly, looked me over with a slightly caustic expression, and said: So, have you really become religious?! With his left hand, he pointed to my clothes, which, aside from my white shirt, were all black, from my kippa to my shoes.

Some people say it's a disguise, I concede. Has it really been that long since we last saw each other?

Evidently, von Dennen said. I've never seen you in a three-piece suit, anyway. He shook his head, unable to hide the fact that he didn't approve of the change. He put down his briefcase, took off his coat, sat down, and waved to the waiter.

So, let's begin the experiment, von Dennen said, interlocking his fingers. He got right to the point: If it's going to be realistic, then I can't mince words . . .

This made me a bit apprehensive. But I agreed. That's just what I have in mind, I told him.

The waiter came. Von Dennen ordered a coffee and some water, and then he leaned back, reflecting for a moment before he provided *his* view of my life story, as far as he knew it.

As it turned out, he could hardly give me any details. He didn't know much more about the basic facts than I had learned online or at the registry office in Munich. He corroborated the year and place of my birth. He claimed that my father was twenty years older than my mother and had died in the early nineties, before I came to von Dennen with the manuscript for my first novel. At the time, I was around thirty, but still living with my mother, something he said he occasionally teased me about.

In light of that, he said, it surprised him that a year after *Masquerades* came out, I pulled up stakes from one day to the next and moved, not only out of my mother's house, but also out of the country, leaving the poor woman behind without a word. Just recently she had called him up in tears, von Dennen said, inquiring about my whereabouts. So he had taken out my letter and given her my telephone number in Munich.

I can't believe you could have been so cold-hearted, keeping her in the dark all these years, he said.

What *I* couldn't believe was how nonchalantly he admitted that he had given out my number. Of course he had no way of knowing what my mother's call had unleashed. And I couldn't give him a hard time about it without blowing my cover. So I swallowed my irritation.

Everything else he knew, von Dennen said, he'd only heard second hand. He told me that another author had run into me on the street in Munich at some point, and he had told him that I had put my old life behind me and become religious.

Most of what he knew about my previous life in Switzerland was also nothing more than hearsay, he told me. After the publication of *Masquerades*, he said, anonymous letters started arriving at the publishing house, and they contained all kinds of more or less credible information about the author Jan Wechsler's dubious past life. He didn't pay much attention to it, von Dennen told me, but he did occasionally wonder whether there was anything to the allegations.

Of course I wanted to know more about this. Von Dennen was a bit hesitant. He asked me if I really wanted to hear about all that nonsense.

Of course, I said, reminding him about the authenticity of the experiment. You admit yourself that the allegations affected your image of me, I said. So I really need to know what was in the letters.

Fine, von Dennen relented. if you insist. One of the anonymous writers, for example, claimed that, during your university days, you infiltrated the left-wing student scene as a confidential informant for the Swiss intelligence service. That's a good example. I didn't find it all that odd that someone with a penchant for investigative journalism might also be employed as a spy.

I furrowed my brow, but I didn't want to stop von Dennen. That can't be all, I objected.

Von Dennen waved his hand: I shouldn't have mentioned it . . .

No, I'm glad you did, I assured him. Go on, I want to know everything.

The wildest claim, von Dennen continued, had to be the one about how, after you were done with the left-wing students, you began to sympathize with the extreme right. The letter named a dueling fraternity that you supposedly belonged to. Enclosed with the letter were clippings from Swiss far-right scandal sheets, which railed against the outrageous demands that the World Jewish Congress was making from Swiss banks, and which referred to Bronfman and Singer as hoodlums. The articles appeared under another name. But the letter writer claimed it was one of your pseudonyms.

Von Dennen leaned back and thought for a moment. You know, Jan, he said, I didn't find that notion so absurd, either. You brought up the same topic in *Masquerades*. Your tone was so strident that we argued about it for days. I couldn't have printed the original version of the manuscript. Of course I wondered why you were so vehement, throwing around phrases that wouldn't have been surprising if they had come from a right-wing parliamentary whip, but which were surprising coming from a poet.

Von Dennen waved to the waiter, ordered another coffee, and asked the way to the restroom. He excused himself, and for a few minutes I was left to my own devices.

These new disclosures made me sick to my stomach. Von Dennen also claimed that it was only after the release of *Masquerades* that I had left for Germany, from one day to the next, burning all my bridges. If that was true, then I couldn't possibly have worked as an editor at a German computer magazine in the mid-nineties. But that didn't necessarily mean that I hadn't engaged in journalistic pursuits. The anonymous letter writer had enclosed articles that were supposedly written by me. I had never even heard the name of the obscure paper in question. But I can't claim that the story didn't fit the image that was starting to take shape in my imagination.

The idea that I had once been a member of a dueling fraternity, on the other hand, struck me as completely absurd. I have a fear of violence and hate everything related to the military. I never even served. I was always horrified by the idea of some idiot ordering me around.

I refused to do my military service in 1988, when they wanted to send me to the border in Berlin. That's why I never published a single word in East Germany, and I never went to university. As a conscientious objector, I was *persona non grata*. My insubordination would have landed me in prison if my grandfather hadn't interceded on my behalf. His word still counted for something in the party apparatus, even after his retirement. I also assume his intervention was the reason I never had to "prove myself" through industrial labor, like my favorite poet Hilbig, who was forced to shovel coal as a boilerman until he left East Germany. I was allowed to do twenty night shifts a month as a custodian in a retirement home. And I earned more than an engineer. Some people viewed this absurd state of affairs as a sign of special appreciation of the working class. But to me, my wages often seemed like hush money: they would leave me alone as long as I kept my mouth shut.

Fables! I said to myself while von Dennen's words reverberated in my mind. Those are all untenable claims, if not flagrant lies. And the fact that I have not owned up to it is the only thing that makes me recalcitrant. The mention of the dueling fraternity was the most important piece of information that von Dennen provided. I only recently read Wechsler's first book. In the stories he told, I recognized the tales of my mother and great-grandmother, and I saw myself in his protagonist—Alexander Rottenstein. I was stunned by the attention to detail in Wechsler's narrative. I had noticed the parallels with my own life; I had paid less attention to the points of divergence.

According to the story, Alexander Rottenstein had joined a corps in Hamburg that stipulated two mandatory duels, both of which he fought enthusiastically. Wechsler described the rapiers, depicted the bout, known as the *Mensur*, and also the first dueling scar, a deep cut on the back of the head, which required stitches on the spot.

Von Dennen undoubtedly recognized me as his author. Consequently, Jan Wechsler's debut was just as much my work as *Masquerades* would be later. As a former corps member, it must have been easy for me to describe the dueling hall and the bout. Von Dennen must have thought the same thing when he read the anonymous letter.

So I am Jan Wechsler, the Swiss author and journalist with the checkered past on the fringes of the political spectrum. After my investigative coup, I fled from my own life. The life story I remember today is a fable that I constructed myself. In my first book, I fanned it out like a panorama of stories, and later, I adopted it as my own. My mother had to vanish from my life, because she knew that my claims were not even remotely true. I am living in a movie that I directed myself. Up until now, it's been a pleasant life. I have been spared from questions and attacks. I must have hoped that I would be able to sustain the fable until I believed in it myself and forgot my old life. Cultivating fables is complicated. You need a good memory. Otherwise, you're sunk.

When von Dennen came back to the table, he seemed to be calm, in a good mood, and completely trusting.

Now, he said, as he sat back down, it's your turn. What came over you that made you decide to become so religious?

The answer was on the tip of my tongue. Withdrawing into a small community where no one knew me, and keeping my contact with the non-Jewish world to a minimum, was the best way to protect my fable. But I didn't say that. Instead, I trotted out a reasonably plausible story about a spiritual awakening that moved me to choose the religious path. I can't remember all the things I told him. I could see that he was having trouble believing it. But he didn't argue with me.

Okay, out with it, he said finally. What's your new book going to be about?

Minsky, I said, and von Dennen's face turned red. I've gained a completely new perspective on the case, I hastened to add. But it was too late. Von Dennen grabbed his coat and his document case and stood up.

You really do have a screw loose! he roared. You're the last person in the world anyone's going to buy a "new perspective" from on the Minsky case, after all these years. I don't want to have anything more to do with this crap. What a ridiculous charade!

He threw a bill onto the table and walked out on me. He may still have held out hope for me when he came to Lindau. That was over now.

.

9

When I got home and walked into the courtyard, I heard a frantic flapping above my head. I stopped and looked up. A pigeon was flying back and forth between the walls. The rear courtyard of our building has a net stretched over it. If it weren't for that net, there would be birds all over the place. There's a restaurant on the ground floor. The garbage cans full of kitchen scraps are like a magnet, and the courtyard is so alluring to the pigeons that they can't stop tearing holes in the net. They manage to gain entry to paradise, but they can't find their way back out. They look around helplessly for a hole, and they rest on the sills of our windows that overlook the courtyard, coating them with a green-and-white patina.

Every now and then the pigeon catcher comes by, rounds up the prisoners, and plugs the holes in the net. But it's never very long before the net is torn again and another pigeon is flying around in paradise. When that happens, it isn't a good idea to open the windows. The urge for freedom makes the birds get bold. They'll even fly right into your apartment.

They peck at the windows, and their wings leave greasy streaks on the glass. You can get frightened out of your wits when you're walking down the hall, and suddenly there's a pigeon in front of you, cooing loudly and staring at you with those iridescent eyes.

Sometimes my daughter bangs on the window to get back at the birds when they scare her, and I have to hold her back.

But what am I supposed to tell her? Don't scare off the Tzaddik? It's not easy to explain something to a child that I took so long to learn myself.

My mother always called pigeons flying rats. When I came to Munich, I wasn't particularly fond of pigeons. I still don't like them, but now I am no longer able to reject them as casually as I once did.

One time a few years ago, I was standing on the street chatting with our mashgiach, and I scared off a pigeon. He immediately turned pale and rebuked me.

A pigeon that approaches us is the soul of a righteous person who is trying to call on us, he said. If you chase it away, you're rejecting a visit from a Tzaddik.

That was news to me. I looked at him incredulously; but he was serious.

The job of a mashgiach is not especially exciting, but it is occasionally bloody. A mashgiach is a guardian of souls. He supervises the kashrut of community institutions. He spends most of his time shuttling between retirement homes, restaurants, and butcher shops, one day he's here, the next day somewhere else. He goes into kitchens and inspects ingredients, he washes the lettuce and checks for bugs, he cracks each egg to make sure there are no blood spots, and he looks over the shoulders of the cooks. He keeps the key to the butcher's walk-in refrigerator and puts the seal of the rabbinate on the shrink-wrapped packages of meat and sausage before they're delivered.

Now and then, when chickens are being slaughtered, the mashgiach is called upon to oversee the draining of the blood. The souls of the birds leave their bodies along with the blood, and they continue to hover in the room as long as the blood is still flowing. It's only when the animal stops moving, and the blood is covered with sand, that the soul departs and you're allowed to pluck the chicken. The legs and wings have to be examined for fractures, and the tiny lungs have to be felt to make sure there are no lesions that could indicate previous illness. On days like those, the mashgiach has to work long hours alongside the shochet, who wields the knife.

At the major yeshivot around the world, the mashgichim don't just watch over the purity of food, but also over the spiritual development of the students. They are counselors, the people to go to when students have doubts, or if someone with an overgrown ego is causing problems. A job like that is a good fit for people who have dedicated themselves to the inexplicable laws of keeping kosher. You have to have an affinity for the spiritual if you're going to watch over rules that can't be justified scientifically, and which only become meaningful in a mystical dimension of obedience, humility, and mental purity.

Our mashgichim don't get to do that job. They just accompany the souls of chickens from the edge of the knife into the sphere of transition. They perform their service to our souls in obscurity. Most of them don't stay in this town very long, which is probably because that type of person can't survive for long in a spiritual desert.

It was surely no accident that the mashgiach who enlightened me about the souls of birds bore the name of an angel: Ariel. Everything I know about the Torah, Talmud, and Kabbalah, I learned from him. He moved on long ago, like the others. I was able to learn with him for two whole years. When he left, we lost contact. I don't even know where he lives now.

If he were here, I would confide in him. I'm sure he would sympathize, and maybe he would even have an explanation for my confused situation.

The souls of the righteous, Ariel once explained to me, don't leave the world as long as they are needed. When a Tzaddik dies, his soul passes into the body of a young dove. It waits there until someone with a suitable body is born. That's how the righteous return to Earth and continue their works.

As part of this theory, Ariel referred to a concept of the transmigration of souls mentioned in the secret books. *Gilgul Ha Neshamot* is a term you're not supposed to say out loud. If you only consider these ideas in passing, they seem too closely related to those of other peoples and religions. If you speculate about them, you run the risk of slipping into error. Maybe that's the reason mystics from every religion always seem to have one foot in the fire.

The wandering soul doesn't displace the soul of the dove or the newborn. Instead, the two souls intermingle during the transition. Ariel compared it to a candle flame that jumps to another wick. It's still fire, but it's no longer the same flame.

Some say it isn't only the righteous, and that all people return to earth many times, commingling with some other thing at the moment of transition, Ariel continued. But there are no guarantees about the outcome of these unions, he said. That portion that comes from someone or something else can be an aid or an obstacle on the road toward perfection that each person must travel.

At the time we didn't just talk about doves and pigeons, but also about sparrows. Ariel told me that many people see them as vessels that hold the souls of children who have been snatched from this life too early. Ariel claimed that, in the early forties the number of sparrows in Poland rose dramatically.

I shuddered, recalling a report I had once read about China's "Great Leap Forward." Mao Zedong blamed the sparrows for the country's famine—they were said to be stealing from the people because they ate grain seeds—so he launched a campaign to have them exterminated. Thousands were shot down out of the sky. To save ammunition, they soon switched to another tactic to hunt down the birds: all around the country, thousands of people came out with rattles, horns, and drums and made so much noise that the sparrows were afraid to land. They stayed up in the air and kept flying until they fell from the sky in exhaustion. Two billion sparrows were killed this way in 1957.

When I was a child, I told Ariel, the trees were full of sparrows, and they sat in clusters on the overhead streetcar wires. Now they've disappeared. I can't even remember the last time I saw a sparrow. It could be that there were more sparrows thirty years ago, Ariel said. But he told me it was more likely that the reason I didn't see them anymore was because I was no longer as close to them as I was when I was a child.

Ariel taught me the Brachot, the blessings, the first thing children learn. The concept of a king of the world, a king of kings, whom all kings serve, was foreign to me. So was waking up and thanking that king for giving me back my soul, which was supposed to have left me partially while I slept. It wasn't easy for me to give thanks—for every sip that I took, for every bite that I ate. Hadn't I paid for all of it with my own money?

Ariel told me that anything we buy is stolen if we enjoy it without a bracha. Talent comes from God, he said, our jobs come from him, the money, and everything I buy with it. It doesn't truly enter into my possession until I give thanks for it. That was difficult to accept. But Ariel insisted.

Everything, he said, begins with this small exercise in humility: saying thank you.

One Sunday, I ran into him on the subway. He was on his way to work.

I was surprised. You're working today? I asked.

Of course, he answered, quoting the Torah, *Sheshet yamim taavod . . .* Six days you shall labor, but the seventh day is a day of rest for the Lord your God.

I realized that, for years, I had worked almost without interruption. There were no days of rest for me, so there was no peace. Could I even afford to take a break like that? The idea of sacrificing a whole day each week so I could do nothing made me really nervous.

Who says it's doing nothing? Ariel asked, taken aback. You learn, you speak with Hashem, you sleep, go for a walk, talk to other people, and return to yourself. It's a full day, only without the car and the TV, the computer or the phone, no appointments or errands. Shabbos is an island in time where you can rest every seven days. You don't lose a second. For every moment you give, you get back twice that much during the week.

He saw a general principle in this: anything you give up consciously comes back to you as a gain, whether it's the donations you make to people in need, or the time you give to others. It's an exercise in letting go, Ariel told me. I only needed to try it.

Of course I immediately came up with a dozen reasons why I couldn't even make an attempt at it. Why I eventually did do it, I can't say. But I did it and stuck with it. On Shabbos afternoons, I would get together with Ariel. We would go walking by the Isar or sit at home, learning and drinking strong tea from the samovar. Keeping Shabbos wasn't a loss, but a gift.

At some point, Ariel got me a tzitzit shirt. He wore his tzitzit so you could see them. I didn't want to be that conspicuous. But he put my mind at ease.

You can wear them under your shirt, he said. No one but you will see them or even know they're there. But for you, they'll serve as a reminder throughout the day, a reminder of the Torah, and of what you can and can't eat.

Just as your body can't digest everything, your soul can't tolerate everything you stuff into it.

Given his profession, it was only logical that he would get around to this subject. I already felt bad if I was even tempted to go to an Italian or Chinese restaurant. I had realized one thing: one mitzvah leads to another. Once you've gotten used to saying a Bracha over everything you eat, you wouldn't even consider eating a pork chop anymore.

You also can't say a blessing if your head isn't covered. And so one day, I didn't take off my kippa when I went out onto the street. As unspectacular as that might seem, it was the most important turning point for me. For the first few days, it was a constant struggle with my own insecurity. In Israel, London, or New York, no one would have noticed me. But in Germany, a kippa is a signal. You're out of the ordinary, you don't fit into the picture. People stop, turn around and stare, sometimes they even talk to you. Usually they're friendly, but not always. I can't say how long it took before I stopped noticing the constant stares on the street. But it was a long time.

Ariel took note of all this without comment. In his eyes, I was just clearing up something that hadn't been sorted out before. At some point he asked me when I had last eaten treyf. I couldn't remember when or what it had been.

Then you're ready, he said. He gave me my first tefillin. Laying them on, he said, will be a bigger step than any of the others you've taken so far. But before he would show me how to do it, he said I needed to go to the mikvah, so I could affirm the transition to my new life symbolically, as well.

I agreed, and I made an appointment with Ariel for the next morning. He said the best time for the tevila was sunrise. He told me to come to the community center at dawn.

During the last night of my old life, I saw Ariel in a dream. I remember that he was taking me across a leaden river in a rotting rowboat. The sky above us was glowing. The only sound I could hear was the creaking of the planks under Ariel's feet and a scraping sound, as if the keel was dragging on the ground. When we reached the other side, we turned the boat around instead of getting out. This happened several times before I noticed that my ferryman had become tired and was leaning on the oar rather than pushing us forward. At some point one of his feet broke through the bottom of the boat. Water started to bubble up into the boat. Ariel let go of his oar. Our boat slowly began to sink. But we just sat there and said nothing. We went down quietly. Under water, I opened my eyes and was amazed. I could breathe, and all around was the garnet red of the sky, with just a few black and gray streaks across it.

As a mashgiach, Ariel often had to be the first person in the kitchen. He had the keys to the community center and knew his way around. The mikvah was in the basement, next to the boiler room. It was humid down there, and it smelled musty. The room was bathed in a dim yellow light. There was a steel handrail around the basin. I had a towel with me and the tefillin that Ariel had given me. In the next room, which was piled high with junk, I put my things on top of a worn out old chair. Then I took off my clothes.

Ariel had explained the procedure. When a person like me returns to Hashem and immerses in the mikvah, he told me, it's as if

I were standing with the ancestors at Mount Sinai at the moment when they received the Torah. Everything that had gone before would no longer apply, he said. I would emerge from the water as a new man.

Over the past few months, while we were studying the laws that deal with conversions, Ariel had returned to the subject of the transmigration of souls. When a stranger enters into the covenant, he takes a new name during the tevila. He also receives a new patronymic and matronymic. The ribbon that binds the generations is cut, and a new one is tied. Changing your name alters your destiny, your future, and your past. The wise men took the view that a soul waiting to return to Earth can pass into a new body not only during a birth, but also during the tevila of a convert. In a sense, Ariel said, that also applies to a person who is returning to Hashem.

I, too, had to pick a name that I could add to my previous one when I went in the water. I decided on Arieh—lion—and Ariel added the Yiddish equivalent, Leyb. What prayer it was that my friend whispered in my ear as I descended the seven steps, he never told me. When I dipped one foot in the water, I was overcome by fear. I believed that two lions were waiting for me in the water, and I wasn't sure whether I was ever going to surface again, or they were going to tear me apart under water.

I am experienced at giving up one life for another. On that point, there's a connection between Wechsler's story and my memories.

I stood in the courtyard for a while watching the pigeon's desperate attempts to escape. Then I went upstairs. When I was hanging up my coat, I saw the pigeon on the windowsill.

What should I do? I heard myself asking. I bent down and looked deep into its stark, yellow-spotted eyes, which seemed to be sizing me up. The pigeon cooed, flapped its wings, and flew away.

If you want to recover something, I thought, you have to go back to the place where you lost it. The word *Berndeutsch* had been enough to remind me where my mother lives. Maybe, I thought, the rest of my lost memories would resurface if I went back to Israel. Whatever it was that had washed them away, it must have happened in Israel, where I went late last year for the first time.

I went online and booked a ticket for the next available flight to Israel. Now, two days later, I'm on an El Al plane on my way to Tel Aviv. I'm traveling light. The only thing I have with me is the pilot suitcase—with everything that was in it when Molina carried it through my door and put it down in my apartment. Since the suitcase no longer shuts properly, I had to put a belt around it to keep it closed. Just like in the old days, I didn't check the suitcase; I rolled it onto the plane as a carry-on. It's under the seat in front of me. I can open it any time if I want to read through any of the books or take out any of the other objects, so I can examine them and try to recall what they're supposed to remind me of.

We're flying high above thick cloud cover. This plane could be going anywhere. I can't say where it's taking me.

I have felt this lost once before. It was about eighteen years ago. In 1990, at a travel agency in East Berlin, I booked my first ticket to Israel and paid for it with East German marks. It was a one-way ticket from Berlin-Schönefeld to Tel Aviv, booked four months in advance for July 6th, 1990, my birthday. I didn't tell anyone about it.

The experience of those few hours of exile on the banks of the Spree in Kreuzberg was still fresh in my mind. Perhaps I thought that now I could consciously say farewell to the Small Country. Everything was going to change. That had become clear to everyone. In some parts of the city, the wall was already being torn down. Helmut Kohl was touring the country, basking in the cheers from the crowds, which had changed from *We are the people!* to *We are one people!* That struck me as an overt threat. The intellectuals who had brought about the changes quickly left the stage. No one was interested in their utopian visions of progressive change in the Small Country. Most people had opted to join the ant columns and were stockpiling goods from the West. Everyone was talking about freedom, and by that they seemed to mean the colorful bills of the West German mark.

I left the Rykestraße synagogue behind. That place had too many unpleasant memories associated with it. I felt more comfortable at the synagogue on the Fraenkelufer in Kreuzberg. I didn't realize how little I knew and how skewed my image of the Jewish world was until I found that congregation, where I was able to at least get close to the kind of normality that I'd always hoped for.

Nevertheless, I believed that it was only in Israel that I would really be able to find out who I was, what my feelings about religion were, and which path I should take. So I started looking for a kibbutz that wasn't too socialist in its orientation, where I could learn Ivrit. At the time, my Hebrew vocabulary was limited to what was in the prayer book, and the grammar I had learned was the grammar of the Torah and the liturgical poems. I was told that nobody spoke that way anymore.

I gave myself four months to pull up stakes in Berlin. My plan was to sell whatever I could—it wasn't much anyway—and start my new life with just one suitcase. The country I had always considered my homeland was about to be dissolved. There was no way to avoid a life in exile, that's how melodramatically I viewed the situation. So I at least wanted to choose the country I was going to live in.

I never used the ticket. I agonized over the decision almost up until the last day. Even on the morning of June 6th, 1990, I looked at the clock and realized that I could still make the flight, if only I wanted to. But I stayed home, and the plane took off without me.

Since I hadn't told anybody about my plans, I didn't have to explain why I had chickened out. But in my own mind, I called my cowardice what it was. The excuse I came up with was that an author who emigrates from the country of his native language runs the risk of permanently losing his voice as an artist. I took it for granted that I was an author. I thought I was talented. I hadn't managed to get anything published, but I attributed that solely to the political conditions. Leaving the country of my mother tongue seemed like a betrayal of my talent. I couldn't imagine ever being able to express myself in another language the way I could in German.

The image on the monitor in front of me claims that we are over the Mediterranean. When I look out the window, I still can't see anything other than thick clouds. The sun is going down. The image on the screen, which shows our speed and estimated time of arrival, could be a trick, as could the captain's announcement that we're about to begin our descent. I feel like I'm floating through nothingness in a steel tube.

I pull the suitcase out from under the seat in front of me, un-buckle the belt, and look around for Hans Macht's book about the Minsky case. I just remembered a passage from it that's related to where I'm going.

Right after *Days of Ashes* came out, the BBC produced a docu-mentary about Minsky. The camera crew accompanied him not only to Minsk, Majdanek, and Auschwitz, but also to Jerusalem, where he visited the digital archives at the Yad Vashem memorial to look for traces of his origins. Macht gives an account of the filming and talks about the reactions when the documentary was shown on Israeli television.

There's one story I remember vividly, even though I only skimmed through Macht's book when I was on that little train to Sentier-Orient. A woman who had seen the documentary in Israel called the TV station, claiming that she recognized Minsky as the son of her sister, who was lost at Majdanek. The family had always thought the boy died along with his mother, she told them. Her brother-in-law, who was the only member of the family to make it back from the camps, never got over the loss of his wife and child, she said, and he did not remarry until much later. She said her brother's name was Yaakov Gelernter, and that he lived with his second family in Bnei Brak. She told the people at the TV station that they absolutely had to inform Minsky.

Minsky and Gelernter talked on the phone. Gelernter read him a letter that he had written to his presumably dead son more than thirty years before, explaining his decision to get married again. *I will never forget you, my darling baby. But if I remain alone, I won't have lived when I reach the end of my days, just as you and Mameh weren't allowed to live. Then we would all have died in Poland, and I don't want that. You understand, don't you?*

Gelernter had been carrying this letter with him ever since. Now, fifty years after he had given up his son for lost, he read the letter to Minsky.

I know, Minsky said. Tateh, I understand everything.

The BBC crew was deeply moved by this development. They decided to produce a second installment of the documentary, so viewers wouldn't miss out on this poignant story of a father and son reunited after a half-century.

They interviewed Gelernter at his house in Bnei Brak. With tears in his eyes, he told them about his first telephone conversation with Minsky: After so many years, I heard my child, he said . . . but he didn't get any further than that, because he choked up.

A member of the film crew suggested that they should get Minsky and Gelernter to take a DNA test. The cameras were rolling at a hospital in Israel as Gelernter pulled up the left sleeve of his white shirt for the blood draw, so the doctors could provide him with the proof of his paternity, which he was already convinced of, anyway. Meanwhile in Zurich, Minsky proclaimed to the cameras that he had done the same and would set off for Israel right away to celebrate the reunion with his new, old family.

When Minsky arrived at Ben Gurion Airport, it wasn't just Gelernter, his second wife, and all their children and grandchildren who were waiting to receive him, but also several camera teams, journalists, and photographers who wanted to capture the moment. The entourage accompanied the convoy of taxis that took the father and son to the hospital, so they could view the blood test results together.

The test was negative. The doctor said there was no room for doubt. Minsky and Gelernter were not related. This revelation only inflamed the throng of reporters all the more. The flurry of camera flashes wouldn't stop. The microphones stretched out toward Minsky.

What do you have to say about the results, Mr. Minsky? Are you disappointed, Mr. Minsky? What are you going to do now, Mr. Minsky?

The important thing, he whispered, is that we've met. We were in the same situation, in the same places, and now we've learned that we have so many of the same memories from that time. It's an extremely powerful feeling, not only of solidarity, but that we belong together. That's more important than biology. What matters is human emotion. Yaakov was looking for his son, and I was looking for my father. He was prepared to accept me, and that's a wonderful confluence of events.

A few days later, the BBC also interviewed Gelernter again. He said he was completely convinced that Misnky was his son. Because of him, he had felt a father's true, deep love for the first time. For years, Gelernter said, Minsky had been trying to reconstruct the image of his mother, but it had never occurred to him that he had also had a father. And now he was experiencing this miracle.

The journalists didn't let up, insisting that the test had conclusively proven the opposite.

The opposite of what? Gelernter asked. Miracles don't care about medical tests, he said. He had brought the case to a rabbinical court, and the rabbonim had reached the unanimous conclusion that the two were father and son. Only his love as a father and the judgment of the rabbonim were relevant for him.

I must have fallen asleep. I am startled awake by a gong and the announcement, *Cabin crew, all doors in park.* I don't know where I am. On the seat next to me, there's a black pilot suitcase. But I can't find the book I was just reading. The belt I had looped around my suitcase is also gone.

I have to get off the plane. I stand up, feeling dazed, and I look in the overhead compartment for my coat. But it's not there, and suddenly I'm not sure whether I even had a coat with me when I boarded the plane in Munich. So I take the suitcase and line up with the other passengers to get off.

I take a number of escalators and go through several winding corridors and empty halls before I end up in a vast crowd of people waiting to have their passports inspected. It seems that I don't understand the local etiquette for how people are supposed to line up. After more than an hour, the hall is nearly empty, but I'm still waiting. All of the people who arrived along with me are gone.

When I get up to the counter, I can see my reflection in the window, and I am startled. I'm not wearing a kippa or a hat. My hair is blond and frizzy. In a panic, I reach for my passport in the inside pocket of my jacket. It's still there.

By the time I realize that it has a white cross on the front instead of the German eagle, I've already pushed the passport halfway through the slot under the window, and the agent is already reaching for it. It's too late to do anything now. Whatever's going to happen, I just have to let it happen.

The agent compares me with my picture, flips through the pages with the visas and the entry and exit stamps, and doesn't seem to find anything suspicious. She stamps the temporary residence permit into my passport and passes it back to me. Everything seems to be in order.

She tells me to move along, I pass through a final set of doors, and I end up in the arrivals area. The first thing I notice is that there are several camera teams and journalists carrying notepads and audio recorders. When they see me, they start calling out things I can't understand in different languages. The crowd begins to move.

Suddenly I recall the image of Valparaíso harbor overflowing with people. I'm standing at the railing of a ship that's entering the harbor, and I'm looking around. But there's no Gabriela. I'm the one who's returning home from exile. The people are waiting for me. They will cheer for me when I come ashore.

I have to wave and say a few words of great significance, I think to myself. But then I am nearly trampled by the horde of journalists. Behind me I can hear the cameras clicking and the agitated reporters asking a wild tangle of questions. When I turn around, a wave of shame, rage, and hatred washes over me. Standing in the center of a family of Hasidim is Minsky, and he's embracing an old man so fervently that his hat falls on the floor. The cameras keep on rolling, documenting every single tear they shed.

This is not my homecoming from exile. And I am not the son who has been found again. For the second time, Minsky has stolen the spotlight from me with his melodrama. My book was never translated. Nobody here even knows my name.

The gong rings again, and I wake up. The captain tells the crew to prepare for landing. It's gotten dark outside. The sea is black below us. Ahead of us, I can see the lights of Tel Aviv.

Macht's book is on my lap. I put it back in my suitcase, buckle the belt back around it, and slide it under the seat.

I think of the pigeon that was flapping around in our courtyard when I came back from Lindau with the incontrovertible truth about my life story. The bird must have known something I didn't know. I have already landed at this airport twice before. My first trip wasn't six months ago, but twelve years ago. And my first arrival here was a disaster.

I saw almost nothing of the country during that visit. For days, until my flight home, I shut myself away in a hotel room in Netanya and stared at the sea, unable to think of anything but Minsky's weak little book and how it was making everyone lose their minds.

He's not an author, he's an actor, I told myself. I couldn't understand why I was the only one who could see the obvious. I decided then and there that I was going to shoot him down. Unapologetically, and mercilessly. Just as mercilessly as he had shot me down.

From that day on, all my writing came from a place of rage, and when that rage was all used up, I had nothing more to say. It must have something to do with this country. The first time I arrived, it robbed me of my hope. During my second visit, I lost my memory, and now I don't know who I am anymore. If I walk into the arrival hall at Ben Gurion Airport a third time, I don't even dare to imagine what awaits me.

It's too late to turn around. I've let all the other passengers get off the plane. I can't put off my arrival any longer. I have to take my hat, my coat, and the suitcase, and get off.

I know the way, and I walk quickly through the corridors to the exit. I pass the baggage claim and go through customs. Just before I enter the hall where passport inspection is, I pass a mirror on the wall. I hazard a quick look, and I feel reassured. I recognize myself. There's no mop of blond curls peeping out from under my hat.

But once again, I can't manage to get to the window without being pushed aside by a hundred other people who are waiting. At least a half an hour goes by before I get a chance to show my German passport. Once again it's a surly Israeli woman in uniform who inspects my documents. She flips through the passport in both directions, gives all the visas and stamps a thorough check, then types my name and passport number into her terminal.

Rega! she orders. Wait a moment! Then she stands up, leaves her booth, and disappears with my passport. When she comes back after a few minutes, she looks me over with undisguised disapproval. Still, she puts a stamp on the last page, slides the passport back through the slot, and waves to the next person in line to step up.

I feel relieved. When I get to the arrivals area, there are no journalists waiting. Nobody notices me, which I now find reassuring. I head right over to the ATM, take out five hundred shekels and go the exit to look for a sherut that will take me to Jerusalem. When I get outside and start looking for my cigarettes, someone speaks to me from behind.

Slicha Adoni, a deep male voice says. Are you Mr. Wechsler? Startled, I turn around and find myself standing face-to-face with a stocky, gray-haired man with a clipped beard and black crocheted kippa, who just about comes up to my chest. Speaking fluent American English, he introduces himself as Gavriel Ben-Or, *Mishteret Yisrael*.

Is there a problem? I ask, suddenly feeling like I'm in a car with failing brakes, speeding toward a wall. The last time a policeman stopped me was twenty years ago. And even that memory—my visit to the library at the American embassy in East Berlin—is now questionable.

Don't worry, Mr. Wechsler, Ben-Or says. I'd just like to ask you a few questions. In a few minutes, you'll be on your way.

He delicately reaches for my arm and leads me back inside. Ben-Or seems very calm. As we walk across the hall, he asks me if I had a pleasant flight.

I nod. The feeling that the brakes are failing is still with me.

10

I hate inspections. I can't even get through the predictable subway ticket checks during the first few days of every month without my heart starting to race, and the adrenaline rush leaves me jittery even several minutes later. It's not that I have a guilty conscience. It's more that I'm afraid of getting caught in an inadvertent slip-up, or having to justify misconduct that I can't explain.

It's not like I make a habit of fare evasion. But when the inspectors get on the train just before the doors close, and they whip out their badges and demand to see people's tickets, I start to panic. What if I forgot to get a new monthly pass, or I left my briefcase at home, and I can't show them my ticket? When I have these recurring thoughts, the threat of being fined scares me less than the embarrassment you have to endure when you get caught and have to submit to the whole procedure where they take down your personal information in front of everyone.

The interviews you have to go through when you're waiting in line to check in at Ben Gurion Airport are similarly unpleasant. A small army of psychologically trained airport employees in plain-clothes ask every departing traveler a number of questions. Their objective is to make people anxious, so they can find out if anyone is traveling with false documents, or perhaps even attempting to commit an act of terrorism. The interviewers don't really care what your grandmother's name is, whether she was the one who taught you the *aleph bet*, and when that was. They also immediately forget the name of your synagogue at home, the ages of your children, and the year you started school. But they keep a very close eye on how people behave. They take note of whether, and how long, a person hesitates before answering questions, and whether a person reacts reluctantly, or even aggressively. And you don't have a choice: you're not allowed to proceed to the baggage check-in until you've convinced the interviewer that you have nothing to hide, and you're really the person your passport says you are.

I'm familiar with the procedure. I know it's necessary, in the interest of security. Still, the questions drive me crazy. "Why is that any of *your* business?" is what goes through my mind at the first indiscrete question. I'm always tempted to say nothing, and I have to force myself to answer. Of course they notice my displeasure and the stress that all their questions are causing me. So my interviews always end up being especially detailed, and the "selectors" purposely take things to extremes, to make sure that I'm not really dangerous, just odd in a very ordinary sort of way.

The fear that an unanticipated inspection will reveal an unwittingly or carefully hidden sin has been with me since childhood. When I was seven or eight years old, I stole an eraser from a stationery store, just because I was feeling cocky. I put it in my pocket and walked out of the store nonchalantly, and I didn't get caught. But when I got home, I didn't dare use it, or even take it out of my coat pocket. If my mother had found the eraser and asked me where I had gotten it, I would have broken down immediately under questioning. She wouldn't have spared me the embarrassment of having to bring the stolen goods back to the store and apologize; and the embarrassment of a public confession seemed far worse than what I imagined a prison term with bread and water would be like.

Walking through the airport with Ben-Or, I expect the kind of unpleasant but routine questioning that I already know from the Israeli security forces. I've never heard of arriving passengers being picked out of the crowd at the exit. But what do I know about this crazy country?

Where are we going? I ask my escort.

It's just a short walk, he reassures me. My colleagues from customs have made a room available.

I've also never heard of criminal investigators from the police department assisting in routine checks at the airport. For a moment, I am tempted to ask Ben-Or if this is normal. But I decide to keep quiet, so that I don't start out with an impertinent question and make the situation even more complicated for myself than it already is.

The entrance to the office wing, which is located at the other end of the arrivals area, is unremarkable. Ben-Or opens the door with an electronic badge, holds the door for me, and then takes me down a long hallway and into an office. The room is empty, except for a desk and an old chair. The desk has an olive green blotter on it and is piled high with forms that have been filled out by hand. On the wall there's a military-looking emblem that I'm not familiar with. I can't make out the stylized abbreviation on it. If I have to stand up while Ben-Or asks his questions, this interrogation won't take long, I think to myself. But then he points to another door, which he also unlocks with his badge, before he asks me to go into the examination room.

This room is also bare and small, hardly bigger than two-and-a-half by four meters. The ceiling is bright white, and the walls are painted lime-green. The paint has started to crack and peel off in some places. In the middle of the room, there's a camping table with a plastic chair on each side. A fluorescent tube is buzzing above the table. There are no windows, just ceiling vents with cool air blowing in through them. In the middle of the table, there's a microphone on a tripod, and next to that a mini cassette recorder, the kind the reporters were carrying on straps over their shoulders when they almost trampled me the first time I arrived here.

Ben-Or asks me to take a seat in front of the microphone. He tells me he has to go get something and will be back in a minute. The door closes, but I don't hear a lock click. I think about whether I should just slip out of there. I don't see any cameras, and there isn't a two-way mirror, either. But I suspect that this moment I'm spending alone is already part of the interrogation. Even if I'm not being watched, Ben-Or could be in the office next door, waiting to see if I'm going to make a move. I don't want to show that kind of weakness. So I set the suitcase aside, lay my coat over it, and sit down.

Ben-Or actually does come back quickly—with a pad of paper and a freshly-sharpened green pencil. He takes off his jacket and hangs it over his chair. The he sits down and meticulously arranges his pad and pencil in front of him. The pencil point is aimed at me.

We don't need the microphone, Ben-Or says, pushing it aside. Then he asks me for my passport. I open it up and slide it across the table. Ben-Or has to stand up to reach it. Just like the agent at passport inspection, he also studies my personal information and looks over each individual exit and entry stamp on the back pages. When he gets to the page where my children are listed, he smiles. Then he thumbs back through the passport and raises his eyes.

What is your name? he asks.

Jan Wechsler, I answer without hesitating, even though the first thing that goes through my head is that this is a dull way to start things off. I assume that he's just reeling off the usual mandatory questions. I guess that should make me feel better.

What is your Jewish name?

The answer to that question is not in my passport. I could give him any name.

Do I have to answer that?

Yes, Ben-Or replies.

I don't know if that's true. But if I want to get out of here quickly, I have to restrain my urge to be difficult and answer his questions without showing any emotion.

Yonah Arieh Leyb ben Dan, I say.

Where and when were you born?

This is dangerous. If I hadn't confirmed just a few days ago that Ramat Gan is listed as the place of birth on all my documents, I would have gotten myself in trouble by answering: Berlin.

So I say: Ramat Gan, June 6th, 1965, a Sunday.

What is the Jewish date of your birthday?

7 Sivan 5725.

Ben-Or maintains his poker face. Where do you live? he continues.

In Germany, I reply, giving him my full address.

What was the starting point of your current trip?

I like this question. It has an almost philosophical dimension. But I'm afraid that Ben-Or prefers direct, clear answers. So I tell him that I started off in Munich and that I went straight from home to the airport without stopping anywhere.

Does this suitcase belong to you? Ben-Or asks. He points to the pilot suitcase underneath my coat, and I'm sure it doesn't escape him that the word "yes" doesn't roll off my tongue quickly.

Did you pack it yourself?

Yes, I continue fibbing. It may be risky, but I can't possibly tell him the truth, which is that the suitcase belongs to me about as much as most of the things inside of it do.

Did anyone give you anything to carry?

No, I say, and I feel relieved to be out of the gray area concerning the ownership of my baggage.

Good. Ben-Or closes the passport and places it next to his pad, arranging it just as meticulously. After a brief pause, he continues to go down the list of the usual questions.

Is the purpose of your visit to Israel business or personal?

Personal, I reply.

And how long do you plan to stay?

I haven't really thought about it. I booked a flight back in a week, but I haven't confirmed it. It could be two weeks, depending.

Depending? Ben-Or leans back. Depending on what? he wants to know.

It depends on how much time I need to get things done here, and when there are seats available.

That was an inept answer. It leaves room for interpretation. But it doesn't seem to bother Ben-Or. He doesn't ask me to elaborate, anyway. Instead, he asks me if I have relatives or friends in Israel.

No, I say.

Where are you going to stay, then?

In Jerusalem, at the Little House in Bakah.

Ah, Ben-Or says, I know that place, it's a nice hotel. Do you have a reservation you could show me?

No, I reply.

So how can you be sure that you'll be able to get a room there?

I'm not sure. I've been there once before. I liked it. I'm just going to give it a try.

By all means, he says. But since you're not sure, you can't provide an address for the duration of your stay. Is that correct?

That's correct.

Why didn't you reserve a room? Ben-Or asks. I clear my throat.

I . . . planned my trip on the spur of the moment, and I only took care of the flight. I don't think it'll be too difficult to find a place to stay in Jerusalem. The Little House is just my first choice, you know?

Yes, of course, he says, trying to reassure me. We must be just about done at this point, I try to persuade myself. But Ben-Or continues without missing a beat.

This is the second time you've been to Israel in six months, he declares. Last time you were in the country for a week, from January 1st until the 7th, 2008.

There's no follow-up question. Ben-Or just looks at me intently. He reaches for his pencil and stands it up vertically. The tip of the pencil is pointed upward.

I'm beginning to feel wary. It's clear from his statement that he didn't pull me out of the crowd randomly. The top page of his pad is blank. So far, Ben-Or hasn't taken any notes. But he's prepared for this conversation, and I'm not. Or maybe he just has a good memory and made a mental note of the dates on the stamps as he went through my passport. He could be testing me to see whether I actually made the trips that are noted there. I confirm the dates for him. But I don't get a chance to catch my breath.

Was the purpose of that trip . . . *personal*? he continues.

Yes, just personal!

And the thing you had *to do* during that trip was the same thing you're planning to do on your current visit?

I don't like this sudden change in tone when he repeats my words back to me. I may not be able to remember every detail of my last trip, but whatever I did, I'm certain it must have been harmless. Ben-Or is not so sure. He thumps on the table with the blunt end of the pencil, lets it slip through his fingers, then turns it around and finally jots something down on his pad. He writes in English, slowly and in big letters, so I can see what he's putting down. It's the date of the last time I left the country: *January 7ᵗʰ, 2008*. He puts an exclamation point after it.

I still remember quite well why I came to Israel last time. I had claimed that it was my first visit to the country after I had allowed my one-way ticket to the kibbutz to lapse eighteen years before. I wanted to have a look around and get a feeling for the country, the people, and the language. The idea was to make a tentative approach, and I hoped that my prejudices would vanish into thin air, and I would feel comfortable in this country that I had steered clear of for so long.

That's how I had explained it to my wife. I came up with another story for my friends and acquaintances, organizing my short trip in such a way that it would seem like I was following a rigorous schedule. I pretended that I was going to Israel to take a tour of historic mikvaot. My interest was genuine. Ever since my tevila at the rundown mikvah in the basement of the old community center on Reichenbachstraße, I hadn't been able to shake the idea of a transition to a new life through the mikvah.

Stories from the *Zohar* and from Luria's *Gates of Reincarnation* wandered through my mind like ghosts. You can't wash yourself clean of shame and disgrace. But if the mikvah is a gateway to another life, then there is a way out—the possibility of getting away from the memory of your own mistakes. That may sound like a kind of escape. But that's not the way I see it, because the life that awaits you when you come out of the water is also full of challenges. They're just different challenges, and the traps you walk into are different, as well.

The feeling of liberation I had when I emerged from the mikvah on Reichenbachstraße was powerful. And yet, I felt like I still hadn't made it to the one true life that was intended for me. And so I wanted to go further. I had my mind set on finding a mikvah that was almost overflowing with memories and inspirations from other souls. I wanted to go through a gate of reincarnation. But I would have to choose carefully if I was going to make it to the place where I belonged.

I went to Cologne and Worms and visited their medieval mikvaot. I was hopeful, but I came away disappointed. What I was looking for can't be found in a museum.

I expected more from a trip to Israel. I imagined a mikvah in a natural setting, preferably fed by a spring and at least old enough that you could trace its history back to the time of the Second Temple. I had friends ask their friends, and I got a few phone numbers and addresses. When I started on my way, I felt upbeat about finding a suitable gateway.

I decide to tell Ben-Or about my passion for mikvaot. And leave out the real motives for my trip. It's a hobby, nothing more, I tell him. Whether he believes me or is even interested in my story, I can't say. His face seems almost immobile. Every now and then he blinks. Otherwise, he looks into my eyes calmly and intently, and he watches my hands.

So, because of this *hobby*, he continues, you spontaneously dropped everything at home to stay here for an indeterminate amount of time? Is that correct?

There it is again, that odd emphasis when Ben-Or repeats my words, a syncopation in the middle of the sentence, as if he were indulging himself by making a joke, or trying to let me know that he thinks my statement is a joke. The next thing he's going to ask is what work it is that I do that gives me such freedom. I'd rather beat him to the punch.

I'm a publisher, I tell him, and the owner of a small literary house in Munich. The information I'm gathering is essential for a book by one of my authors.

I finally see some movement in my counterpart's face. He puts the pencil down on top of his pad, leans back, and clasps his hands in front of his chest. I think I even detect a faint, satisfied smile on his lips, a tiny moment of thawing.

That's interesting, Mr. Wechsler, very interesting. I also read novels occasionally. Putting out books must be a fascinating job.

Yes, it is, I reply. And now I'm smiling.

Yes, Ben-Or says, I believe it. Then he sits up straight at the table again, reaches for the pencil, and while he's writing down the word *publisher*, without even looking up at me, he adds: That's a *profession*, Mr. Wechsler. So it seems to me that both your trip to Israel in January and your current visit are of a *professional* nature.

He stretches out the word *professional* as if he were sounding out the syllables, while he notes it down like a quibbler.

If you want to look at it like that . . . I retort irritably. Ben-Or still doesn't look up. He's correcting this and that letter in the word *publisher* and murmuring, as if his words weren't intended for me: I have to advise you that the statements you make must be truthful.

I didn't know details like those mattered, I say, attempting an apology, but I'm sure I still sound irritated. Now Ben-Or looks up, scratches his temple with the pencil, and responds, this time clearly and directed at me.

Nine times out of ten it's the details that matter most, he says. Being a man of the written word, you must know that. So I would ask you to be precise in your answers from now on.

I feel like I've been caught red-handed, and I nod in shame.

Good, Ben-Or says. Obviously sensing that I'm on the defensive, he ups the ante: So you're in Israel on business, looking for information?

This can't be happening! I think to myself. Suddenly, I get that subway-ticket-inspection feeling. What is he getting at by phrasing it that way?

I'm visiting mikvaot, Adon Ben-Or! I reply, my voice shaking slightly as I struggle to regain my composure. Surely you don't consider that espionage!

You're the one who brought up the word "espionage," Mr. Wechsler.

I'm doing research for a book! I protest.

You've already said that, he says, and he asks me what kind of book it is.

A novel.

A project of one of your authors?

Exactly.

What's this novel about? he asks.

I . . . I don't exactly know yet, I have to admit. Ben-Or puts the pencil in the breast pocket of his shirt with the point sticking out, and he rubs his forehead. Then there's a pause. I'm on pins and needles. My palms are sweaty. I'd like to wash my hands, but this is certainly not the right moment to ask Ben-Or for a break.

He resumes his questioning: Isn't it unusual for you, as a publisher, to do research for an author's project, a novel that you don't even have a vague notion about yet?

I am too flustered to talk my way out of that one. So I agree. He takes note of this impassively. Then he asks which places I plan to visit, and he takes the pencil out of his pocket and puts the point to the paper so he can take down the locations of my planned research.

Jerusalem, I say. Ben-Or makes a note of it. I continue the list with Masada, and Ben-Or writes that down. Motza, I add. When he hears that name, he pauses for a moment.

Why Motza? he asks.

I stop short. The name had slipped my mind. But now that Ben-Or is specifically asking about it, I can picture the stop I made on my last trip.

Actually, it's not right in Motza, I say. It's a grove nearby. There's a stone mikvah there that's more than two thousand years old, it has three pools that are arranged like steps, right next to a spring. I was there at night, on the second-to-last day of my trip. It was a place with an unbelievable atmosphere. The mikvah drew me in like a magnet, and the water was so miserably cold that, when I was standing in it, I felt like I was being pricked by a thousand needles.

Ben-Or is listening attentively to me. Since I have finally started to talk willingly and coherently, he asks me to tell him about the results of my research in Jerusalem and Masada. I have the feeling that I'm getting back onto solid ground, and the situation between us is beginning to ease. So I tell him what I can remember. And the more I tell him, the more details come back to me. I am happy to be able to talk instead of having to answer questions, so I run down the list of all the places I visited six months ago, mikvah by mikvah.

My tour started in Jerusalem. I spent two days meandering around the Old City and walking along the outside of the ancient city wall, looking at the innumerable mikvaot from the era of the Temple. They're built along the wall like caves in the earth and are unusable. The mikvah pools were empty, and some of the caves had decomposed to the point that they were no longer sound, or they had collapsed altogether. Not all of them were cordoned off, but there were signs warning people not to enter.

To get to Masada, I took a bus through the Judean desert, passing by the oasis of Ein Gedi and Ein Gedi Beach, which is on the Dead Sea and has an apocalyptic feeling to it. The trip took two hours. The other passengers were tourists, soldiers, and Arab goatherds, who tied their goats to stakes and left them at the bus stop.

Masada is a cliff fortress in the Judean desert. The fortifications are on a rock plateau about 450 meters above the Dead Sea. I didn't try to prove my physical prowess by going up on foot. When I reached the top on the cable car, I met a group of young men who had taken the steep, narrow path up to the plateau. And I got the impression that it was going to take them a while to recover from the climb.

The panoramic view from the plateau is breathtaking. Unfortunately, it was a bit hazy, so it was hard to get a good view of the Dead Sea. Still, I could have spent the whole day looking at the cliffs all around.

Masada is a place full of history and stories. The fortress built by Herod, King of Judea, was the last bastion of Jewish resistance against the Romans. The most well-known story comes from Josephus Flavius's account of the last days of the Zealots of Masada, whose defeat sealed the fate of the Kingdom of Judea.

According to Josephus Flavius, the rebels refused to surrender. They swore that they would sooner die by their own hands. But because they considered suicide dishonorable, they decided to write their names on shards of pottery. They drew lots to determine who would have the task of killing a certain number of their fellow rebels. The drawing was repeated until there were only ten men left. They drew lots again to decide which man would kill the rest, and then himself. Thus only one man had to bear the burden of suicide.

The fortress faded into obscurity. It wasn't until the 1960s that the buried fortifications were excavated, by a team of archaeologists from the Hebrew University, led by Yigal Yadin. When he began his scientific career, he had already spent years as a military officer. He had risen to the level of chief of staff when he retired from the service and devoted his attention to science.

When his team got to Masada, they didn't just find well-preserved textile remains and baskets. Yadin also presented the public with the sensational discovery of several ostraca with names on them. He proclaimed that these pottery shards were the lots that the rebels had drawn during the siege, saying this conclusively proved the veracity of Josephus Flavius's account, which had been challenged again and again.

Mostly due to the strength of that reputable evidence, the myth of Zealot resistance at Masada once again gained tremendous power. Ever since the excavation, the Tzahal's yearly graduation maneuvers after basic training have ended with the ceremonial swearing-in of new recruits on the cliff plateau. "Masada must never fall again!" is the message to the soldiers.

When it came to the Mikvah, however, Masada was a failure. The only thing I could find was a dried-out, shallow hole full of rubble. In the fortress museum, on the other hand, I came across an incredible story: While Yigal Yadin was still alive, some historians had cast doubt on the authenticity of the ostraca. And in the end, those historians managed to prove beyond a doubt that they were forgeries. A national myth and the swearing-in ceremony of a whole army were based on a hoax.

You can still see photos of the phony ostraca at the fortress museum. I had heard about the myth a long time before. The false discovery had bolstered it, and the revelation that it was a hoax did nothing to damage the myth. I took that as proof that the written word, even when it's centuries old, is more powerful than any scientific evidence—or lack of evidence. The story that people tell is what counts in the end.

Ben-Or has been listening to me attentively. I think I can even detect a little excitement on his face. He tells me that he was also sworn in at Masada, and that he's seen the original—fake—ostraca. It never would have occurred to him or any of his colleagues back then that they might not be real, he says. When the news of the fraud came out, there was an outcry, he tells me. But people quickly forgot that one unpleasant detail in the great story.

Ben-Or goes on to say that he's impressed by how enthusiastic I am when I talk about my research topic. He asks me whether I've also been to the Arizal mikvah in Sfad.

No, I reply. I didn't have enough time for a day-trip to the far North.

Are you planning to go to Sfad this time?

I don't know, I say. I don't think I'm going to make it.

Ben-Or is playing with his pencil. He's tapping the table with it as if he were sending Morse code. Maybe it's the rhythm from a military march that came back to him when we started talking about Masada. In any event, the tapping seems like an attack to me. And sure enough, my counterpart returns to the subject of the interrogation.

You know, Mr. Wechsler, he says, putting the pencil down, you talk about your research so enthusiastically and in such detail that I find it hard to believe that it's not your *own* project you're working on here. Could it be that you are the author of the novel you told me about?

I tried to put Ben-Or on the wrong trail by talking about the Zealots, but there's no fooling him. And now he's standing in front of me, the inspector, waving his badge at me. And I know that I don't have a ticket. There's no point in denying it. I sigh and admit that I'm doing the research on my own behalf, but Ben-Or doesn't dwell on that confession for long.

Your itinerary, he continues, matches the stops you made on your last trip. I don't have the sense that you're looking for anything new. Rather, it seems to me that you merely forgot something at one of the places you visited in January.

I admit that, too, but without explaining myself further. Ben-Or has no way of knowing what I lost the last time I was here: memories, and along with them, my previous identity. Perhaps I should even be grateful to him for finally refreshing my memory with his questions.

For the first time since we started talking, I notice a testy look on his face. He gets up.

I thought we agreed to stick to the truth, he says, but you've already lied twice during this examination.

I don't know how to respond, but I have the feeling that I'm flushed and have a nervous twitch in my neck. Ben-Or points the pencil at my suitcase and tells me to open it, put the contents on the table where he can see them, and then step back.

I don't dare argue with him. I put the velvet bag with my tefillin on the table. I add my shirts, underpants, socks, and a small bag of toiletries. Then I take out the jellabas, the cotton gloves, the books, and the things that were in the suitcase when it was delivered to my apartment. The last thing I put on the table is the little black cardboard box. Then I step back, as I have been instructed to do.

Ben-Or picks up the cardboard box first. He opens it up and looks at the large gemstone on the ruby-colored velvet cushion, without touching it. He leaves the box open, puts it back on the table, rubs his earlobe, and fixes his gaze on the wall I'm standing in front of, as if he were looking right through me.

Mr. Wechsler, he says, I would like to begin recording our conversation at this point. Will you consent to that?

I don't know if such a recording is legal. But I'm not in the mood for a confrontation. So I give my consent in the hope that it will make him go easier on me.

He asks me to sit back down while he fiddles with the tape recorder. He checks the cassette and tries to record: *Testing, one, two, three, testing, testing . . .* Then he rewinds and gives a satisfied nod when he hears his own voice. He rewinds again and then uses the pencil to press the button with the red dot. Continuing to stand, he records his first words: his name and rank, the number of the office, and the location of the examination. He repeats my name, place and date of birth, citizenship, and home address, all from memory. When he's finished, he asks me to confirm the information. I indicate that everything is correct. With the subject's consent, Ben-Or continues, this interview will be conducted in English. A translator will not be provided. The subject agrees. Is that correct, Mr. Wechsler?

Yes, I agree.

Ben-Or takes his chair and puts it next to the long side of the table, so that we are now facing each other at the corner. He leaves his pad on the table and puts the pencil in his pocket. Once again I am asked to confirm that the suitcase and the objects I have taken out and put on the table belong to me. Ben-Or lists them, names the authors and titles of the books and the manuscript. He opens the bag of toiletries and describes its contents with the words "for regular cosmetic needs." Then he turns his attention to the jellabas and asks me who they're for.

My wife and kids, I answer.

Since the tags are in Arabic, I suppose it's more likely they were purchased in Israel than in Munich, Ben-Or says.

That's right.

So why did you bring them back? he asks.

I bought them during my last visit and forgot to unpack them, I lie, even though I am now sure that he can tell. But there's something else bothering me. At the moment when I was lying about having bought the jellabas myself, the lie felt like the truth to me. And I suddenly remembered where I had seen them before.

When I was wandering around in the Old City, I also walked through the Arab market. Even though I hate getting lost in big crowds, I was fascinated by the colorful hustle and bustle. I spent hours walking through the narrow streets of the shuk, and I stopped outside just about every shop to take a look at the merchandise: household items, shoes, spices, jewelry, CDs, electrical goods, and worthless things.

At one Arab butcher shop, there was half a sheep carcass hanging in the window. On its shoulder, in blue ink, was the Hechscher of the Beis Din Tzedek. I was surprised, because I had expected that the worlds of Jews and Arabs would be absolutely separate. People had even warned me not to go to the shuk by myself. The fact that a Muslim butcher was selling kosher meat came as a surprise, but it was also a comfort to me, because it seemed to confirm the impression of peaceful neighborliness that I got from the mix of people at the market. Women in sheitels walked by women in veils, Yeshiva bochers and Hasidim passed men wearing turbans and carrying tesbih. The voice of the muezzin echoed through the streets from loudspeakers, calling the people to prayer.

The jellabas hung on poles at one vendor's stand. A Jewish tourist was looking them over. I stood across the way and watched the scene. The price the Arab was asking was exorbitant. When the tourist waved him off with a laugh and started to walk away, the seller changed his tone.

Why are you laughing? he asked, acting insulted, I sell only the best. Look at the embroidery, feel the quality of the material! He grabbed the tourist's arm and pressed the hem of a gown into his hand.

The price was outrageous, and the tourist didn't look very interested. But for a tenth of the price, he said, he'd think about it.

I was fascinated. Never in a million years would I have been able to haggle with any of these traders, and on top of that, boldly start negotiating over such a small amount of money. I continued to eavesdrop on the argument the two men were having, and I jumped for joy when the tourist left the stand a half hour later with jellabas for his wife and two kids, for a third of the original asking price.

While I'm looking at the jellabas on the table in front of me, I wonder if that tourist couldn't have been me. Maybe I had actually bought those gowns. That would explain why the sizes are just right for my wife and kids. And perhaps my memory of the shuk, which is now slowly coming back, is trying to tell me something by placing me in the scene as an observer. For a long time, I looked at the part of myself that I wanted to get rid of as if I was looking at a stranger. Could it be that that stranger had taken his memories and the jellabas in the suitcase and left me, so that from then on he could go his own way?

Ben-Or doesn't give me any time to pursue the thought about my potentially divided self any further. He thumbs through the manuscript and asks me the name of the author.

Amnon Zichroni, I answer automatically, and I tell Ben-Or that the study was sent to me months ago.

Do you know the author?

No.

Are you planning to publish the study?

No, I reply, puzzled. I publish literature. Medical case studies aren't my department.

So why do you have the manuscript with you?

I'd like to read it.

So if you haven't read it yet, how do you know it's not a literary work after all?

I don't know that, I admit.

Where did you get the demantoid? Ben-Or asks, looking me right in the eyes.

The what? I ask.

Ben-Or reaches for the jewelry box and holds it up in front of my face.

It's an heirloom . . . I stammer.

Why did you bring such a valuable gemstone with you on your *spur-of-the-moment* trip? he fires back.

I don't know, I hear myself say.

And what do you need these gloves for, Mr. Wechsler?

I have no answer for him, and I give up. Even if I knew, I wouldn't be able to handle these questions anymore.

Ben-Or is standing up now. He doesn't let me out of his sight. After an agonizingly long pause, he puts his hands in his pockets, and he finally tells why I'm being interrogated.

Amnon Zichroni, he informs me, is an Israeli citizen, a resident of Ofra, a settlement in the West Bank, north of Beth-El. It's presumed that his house was broken into on January 6th of this year. The thief, or thieves, made off with a demantoid garnet of approximately three-and-a-half carats, and the manuscript of an unpublished medical study. The break-in was discovered by some of his neighbors. Amnon Zichroni was last seen leaving the settlement in his car on January 5th, about an hour after the end of Shabbat. He was accompanied by a visitor from Germany, who had been staying with him over Shabbat. Zichroni's car was found in a grove near Motza. He has been considered a missing person since then.

Mr. Weschsler, you were in Israel during the time in question. Your suitcase contains items that belong to Zichroni. Furthermore, you have lied continually during this examination. I am going to retain your passport and any means of communication, such as mobile phones and pagers. You are not under arrest, but you will remain in custody overnight. We will resume questioning in the morning. I urge you to take some time tonight and think very carefully about what you're going to say to me tomorrow, Mr. Wechsler. You're not going to get anywhere by lying.

11

I never dreamed that I would end up in jail one day. The night-mares I used to have when I was a child and a teenager always ended when my guilt was discovered. The moment that Ben-Or confronted me with the facts and made me turn in my cell phone was the instant when I should have awakened. But the reality of the situation exceeds my worst nightmares. Or else I'm still dream-ing, and I just haven't realized the true magnitude of my guilt.

Ben-Or isn't bluffing. He puts my things back into the suitcase and carries it as he escorts me to the airport exit. I'm put into a patrol car and taken to a police station in the center of Tel Aviv. When we get there, Ben-Or hands my suitcase over to a colleague and takes me to my cell.

The room is bare, cold, and small, though the ceiling is high. Across from the door, there are two narrow windows, but they're so high up that I can't reach them. Against the side wall, there's a cot. It's bolted to the floor. On top of it, folded neatly, is an army blanket. There's no pillow. There's a sink attached to the wall. The toilet next to it doesn't have a cover, or even a seat.

This must be the waiting room to Hell, I think to myself as Ben-Or shoves me into the cell. My claim that I grew up in captiv-ity like Rilke's panther doesn't hold up. But my aversion to bars, and to the feeling of being confined and caged, is real.

Ben-Or is standing in the doorway with his hand on the knob, ready to lock me in. There's no way he'd know it, but I have the feeling that I'm not going to see him again. It's inconceivable to me that I could even get through an hour in this cell, let alone an entire night.

How bad do things look for me? I ask him softly, almost inaudibly.

Only you can answer that question, Mr. Wechsler, he replies, unmoved. I'll see you tomorrow.

And with that, he shuts the door. I hear the bolt slide into place. Then I'm on my own.

Just recently an author told me about the snake pit in the temple of Asklepios in ancient Epidaurus, with an enthusiasm that bordered on the hysterical. During excavations, she told me, they found small stone tablets where the dreams of patients were immortalized—the only thing that remained of those people. They had made a pilgrimage to Epidaurus in the hope of curing afflictions of the soul. The treatment began with a ritual purification in the well house. My author told me she saw a parallel to the concept of the mikvah.

Once she got going, she also described the way they used to treat psychotics there. They were wrapped in burial garments and tied to boards. Pieces of bread with honey were laid on top of their stomachs—provisions for the ferryman who would take them across the River of Forgetfulness in a rotting boat. Once they had been prepared in this way, they were lowered into a well. They floated on the water, and soon they found themselves face to face with death. Countless reptiles swam toward them. But the patients could not move. The shock abruptly freed many of them from their delusions. They screamed their heads off, begging to be brought back to life. When confronted with death, they found that they would rather face reality than be at the mercy of the snakes in the underworld.

That's just the kind of trap I'm in now.

I'm convinced that this cell is alive. The sink is filling up with emerald green slime. It comes up out of the drain, quickly fills the basin, and flows over the edge, soon covering the floor of the cell. Black-and-yellow snakes slither out of the toilet with scarlet markings on the backs of their heads, baring outlandishly large fangs. They swim around the cot, acting like they're ignoring me. But I don't believe them. The more slime floods into the cell, the closer they get to me. And soon they're going to bite me.

Of course I don't get any sleep, even though I'm overwrought and completely exhausted. As soon as I close my eyes, even for a second, I feel the cold skin of a reptile against my neck, and I wake up in a panic. Every time this happens, I become more determined to clear this whole thing up, admit my guilt, and accept the punishment, if they would just release me from this torture chamber.

My guilt has a name: Minsky. I must have always known that. I gave him an identity that can be verified and has no holes in it. But I robbed him of his memories. Now he sits at home, forsaken and resentful, living a life that he never wanted. I blotted out the other life that he thought was his. Minsky can't get his revenge, but I'm still afraid of being discovered and enduring a punishment that I don't even dare to imagine.

The snakes won't go away. I can hear them hissing, and I can see their fangs. I am prepared to go back to L'Abbaye to ask Minsky for forgiveness. I will return to my old life and repent. I will tell my wife everything, even if she kicks me out and I never see my children again. If that's the punishment, I'll have to live with it. But get me out of this snake pit!

My begging is futile. Of course, no angel comes to open the door. It's going to be hours before Ben-Or returns to let me out and put an end to this horrible episode. And even then, I suddenly realize, there will be no relief.

A man was robbed and has been missing ever since. The evidence points to me. Ben-Or hasn't said anything about a body, but he'll find it. It didn't even take him an hour to expose me as a notorious liar. He'll prove me guilty of the murder, too, if I really committed it.

Maybe, I think to myself, I'll be able to keep the snakes at bay if I can reconstruct where I went during the last few days of my trip in January. Maybe they'll leave me alone if I try as hard as I can to remember who Zichroni is, whether and when I saw him, and what we talked about.

It seems to work. Just making up my mind causes the snakes to back off a bit. And this time, I don't feel anything against my skin when I close my eyes to listen to a melody that's ringing in my ear . . .

It's Shabbos, late at night. I'm sitting in a Sephardic shul, listening to the singing of three peytanim, two baritones and a tenor. The oldest one is around sixty, and he's a Hasid, which confuses me, since the *Shirei ha-Vakashot* they're singing are Moroccan melodies. The other two—the second baritone, who's about forty, and the tenor, who can't be older than twenty-five—look more like Sephardim from North Africa. The Hasid sounds wise and caring. Poetry pours out of the young singer. The third one seems to be acting as an intermediary, as if he were trying to link their songs together.

Spoken Hebrew always sounds stiff and cold to me. But in the songs of the peytanim, the guttural sounds are woven into poetic figures that pulse and float in the room.

They're masters, my companion whispers to me. They start with a psalm, then they improvise. They let the mood of the night and the place guide them. The songs only sound this way here and now. On another night, they will be different.

I like this thought. It's the first time I've ever heard anything like it. The act of willingly offering up the most beautiful creation, while accepting that it will fade away irretrievably, is true devotion.

The man next to me must be Zichroni. I am in Ofra. Just this morning, I didn't know I would be spending Shabbos here. I walked around the Ben Yehuda pedestrian mall in Jerusalem, I ate shawarma, I daydreamed . . . and at some point, I got lost in the sidestreets. And then I got the call.

During my first trip to Israel, I wanted to spend Shabbos in a place where everyone keeps Shabbos, where the street turns into a playground during the day, because there are no cars out. A friend's son is studying at a Yeshiva in Jerusalem. He asked around for me. Taking in travelers over Shabbos is a great mitzvah. There's no need to be embarrassed about asking for an invitation.

I didn't know what to expect. I was a bit afraid of Haredi areas and neighborhoods. Because of my clothes—a black suit with a vest, a white shirt, and a large black velvet kippa—people here in Israel think I'm Haredi. But the dress code is imported from Munich and is misleading.

I would feel out of place around people who don't know anything other than the yeshiva. I live a modern life, I work in literature, and this is my first time in the country. I think it would be better for me to stay with a modern Orthodox family, people who are religious but also have regular jobs.

My friend's son said he'd found something suitable. The idea of visiting a settlement in the West Bank scared me at first. In my mind, it was a war zone. But he reassured me that nothing had happened there for years and that the settlements were well-guarded. There was nothing to worry about, he said.

There wasn't much time. I caught the next taxi and made it to the bus station just in time to get the last bus.

There was a cluster of students and soldiers waiting at the gate, and I had to overcome my reticence and push my way up to the front, so I wouldn't be the last one to the door and possibly not make it on. I had been warned: the buses to the occupied territories have windows that are reinforced with bulletproof glass. If all the seats are taken, they won't let anyone else on, because passengers on these trips aren't allowed to stand in the aisle. I grabbed my seat.

Since it was the last bus before Shabbos, the driver made an exception. A few soldiers were allowed to sit on top of their bags in the center aisle. I had never seen a submachine gun up close before. Now I was surrounded by them.

All of this *did* seem like an excursion into enemy territory. The only thing that made me feel a little bit better was the fact that there were so many students on the bus who were evidently studying in Jerusalem and were now going home for Shabbos as a matter of course. No one besides me seemed afraid. So I tried to calm down, too.

The Israelis are crazy about their cell phones. On the bus and on the street, you can hear them ringing constantly from every direction, and half the people you see have phones pressed against their ears and are yakking incessantly. Nobody's embarrassed about it. Still, I didn't want to make a call on the bus. But I didn't have anything but the name of the settlement, the first name of my host—Amnon—and his cell phone number. I decided to send him a text message. He answered right away. He said he would be waiting for me at the gate, and he asked how he would recognize me. I looked around and wrote back that I was the only Yekke on the bus.

Ha ha! he answered. I've been there before. See you soon.

Now I was really curious. My host spoke German. My friend hadn't mentioned that.

The trip was about an hour long. It took around twenty minutes just to get out of Jerusalem. When we passed through the wall that has separated the West Bank from Israel proper for the last few years, I felt like I was back in the days of the Cold War.

In Berlin, I often walked alongside the Wall on Mühlenstraße. It was a part of the streetscape. I didn't know that the Spree flowed behind it, and that there was a district called Kreuzberg on the other side of the river. It didn't even interest me. I didn't realize how limited my perspective was until I ended up in Kreuzberg for the first time, that evening when the welders were opening the gates of the border crossing at the Oberbaum Bridge, and I spent hours on the other side of the Wall, waiting for them to let me go back home.

This harmless association upsets the snakes in my cell. Now they're hissing and trying to get onto my cot. Apparently I can no longer indulge in stolen memories with impunity. I pull my legs in, sit up against the wall, and try to pick up the thread again and remember what happened in Ofra.

That's where most of the passengers were headed. When we arrived, the bus emptied out abruptly. I was the last one off, and I looked around. There were a few cars waiting at the bus stop. Fathers were gathering up their children. Only one man had come on foot, and he was standing right at the automatic iron gate. That had to be Amnon. I walked over to him, introduced myself, and thanked him for the invitation. His reaction confused me.

From what everyone had told me, he was supposedly an expert on mikvaot and was excited about my visit. They had said he lived alone and didn't get many visitors. Hosting me over Shabbos would be a welcome change for him, they had told me. But when I met him, he was so aloof—cold, really—that I didn't get the impression that I was really welcome. He told me I was, but it sure didn't feel that way.

Of course, it was too late to turn back, or to look for another place to stay in Ofra. It was only about forty-five minutes before Shabbos. Besides, it would have felt impolite for me to back out just because I had a vague feeling that I was now being rejected, after I had been invited so eagerly.

Zichroni told me we'd have to walk for a few minutes, and he turned to go. Those were just about the only words I heard out of him all evening. He hardly said anything, and he only answered my questions about the settlement and the situation in the West Bank reluctantly. So I resorted to telling stories. I told him I was amazed by the wall and by the fact that it was so easy to distinguish the Arab areas from the Jewish ones. They didn't seem to have gable roofs on the Arab side. From a distance, you could make out gray concrete blocks with flat roofs, dreary places I wouldn't have been tempted to visit even if people hadn't told me that, as a Jew, I wouldn't survive for an hour there. I asked him if it was really true that any Yehudi who went to a place like that could expect to be shot dead in broad daylight.

Yes, Amnon told me tersely. The wall and the high fence around the settlement weren't there for decoration, he quipped. There was no shooting, he continued, but only as long as everyone stuck to their territory. He told me Arabs didn't enter the settlement often: construction workers, electricians, and handymen. And the workers who helped build Jewish houses were never from nearby villages. They came from Jerusalem.

When we got to the house, I felt at home. Amnon had cooked. The table was set. Everything was ready for Shabbos. He showed me my room for the night. I took a shower. Then we lit the candles and set off for the synagogue.

I felt like an alien among the settlers. Nobody had a suit on. Even the prayer leader was wearing jeans at the lectern. And a friend of Amnon's came right out and asked why I was so "overdressed." Amnon told him I was from Germany. That was apparently explanation enough.

Ah, his friend whispered, shaking my hand. His grandparents had lived in Germany, he said. What a terrible country. He asked me how I could stand it there . . .

Things in Germany were no longer quite the way he might imagine, I told him, in an attempt to smooth things over. But he shook his head. Living as a Jew anywhere outside of Israel seemed strange enough to him. But in Germany? That was a completely absurd notion.

After services, we walked back to the house in the warm night air. Once again, Amnon said nothing, so I started telling stories again, to cut through the icy silence between us. I unfurled my entire family saga before him while we ate, all the stories I had heard from my mother. He didn't really seem interested, no matter how artfully I embellished the stories with details and emotion. He didn't tell me anything about himself.

At around eleven, he came up with the idea of going back out again, to the main synagogue, the Sephardic shul, so we could hear the peytanim perform the *Shirei ha Vakashot*. I was tired, but

I agreed to go along. I must have hoped, just a little, that if we shared the experience it might give us something to talk about.

I don't know how long the peytanim sang that night. We left after two hours, because my eyes kept closing. I walked in silence beside Amnon. When we got back to his house, I went right to bed.

He woke me up in the morning. We had a piece of cake and some coffee before we went back to the synagogue. But once again, during our little breakfast and on the road, Amnon hardly said a word. I chalked it up to his religiosity. Before the morning prayer, you're only supposed to talk to others if it's absolutely necessary. That was fine with me. I wouldn't have known what to say.

The Shabbos atmosphere in Ofra was a revelation for me. Children were playing in the street. Because of the fence around the settlement, and the gate at the entrance, which was closed at nightfall, you're allowed to carry on Shabbos in Ofra. That would be unthinkable in Munich. When I'm at home, I even have to hook my house keys onto a special belt, so I can keep them with me. But Shabbos belts are unknown in Ofra. The kids play ball. Families can go for walks with their strollers. In Munich, mothers are chained to the house on Shabbos if their children can't walk by themselves. What I saw in Ofra was like paradise to me. It could have been the best Shabbos of my life, if only Amnon hadn't been so chilly and taciturn.

He warmed up a little in the afternoon, at least. He showed me his garden. It looked a bit overgrown, but Amnon assured me that that was only because of the Shmita year. He wasn't allowed to prune the trees or trim the bushes, which was hard for him, because he obviously loved his plants more than anything else.

He had imported the tree and shrub saplings. Most of them came from subtropical regions, so they needed loving care to thrive in the relatively cool climate of the West Bank. Thanks to Amnon's efforts, there were various fruits growing, but I had never heard of most of them. I don't know anything about botany. But I pretended that I was really interested in exotic plants, just so he would keep talking. I had run out of stories to tell. And so we spent the hours before sunset in the garden and walking through the neighborhood, where he had found more fruit trees. He wanted to take saplings from them and plant them in his garden after the Shmita Year.

As soon as Shabbos was over, he seemed restless. He told me about the mikvah he wanted to show me. We hadn't actually planned to go see it until Sunday. But suddenly Amnon insisted that we leave immediately. He said the place he wanted to show me was indescribably beautiful at night.

How could I object? In spite of the dragging conversation, I had spent a wonderful Shabbos in Ofra. If I was able to see this mikvah now, I could go back to Jerusalem that same night. Why should I overtax Amnon's hospitality, which hadn't been all that warm anyway?

So I agreed and got my things together. Amnon packed some towels. We put everything in the trunk of his old Peugeot and set off for Motza.

I am startled awake. It sounds like someone is opening the cell door. There is sunlight coming through the narrow windows under the ceiling. The floor is dry, not a snake in sight. Maybe I did get a little sleep after all.

As soon as I see Ben-Or standing in the open doorway, I start sputtering. It's all true, I tell him. I know Zichroni. I did actually spend a Shabbos at his house in Ofra, and I went to Motza with him.

I assure him that I'm willing to confess everything. Except I can't tell him what happened in Motza. Even my experiences in the settlement had been difficult to reconstruct during the night, I tell him.

Ben-Or must think I'm a lunatic. What I'm saying probably sounds crazy to him—nothing but incoherent confessions. I tell him that the word *Berndeutsch* recently reminded me of my mother and our apartment in Switzerland; and it was only in the snake pit that I was able to remember Zichroni.

Maybe it would help me to go to Motza, I tell Ben-Or. If I look at the mikvah, I say, maybe I'll remember what happened in the grove there. And I wouldn't hesitate to tell you.

My sudden willingness to cooperate doesn't seem to surprise him. I assume he knows the effect that a night in a narrow holding cell can have on someone who has never seen the inside of a prison. He thinks about it for a moment. Then he agrees. If it helps establish the truth, he says, he'd be happy to invest a couple of hours in the trip.

I hold my hands out, assuming that he's going to put me in handcuffs. After all, I've acknowledged that his suspicion didn't just come out of thin air. I really could be the person behind Zichroni's disappearance, I say. And I assume you wouldn't let a potential murderer out of his cell without handcuffs.

But Ben-Or just chuckles, steps aside, and waves me out.

That won't be necessary, he says. A person like you might try to escape. But we'd catch you again before you could count to three.

I assure him that I won't give him any trouble. And he nods as he leads me out. We leave through the back door and get into Ben-Or's car, an almost ancient-looking gray Mercedes coupe with chrome bumpers and door handles. Ben-Or opens the passenger door and asks me to put on my seatbelt. He takes his suit jacket off and puts it in the trunk. When he sits down at the wheel, I notice that he's wearing a shoulder holster. I can't see the pistol. But I'm sure it's under his left armpit.

We take Highway 1. We get off just before Jerusalem, take an underpass, and get back on the highway going in the opposite direction. Luckily, Ben-Or knows the way. I certainly wouldn't have recognized that rugged exit near Motza.

Zichroni also knew exactly where he was going that night. There were no lights at the exit, but he slowed down in time and turned carefully onto a dirt road that led into the woods. Unlike Zichroni, however, Ben-Or seems worried about his car. He stops right after the exit and tells me to get out.

I think it would be better if we walk the last hundred meters, he says.

It was pitch-black when I was here with Zichroni. The head-lights lit up the path for us. But on either side, the trees stood like walls. Now, in the daylight, the grove feels serene. It's not even nine in the morning, but it's already hot.

Ben-Or leaves his jacket in the car. When he walks up to me and points his left hand toward the mikvah that I can just make out at the end of the trail, I see his pistol. I wonder if he'd use it on me if I tried to escape. But I wasn't lying, maybe for the first time in years, when I assured him that I am only interested in the truth. I am going to look into the water of the mikvah, no matter what I find looking back at me in the mirror.

Let's take it slow, Ben-Or says. Let everything sink in. There's no rush.

Last time, I remember, I was in a big hurry. I was eager to get undressed and jump into the mikvah. It was cold and windy, and there were almost no clouds in the sky. I remember the moon, because the fine, bright crescent was almost horizontal in the darkness, instead of vertical, the way it looks in Munich. Zichroni had driven right up to the edge of the mikvah and had pointed his headlights at the steps. I got undressed next to the car, threw my things onto the passenger seat, took off my glasses, my rings and my watch, and stood naked in the dark.

I asked Zichroni if he wanted to go in, too. But he told me he'd prefer not to. It was definitely too cold, he said. Then I walked up to the pool. The water was freezing. I lowered myself in very slowly, and I started huffing. But I wanted to know. I was already wet, anyway. Now I just needed to submerge . . .

There are only a few meters to go before we get to the mikvah. Ben-Or stops and looks around. I also pause for a moment. I cross my arms in front of my chest like I did that night, and I move my lips the same way I did then, when I shivered as I said the bracha that Ariel had taught me.

During my first tevila at the mikvah in Munich, I was afraid that the lions I had added to my name were lurking in the water and were going to attack me, but nothing like that had happened. They had waited. For years, I thought I was safe. It was only when I got to the mikvah at Motza that night that the lions attacked me. When I surfaced, they batted at me with their paws and pushed me back into the water.

I fought back with all my strength. I don't know how long it took, I only know that at some point they stopped attacking, and I surfaced, and without looking around again, I crawled out of the pool and ran to the car, got in, and locked the doors. I sat naked on the seat, shivering and staring at the entrance to the mikvah, which, in the ghostly illumination of the headlights, looked like a dark lion's mouth, open wide and snarling at me.

Zichroni was gone.

•

I don't know if I should tell Ben-Or what I have just seen. What if I didn't fight with lions that night, but with Amnon? And who's to say that that wasn't the reason I ended up alone in the car, because Amnon had drowned in the mikvah?

I have still only seen a fragment from the image of my past. The largest part is still covered with a black cloth. I am back in the grove near Motza where Amnon took me, I have to assume that I am his killer, and I still don't know who I really am.

But over there, in the water, is my lost self. It's waiting for me. I just have to reach for it.

I don't think Ben-Or will allow me to immerse in this mikvah again. But there's no other way, if I want to get back to myself. So I push him aside, as hard as I can, and I start running. I hold my breath and jump. In a second I'll be sinking in the ice-cold water, and everything will be the way it was before.

But I don't sink. I fall.

The pool I'm plunging into is empty.

Munich/Jerusalem
February—October 2008

Glossary

Aggadic: from *Aggadah*, Aramaic for tales or lore. Rabbinic texts on biblical characters and ethical ideas recorded in the Talmud and **Midrash**.

Arizal: Yitzhak Ben Sh'lomo Luria Ashkenazi (1534-1572), a rabbi and mystic in the community of Sfad in the Galilee, considered the father of the mystical discipline known as **Kabbalah**.

Ashkenazim: Jews descended from the medieval communities along the Rhine in Germany and Northern France. Used broadly to describe the Jews of Central and Eastern Europe, and their descendants.

Atara (*plural* Atarot): crown. A neckband on a **tallis** (prayer shawl).

Aufruf: Yiddish name for a ceremony held just before a wedding, where a groom is "called up" to recite a blessing over the Torah.

Bracha (*plural* Brachot): Hebrew, a blessing

Chavrusa: Yiddish/Ashkenazic pronunciation of Hebrew *Chavruta*, from the Aramaic for "friendship" or "companionship." A method of Talmud study where two students discuss a text.

Cheder: an elementary school where children learn Hebrew and the basics of Judaism.

Chometz: Yiddish/Ashkenazic pronunciation of *Chametz*, leavened foods prohibited during Passover. Describes any product made from one of five kinds of grain, which has been combined with water and left to stand raw for longer than eighteen minutes. Must be removed from the home before the holiday and sold temporarily to a non-Jew, because Jews are not allowed to own *chometz* during the eight-day festival.

Droshe: Yiddish/Ashkenazic pronunciation of *d'rash*, a sermon or brief exposition of the Torah portion or rabbinic literature.

Gedolim: Plural of the Hebrew *Gadol*, or "great," a term used mostly by **Haredi** Jews to refer to revered and learned rabbis of their generation.

Gehinnom: the name given to Hell in rabbinic literature.

Gemara: From the Aramaic "to study," the component of the Talmud that comprises rabbinical analysis of and commentary on the **Mishna**.

Get: a document presented by a husband to his wife to effect a divorce.

Gilgul ha-Neshamot: Kabbalistic concept of the reincarnation of souls.

Halacha: the collective body of Jewish law.

Haredim: Jews associated with the most conservative forms of orthodoxy.

Hasidim: literally "the pious." Jews associated with orthodox movements of Eastern European origin that promote mysticism along with strict adherence to Jewish law.

Hechscher: a kosher certification.

Ivrit: the Hebrew language.

Kabbalah: literally "receiving." An overarching term for a range of mystical activity in Judaism.

Kasher: to make kosher.

Kashrut: Jewish dietary laws.

Kohanim: Priests, direct male descendants of the Biblical Aaron, the brother of Moses and first high priest.

Kollel: an institute where married men study Talmud and rabbinic literature.

Mashgiach: person who inspects and supervises the production of kosher food.

Mezuzah: literally "doorpost." A piece of parchment inscribed by hand with two portions of Torah, contained in a small case which is affixed to door-frames in Jewish homes. The portions are the *Shema*, Deuteronomy 6:4-9 and 11:13-21, both of which include the verse: "And you shall inscribe these words upon the doorposts of your house and upon your gates."

Midrash: from the verb "to investigate" or "to study." A form of storytelling, a tool of interpretation that explores ethics and values in biblical texts.

Mikvah (*plural* mikvaot): ritual bath.

Minyan: Congregational quorum of ten adult (traditionally male) Jews required for a public prayer service and certain other religious obligations.

Mishna: literally "repetition." Judaism's first major canonical document after the Bible. The written compilation of the oral laws known as the "Oral Torah."

Mishteret Yisrael: The Israel Police. Its duties include crime fighting, traffic control, and maintaining public safety.

Mossad: Israeli secret service.

Muezzin: Arabic for the person who leads the call to prayer at a mosque.

Mussar: literally moral conduct, instruction, or discipline. An ethical movement that developed in 19th century Eastern Europe. The term is used for didactic Jewish ethical literature.

Peyes: Yiddish for sidelocks or sidecurls worn by some Orthodox Jewish men.

Perushim: commentaries to the Bible and the Talmud.

Pesach: Passover.

Peytanim: a cappella singers who perform liturgical poems.

Piyyutim (*singular* Piyyut): Jewish liturgical poems, usually sung or chanted.

Rav (*plural* rabbonim): rabbi.

Ramchal: an abbreviation for Rav Moshe Chaim Luzzatto (1707-1746), a prominent Italian rabbi, philosopher, and Kabbalist whose magnum opus is the ethical treatise *Mesillat Yesharim* (1740).

Rega!: Hebrew, "Just a moment!"

Rosh Yeshiva: The dean of a Talmudic academy.

Sanhedrin: from the Greek *Synhedrion* (assembly or council). The high court in ancient Israel, made up of seventeen judges.

Shabak: an acronym for *Sherut haBitachon haKlali*, Israel's internal security agency, also known as Shin Bet.

Shachris: Yiddish/Ashkenazic pronunciation of *Shacharit*, the morning prayer.

Sheitel: Yiddish name for the wig worn by some married Orthodox Jewish women.

Shuk: Hebrew rendering of *souq*, the Arabic word for market.

Seder (*plural* Sedorim): order or sequence. In this case, a study session at a **Yeshiva**.

Sfardim: Descendents of Jews who lived on the Iberian Peninsula before the expulsion in 1492, many of whom later settled in North Africa, Turkey, Greece, and other parts the Ottoman Empire.

Slicha Adoni: Hebrew for "excuse me, sir"

Smicha: Hebrew for "leaning (of the hands)." Formal ordination of a rabbi. Grants authority to give advice or judgment in *Halacha*, Jewish law.

Sukkot: "Festival of booths" or "Feast of Tabernacles," a Jewish holiday celebrated for seven days. Commemorates the forty-year period when the Israelites wandered the desert and lived in temporary shelters.

Tallis: Ashkenazic/Yiddish pronunciation of the Hebrew *Tallit*, a prayer shawl. In Yiddish, the plural is *Talesim*.

Tateh: Yiddish for "papa."

Tayves: Yiddish, morally questionable urges.

Tehillim: psalms.

Tesbih: Islamic prayer beads.

Tevila: immersion in a ritual bath.

Tikkun: Hebrew for "fixing" or "rectification." Often used in the phrase *Tikkun Olam*, or "mending the world," a concept central to **Kabbalah**.

Treif: Yiddish for not kosher.

Tzaddik: Hebrew for "righteous one."

Tzahal: Hebrew acronym for the Israel Defense Forces.

Tzitzes: Ashkenazic/Yiddish pronunciation of the Hebrew *Tzitzit*, knotted ritual fringes on the four corners of the prayer shawl (**Tallis**) or on a *tallit katan*, a garment worn under or over a man's shirt.

Yeshiva: a Jewish school where students focus on traditional religious texts. A *Yeshiva Bocher* is a young man studying at a Yeshiva.